Beware
the Dither Bird

Russell H. Plante

Whimsical Publications, LLC

Florida

To purchase the authorized electronic edition of
Beware the Dither Bird, visit
www.whimsicalpublications.com

The Paul Harvey's 1996 commentary version of *If I Were the Devil... was* included as a courtesy from *World Net Daily* with permission, copyright WND.com
(http://www.wnd.com/1999/08/2815/)

The excerpt from the lyrics of his song entitled *We Will* by Gilbert O'Sullivan, published by Sony/ATV Music Publishing Ltd. All Rights Reserved, was used with permission from Gilbert O'Sullivan.

Cover art by Shyanne England
Editing by Melissa Hosack and Janet Durbin

ISBN-13: 978-1-63495-014-5

Published by
Whimsical Publications, LLC
Florida

The old man was unaware I was watching him from the top of a nearby hill across from a ravine that separated us. I was usually at that same spot on as many mornings as the old man was, enjoying the first rays of sunshine and the friendly quietness that accompanied those moments. I don't believe he ever noticed me as I watched his usual journey.

We didn't live very far from one another, and I could usually hear him working in his garden during the spring and summer days. During those seasons, he always wore the same old straw hat that he wore this day. On many occasions, he had a corncob pipe in his mouth. He didn't smoke it anymore, but just had it in his mouth, a habit hard to break I imagine.

I saw it was the garden that brought about the slight smile he always seemed to have. But that smile also made you wonder what else he might be thinking about. I overheard the people who knew him well call him Donny.

Neither of us made much noise as we traveled along our respective pathways, Donny always on one side of a ridge while I traveled the other. If you listened closely, you could hear the leaves come alive as each step turned dew to mist, evaporating into the air as they warmed and curled from the rising sun. Inhaling the smells of dried leaves and autumn earth provided him and me with a sense of invigoration and new life.

I watched as the forest stirred, awakening at his every step, his footsteps resounding upon the old trail. To his right, the land sloped downward toward a large wooded wetland, where ferns and false nettle dominated the shallow end. Jewelweed hidden from the first sunlight at the edge of the water was also seen from the trail.

These shallow depressions contained small rivulets of water shimmering in the early morning sun, a trickling of water from the surrounding hills, slowly increasing the volume from the earlier fall rains. They were home to a few wood frogs and spotted salamanders, and if anyone took the time to closely watch, the ripples in the water ultimately could be sourced to their inhabitants.

The overgrown path continued with serried rows of small poplars on either side, and off to one side was an old wooden bench that provided a distinct resting place for any aging, weary traveler. A large maple tree separated itself from all others at the end of this hall-like extension and stood out alone as if to make a statement.

I watched Donny slowly proceed along the aged pathway, passing the bench, not stopping to rest until he reached the maple and abruptly halted his steady advance. Facing the wide trunk, he paused as if to think about the many years it had seen. He knelt down on one knee for a closer examination. Inscribed on its withering bark were many names scrawled by his pocketknife from years past, made during his younger days.

Time had not been a friend to the weathered bark. It had expanded and stretched over time making it difficult to read some of the names and dates. Many of the letters were split, but some were still discernable, even though they were over thirty years old.

Donny ran his fingers over the words and read the names once again, remembering those he himself had inscribed. He had lived in the area all his life. In fact, he had been born there and his wife had died there fifteen years earlier. I recall his daughter's name, Sarah, was engraved in the bark. There were also the names of former pets. Heidi, Mittens, Kali, Wickett, and Stimpson were a few of the many inscriptions that would remain within the weathered bark for years, never to be forgotten.

The old man wiped tears from his blue eyes as he stared off into the past, but a slight smile returned to his face as happy memories replaced the void. I know Donny often stopped here to reflect upon those times in his life, but how quickly they had passed. Even though he couldn't stop the progression of time and the changes that went with them, he could always cherish the memories.

Voices from a nearby, large wetland area interrupted his reflections, causing past images to disappear. There were other people in the woods. Donny descried their approach off to his right as he overheard portions of their conversation. Below him, in one of the small ravines that ran though the eastern part of the forest, I saw two men.

It was surprising that anyone else would be in the forest this early in the morning.

Dedication

☙

In memory of
Alton N. Donnell
A World War II Veteran
~ His straw hat and ubiquitous smile –
always remembered ~

And to all the men and women in the armed forces
who protect a nation.

Acknowledgements

I want to thank my wife, Kathy, for her suggestions throughout the many, many drafts of the manuscript. An avid reader, her comments gave me pause to reflect upon the characters and the messages conveyed within this story. Additionally, I want to thank my longtime friend Carl Corsello who provided many helpful suggestions during the initial revisions.

Credit is also given for the cover design by Shyanne England. And thanks are also extended to my editors, Melissa Hosack, whose suggestions and comments were helpful in ensuring a comprehensive manuscript and Janet Durbin, whose recommendations, corrections, and efforts to bring the characters and storyline together were essential in the final revisions to this publication. Janet's belief in this book and her demand for the very best from me were tireless.

Grateful acknowledgement is made to World Net Daily for permission to reprint Paul Harvey's 1996 commentary version of 'If I Were the Devil...' This excerpt was included as a courtesy from World Net Daily with permission, copyright WND.com (http://www.wnd.com/1999/08/2815/)

Grateful acknowledgement is made to Gilbert O'Sullivan for permission to print an excerpt from the lyrics of his song entitled "We Will", published by Sony/ATV Music Publishing Ltd. All Rights Reserved.

BEWARE
THE DITHER BIRD

☙

Dither Birds are amiable, normally flightless birds found foraging for food on the ground in the rain forests of Central and South America. They are remarkable in their inability to make a firm decision, hence their name. Given any change in their natural environment, they will continue to behave as if there are no changes occurring and will lack any real focus in reacting to those changing conditions, whether harmful or not...

☙

Have you never heard of a Dither bird? Ask yourself: do they even exist? If you look very carefully, you can find one. They're not as rare as you might think.

Come with me and I'll tell you a story. I'll tell you of things that were never meant to be but were, of things that should have been done but weren't, and of things that were done and shouldn't have been.

We exist as an anomaly of time, and this story is but one of those historical periods where apathy has consequences—a story developed from our past and extended from a state of anomie toward an outcome that only you can determine.

Contemplate its message, respect the past, remembering that it was once the future, and never stop looking for what's not there.

Russell H. Plante
May 13, 2029

Prologue

"Only the keeper sees that,
where the ring-dove broods
and the badgers roll at ease,
there was once a road through the woods."

— Rudyard Kipling

A Church in the Forest

L

The forest was an ecosystem of plants and wildlife surrounded and captured by humanity. There were tall oaks, maples, pine, and hemlock trees, all contributing their own particular essence to the silent composure of the forest. It was a separate world hidden from the daily routines of cell phones, automobiles, and people.

Since the nearby ocean waters normally kept the first few miles of the coastline warmer and more tempered than the inland regions, snow accumulations were usually less here. There were only a few forested areas left in this residential community still in their natural state, but those areas were becoming even rarer over the years.

Surrounding this small forest in Maine was the tiny coastal town of Laslo, located just north of the city of Portland. There were about six thousand residents within the town, with not much of a downtown area, consisting of only a few retail shops, two restaurants, and a barber shop.

The town hall was the largest structure, and the majority of people called it the Taj Mahal. It was imposing in appearance, resembling a large stark shopping mall. It was funded by appropriated property tax revenue and built without public input or support, with only the pretense of a previous town manager desiring a new office space.

The forest had been split into two distinct parcels of land that were deeded and identified separately by the town.

The southern parcel consisted of about thirty-two acres, where there were two large open wetland areas, as well as several smaller vernal pools throughout. That section of land was connected by a twenty-five-foot wide piece of wetland property that extended several hundred feet into its northern counterpart of just over twelve acres; a parcel of land that had already been heavily developed by a senior housing apartment complex.

The only untouched land remaining in the northern parcel was the wooded wetland area that abutted its southern counterpart. Both parcels connected were reminiscent of a disproportionately shaped hourglass with the top slightly smaller than its bottom.

The majority of the remaining forest was characterized by uneven terrain and by shallow depths of soil to bedrock, and by the plentiful outcropping of ledge, yielding a diverse, natural character to the land. Both southern and northern parcels of land were owned by the same corporation and not by any one individual.

In the past, there were a number of wetlands found throughout the small town of Laslo. These wetlands included swamps, marshes, bogs, and similar areas. They were considered wastelands, something to be filled or drained. Increased understanding of their ecological role had changed that perception by many people over the years. However, there were still those who maintained a mindset to fill and drain whatever portions of land were necessary in order to make a profit, no matter the outcome.

They didn't care whether or not controls were in place against such issues as erosion, nutrient recycling, flood-water retention, or filtering pollutants in ground water. The idea of providing open spaces and wildlife habitats was far removed from the concept of making money. They were the inveterate liars who would omit crucial information, undermining responsible conclusions.

There were over two acres of definable wetlands in this section of the forest, owned by a company called Caring Home Services, Inc.

ii.

The air was crisp and leaves crackled underfoot like parchment paper as the old man slowly walked along the overgrown path that at one time had been a narrow forest road. The woods were thick with branches reaching out, touching his thin fleece-lined coat as if to welcome him back. It had been some time since his last visit. His usual daily trek was obviated by the unconditional result of old age.

His walking staff carefully guided him along the trail,

missing the small ruts left by earlier weeks of rain. The white stubble on his face showed his indifference to shaving every day, and his thinning white hair, mostly covered by an old straw hat, reflected the unstopping progression of time.

Nonetheless, the seasons had been kind to him, leaving him with enough energy and motivation to take his walks in the forest and appreciate his surroundings. Slightly bent in form but very spry for his seventy-nine years, he steadily continued on his course with the added assurance of his wooden staff.

He was a finish carpenter in his younger days, and occasionally still managed to practice his craftsmanship by fabricating useful items, like the staff he had formed from a youthful cherry tree that hadn't survived the previous harsh winter.

It was always with him during his daily walks. The wood was strong and helped support and steady his light frame. The sunshine exposed the real beauty of the wood, defining its natural grains. It moved as he did, in step with him, as if it had a life of its own. He had rather the tree grown strong and tall, but it had died early. He remembered when he had first planted the tree, wanting to retain its original beauty, only to reconcile a change to its final purpose.

It was the end of fall, and with the season were the smells of the earth from the decay of fallen leaves. The cool air whispered along the old trail, wanting to find an end to its journey, but then refreshing itself and starting over once again.

iii.

No one seemed to exist in this southern part of the forest except for the old man who had entered this quiet domain as he had done so on many early mornings. Only the harshest of winters and his age hindered his normal weekly jaunt. He walked on enjoying the quiet morning as the sun peeked through the trees and filtered the earlier night sky from darkness into early blues and reds. He seemed to know the best time to visit the forest was either at sunrise or sunset, when most animals either began to awaken or bed down for the night.

The forest was within the town limits, and hunting wasn't allowed here. The few natural predators were owls, hawks, fox, and an occasional coyote. Normally, it was the deer mice, chipmunks, and squirrels that had to take notice of their neighbors. Most residents knew to keep their cats from meandering outside.

The old man was unaware I was watching him from the top of a nearby hill across from a ravine that separated us. I was usually at that same spot on as many mornings as the old man was, enjoying the first rays of sunshine and the friendly quietness that accompanied those moments. I don't believe he ever noticed me as I watched his usual journey.

We didn't live very far from one another, and I could usually hear him working in his garden during the spring and summer days. During those seasons, he always wore the same old straw hat that he wore this day. On many occasions, he had a corncob pipe in his mouth. He didn't smoke it anymore, but just had it in his mouth, a habit hard to break I imagine.

I saw it was the garden that brought about the slight smile he always seemed to have. But that smile also made you wonder what else he might be thinking about. I overheard the people who knew him well call him Donny.

Neither of us made much noise as we traveled along our respective pathways, Donny always on one side of a ridge while I traveled the other. If you listened closely, you could hear the leaves come alive as each step turned dew to mist, evaporating into the air as they warmed and curled from the rising sun. Inhaling the smells of dried leaves and autumn earth provided him and me with a sense of invigoration and new life.

I watched as the forest stirred, awakening at his every step, his footsteps resounding upon the old trail. To his right, the land sloped downward toward a large wooded wetland, where ferns and false nettle dominated the shallow end. Jewelweed hidden from the first sunlight at the edge of the water was also seen from the trail.

These shallow depressions contained small rivulets of water shimmering in the early morning sun, a trickling of water from the surrounding hills, slowly increasing the volume from the earlier fall rains. They were home to a few wood frogs and spotted salamanders, and if anyone took the time to closely watch, the ripples in the water ultimately could be sourced to their inhabitants.

The overgrown path continued with serried rows of small poplars on either side, and off to one side was an old wooden bench that provided a distinct resting place for any aging, weary traveler. A large maple tree separated itself from all others at the end of this hall-like extension and stood out alone as if to make a statement.

I watched Donny slowly proceed along the aged pathway, passing the bench, not stopping to rest until he reached the maple and abruptly halted his steady advance. Facing the wide trunk, he paused as if to think about the many years it had seen. He knelt down on one knee for a closer examination. Inscribed on its withering bark were many names scrawled by his pocketknife from years past, made during his younger days.

Time had not been a friend to the weathered bark. It had expanded and stretched over time making it difficult to read some of the names and dates. Many of the letters were split, but some were still discernable, even though they were over thirty years old.

Donny ran his fingers over the words and read the names once again, remembering those he himself had inscribed. He had lived in the area all his life. In fact, he had been born there and his wife had died there fifteen years earlier. I recall his daughter's name, Sarah, was engraved in the bark. There were also the names of former pets. Heidi, Mittens, Kali, Wickett, and Stimpson were a few of the many inscriptions that would remain within the weathered bark for years, never to be forgotten.

The old man wiped tears from his blue eyes as he stared off into the past, but a slight smile returned to his face as happy memories replaced the void. I know Donny often stopped here to reflect upon those times in his life, but how quickly they had passed. Even though he couldn't stop the progression of time and the changes that went with them, he could always cherish the memories.

Voices from a nearby, large wetland area interrupted his reflections, causing past images to disappear. There were other people in the woods. Donny descried their approach off to his right as he overheard portions of their conversation. Below him, in one of the small ravines that ran though the eastern part of the forest, I saw two men.

It was surprising that anyone else would be in the forest this early in the morning.

iv.

Morty Myers and his boss, Kurt Tussi, were self-absorbed in their task as they trampled through the thick underbrush, unaware of the watchful eyes of the old man. Morty was in his early thirties, short, and a little pudgy for his early years—perhaps too much beer, Donny imagined. Morty's boss, on the other hand, was a thin, slender man in his late forties. He had a darker complexion than his counterpart and brandished a graying beard from its once intense brackish black. His eyes had a dark, coal black intense look, and he curtly remarked, "This shouldn't take more than about a week to survey."

Morty caught himself from stumbling backwards and grumbled under his breath about handling the sixteen-foot long rod he had to carry in order to take the graduated readings needed for their survey. The oversized rod kept getting hung up in the dense underbrush whenever he turned or tried to move forward, as if the forest wanted to prevent him from following the ravine. Even a ringed bog haunter dragonfly that had land delicately on the end had to set flight, disturbed by the rough ride from the continued challenges of the undergrowth and ferns.

"We'll place a few survey flags in some of the areas we need to mark for the DEP so they'll know we have properly surveyed the area. I don't anticipate any issues with the Department of Environmental Protection." The old man overheard Kurt emphasize what the abbreviation stood for just to make sure his new assistant understood. "We'll provide them with the information they require in order to get approval for this development."

Kurt motioned for his subordinate to measure off the hundred-foot survey line to the edge of the first wetland area, a definitive measure Donny knew was required by town ordinances.

Morty made the first mark on a tree and continued toward the water's edge. The forest remained quiet, as if it anticipated some immediate action to the conversation. Nothing stirred except for a few leaves that continued to fall, announcing their call of an approaching winter. Even the ripples in the shallow wetland waters disappeared from view and hid from the intruders.

Morty slowly made his way toward an area of the marsh littered with multiple dead tree snags, providing homes for many cavity-nesting birds. A pileated woodpecker was loudly evacuating a nearby section of decaying wood when he stammered, "What's that hole I see in the embankment ahead of us?"

"It looks like a fox hole to me," said his boss. Each step along the water's edge brought them closer to the small irregular opening in the hillside. "We'll go around it just in case we come across an irate parent. We may encounter more dens like this throughout the day so keep an eye out."

Morty tugged at the survey rod caught in the underbrush that grew thicker the higher they continued up the ravine, bypassing the partially concealed burrow. He mumbled out loud about the constant entanglement.

Donny finished his reminiscent scan of the inscriptions in the bark of the old maple tree and pulled the straw hat he always wore down a little lower over his eyes, as if to prevent the glare from a rising sun. In reality, his purpose was to pause within his own reflections and isolate his thoughts, a separation of man and humility.

He stepped back onto the well-worn path to continue his morning trek, leaving the two intruders of the morning behind. He wandered onto a small pile of wood chips created many years before by an old sawmill. There was nothing left now except for those small piles scattered about the woods and embedded into the soil.

A red tail hawk flew overhead and guided him onward. Other animals stirred, relinquishing their locations. He could see a group of five deer in the distance on a small hill that overlooked the ravine to his right. He kept walking. They had already seen him but didn't stir because they knew he posed no threat to them. They had seen him here before.

The thick growth along each side of the path finally gave

way to a large clearing, where he came to a sudden stop. A high embankment greeted the old traveler, causing him to change his smooth gate into one involving a steep climb. With each step he took upward, rocks of all sizes kept sliding down the hill. It was twenty feet from the bottom to the top of the added earth fill, and it was like walking uphill in quicksand.

When he reached the top, he was greeted by a totally different view than he remembered. The old worn portion of the path, which at one time had continued to the edge of the forest, was gone, replaced with six large housing complexes and a church at the far end of a newly developed mini-village. A large swath of trees had been cut away from around the buildings.

The church gave the area a somewhat tranquil appearance. It looked a little out of place but nonetheless calmed the deforested area. Its steeple soared above the trees that remained. Donny fixated his look at the steeple and shook his head as his morning journey into tranquility relinquished itself to the changes that faced him.

The slight smile he usually wore disappeared; a dissatisfied and disdainful smirk took its place. He stopped, turned away, slightly shook his head again from side to side with a noticeable repugnance, and retraced his steps down the embankment, trying not to stumble over the loose stone. Once again at the bottom, he stepped back onto the worn path into the familiar surroundings of the remaining untouched forest and continued on his way.

I watched him as he faded from view. Then I turned and choose a different path in the opposite direction.

Year Eight

October 19 - Morning

"The point of philosophy is to start with something so simple as to not seem worth stating, and to end with something so paradoxical that no one will believe it."

—Bertrand Russell

Chapter One

Conceivability

i.

What if Maxwell was right? Nelson looked at his watch and quickened his pace. He hated being late for appointments.

People might have a difficult time believing the story about confrontations with his own home-town bureaucracy, but his real fear was that no one would ever believe Maxwell's predictions—the ones that were real, not imagined—outcomes that would affect more than just himself.

Despite Nelson's proclivity to dwell upon the lies and twisted truths he had witnessed over the last seven years, his past communications with Maxwell suffocated those thoughts. He looked at his watch again, attempted to clear his mind from thoughts of a yet unfulfilled prophesy, and crossed the busy intersection, eluding the final flicker of a pedestrian traffic light.

The chaos of it all was new to Nelson Quip. He wove his way throughout the heavy traffic and jostled his way toward open space on the crowded sidewalks. In his mind the city eagerly anticipated the hustle of people and welcomed the commotion as a natural order to the daily business routine. They rushed, shoulder to shoulder, across the streets of Manhattan with downcast eyes dwelling upon cell phones in hand, talking, texting, tweeting.

Nelson realized his bias, his first impression: callous.

He viewed city life as one of daily irritation, not from the perspective of those who appeared to relish the unpredictability of what they considered to be a normal work day. He just wasn't used to such commotion, nor did he like it. He wondered if such daily confusion prevented people from paying attention, causing them to ignore the changing world around them, never thinking about the unintended consequences of inaction.

Shifting shadows from the early morning sunlight were augmented by Nelson's brisk walk, and by the buildings that towered over fifty stories high. The streets were glassy with water, a reminder of last night's late downpour. Cars whooshed by the crowded sidewalks, fanning water from nearby puddles. Dyspeptic faces were obvious results from the unwanted spray, followed by the dank smell from remnants of wet, dirty pavement.

Nelson crossed another street, jumped a sheet of water at a curb, and paused to observe his surroundings, thoughtfully comparing the daily environment of his own home-town to his impression of the city and its inhabitants. Horns and nearby sirens added to the forlorn cries of the city as they chased and shoved the crowds together, and he wondered what role the greed of landowning developers, city politics, and assorted idiots had in sculpting the physical landscape of this cement forest.

Nelson quickened his step once again, and he darted among the people, avoiding any attempt to belong. He was inherently apprehensive about his predestined appointment, compounded by the immensity of the unfamiliar city and the ocean of humanity that surrounded him. He was naturally shy and if anyone was to review the results of any Myers-Briggs assessment regarding his psyche, they would conclude he was somewhat of an introvert.

He was in Manhattan for one specific reason. He was asked to come. He had written a novel, contrived from meetings, backyard conversations, e-mails, and letters spanning a seven-year period, that he had sent to a major publishing house. He'd sent it as an unsolicited manuscript for review, knowing he might never get a response or even any recognition that it had ever been received.

He wrote it because he wanted to warn people of what he thought was a consequential and prophetic story—a true story about events that had already occurred and of events yet to happen that could ultimately affect the lives of everyone—including himself.

ii.

Nelson stopped amid the throngs of people to verify the address he had scribbled onto a small torn piece of notepad paper earlier that morning with the address on the skyscraper on Fifth Avenue. He entered and the plate glass doors glided shut behind him—giving him a quiet oasis from the chaos outside.

The lobby glistened as sunlight reflected off polished marble floors and an abundance of stainless steel. Glass barriers provided an airport-like walkway that led to a security desk, separating two banks of elevators from the entrance. Signs were posted, notifying visitors of their requirement to register at the desk in order to proceed. A colorful mural—a frenetic abstract in composition—adorned the wall directly behind the desk, in stark contrast to the building's monotonous, inordinate black and white letters of a wall-mounted business directory.

Nelson scrutinized the list, located his destination, Block Publishing, and handed a security guard his driver's license for identification. The guard typed Nelson's name into a computer system, observed his monitor to validate his appointment, and courteously directed him toward the metal detectors and the section of elevators for the appropriate floor.

Can't be too careful these days, Nelson thought to himself as he passed through without hesitation, skated across the slick variegated floor, and stepped into one of the ten elevators that lined two sides of the wide hallway, crowded with at least a dozen other people. Being the last one to enter, Nelson pressed the button for his designated floor, and the door silently closed.

It was then that he felt the overwhelming sensation of being incarcerated, as if his shared living space was suddenly defined to a mere thirty-six square feet. He wasn't claustrophobic, just not use to the constant crowds and restricted surroundings, and he felt relief when he noticed there are only four stops before reaching the 43rd floor.

He squirmed in his new environment, and the quiet, almost motionless ride put time on hold for Nelson until the elevator finally reached his destination. To his surprise, the doors opened on the opposite side from which he had entered, and grateful to escape his confinement, he proceeded to the receptionist's desk before him.

"My name is Nelson Quip," he stammered to the girl who looked up from her computer screen, raising one eyebrow. "I have an appointment with Mr. Paul Whitman," he added with hesitation and a hint of anxiety in his voice.

The girl quickly checked her on-line appointment list. "Yes, Mr. Quip." She pointed to her right, and said, "You can go straight down that hallway where you'll find Mr. Whitman's secretary. I'll let her know you're here. You're right on time. They're expecting you."

"Thank you."

"Have a good day, sir, and welcome to Block Publishing."

She is very nice, he thought. He turned in the direction given and started down the long corridor. Offices extended on both sides as he walked past open doors to secretaries, editors, and waiting rooms. When he reached the end of the wide passageway, arched mahogany double doors automatically opened inward to a lavish office, more expansive and detailed than the others he had just observed. A young woman stood up from behind an ornate executive desk and introduced herself when he entered the room.

"Good morning, Mr. Quip. I'm Sherry Nolan," she said as she extended a warm handshake. "We've been expecting you. How was your flight from Maine?"

Nelson was surprised and somewhat pleased to receive what appeared to be a sincere welcome, helping to diminish his pent-up anxiety. "Good morning," he replied. "The flight was very smooth. I actually left from Portland last night and stayed at a nearby hotel so that I wouldn't be rushed this morning. Luckily, I arrived just before the rainstorm. I've never been to New York City before," he quickly added, "so I didn't know what to expect for delays in traffic or how much time it would take for me to find your offices."

"I'm glad to hear your trip down here went well. Airports can be such a hassle these days, particularly with all the security checks we have to endure. Mr. Whitman will be glad to see you. I'll buzz him to let him know you're here."

"Thank you."

"Please take a seat if you'd like." She gestured to the area on her left as she picked up her phone to announce Nelson's arrival, then answered, "Thank you, Mr. Whitman, I'll let him know.

"He's on the phone, Mr. Quip, but I'm sure he'll be with you in a few moments. He's looking forward to meeting you."

"Thank you," said Nelson as he looked about the large office. The size of the room itself was reminiscent of a town meeting hall, the familiarity being a recent consequence of local politics and public hearings. However, instead of having long tables, uncomfortable metal chairs, and stark walls, as he was used to in his local town hall, this space was filled with dark mahogany bookcases and volumes of books that line the shelves. Tastefully placed paintings provided color to the room and narrow streams of light from hidden fixtures in the ceiling accentuated the contrasting deep blue walls. Some book editions looked old from the condition of their bindings, while others appeared like they had just come off the press. There was a pleasant earthy scent to the room, as if rain had recently fallen onto dry soil.

His first thought was there were enough books in that one room to fill his entire local library. To his right, where Sherry had offered him a seat, were four oversized, high-back chairs, creating somewhat of an alcove next to a wall that had three large windows extending from floor to ceiling.

"I've never been to New York City before," he commented to Sherry once again, then, slightly embarrassed, realized he had repeated himself.

He turned and slowly walked toward the windows at the end of the room. He noticed a slight movement in the heavy, light blue colored drapes that lined each side of the windows, caused by the air conditioning quietly pumping cool air throughout the room, maintaining a constant temperature, possibly as much for the books as for the people he thought.

"There sure are a lot more people living here in such a relatively small space than in *my* home town," he commented as he walked toward the windows. "There are simply too many people here to ever personally know even a small portion of them. You could only settle for a glimpse of their lives as they come and go, unlike the relatively few people who live in a much larger space where I'm from." Nelson paused, waiting for her to consider a response to his philosophical remark.

"I've been to Maine before," she said, as if simply to add

a personal touch to the conversation. "Pretty up there in the summer. I like those small towns on the coast. They're a great place for a relaxing vacation away from the hubbub of city life. I'll grant you that."

He smiled at her remark and unbuttoned his sports jacket so he could comfortably walk with his hands in his pockets.

The cool air was refreshing under his jacket, an English tweed, more casual than a suit jacket. He never wore a tie, believing it to be a 20th century affectation. The top button on his shirt served the same purpose, and he fidgeted with it to ensure it indeed remained open, not tight to his neck. He figured he was uncomfortable enough being out of his own environment.

He shuffled across the thick carpet to the end of the room and stood with his nose almost touching the window, looking down at the city. The people and cars below reminded him of the board game Monopoly®, with all the hotels and game pieces neatly arranged but their sizes incongruous with one another. His thoughts were interrupted by Sherry's voice.

"Mr. Quip, Mr. Whitman can see you now."

Nelson turned and quickly walked back toward Paul Whitman's office, still collecting and associating his thoughts with the reality of the game pieces he had been contemplating.

"Please go right in." With that announcement, she opened the door for him.

"This is Nelson Quip, Mr. Whitman."

"Thanks, Sherry."

Extending his hand, he stood to introduce himself. "Good morning, Mr. Quip. I'm Paul Whitman. It's great to finally meet you, especially after the many phone conversations we've had and emails we've exchanged. Thanks for flying down here to talk with me about your book. We think the story is unique enough to warrant your time as well as ours to discuss publication. I also want to discuss the story itself with you as well as finalize a contract agreement for the rights and a possible publishing schedule. Please, have a seat. Let's talk."

He shook hands then glanced about the office. There were two chairs in front of the desk and Nelson hesitated while he contemplated in which to sit. That was his very na-

ture. He always had to methodically evaluate everything before committing to an action. He quickly made his decision
and chose the chair on the right. Paul Whitman sat behind
his desk directly across from him.

Paul was a thin, balding man. He had gray peppered hair
on top with more gray on the sides than the top. His high
forehead, however, seemed to exaggerate the little hair remaining. Nelson observed the thinning hair was a feature
shared by them both. Paul also had a pleasant, calming, well
pronounced voice, with a bit of an English accent. His rimless
glasses slowly inched down from the bridge of his nose while
he spoke.

"As you know, Mr. Quip, from our previous phone conversations, I'm the senior acquisitions editor of Block Publishing
House. A small executive staff and myself have the daunting
responsibility of deciding which manuscripts to publish."

Nelson interrupted before the editor could continue.
"Please, just call me Nelson. Mr. Quip is too formal for me.
I'm a bit curious about you wanting to meet me here and
paying for my flight and accommodations. It was very nice of
you, but isn't this a little unusual—I mean...to fly a first-time
novelist down to New York City...to discuss a book that
has...just recently...been completed?"

Nelson nervously stuttered his statement, and the last
word, completed, mistakenly sounded like competed. Mr.
Whitman seemed to notice his hesitancy and ensured the
conversation remained at a comfortable level.

"By all means, please call me Paul, and yes, it is a little
unusual for us to do this—very unusual—highly unusual. But
after reading what you sent us, I decided it would really be
best to meet with you and talk to you in person. There are
some disturbing things about your story. I'll be up front with
you. I liked your manuscript. It needs a bit of editing, but the
overall story intrigues me. I had an opportunity similar to
this one several years ago and let it slip through my fingers.

"There's a certain feeling you get as an editor and publisher, one of missed opportunity, and it doesn't let go. You
say to yourself—never again. Of course, it's really never only
a one-time thing. I've made my share of regretful calls. The
author found another publisher after I turned him down and
his manuscript became a best-selling book. He wrote several

others after that but he never came back to us. I think your book has the same potential."

"Well, I'm happy to hear you like it. I've been working on it for over seven years on and off. It's just a story I needed to tell even though I think people will find it difficult to believe."

Whitman's voice took on a more serious tone. "The reason I wanted to see you was to discuss the letters and e-mails addressed in your story."

"Do you mean the exchanges I had with town officials? Or those I received from Maxwell Draper?"

"I mean the letters and e-mails Maxwell Draper sent you."

"What about them?" Nelson questioned. Past conversations and hypothetical conjectures invaded his thoughts once again.

"As I read them, I realized there was a persistent theme that emerged over the years. I realized the effects of circumstances and their causal relationships had a natural trend of events—ones that had occurred and ones that hadn't at the time, and then later did."

"I don't understand what you're getting at."

"I'll explain. You didn't fully define the months and years associated with the letters and e-mails in your story. Your story only addressed events in terms of years, months, and seasons as a sequence of time, but not by any specific year. Based upon your storyline, however, particularly those issues addressed on a national level, I can hazard a guess as to what year events actually happened, and in many cases, I know exactly when they *did* happen.

"You sent me copies after I asked to see the originals. That's when I happened to notice the actual dates and from some of the e-mails, the times when they were sent to you. In many circumstances, the situations and events described in newspapers, Associated Press releases, government and other sources occurred *after* Maxwell wrote his information, indicating those certain events would happen. Notice I used the phrase 'would happen', not 'could happen'. There's a subtle difference between those two phrases, and I'll tell you why. Many of his writings appeared to be warnings. Then those things he warned you about actually happened. In many situations, they seemed more than just coincidental."

"I didn't date the correspondence because I never considered any of it relevant to the main part of the story. As you know, one of the two themes concerns the destruction of a forest and the idea that people can make a difference if they pay attention, are aware of what's going on around them, if they represent themselves together as a common voice. I only needed to keep track of time and the sequence of events by designating the years as one, two, three, and so on, and at times, I included the months in which they occurred."

"I understand your reasoning, and I don't disagree with you," Paul said. "According to your time sequence, this meeting today would actually be Year Eight, the year in which you completed your manuscript. You really don't need to provide the reader with the actual year in which the chronicled events occurred. The situations regarding the forest where people were trying to save it and their interactions with zoning and planning boards could have taken place at any time and in any town. Besides, the events in your story that occur on a *national basis* can actually define the years in which your story really *does* take place. The local and national themes are an allegory to one another."

He leaned back, rested his elbows on the arm of his chair and steepled his fingers before continuing. "Maxwell's information does emphasize the relevance of time, however, pursuant to your point as to what can happen when people don't pay attention and remain apathetic. He warns us about the dilemmas that have been created over the last seven years; situations that escalate toward harmful consequences. No matter the actual year, the relevance of your story is true for any interval of time—not just now, but in the future as well—whether it involves changes that evolve during a public hearing or changes that evolve during terms of any particular political office. Your story is really about harmful consequences that can occur when no one pays attention. It is about people believing in rhetoric and not substantive information when forming an opinion. However, if you think a particular year is pertinent in order to emphasize a prediction, you could always reference it anywhere in the story.

"How did you meet Maxwell Draper, and how well do you know him?" Paul leaned forward and queried.

"He was in several of my classes at the University of

Maine during our undergraduate years. We studied together at times and became good friends. I got my degree in Electrical Engineering and he got his in Engineering Physics. I went on to get a Master's Degree in Business and became a CPA. He went on to other colleges and earned PhD's in both Nuclear and Astrophysics. There's a bit of diversity in our backgrounds, but we've always had common interests. We had not talked with one another for a while, not until these last few years, but we've always managed to keep in touch."

"What about the man personally?"

"Like I said, I consider him to be a good friend, even though I don't see much of him. We've always had some sort of connection. He's a brilliant guy, a little quirky at times, but honest and straight-forward. That's what I like about him. He's real and sincere—and for the most part, a private individual. He's a research scientist for a research microwave and satellite technology company, funded by several grants from the National Security Agency and the National Science Foundation in a little town about a two-hour drive north of where I live.

"One thing I always thought interesting about him is he's one of the few people I know who can remember his dreams—in great detail I might add. If I dream about something, it disappears from my memory within minutes after I wake up. Not Maxwell. He remembers everything. It appears he has a photographic memory, even when he dreams. The warnings contained in his e-mails and letters, however, weren't based on his dreams, visions, or premonitions, but rather predictions based on scientific anomalies."

Nelson paused briefly, rubbing his thumb and index finger on the bottom of his chin. He thought about the choice of his next words before continuing.

"I e-mailed Max on several occasions just to keep in touch. Then this thing with the town started. I vented my frustrations to him over the false and misconstrued information being presented to the public, and told him about the resident's responses to the town's Planning and Zoning Boards discussions being ignored. I simply started to write about it. Actually, Maxwell gave me the idea to take notes and keep track of events as they unfolded.

"It's difficult to believe such conversations, twisted truths, and outright lies actually transpired during the public hearings I attended. I was involved in it, and I *still* find it to be incredulous. It would be difficult to even *fabricate* such a sequence of events. Perhaps it's just the reality of life, and I'm just too naive to believe such things can happen. I'm sure many people in many other towns can relate to similar situations that occur in my story; you know, with developers, the taking of land, and the flagrant disregard for zoning and land use regulations. But why do you ask about Max?"

"I asked about Maxwell because in our previous correspondence, you mentioned you had forwarded a draft of your story to him. Why *did* you send your manuscript to Maxwell?"

"I simply wanted to get his opinion. Besides, he urged me to write it. I had used some of his observations regarding national incidents throughout the story because they were similar to what I was experiencing. Maxwell compared our local public hearings to the negative and damaging political policies that occur when people don't pay attention. I guess you could say he was looking ahead at potential repercussions from poor decisions and an unchecked expansion of government. Those discussions I had with him reinforced the message I attempted to convey throughout the book. I just wanted to make sure he didn't have a problem with me using some of the material."

"And did he mind?"

"No, not at all. In fact, he encouraged me to use whatever I wanted and insisted on giving me written permission to use any and all e-mails and letters for any time period."

"Your query letter to us mentioned that after Maxwell Draper read your story, he suggested that you send it to us. The mention of his name raised our eyebrows a little. You may not realize it, but Maxwell Draper has written several books, both fiction and non-fiction. His first novel was the one that slipped through my fingers. With the reference to his name in mind, I took the time to read your entire manuscript, not wanting to make the same mistake again. I'll be honest with you. I may not have read your book had it not been for his referral. Good chance it would have ended up in the circular file. We normally work exclusively with literary agents."

"That wasn't my intent, I mean, to use his name as a referral. I knew he had written a few non-fiction, technical books, but never knew he had written novels as well. Like I've mentioned, he's a fairly private individual, not a recluse, just unpretentious."

"He suggested that you send your manuscript to us because he knew I'd look at your book. He wanted you to have a better opportunity of getting it published right away. Apparently time was an important consideration for him, wanting to get a message out to people to avoid short-term, harmful consequences. He understood why you wrote it and purposely provided you with additional material he knew you'd include in your story, whether or not you understood the reasons for his intended additions yourself. It's the last letter he mailed you a year ago and the accompanying audio transcription that bothers me."

"I know the one you're talking about."

"Yes, I'm sure you do. Why did you leave that out of your story?"

Year One

"We must welcome the future, remembering that soon it will be the past; and we must respect the past, remembering that it was once all that was humanly possible."

—George Santayana

Chapter Two

The Notice

L

Nelson Quip reflected on his life with his wife Sarah and their two young sons. They lived on two acres of land surrounded mostly by forest in the small town of Laslo, Maine. Their two-story house was nestled back in the woods, modestly separating itself from view of other residences, and their dirt driveway turned onto a short private road that led onto a paved town road.

Their property abutted a thirty-two-acre parcel of land owned by a non-profit company called Caring Home Services, which was affiliated and had been originally owned by another non-profit organization known as the Salvation for the Society of Churches.

He and Sarah were close to the same age, both in their mid-forties. Nelson's only sign of aging was the recent thinning of his once thick brown hair. Sarah's features never seemed to change much. She was short, rather petite, with shoulder length dirty blonde hair. She was an energetic woman, a good match for him, keeping him on his toes. She was also a good counterpart for him because Nelson had a tendency to dwell on minute details, and she'd remind him to refocus and move along to other matters.

He was a tax accountant, a far cry from his undergraduate degree in physics and electrical engineering, but none-the-less a profession satisfying his penchant for numbers, and at least a light use of mathematics. He owned a small accounting office within the town and on occasion enjoyed writing. He even had some success in having a few of his technical books published as well as magazine articles.

In his mind, Sarah held the more difficult job as a housewife: raising their two boys, Karl and Preston who were ten and twelve years old. Sarah often complained she should be contributing more financially to the family. Nelson always joked with her that she had the more important full-time job but that the pay was lousy. Besides, it was more important to spend time with the boys while they were growing.

Nelson always had an extensive to-do list and had finally gotten around to working outside after several years of establishing his accounting practice. Only in the last few years had any landscaping been done. He spent many Saturday afternoons in the summer with his sons, while they all worked together and helped build decking around the house, created cobblestone pathways, assembled a patio with a small fire pit for cooler fall evenings, and cultivated a vegetable garden.

There were always those special afternoons after work, particularly in the Spring and Fall, when Nelson and his sons would walk along the forest trail near their house and visit what Nelson called Karl and Preston's Treasure Rock. They'd talk about the animals in the forest and every once in a while, by some mystical circumstance, a few pieces of their favorite candies would appear on a large boulder located next to the winding pathway.

In addition to the many varieties of trees in the forest, Nelson fenced off a section of his property and planted a few apple and pear trees. The entire family had a love for animals and placated their indoor cats by hanging bird feeders outside, underneath a second story deck that ran the length of the house. The sunflower and thistle seeds attracted many types of birds from the nearby forest including finches, chickadees, nut-hatch, and morning doves, to name a few. Occasional blue jays and cardinals would also join the fray. Their three cats spent much of their time watching the birds, and the two boys, in turn, enjoyed watching their cat's reactions to the outside activity.

Nelson's closest neighbors were an older fellow, Donny, who lived alone, Joe and Mary Vaschon, who were retired veterans and lived next door to Donny, Will Penton and his wife Barbara, who lived several houses from the Quips, and Josh Gosling and his wife Joan, who lived across the short private driveway that led from the town road to both houses.

"Did you read this notice we got from the town?" Nelson

asked Sarah. He stared out the kitchen bay window at the forest. It was noontime on Saturday and Sarah had just returned from walking down to their mailbox at the end of the driveway to retrieve the mail.

"That's the first letter I opened as I walked back to the house," she replied. "I saw it was from the town and wondered, what now? There's an agenda item from the Zoning Board of Appeals stating that a company called Caring Home Services is requesting a special exception to the town's zoning ordinance. It says they're affiliated with an organization called the Salvation for the Society of Churches, which is a charitable development company that once owned the entire forest in back of us then sold it for development. I haven't read the whole thing yet."

Nelson held the letter in his hand and alternately kept reading and looking out at the forest. It was the latter part of November, just after Thanksgiving, and the first brushing of snow had covered the ground from the previous night. The real winter snow had not yet begun.

"This notice says that Caring Home Services wants a special exception to the terms of Title 10, Section 14.060, Subsection E.1, of the town's Land Use Code. Guess I'll have to get a copy of the ordinance so I can find out the details. Apparently, they want to construct five buildings containing sixteen total apartments, as well as a community building at their property located off Baker Street. That's the street that goes directly from Route 2. It dead-ends at the entrance to an old wood's road that crosses a shallow wetland at the northern tip of this section of the forest. That's a distance from us."

"I know where that is," Sarah said. "We've walked up that way before. That's the street where Millie Hodgdon lives."

"You're right—very nice lady. I don't remember where we first met her. It must have been at some earlier town meeting. She reminds me of my grandmother—rather petite with pure white hair."

Nelson's thoughts turned back to the notice in his hands. "The town has even attached a copy of the Caring Home Services mission and purpose statement. It's almost like they're promoting this whole thing."

"What's it say about them?" asked Sarah.

"Well, there's about six pages of information here."

"How worried should we be about a massive number of buildings approaching our property lines?"

"I'm not sure. I'll read you a few parts of this."

Nelson stepped back from the window and walked over to their old but sturdy oak kitchen table and sat down. "Their mission statement states that Caring Home Services is a non-profit, non-denominational retirement community established for benevolent purposes. They use the acronym of CHS throughout their literature. It says they're established exclusively for the care of elderly people. They're approved by the IRS, known as a 501(c)3 corporation."

"What's a 501(c)3 corporation?"

"They're companies that meet certain established IRS tax guidelines, designated as non-profit, and pay no federal, state, or property taxes. Although most are legitimate, I have seen a few that really shouldn't qualify under the IRS rules and should be paying taxes, not getting a free ride on the shoulders of tax paying citizens. If they qualify as non-profit, they get services from a town like fire and police and pay nothing for those services. It can also put a strain on water and sewage expansions needed to accommodate and support their facilities. I'd give this company, CHS, the benefit of doubt at this point. But I'm always wary about this kind of tax status.

"There's a statement in here that says they pay a fee for services in lieu of taxes based upon the amount of rental income, but they neglect to say what that percentage is or how much they pay. That could be kind of a red flag, all by itself. The letter goes on to say that their facilities are open to all people regardless of their religious convictions and affiliations. It also proposes they'll establish a chapel as a community building."

"I don't see a problem with it as long as they somehow pay for some of the town services and don't make a clustered mess out of the whole thing like they did on their northern section, of what used to be a forest," Sarah said.

"Neither do I, at least not at this point. I'll have to find out why they want a special exception to the town's land use ordinance. Nothing mentions what that special exception is."

"Do they say anything else?"

"Well, they've provided information about what they did on that separate northern parcel of land...the one you think is a clustered mess. They kept adding to the number of apartments, so now there are sixty units in two buildings on the twelve and a half acres. Then they state they purchased the abutting thirty-two-acre parcel from the Salvation for the Society of Churches, which is the section that borders our property, and they want to develop that as well. They're going to call the northern parcel their North Campus and the southern parcel their South Campus. It makes me wonder—how big is this development going to get?"

Sarah sat down across from Nelson to absorb the conversation. "Does any of their propaganda tell us what they have in mind?"

Looking up at her from the paperwork, Nelson replied. "It does, in a way. Like I mentioned, they state they'd like to build sixteen apartments in five buildings plus a community building, but they also indicate that this is the first phase to the development of their South Campus. They don't say anything about the additional phases they intend to propose. Then they go into an explanation as to the need for this type of project, categorizing themselves as elderly housing for middle-income people. You know—a sales pitch."

Nelson shook his head and continued. "Once their additional apartment buildings are built on this South Campus, it looks like they want to connect their two developments with a bridge by crossing the wetlands into the northern parcel."

Sarah winced at the idea of a bridge being built to connect the two properties. "We've walked around that section of the property on some of the old wood's roads. There's a lot of water in that area."

"Yeah, I would think the town's Conservation Commission would have a few things to say about the idea of building a bridge across such a large section of wetlands. The Zoning Board of Appeals meeting is scheduled on Tuesday in the second week of December. Guess I'd better figure out what the special exception is all about. I remember when their development was proposed for their so-called North Campus. There was only a planning board meeting at that time. I don't remember any special exceptions to zoning in that case. I didn't realize until now that they don't pay property taxes on those buildings."

"Oh, by the way," said Sarah, changing the subject, "you got an e-mail from Maxwell Draper early this morning. I printed it out for you."

"I haven't heard from Max since I did his income taxes early last spring. What's he say?"

"Here. You read it. He's always interesting. I'm just not always sure what he's talking about, though."

"At times, neither do I," replied Nelson. He smiled and took the printout.

ii.

E-mail:Nov 27
To: NelsonQuip
From: Mdraper
Subject: Taxes

Hi, Nelson. Wishing you and Sarah an early Merry Christmas. I know you're starting to get busy with the tax season gearing up once again. I'll mail my stuff down to you shortly so I can get ahead of the crowd. Thought I'd keep in touch and let you know what I've been doing lately.

Currently working on some new microwave satellite triggering devices and gravitational sensing transmitters for black hole theory analysis—interesting technology. I've also been focusing on behavior based control systems for individual satellites which allows a reactive intelligence to flight control. The research center actually developed a rudimentary prototype for two of our satellites many years ago.

The satellites can follow a prearranged plan while remaining aware of the unexpected. This allows the systems to recognize features of their environment, giving them more capability and flexibility in allowing changes to adapt to external conditions. There are advantages in using this technology for deep space exploration, including alleviating communication command delays from us at home.

By incorporating what you might call 'fuzzy' logic into the system technology, the satellites can respond to visual or radio signals in their current environment. It's like having their own neural network so the satellite operates on its own from afar and also has what you might call telepresence, providing the appearance that we, on earth, are right there. Such behavior-based control allows us to function without relying much on human commands to address abnormal and distant environment issues.

Remember some of those late study nights and the partial differentiation and tensor analysis courses we took? Those were our days of classical physics awakening. And those quantum mechanics courses—an awful lot of theoretical stuff for us to contemplate back then. Some of it really does have practicality.

Been experimenting with the concept of bending light and data transmissions near black hole gravitational anomalies. Of course, creating those anomalies is only one issue. I've been designing expanded capabilities to a new powerful particle accelerator we've built over the last ten years. Perhaps we'll be able to confirm some of this theoretical physics with potential observations in order to quantify some of these theories—you know—the potential of creating a miniature black hole at a certain energy level, lasting only a thousandth of a trillionth of a trillionth of a second.

This could suggest that the universe stretches back in time infinitely with no singular point where it started—no Big Bang theory.

We've managed to get funding from private sources, as well as from the National Security Agency and the National Science Foundation. We've built a massive particle accelerator, over three times the size of the Large Hadron Collider. It has a housing tunnel that's about 54 miles in circumference for particle acceleration and a detection aperture larger than a person—not quite unlike the appearance of the Stargate you've seen on television, but reminiscent of that. We're hoping to discover evidence of dimensions to space-time. You'd find this research intriguing!

In addition to that, we've kind of been experimenting with the real thing, as well.

Over fifty years ago, our company sent two satellites, named Sagittarius-A-21132 and Turing-B-21133, six years apart, toward what we believe is a black hole that's in a region called Sagittarius-A, about 26,000 light years from our *solar system. Considering the distance of such a journey, we know it's gonna be a long time before either of them get anywhere close.*

But both satellites are beyond Voyager, which is now well into interstellar space—a region between the stars, filled with material ejected by the death of nearby stars. For some reason, however, both our satellites are farther from us than they should be—almost like they decided to take a faster vehicle in order to make such a long trip. I'll tell you more about that later...

Anyway, their purpose is to see if there is any variation in transmitting data to a satellite and then retrieving that same transmission as a satellite approaches any resultant increase in gravity due to a black hole. In other words, will there be any time anomalies due to massive gravity deflections?

A few years ago, we believe we inadvertently discovered a second black hole much closer than the one in Sagittarius; in fact, both satellites appear to have come across several small black holes during their travel. I use the word inadvertently because the second satellite, Turing-B, appears to have gotten caught in what I would describe as a traversable wormhole; you know—one that connects two points in space time—in principle allowing travel in time as well as in space.

Although we have no observational evidence of such a notion, the equations of the theory of general relativity have valid solutions that contain wormholes—you know—the hypothetical Einstein-Rosen Bridge. So, we've sent news media streams out to both satellites and are waiting to compare the times of return transmissions. I'll tell you more as we learn more. Thought you'd be interested.

Keep in touch
—Max

iii.

One week after receiving Maxwell's e-mail, Nelson attended a Zoning Board of Appeals public hearing. Without knowing much about the developer's intent prior to the hearing, Phase One of the Southern Campus project was approved for zoning. The Planning Board approved the development the following week. One week after that, Nelson finally responded to Maxwell's e-mail.

E-mail:Dec 18
To: Mdraper
From: NelsonQuip
Subject: Concerns

Hi, Max. Sorry for my late response to your last e-mail. Things have been hectic at my office as well as on the home front with town issues.

Your work sounds a lot more exciting than my seemingly mundane tax computations and town development issues. There are times when I think I should have stuck with the engineering—science related work. But I do prefer to work for myself, rather than any grant-based employer. You're pretty lucky though, 'cause you seem to be your own boss most of the time. They kind of leave you alone to design what they're interested in. All you have to do is make what-ever it is you're designing—work. I guess that's not always an easy thing to do, however. On the negative side, you al-ways have to be concerned about getting massive funding for those projects.

While you're working on some highly technical, experi-mental stuff, I'm down here in my spare time proverbially fighting city hall. I'm becoming a little concerned about a de-velopment project that's taking place in the forest behind us.

There's an outfit called Caring Home Services, which is affiliated with an organization called the Salvation for the So-ciety of Churches. They're both non-profit 501(c)3 organiza-tions that want to build an elderly housing development con-sisting of 16 apartments somewhere in back of our property. We had a public hearing before the Zoning Board of Appeals because they wanted a special exception for zoning in order to construct elderly housing in a residential zone. I'm a bit concerned because they don't pay property taxes to the town because they say they're exempt due to their federal tax sta-tus. That means the rest of the property owners will have to pay more in property taxes in order to supply additional town services for them.

Since they appear to have met all conditions and there was very little dissent from any residents during the hearing, they were able to get approval from both the Zoning and Planning Boards for what they call their Phase One construction for the Southern Campus. I expect they'll start building next spring right through next summer and fall.

Not much I can do about this now. Talk with you later. Don't forget to send me your tax stuff before April 15th! And keep me informed about the anomalies you observe with gravity deflections and their effect on radio transmissions traveling at the speed of light. I am still scientifically curious; like you mentioned, results will be very interesting.

–Nelson

Chapter Three

Maxwell's Theory

i.

It was almost 3 a.m. when Maxwell Draper decided to start his first test of the day. He had received an e-mail from Nelson only a few hours earlier and, after a short nap and a bite to eat, he thought he would reply then get back to work. He slid his badge through the wall reader and received a no access light.

"Morn'n, Dr. Draper. You having problems with that old badge reader again?"

Maxwell turned around and looked up to see the skinny security guard who stood six foot-four inches tall, a man in his late forties with a slight southern accent. "Hi, George. Yeah, for some reason, these badges always seem to slide at the wrong angle for me, and the readers don't respond. Guess I'm just a little tired."

"Keeping another late night, huh?"

"Yeah, or the start of an early morning. Sometimes I just don't pay much attention to the time. One day seems to drift into another," replied Maxwell, "especially when I become too focused with what I'm doing. Of course, it doesn't help, not having any sunlight down here. I just left my office on level two and have one more test to run on the accelerator before I quit for the day—or night—or whatever it is now."

"Where's the rest of your staff?" asked George. "Don't you have at least a dozen people on your accelerator project?"

"Yes, but I prefer to have them work during regular day-time hours," Maxwell said as he slid his badge through the wall reader and once again received a no access light. "I'm a workaholic, so I don't expect them to maintain the same weird hours unless we have a predetermined event that re-quires everyone to be in the lab. Most of them maintain the four floors of computer servers and systems that control and monitor power to the detectors and the optical fibers for the massive amount of data received during experimental runs.

"Only two people on my staff keep the same kind of hours I do. That's Harold Lang, our information technology technician, and our data analyst, Dora. Harold integrates our software and hardware and is taking care of a special project I have him working on. I also think he prefers his alone time. In fact, I think he's still in the lab tonight. So is Dora, who analyzes all the data Harold produces. They've both worked with me for about three years now. Time sure goes by fast, doesn't it? You've also worked down here on this level with me for quite a few years now, haven't you?"

"Go'n on about six years now, I'd say. You were working here before I came, and for all the time I've been here, you've always fought with these badge readers. Let me open that door for you. Personally, I really think they installed these things too high up on the wall, at least for most people. Besides, these are an old technology and should be updated sometime soon."

"Thanks, George. Sometimes they seem to work for me. But even when I exit the main lab, the system doesn't always seem to properly log me back out. Maybe that's why I always seem to be here. According to the system, I am."

George chuckled at Max's comment. "You would think with all that computer power you got down here, simple things like these openers and tracking systems would work better."

"You'd think so. And we keep adding more hardware. We're just finishing up linking to the National Nuclear Security Administration system called 'Dawn' so we'll have a capacity of over five hundred teraFlops. That's a lot of computer power."

"Don't know nothin' about flip-flops or whatever they call them, but it sure sounds like a lot."

As the thick steel door quietly slid open, Maxwell proceeded down the long corridor toward the main lab. He heard George call after him, "You should get some sleep, Dr. Draper." Maxwell smiled at the thoughtfulness behind the comment.

The video cameras mounted on the ceiling surveyed his

profile as he approached the entrance to the main part of the laboratory, and a second wide, solid steel door slid open automatically. He entered and was greeted with the same monotone voice he had heard for several years.

"Good morning, Doctor Draper. It's another early day for you at three in the morning." This was her only matter-of-fact response to his entry.

Dora had little inflection in her voice from expressing scientific facts over the years with not a lot of personality behind the voice, but she was a very attractive woman with long flowing dark brown hair, whose framed photograph was a distinctive addition to Harold's desk.

"Good morning, Dora," Nelson said loudly to his unseen but reliable assistant, who by the sound of her voice appeared to be at the far end of the lab, which was well over two hundred feet in length.

"I've logged you in this time. I didn't forget," she said. Then she added one additional comment, almost as an afterthought. "I have a system status update for you. Harold is currently working on the network links. He's made significant progress."

You'd say that no matter what, Max thought to himself, knowing full well the extent of their relationship with one another.

The main lab was a room filled with file servers, monitors, and control panels reminiscent of a nuclear reactor operation center. The particle accelerator itself used so much power the lab had to generate its own electricity, produced by a small nuclear reactor located several levels below the accelerator's control center. That was where three shifts of technical personnel monitored power generation around the clock.

On Maxwell's floor, however, there were no engineers or operators constantly monitoring system functions, only one technician, Harold, at the far end of the lab reconfiguring one of the banks of computers that lined twenty aisles of the room. And of course, there was Dora, who always seemed willing to help out in any way she could.

"Hi, Harold!" Max shouted, not sure the computer technician heard him because of the distance, the amount of hardware dividing the room, and Harold's total involvement with the work at hand.

From the far back reaches of the room, Max heard, "Good morning, Dr. Draper, I see you're still here this morning. You always seem to be here. Don't you ever go home or get any sleep?"

"I've got some things to work out, Harold. Besides, Dora's still here, as well." He smiled at the thought behind his comment. "You'll have to admit, she's worse than me at being here all the time. I guess you're becoming just as bad," he stated as he methodically walked over to one of the larger work stations. "I'm here because some of the data we've been receiving from one of our satellites doesn't seem to be making much sense. And we haven't heard from the farthest one out there in quite some time."

"Okay, Dr. Draper. If there's anything you need, just holler. I'm just finishing the data links to the systems at MIT Lincoln Labs, Lawrence Livermore Labs, and the NSA. Those connections and the updated processors will boost our data crunching availability. We've also finished tying in the news outlets and the major media broadcast networks you requested."

"How about the cable news outlets, both national and local?"

"Yep. Added those links as well. I included cable Channel 17 you asked about. You said you wanted to keep tabs on that particular channel so the local public broadcasts can be monitored, too."

"Harold, did you manage to find out anything about including the surveillance of domestic and international communications?"

"Yes, Dr. Draper. Well, not just me, actually. Both Dora and I managed to develop unique links into both domestic and foreign communication networks. There's a system called 'Thinthread' that's used by the NSA. They're funding a portion of our project, and they've allowed us to tap into it. There's also what you might call a massive domestic spying program called 'Stellar Wind' that intercepts communications. We have that on-line as well. Their upper echelon has provided encryption codes, allowing us to send any type of encoded radio signal to a satellite and analyze any changes to a returned signal. I just wonder if that program is grouped under a terrorist surveillance agenda in order to mask the possibility that it might not be constitutional. Dora can even monitor some of the e-mails and audio files from other government agencies, including our own—even the Secretary of States linked server. International billing records and password protected data and documents can now be analyzed. Tell me, Dr. Draper, why are we analyzing such a wide range of events as they happen?"

"I'm working with space-time relationships in association with our particle accelerator and two of our satellites as they approach high gravity situations. Each satellite is unique, in that it supports a data rate that automatically provides error correcting codes and protocol management for automatic retransmission. I'm looking for time correlation and variations as to when news outlets as well as other sources transmit events, when those transmissions are received, and when they're transmitted back to us. Sending our own directed transmission signals as well as random news media and government signals allows an enormous variety of data we can examine."

"I'm almost sorry I asked," said Harold. "Anyway, every time I add more processing power, Dora and I are able to analyze more strings of data. Comparisons of signals and their transmission times will be interesting."

Max smiled at Harold's response. He looked over at the photo of Dora on Harold's nearby desk, briefly thought about their tepid relationship, and then sat down in front of one of the ninety-inch LED monitors.

"Thanks, Harold. I don't know how I'd manage without you two. Which file server is she working on anyway? I can barely hear her voice from the back of the lab."

"I think she's avoiding being in the same room with us, afraid we'll give her more work to do," he said, a smile on his face.

Max proceeded to type in a security code in order to access his e-mail account. Thoughtful about the definition of his password, Maxwell typed each capital letter—ENTELECHY—then typed a name, pressed the enter key, and the system immediately responded, bringing up Nelson Quip's e-mail address.

ii.

Nelson,
Just wanted to share some background information with you, regarding the highly technical experimental stuff you referred to in your last e-mail—my thoughts on what I'm pursuing at the moment—thought you'd be interested in some scientific chatter.

As I mentioned in my previous e-mail, our particle accelerator is more than three times the size of the LHC (Large Hadron Collider). What I didn't tell you was that not many people know our collider exists—not yet anyway. With a circumference of fifty-four miles, it's similar to the Superconducting Super Collider proposed back in the 1980's that was started in Texas but never completed.

I guess you could say you have your CHS (Caring Home Services) to deal with and I have my LHC to deal with. You have fundamental people issues and I have fundamental technical issues. They both can be hard to deal with at times, frustrating, and difficult to understand. Everything is relative, I guess. I know—bad joke.

The tunnel for the accelerator is an amazing piece of construction. We have to use scooters just to get to different areas of the complex. Otherwise, I'd have to take a backpack and use my hiking boots—another joke.

Our reactor generates enormous electric fields that accelerate the subatomic particles into controlled head-on collisions. We need to keep the protons racing almost at the speed of light in order to create the conditions we're looking for. The particles travel through vacuum pipes and the cryogenic refrigeration plants reduce the superconducting magnets' temperature close to absolute zero. We hope to observe particle collisions and understand why the particles exist and how they interact with one another.

In addition, I have two assistants working on what you might call a time dilation experiment. They've connected several media sources as well as government agencies and have been transmitting that media as coded radio signals/broadcasts toward our two satellites, Sagittarius–A and Turing–B. In turn, we hope to analyze any time differences when those signals are transmitted back to us. As you requested, I'll keep you informed about the anomalies I observe with gravity deflections and their effect on radio transmissions traveling at the speed of light.

Since we've recently started reviewing news media and government agency chatter while analyzing transmission times, I've also started to pay attention to the actual news media received. As a result, I've noticed some disturbing world news that I hadn't paid much attention to before.

For instance, back last February, were you aware that the country of Iran carried out its first satellite launch? I didn't— not until now. I just wonder if their satellite launch has anything to do with ballistic missile development.

There have also been reports that they're constructing a secret uranium-enrichment facility at Fordow, and they only offered confirmation after learning we had discovered it. Guess I haven't been paying attention to what is going on in our world. Anyway, I'll let you know how this separate experiment is progressing.

–Max

Year Two

"The obscure we see eventually. The completely Obvious, it seems, takes longer."

— Edward R. Murrow

Chapter Four

Phase One

i.

It was the first week of December and although the town had approved both a special exception and the site plans for Phase One of CHS's South Campus development the previous December, nothing had changed during the entire year. Anticipated construction during the summer months had not begun, and the forest had remained quiet. Seasons had come and gone, and Nelson was busy preparing his office for the rush of quarterly tax returns while he knew Maxwell remained preoccupied with his research. Neither had talked with one another for several months.

"Sorry I'm late," Nelson said to Sarah as he brushed the snow off his coat and hung it up in the hallway closet. "I had to finish off a few things at the office, and it took me longer to clear the snow off the car than I thought it would. It's really coming down out there. Looks like we may get a lot more snow this winter than last. I guess the long-term effect of winter will start early this year."

"We got a notice from the town," Sarah said. She came from the kitchen and waited until after he unclasped and removed the old pair of rubber boots to hand him a letter. "It's about another Zoning Board of Appeals meeting for Caring Home Services."

"Another one?" Nelson asked. "I thought they had all the approvals they needed."

"This one's similar to the last one except it mentions two special exceptions to the ordinance; the one they mentioned last time plus another one under a Subsection E.2."

"But they haven't even started the first Phase that was already approved. Last year, we found out Subsection E.1 meant they had to get a special exception to build elderly housing in an urban residential zone. They were granted that exception last December on the northern corner of the thirty-two acres behind us. The Planning Board even considered letting them build a bridge over wetlands into their other parcel of land that's already been developed, even though the Conservation Commission said no to the idea. The bridge itself wasn't actually voted upon, but the Phase One project was. That bridge would connect their two developments, allowing access across into their North Campus of housing already completed. But like I just said, since the time of the approval of Phase One, they've never done anything. There simply hasn't been any construction, which I don't understand."

"I don't get it either," Sarah said, "but we do have a copy of the Land Use Ordinance booklet now so we can figure out what the additional exception is they're requesting under Subsection E.2."

"Yeah, I had to pay twenty-five bucks for that stupid thing."

After the family had supper and their two sons were settled in their beds for the night, Nelson retrieved the Land Code Use Ordinance booklet from one of his filing cabinets and sat down at the kitchen table with Sarah to review the additional reference.

"This is interesting," Nelson commented after he opened the booklet to the new section. "Subsection E.2 specifies design and performance standards for buildings in an urban residential zone. It lists such things as minimum land area per dwelling and maximum building heights, and buried in the statute is a separate caveat specific to elderly housing. The maximum net density for elderly housing allows a special exception of up to eight dwelling units per net residential acre. For all other construction, the allowance is only three dwelling units. It makes sense to me now why they want to define their apartments as elderly housing units—more bang for the construction buck! I wonder if they'll try to increase the number of apartments and expand the size of the number of buildings they're proposing to build. Of course, there's still the question of why they haven't yet started to build Phase One."

"When's the meeting?" Sarah asked.

"Next week. Guess we'd better go and find out what they intend to do."

ii.

It was snowing the evening of the Zoning Board of Appeals hearing. Nelson and Sarah arrived at the town hall fifteen minutes early, shaking the wet snow from their coats as they sat down toward the back of the meeting room.

"There's Kurt Tussi," said Sarah. "He's the guy who owns Tussi Engineering and Architecture. And next to him is his client, Phil Dwyer, who's the representative of the Board of Directors for Caring Home Services."

"Where?" asked Nelson. He removed his snow covered hat and dropped it to the floor.

"Down there in the front," replied Sarah. She quickly pointed with her wet glove.

"How do you know who they are?"

"Their pictures were in the paper a couple of weeks ago. I forgot to show you."

Nelson looked toward the front of the room, finally recognizing who Sarah had pointed toward.

Kurt Tussi sat in the front row of the large public meeting room of the Laslo Town Hall, waiting his turn to make his presentation before the five members of the Zoning Board of Appeals. Nelson didn't think he appeared to be nervous. Probably, he thought, because Tussi had requested special exceptions in the past. This request was no different for him than others. It was just another job that paid good money.

Seated next to him was Phil Dwyer, a representative of the Board of Directors for Caring Home Services. He was an older man, in his late 60's, slightly stout, short in stature, and bald. His black round-framed glasses made a noticeable contrast against his pale face.

The posted agenda listed three public hearings for the evening. To Nelson's relief, Phil Dwyer's project was first. He remembered most public hearings started at 7 p.m. and ended at 10 p.m., unless a motion was carried by the board members to extend the discussion time.

There was one large public meeting room used for the various boards and committee hearings. The Town Council met twice a month on the second and fourth Mondays, the Planning Board usually met twice a month on the second and fourth Thursdays, and the Zoning Board of Appeals met the second and fourth Tuesdays as needed. The residents of Laslo elected board members during regular election cycles, twice a year.

In his mind, there were always a few members who had hidden agendas for being on specific boards, but for the most part, many were trying to uphold their civic duties as residents of the town. Unfortunately, there were never sufficient numbers of residents who would take the time to fill the positions when they became vacant. Board members were paid only a small stipend by the town for travel.

A curved, elongated table was at the end of the meeting room for the five members of the ZBA. It faced uncomfortable looking metal chairs available for the public. Having lived in the area for a while, Nelson knew the room accommodated enough seating for one hundred and fifty people. The light wood-paneled walls made the place look almost clinical in appearance. An oak lectern stood to one side as an option for public use.

Nelson mentally went over the hearing rules, knowing they were quite simple. In the case of both the Planning Board and ZBA, a developer or person attempting to obtain approval for a project or request a waiver to deviate from the Land Use and Development Code would first discuss their project before the board members. The hearing would then be opened for public discussion.

If a person wanted to speak about an issue before either the ZBA or the Planning Board, they had to be recognized by the chairperson and were allowed to speak for three minutes. Once the public opinions were heard and the public hearing was closed, they could no longer partake in any further discussions. The developer would then be allowed to respond.

The only problem with this procedure was the public had no recourse to counter what a developer said. If a response to the public's question was false, nothing could be done at the time to correct a misleading answer.

He glanced at the clock; it was 7 p.m. when the five board members entered the room and settled into their respective chairs. Facing the public from left to right, were Eu-

gene Orin, Ron Davis, Chairperson Peter Bolduc, Henry Severs, and Julie Mills.

Chairperson Bolduc was a distinguished looking gentle-
man, with a close cropped white beard, well trimmed mustache, white crew haircut, and a dark tan complexion in stark
contrast to his bright blue eyes. He leaned into his micro-
phone, called the public hearing to order, and made a preliminary statement to the board members and the public.

"I am going to disqualify myself for this appeal, but I'll
stay on as chairperson only to direct the hearing. I'll have no
input for discussion beyond that."

Without any further explanation as to his reason for dis-
qualification, he asked if there was anyone present who objected to him remaining as chairperson. There weren't any.

Sarah and Nelson sat in the audience, both glad the CHS
issue was the first to be discussed. The metal chairs were
uncomfortable. There were only a handful of residents attending the public hearing. Perhaps it was the ice and accumulated snow that had discouraged travel to the town hall,
or perhaps it was just a matter of indifference.

Chairperson Bolduc read the application. "Caring Home
Services Incorporated, an organization that represents itself
as an elderly charitable housing development, is requesting a
special exception to the terms of Title 10, Section 14.060,
Subsection E.1 and Subsection E.2 of the Land Use and Development Code Zoning Ordinance. They wish to construct
twenty-six units of elderly housing in six buildings on property located at U.S. Route 2, Map 2, Lot 35, in our town of Laslo, zoned as urban residential. I'll provide the audience with
the previous background regarding this proposal.

"An organization under the name of the Salvation for the
Society of Churches originally owned two distinct parcels of
forested land, including Lot 35. They, in turn, sold the land to
Caring Home Services, which is a company incorporated in
another state and whose board of directors consists of several officers from the Salvation Society of Churches organization.

"Mr. Phil Dwyer is here, representing Caring Home Services. He appeared before this Zoning Board of Appeals
twelve months ago. This proposal tonight is similar to the
one we approved last time. Now it's in a different location on

the same lot of land.

"The northern and southern lots of land they own are ad-joined by a small twenty-five-foot-wide common strip of wet-land. The northern parcel has already been developed by CHS. A large wetland area encompasses the southern most section of the northern developed property and extends down to the upper border of the undeveloped southern par-cel. It includes the common strip of wetland connecting both properties. At that very border, an old unused road in the woods accesses the southern parcel where Phase One was originally proposed to be built. That road feeds into the dead end of a paved town road, which is Baker Street.

"Last year," Bolduc continued, "the ZBA granted a special exception for their proposed development called Phase One, but without the use of Baker Street as an access road. Even though Baker Street is a paved town road that stops at the border of their two properties and exits onto the main road, Route 2, you must remember Baker Street is a substandard road. There would be traffic issues and safety considerations due to heavy usage, and this board decided it could not be used as an access road to the project."

Phil Dwyer quickly stood up to address the chairperson. In a somewhat hoarse, torpid, high pitched voice, he said, "I'd like to explain why we're seeking approval once again."

"Go right ahead, Mr. Dwyer," said Bolduc.

"We were here about a year ago last December. The pro-ject we're proposing tonight is similar to the one this board previously approved but in a different location on the same property. The ZBA granted our request for a special excep-tion under Section E.1, with the condition that Baker Street not be used as an access. They suggested two options to ad-dress the access to our Phase One project. The first was to use a sixty-foot right of way at the southern end of our southern parcel off the main highway, which is Route 2. The second option was to build a bridge across the wetland and connect the northern and southern lots in order to access the proposed Phase One build-out on our southern undeveloped land. We then took this project to the Planning Board, not using Baker Street as an access but rather crossing the wet-land connecting the two lots. Even though the Laslo Conser-vation Commission didn't want the wetland to be crossed, the Planning Board approved our Phase One project."

Phil Dwyer paused briefly, looked around the room to en-sure the audience was listening, and continued the delivery of his proposal.

"After careful review, we realized constructing a bridge made the project financially not feasible, so we started all over again. That's why we haven't started building Phase One yet. We've redesigned the project using the suggested sixty-foot right of way at the far end of our southern lot, a completely different location for Phase One.

"We are therefore bringing this revamped proposal in front of the ZBA tonight for twenty-six apartments in six buildings, to be located near the main highway at the farther end of the southern parcel of land we own. This is an in-crease in the originally proposed sixteen apartments. This number of apartments is necessary in order for CHS to break even, cost-wise. Included in those buildings in what we call the Southern Campus is a community house with a chapel and common areas for community rooms, offices, and so forth. From an architectural viewpoint, we are trying to cre-ate the look of a colonial village."

Dwyer's voice became increasingly raspy and hoarse, emanating a perfidious personification as he continued. "We expect to continue to develop this site over a period of sev-eral years in seven phases. It is estimated to take fifteen years before the entire southern site is fully developed. At some point, we would like to connect the two developments in the south and north with a road for vehicular traffic.

Upon hearing Dwyer's explanations of future plans, Nel-son was annoyed to learn there could be a large complex built that would destroy the nearby woodland. In one year, the location of the previously proposed Phase One complex had changed from the northern part of the property to the southern part, much closer to his property line. His first thought was there goes Treasure Rock and the walks in the forest with the boys.

He looked around the room as Sarah had done when they first arrived and was surprised to see there were only a handful of residents attending the public hearing. Seven out of over sixty people who owned property abutting the pro-posed housing complex were present. He fidgeted on his uncomfortable, cold metal chair and continued to listen with increased interest to the corporate representative.

"I'd like to emphasize how great the need is for elderly housing," Dwyer continued. "We don't do any advertising, yet our waiting lists continue to grow, with the average age of the applicants being seventy-eight. Because the majority of our residents would be from this town or other nearby towns, this project serves the local population. The use of this project is low impact in terms of affecting the environment and traffic. It is also for people of modest means, low to middle income, which is where most of the retired people fall. Mr. Kurt Tussi, the owner of Tussi Engineering and Architecture, is the project's engineer. He will be presenting more information to the board."

At that point, Kurt Tussi stood up next to Dwyer and asked the chairperson permission to discuss the proposed development.

Chairperson Bolduc recognized the civil engineering firm's owner and asked him to present the proposed plans to the board members. Kurt quickly set several large blueprints of the complex on an existing easel located next to the lectern so it could be seen by the board members. Because it was farther away from the public, however, Nelson and the audience couldn't read all of the details, including the notes attached to the drawings.

"It seems we're at a disadvantage by not being able to see their drawings and notes close up while they're being discussed," Nelson whispered to Sarah as Kurt continued his presentation.

"I think that's the guy Donny told us about," replied Sarah, just as Kurt started to speak. "He's seen him in the forest on several occasions, surveying the property."

"I want to thank the board for the opportunity to present this project to you. As Mr. Dwyer mentioned, this proposal represents the build-out of seven phases of construction for the South Campus of Caring Home Services. Phase One consists of six buildings with twenty-six apartments for our fifty-five-year-old retirement community. We have previously built sixty apartments on the twelve and a half acres of the North Campus. The plan presented today provides details for additional elderly housing on a second parcel of land consisting of 32.7 acres. The proposed use for that site is a multi-unit residential complex. As previously mentioned, we would have constructed Phase One last year, but building a bridge across the wetlands in order to obtain access to Phase One from the northern lot was not financially feasible.

"The rest of the proposed seven phase project for the South Campus will consist of the following. Phase Two contains four buildings with forty-two apartments. Phase Three contains seven buildings with thirty apartments. Phase Four contains two buildings with thirty-two apartments. Phase Five contains one building initially having fifty-two apartments. Phase Six creates an additional wing to Phase Five consisting of thirty-six more apartments, and Phase Seven creates a third wing to Phase Five consisting of another thirty apartments. That totals two hundred and forty-eight units for all seven phases. Since the ordinance allows eight units per acre under Subsection E.2 to the town ordinance, we are allowed two hundred and sixty-one units for 32.7 acres. This concludes my presentation of the Caring Home Services project. I will be happy to answer any of the questions the zoning board members may have."

"Thank you for your summation, Mr. Tussi," Chairperson Bolduc said. He turned to address the public. "I would just like to remind members of the public that once you make a presentation, the only way you can be recognized again is if one of the board members chooses to do so. I am now opening the hearing to members of the public. Does anyone wish to speak for or against the application?"

iii.

Silence enveloped the room. No one spoke. Nelson had never seen the plans before and could not think of any violations to the town's ordinances or reasons to question the addition of six buildings on the thirty-two plus acres. Except that Phase One was now located in a different area of the property—a position much closer to him. Besides, the same number of buildings had been approved once before.

He didn't like the idea, however, that the forest abutting his property and its wildlife would be impacted by the proposal. Even so, it was difficult to provide any worthwhile comments or arguments without more information. Nelson had come to the hearing unaware of the extent of the proposed development.

Taking advantage of the lackluster response from the audience, Chairperson Bolduc quickly said, "There being no comments, I am closing the public hearing."

Well, that was quick and succinct, Nelson thought to himself.

"Do any town officials have anything to say?" asked Bolduc.

The town's code enforcement officer, Allen Treble, stood up to address the board members. Allen was a short individual with a curly mop of black hair, black rimmed round glasses, and a noticeable swagger when he walked up to the lectern. He had what Nelson considered a slight Napoleon complex, a slight arrogant air about him, and clearly loved his position of authority for code enforcement.

"Mr. Chairperson, it should be noted that this proposal also has a special exception regarding the inclusion of a steeple for their chapel, which is one of their proposed buildings. In order to allow this to be like a New England village, the Zoning Board was previously asked to ignore the height limitations in the Land Use Code so there could be a steeple. The town's philosophy on their previous request should be the same as last time. People will use this community building for religious service and at an average age of seventy-eight, I think they would have gained enough wisdom in life not to feel slighted because this development didn't have a steeple. I can point out some very nice New England villages that have churches without one. Apart from that, I don't have any concerns regarding this application."

Nelson chuckled to himself at Allen Treble's commentary. The chairperson thanked Allen for his comment, who returned to his seat, happy to contribute to the consideration process.

The chairperson spoke up once again. "Since there were members of the audience who didn't raise their hands during the public hearing, I would now again allow members of the public the opportunity to comment for, against, or about the application."

An elderly woman Nelson recognized as Millie Hodgdon

raised her hand and was recognized by Chairperson Bolduc.

She was in her early eighties and aware of both the national and local news and more informed than most people half her age. Her pure white hair made her stand out despite her petit stature. She had a keen, sharp mind with a perspicacious wit and an ability to stand her own ground in any conversation.

Her husband had died twenty years earlier, so she was there to represent her home by herself. She appeared to be somewhat disgruntled as she spoke, and addressed her concern about the proposed Phase Seven of the complex, because of its location near to her property on Baker Street. Surely, the cold metal chairs didn't help her demeanor either.

"I can speak for the elderly people living on Baker Street. I would like to know if there will be a traffic light placed at the proposed access onto the main road, Route 2, from this project. Everyone knows that Route 2 is very congested in this area, with entrances to the Rotary Club on the opposite side of the road and the small businesses that exist on both sides."

She continued. "Elderly people entering and exiting an elderly housing complex don't always have good vision. I should know; I'm one of them. When it's icy in the winter, it could be difficult to stop at the end of Baker Street onto Route 2. I'm just worried about the additional phases of this development wanting to enter and exit using this road." With a concerted and adamant emphasis to the board members, she added, "I am concerned about that." Then she curtly sat down.

"Why did Millie ask about a traffic light when the ZBA previously denied access to her road for this project?" Sarah whispered to Nelson.

"I'm not sure. She's pretty sharp. Maybe she believes they'll try and use it as they develop additional phases to the development. But you're right, that access has already been denied," said Nelson.

"Are there any other comments by members of the public?" asked the chairperson.

After listening to Millie, Nelson thought he should at least say something to the ZBA. If more concerned citizens like Millie paid attention to changes, Nelson figured the community would be much better represented. He stood, somewhat reluctant to speak in front of the public. He stated his name and was recognized by Bolduc to make his statement.

"The number of apartments discussed this year has been increased from sixteen units last year to twenty-six units this year due to the request for an additional special exception under Subsection E.2. Mr. Dwyer and Mr. Tussi have now introduced additional building phases for this property. We have never heard about these substantial increases to this development until tonight.

"This property is pretty much landlocked by other properties surrounding it for road accessibility, especially considering the number of buildings and apartments being proposed. Only a very small portion of their property borders Route 2. I have concerns about fire and emergency access to this housing development. If other building phases are intended in the future, I foresee a real problem with taking care of people living in those areas if there is an emergency."

Nelson hesitated, trying to formulate his comments into somewhat of an orderly manner. He disliked speaking in public, especially when he didn't have any time to prepare for what he was going to say.

"One of my neighbors took a measurement of the wetland behind my own abutting property, and I understand there appears to be a problem with the setbacks from where these buildings are proposed to be built to its edge. I haven't seen the blueprints showing the setbacks or the design notes so I can't confirm or deny the possible problem. I realize these issues will have to go before the Planning Board, but I think this ZBA should be concerned about these areas as well. I also have concerns about the number of people living in Phase One of the development as well as the other phases just mentioned tonight, particularly in regard to having only one access road to such a huge complex." Deciding he had said enough, and unable to think of anything more to add, Nelson stopped, politely thanked the board for the opportunity to speak, and quickly sat down, relieved he had completed his quickly mustered statements.

"Are there any further comments from the public?" asked Chairperson Bolduc. No hands were raised and the audience remained quiet. "There being no further comments, does Mr.

Treble have any further issues he would like to present?"

Allen Treble stood up again, enjoying the recognition. "I just find it interesting to note that there is no further discussion regarding the use of Baker Street from the development onto the main highway, Route 2. This is the only access from the future phases of this project, and I understand the board was specific with the last plan that Baker Street was not to be used. I thought that requirement followed through to any future development. Since the terms of access to Route 2 from this Phase One as well as additional phases haven't been agreed upon, the board doesn't know what it's approving. In addition, the previous comment by the elderly lady who lives on Baker Street regarding a traffic light can't happen until the Maine Department of Transportation approves it, because it's a state road. I don't know at what point in such a development that a second access would be required."

"Thank you for your comment, Mr. Treble. Are there any other comments from the board members?" asked the chairperson.

iv.

Eugene Orin was a notable resident of the town. His rather large frame and round face with an untrimmed scraggly, gray beard stood out from all others on the board. He was a retired doctor, always quick to the point in any discussion. "Mr. Tussi, has this plan gone before the Planning Board?"

"Yes, as a sketch plan," Kurt responded. "The traffic count for this use was less than eighty, and two means of access are required per town ordinance when the traffic count is over two-hundred. We therefore are required to have only one access road."

"How does the Planning Board feel about this possible access issue?" asked Henry Severs, another ZBA member.

Kurt was quick to answer. "There's ample room to construct a road at the southern portion of the property through a sixty foot right of way onto Route 2. The remainder of the property is landlocked by the adjacent abutters. There is a solid granite ledge outcropping at that southern section, but enough can be removed in order to construct an access road."

"What do you do about fire access if this main access road is cut off?" asked Eugene.

"An emergency access is not required for this plan," Kurt replied. "As I stated a few minutes ago, the Town Land Use Code requires two means of access when the traffic counts are greater than two-hundred trips per day. This plan is for six buildings and twenty-six units, which figures out to less than eighty trips per day. I don't believe Fire Chief Gerard would require a second means of access for a project of this size, and one wasn't proposed."

Nelson turned to Sarah. "How do they figure the number of trips per day? What's it based on?"

"I don't know. I guess we'll have to figure it out after the hearing, so we can understand what they're talking about."

"Yeah, I'm really in the dark about this," he whispered.

Completely ignoring the topic of road accessibility, Henry Severs asked a second question. "What should the height of the steeple be?"

"Eighty-six feet," Kurt said.

"And what did the board do last time about the steeple that was built in the northern development, or what you call the North Campus?"

Still sitting, Allen Treble spoke up to answer Severs' question. "I don't remember the reason for allowing a variance to the Code in order to justify the steeple."

Ron Davis of the Zoning Board interjected. "I believe the steeple was approved based upon some religious aspect attached to it."

Slightly agitated, Dwyer stood and with a harsh, hoarse voice said, "The steeple was approved for the North Campus not on the basis of variance but because the Land Use Code allowed churches, and a church is allowed to have a steeple. The discussion at the public hearing regarding the building in question on the North Campus was whether or not it was a church. The development has a chaplain and services are held there regularly."

Ron Davis responded to Dwyer's comment. "Since Caring Home Services already has a church on the North Campus, is it felt necessary to have another church on the South Campus—two churches and two steeples?"

Nelson turned to Sarah and whispered, "I can't believe

we're talking about the height of steeples over more important issues like road access, safety, and the size of this major development." He felt helpless, as if quicksand were forming about his ankles with nothing to hold onto in order to keep himself from sinking farther into unknown muck.

Dwyer fidgeted noticeably in his chair before responding. "Yes, we need two churches. This South Campus complex would act as a separate community."

"But both communities are under the same umbrella," said Davis.

"That's true, but these residents won't go from the southern complex to the northern complex for their activities."

"But every church doesn't have a steeple," Davis continued.

Dwyer carefully thought out his next response. "I agree with you. But if the Land Use Code allows a steeple for a church and this is a church, how can the request for a steeple be denied?"

Henry Severs quickly glanced at the code enforcement officer and asked, "Is it in the Code that a church could have a steeple?"

"I don't know about that," replied Treble.

Chairperson Bolduc intervened. "The definition of the height of a building is on page 211 of the Town's Land Use Code. At one point in past conversations, Mr. Severs asked if the church itself had a living space in it. Mr. Dwyer said part of the building was a chapel, and the steeple was part of the chapel."

Julie Mills, the board member to the right of Bolduc, and who had been quiet throughout the proceedings, asked, "Mr. Dwyer, are there apartments between the chapel and the steeple in the already developed northern complex?"

"Yes," Dwyer answered. "Since the sixty apartments on the North Campus are contained in only two buildings, we had to combine the chapel and steeple in one of those buildings."

Treble addressed the board again. "It's my understanding that the Salvation for the Society of Churches and Caring Home Services are nondenominational. There are some religious groups that don't have a steeple on their place of worship. If the board wants to grant a steeple, I suppose they could. I was just trying to make a point."

Eugene Orin spoke up addressing Phil Dwyer. "When was the church and steeple built on the North Campus of this development?"

"It was built four years ago. I have the approval letter from the previous Zoning board if you would like to see it."

"I'd like to see that letter," interjected Julie Mills.

Dwyer methodically searched through a manilla folder, pulled out the letter, and handed it to her.

She read it, then said, "This is important, but I am more concerned about the ledge outcropping accessing the property from Route 2. It runs parallel to the property and blocks the view onto the highway. I wonder if the proposed access road can truly be accessed without sight distance problems." She added, "I don't have an issue with the concept of elderly housing, but insufficient removal of the ledge could create problems.

Almost interrupting, Eugene Orin spoke again. "The access onto Route 2 is the more important issue. The steeple is just a matter of personal choice."

"Finally," Nelson whispered to Sarah. "Perhaps we'll get back on topic."

"Can Mr. Treble give a permit to a plan which has an unsafe road and perhaps doesn't meet the Town Land Use and Development Code?" asked Eugene.

As if personally attacked by such a question, the code enforcement officer was quick to respond. "If the road is approved by the Planning Board, what could *I* do? Would I take the Planning Board to court?" asked Treble.

"We don't decide road standards," Eugene said. "The Planning Board does. Ms. Mills' issue is that if the road exited the southern portion of this property where there is a ledge on the left-hand side as well as on the right, would a driver be able to see around each section upon accessing Route 2?"

"I understand the concerns for safety, but is it this board's bailiwick?" asked Ron Davis. "When the board originally reviewed this project when the proposed access was off Baker Street, safety was the primary issue. It was why the board didn't want the access there. Since the only other access to this parcel is a narrow sixty-foot right of way onto Route 2, bordered by ledge on either side, there still might be a safety issue. Also, what about fire access if the main road is cut off for any reason? Mr. Tussi previously stated that an emergency access wasn't required for this plan. He said that the Land Use Code required two means of access when the traffic counts were above two hundred trips per day. If you add the Phase One and Phase Two units, it appears you would exceed that traffic count."

"There's a difference between the original Baker Street proposal and this one," interrupted Tussi. "This proposal involves a right of way access from the southernmost part of this land onto Route 2, around a large granite ledge outcropping in order to enter the Phase One apartments. Most of the ledge that would cause a sight disturbance will be removed and the area will be graded. As a reminder, this proposal is only about Phase One, not about additional buildings that will be included during a Phase Two proposal. We'll submit a separate right of way plan as well as a site plan for the Phase Two project."

At that point, the Zoning Board members looked at one another with approving nods and concluded there would be no further issue with the proposed access road or the ledge surrounding the opening onto Route 2. The abrupt end to their discussions surprised Nelson, as to how the ZBA could have settled on any conclusions from the topics discussed.

"As long as there appears to be no safety issues," said Chairperson Bolduc, "the board will approve this as presented as a special exception, including the steeple. I guess the only thing left is to put this to a motion, understanding that the steeple is a part of that motion. The only condition of not approving this project would be if the plan changes. If that happens, it must come back before the board."

Henry Severs introduced a motion to the board members. "I make a motion to approve the application for Caring Home Services, otherwise referred to as CHS, for their request of a miscellaneous appeal to the terms of the Town Use and Development Code, Title 10, Section 14.060, Subsections E.1 and E.2. They are to be approved to construct twenty-six units of elderly housing in six buildings at property located off Route 2, Map 2, Lot 35, zoned urban residential, with the condition that any changes to the site plan must come back before this board for approval. Construction shall be in accordance with the sketch plan submitted and signed and dated by Phil Dwyer and Chairperson Bolduc."

Eugene Orin quickly seconded the motion. There was no further discussion and the motion was approved by a show of hands, with Mr. Orin, Mr. Davis, and Ms. Mills voting in favor, Mr. Severs voting in opposition, and Chairperson Bolduc abstaining himself from voting, as he had promised.

After finalizing the vote, Chairperson Bolduc said, "The applicant will receive written notice confirming the board's decision in one week. Any interested party can appeal this decision within forty-five days in Superior Court."

At the conclusion of the public hearing, Nelson and Sarah slowly stood, bundled up in their winter coats, and walked out into the cold night air.

"I don't see there's much we can do to stop this project," Nelson complained to Sarah. He gripped her hand and they walked from the town hall toward their car. "I assume they'll start construction next year, as early in the spring as possible."

"I was surprised no one brought up the issue of the effect on wildlife in the forest and the potential wetland issues," Sarah said.

"This development will certainly change several of the acres of forest that abut our property. I'm just not sure what those changes will be like. I didn't realize there was an intended build-out into seven phases. We need to look at their plans regarding the extended development they mentioned before they present their next phases to the planning and zoning boards."

They arrived at the car and Nelson opened her side, allowing her to get in, then closed it. He rounded the vehicle to his side, got in and shut the door before turning the ignition. He reached over and turned up the heat to ward off the bitter cold.

V.

A new year was about to begin, and the snow from recent storms was already over two feet deep; unknowingly, an inference that things could get worse.

It had been almost a year since Nelson received any

communication from Max, which wasn't unusual, so he decided to send a short e-mail. A few hours later, Maxwell replied.

E-mail: Dec 15 – 21:04
To: Mdraper
From: NelsonQuip
Subject: Taxes – Yet Again

Hi, Maxwell,

I haven't heard from you since I did your taxes last February. I had hoped you would have been able to visit last summer, but I know you've been busy. How's the research going?

We've all been well here. Having some issues though with a very large development being constructed on the 32 plus acres that borders our property. Phase One of their plans has already been approved, but now I understand there are many more phases we'll have to worry about. Guess I'll have to take a closer look at what's being proposed so it hopefully won't get out of control. Our property taxes keep increasing and people in the community don't seem to be paying attention to potentially detrimental changes.

–Nelson

E-mail: Dec 15 – 23:20
To: NelsonQuip
From: Mdraper
Subject: Taxes – Yet Again – Reply

Thanks for the reminder. I'll be sending you my stuff so you can do my taxes again at the end of next month. I just hate doing them. That's why I'm glad to have you working on them.

It's hard to understand the mess our country appears to be in at this point in regard to debt and taxes. We are accumulating more debt than anyone can imagine. I'm concerned that we'll spend trillions of dollars toward stimulus just to try and kick-start an economy. It's a bad idea and a waste of printed dollars. Just looking at the numbers, I can tell you it won't work. I know congress continues to talk about it— again, a real dumb idea.

As to detrimental changes, I keep looking at issues regarding Iran's nuclear program. I noted that last June, Congress adopted the Comprehensive Sanctions, Accountability, and Divestment Act, tightening sanctions against firms investing in Iran's energy sector. This gives me hope that perhaps someone is paying attention to a potential problem.

Regards,
–Max

Year Three

*"There are things known and
There are things unknown,
And in between are the
Doors of perception."*

– Aldus Huxley

Chapter Five

Concerns

i.

Springtime was cacophonous, as hydraulic excavator hammers and dynamiting chipped away sections of ledge and rock outcroppings, leveling large portions of forest at the same time. I watched from a short distance as bulldozers raped the earth and continuous mounds of fill were delivered with the loud roar of an endless collection of dump trucks. The amount of earth moved by the enormous machines seemed to be never-ending.

The larger animals, like deer, fled to the northern part of the forest in fear from the pillage of their homes, and the smaller inhabitants sought whatever nearby shelter they could find.

The forest opened to the unyielding whine of chainsaws that continued for weeks, never stopping. From the early morning hours to dusk, the rasping sounds never seemed to languish.

By early summer, the leaves from the trees along the embankment of the Quip's property provided the only green blanket of shelter, hiding the ongoing deforestation and construction build out. An open wetland and a shallow ravine were the only barriers separating Phase One construction from the total deforestation to Quip's borders.

Undaunted, Donny still took his early morning walks along the old paths; he talked aloud to the forest as if it was alive, capable of hearing and understanding what he had to say. I watched him every day and enjoyed his one-sided conversation with the forest, not interrupting his private moments, keeping to myself, and never attempting to answer back or distract him in any way.

Every now and then, I also saw Donny's neighbor, Nelson, walking near the construction site, checking on its progress. He didn't look very happy about the land-fill being used to create a new, higher ground level. Several acres of the forest simply disappeared, replaced by progress.

By early fall, Phase One of the development was completed.

ii.

It was late afternoon, during one of my walks, when I noticed Nelson, Sarah, and Donny sitting outside on Nelson's cobblestone patio with three of their neighbors: Will Penton, Joe Vaschon, and his wife, Mary. The sound of their voices carried into the forest, and without any intention to purposely eavesdrop, I found it difficult to ignore their conversation. Curiosity prevailed and I stopped to listen.

It wasn't unusual for them to get together on a Friday afternoon. It just seemed like a good time for everyone to unwind from their jobs, their daily routines, and share their thoughts with one another. Politics was the issue of the day, a topic of which I never had much interest. I had heard similar afternoon discussions on several other occasions.

Donny was the only retired person among them. He had just finished tilling his garden and pulling weeds, getting it ready for the next spring's planting.

Will Penton, who normally worked as a crane and backhoe operator for a landscaping company, and had just finished a big stump clearing job, took the afternoon off to help Donny. Will was the kind of guy who enjoyed helping anyone who needed it.

"I stopped by to see my old friend, Charley, yesterday," said Donny. "He lives in the church in that new Phase One construction."

"He lives in the church?" asked Nelson, surprised by the reference.

"Yeah, it's not really a church. It's an apartment building that looks like a church—kind of a facade to its real purpose. I personally think the developer used it to their own advantage in justifying another addition to their Phase One development during the public hearings. But enough said about our recent construction zone. This economic recession we're experiencing has been one of the worst I've ever seen,"

Donny continued, as he pulled his straw hat down to shade his eyes from the late afternoon sun.

"At my age, I've seen a lot of things—from the economic depression of the 30's, to World War II and navigating B-52's, to the Cuban missile crisis. I try to keep up with current events by reading a lot. Now we appear to be heading toward another crisis—one of economics once again. According to the latest news reports, two thirds of Americans report that their family's income has now fallen behind the cost of living, and a quarter of Americans say their income is barely staying even."

"Well, I don't believe the excessive government spending in the way of a stimulus bill has done much except to increase the national deficit," said Nelson. "In just one year it's increased by almost two trillion dollars. That's about a twenty percent increase in only one year."

"This whole thing started when a few members of congress thought it was a great idea if everyone owned their own home," Joe Vaschon said.

His wife, Mary, was also quick to enter the discussion. "Yeah, even when they really couldn't afford it."

"It was all those sub-prime mortgages that started with low interest rates and then ballooned into unaffordable notes that triggered the financial meltdown we're witnessing in this recession," Nelson said. "I see the results of those financial losses every day with my clients. Some of those people just wanted to make a quick buck and flip a house for resale in a growing market. I feel bad for those families who got caught in the same market fallout."

"So what do we do to stimulate the economy?" Will asked. Then thinking about it, answered his own question. "I guess we could throw more money at it in another stimulus package. It could help. If it was managed properly, it could create a few jobs. But I'm not talking about just increasing federal employment. I'm talking about creating jobs that make a product."

"There's been a lot of money wasted and mismanagement with that program," said Joe. "There's been some crazy spending. Two million dollars were spent to send researchers to study exotic ants on islands in the Indian Ocean. Over a million dollars was spent to create a museum in an abandoned train station in New Jersey, and seven million dollars were spent for repairs to an old eighteen hundred's brick fort marooned at the end of the Florida Keys. Sounds good but the only way you could get there is by boat. And ninety thousand dollars were spent to replace sidewalks in the small town of Boynton, Oklahoma. Sidewalks that were replaced just five years ago. How would you like to have some of that ill-spent money?"

"How do you know all that?" asked Sarah.

"I read a lot," said Joe. "And I'm pissed off about this nonsense spending spree the country seems to be on. I browsed the internet to find out where some of this spending was going and purposely remembered some of them to tell you guys. Even the signs that advertise the fact that stimulus funding was used for highway programs cost around ten thousand each. At least the sign companies are making money. There was one large sign at Dulles airport that cost nearly fifteen million dollars. While it was being constructed, it created seventeen new jobs. Pretty pricey cost per person—if that's true. Lot of waste in those packages, wouldn't you say?

"And did all that spending really do any good? The unemployment rate's now almost ten percent. A portion of the two hundred and thirty-million-dollar stimulus expenditure was like flushing a good portion of printed money right into the Potomac River. And don't forget, we're paying China interest from all that borrowed money."

"You left out the two million dollars spent on research for swine odor and manure management research," Will interjected, with a somewhat disgruntled laugh at his own comment. "We're spending money we don't have on studies we don't need."

Mary spoke up. "Shit management—that's something the administration could *probably* use." Her comment brought additional chuckles and mumbles.

"Don't forget about the Detroit auto industry bailout," Sarah said. "It was like seventeen billion dollars at first and then another thirty billion when one of the companies went bankrupt. There's also bailouts to banks and financial institutions."

"Are we being too critical?" asked Donny. Everyone paused, glanced at one another, and then shook their heads in the negative. "Guess not then."

iii.

I laughed to myself at the remarks from my neighbors, keeping quiet to avoid detection. It was then that Nelson decided to expand the topic of conversation.

"There are issues other than our economy. We've got problems overseas as well. We keep apologizing to every country we've ever assisted. It makes us look weak, as if we did something terribly wrong all these years. I'm sure the country of Iran is laughing at us these days. We keep talking about what we might do if they continue on their path to manufacturing enough material to produce their own nuclear weapons. With all our apologies, do you think they'll ever believe we're serious about anything?"

"Seems to be an awful lot of just plain rhetoric to me," said Sarah. "Look at the climate change issue. You would think we might want to truly investigate and study the climate, without falsifying numbers. Some people are doing that, just to make money. First it's called global warming and then, in order to substantiate the real facts, it's called climate change. Of course there's climate change, but the question is, what percentage is actually caused by people? I wouldn't be surprised to hear someone say that climate change is worse than weapons of mass destruction. Yet we certainly have more control over one than we do the other. And we go about voting for congressional bills from climate change and carbon tax issues to health care that are thousands of pages, and our politicians don't even read those bills before they vote on them."

"Makes you wonder what our policies really are," Nelson added. "We appear to have little direction except to try and placate everyone. Look at the Honduras incident that happened a while ago and the reckless action made by our own Secretary of State."

"What do you mean?" asked Will. "What reckless action did she do? I didn't hear about that one."

"Probably not many people have. At times, a lot of our

media doesn't seem to report any real news," Nelson said.
"From news reported on CNN, the President of Honduras or-
dered their military to distribute information regarding a non-
binding referendum asking their citizens to vote on whether
or not they were in favor of including a proposal for a con-
stituent assembly to redraft their constitution on their up-
coming voting ballot. He wanted to end term limits, violating
their constitution, in order to continue as President."

"That sounds like an intended dictatorship," Will said.

Nodding his head in agreement, Nelson continued.

"Other people, like Hugo Chevez in Venezuela, would certainly laud that type of regime—to always be the President.
The head of the Honduras military refused to carry out the
order and was fired. Their Supreme Court ruled that it was
illegal to fire the head of the military, and they also ruled
against the referendum even though it was non-binding.
About a month later, the President of Honduras was kid-
napped and flown out of the country into exile by a military
coup, and civil liberties were suspended."

"What did our Secretary of State have to do with that?"
asked Will.

"I'm getting to that," said Nelson. "Our State Department
freely admitted it had consulted with the perpetrators prior to
the coup. It was also reported that the coup government was
responsible for the targeted killing of at least four individuals,
including two political opposition leaders. Over a hundred
people were assaulted by the military and over a thousand
were detained. The problem is that the military is not the ar-
biter of a constitutional dispute between various branches of
their government. There essentially was a media blackout
within the country. By controlling the information and re-
pressing dissent, the coup regime set the stage for unfair
elections. Our government remained quiet on this issue."

"So what did the Secretary of State have to do with
that?" Will asked, repeating his earlier question.

"On the day of the coup, our Secretary of State published
a statement not recognizing the events that took place as a
regime coup and refused to legally classify it as such. In that
way, we could continue economic aid to the country and their
military. In that regard, we were complicit. We actually violated our own congressional law, which states that any dem-

ocratic government that is a victim of a military takeover is denied military and economic aid."

"Continuing to aid their country in this situation doesn't seem to justify breaking our own laws, does it?" asked Will.

"It doesn't seem to matter much," Nelson said. "I think you'll see more federal laws broken as time continues. That's why I brought this matter up."

Disturbed with the pessimism of the conversation, I continued on with my walk, thinking about what was said. The forest absorbed the sounds of their discussions as I distanced myself. I glanced back to look at my neighbors before they disappeared from sight, and noticed they had all finally decided to call it quits for the afternoon. I watched them leave for their respective homes. Just more politics, I thought—turmoil everywhere.

Then I wondered what direct effect continued development of the forest would have on everyone, including myself.

iv.

It was late when Nelson e-mailed Maxwell about the afternoon's conversation with his neighbors. He was asleep when a reply arrived at 2 a.m., per the time stamp on the message he read the next day.

E-mail: Sep 02
To: NelsonQuip
From: Mdraper
Subject: Your Concerns

Hi Nelson,

That's quite a conversation you had with your neighbors earlier today, or should I say yesterday, at this early hour of the morning. I thought your political and domestic issues were strictly with Laslo, but it appears you've expanded your discussions—even about the country's economics.

Unfortunately, the current debt of our country is small compared to what it will be in just a few years. There will be record deficits. The S&P triple A ranking for the country was recently reduced one level to AA+ for the first time, reflecting an opinion that the fiscal consolidation that Congress and the Administration would agree to, would fall short of what would be necessary to stabilize the government's medium-term debt dynamics.

And now, even though two of the three major car manufacturers were bailed out, you'll find that cities like Detroit will eventually become bankrupt.

Based upon the premise that continued spending will solve economic problems, you'll find that the number of jobs will not significantly increase.

Increased government regulations and control over major industries and the banks will actually make things worse. Using the global economic crisis as an excuse to revolutionize our economy and orchestrate a redistribution of wealth by raising taxes on a very small percentage of citizens who make more income and providing tax credits for those who don't, who won't make up the difference for excessive spending.

The over regulation of emission standards and government attempts to curtail the coal industry will cost additional jobs, increase utility costs, and further stagnate the economic growth no matter how much paper money is printed every month.

I foresee we'll continue those policies, rendering a false economy. Before we get a chance to repair all the damages done by such policies, Iran will be well on their way to developing a nuclear weapon. And that will create a whole new scenario of other problems.

There will also be more issues in the mid-east, with uprisings in countries like Egypt and Syria, where we will become more ineffective and uninfluential. There will be more attempts at terrorism.

And you're correct about our continued apologies. There will be a point in time when we won't even call the terrorists, terrorists. We'll want to be more sensitive and call it workplace violence or better yet, man-caused disasters. I wouldn't be surprised if we don't have terrorist attacks within some of our major cities like New York, Los Angeles, or Boston in the future—even in major cities in other countries. Then you'll witness some of our own brainwashed population supporting the perpetrators and demonizing the actual victims in those attacks who have lost limbs and lives. The vic-

tims will be the ones to suffer in those cases.

There will be a price to pay for the ideology we're sinking into, and it will affect us all. I'm simply amazed that more people aren't aware of our potential decadence and that your friends are so well versed in current events. I've become more cognizant because of radio broadcasts from the Turing-B satellite, where we appear to be receiving news about events yet to happen. I am assembling a timeline of events reported with their actual occurrence.

In many aspects, these national issues aren't unlike those you are experiencing on a local level, particularly regarding the manipulation of information. Keep in touch and let me know about that construction development in your town. It appears like it could go out of control as hearings progress, not unlike the country.

Again, I can see many similarities between the progression of both. Keep notes to yourself about the planning and zoning board discussions. You might want to write a book comparing similarities of harmful changes. It might make an interesting chapter in our history. You never know.

Well, I've got one more accelerator test to perform before I shut down this morning and get some sleep. Been busy here—day and night, seven days a week for some time now.

–Max

Chapter Six

Phase Two

i.

Nelson and Sarah received another notice from the ZBA one week after Thanksgiving, informing the abutters of another public hearing and once again requesting a special exception to the town's ordinance for the continued expansion of the CHS development.

"Another one!" Nelson exclaimed as he sorted through the day's mail.

"Afraid so," Sarah answered. "This time the letter mentions an expansion of the Phase One construction into six more phases. I assume that means the site plans for the development are ready for Phases Two through Seven, which they mentioned at the last ZBA meeting. I'll go down to the town hall and get copies of the plans so we can see what they're proposing. Last time we never got much of a chance to review them. The meeting is scheduled for the second week of December."

"I can see we're going to have a lot more of these hearings as time goes on," said Nelson. "From what I gather, this Phase Two will be right in our backyard; Merry Christmas to *us.*"

Cஃ Cஃ

Three days later, Sarah obtained a set of eight large blueprints from the code enforcement officer. Since he had an extra set of prints, he provided them at no cost. The plans showed that Phase Two consisted of forty-four units in five additional buildings.

"These general notes on the site plan for Phase Two are interesting," Nelson said to Sarah while he looked at the first of several blueprints. "It shows the number of trips generated are 3.48 trips per unit. That's the same number they used for their North campus. And the drawing still shows a bridge connecting their two so-called campus' together, even though they mentioned at the last ZBA hearing that it wasn't financially feasible. I realize the Planning Board considered it, even though the Conservation Commission previously said no. But why bother leaving the annotation on the site plans at all? The plan also calls this an elderly housing complex.

"These two lots of land they call the North and South Campus' are actually independent of one another, but it appears that they've combined the total area of both lots in order to get a greater number of units per acre. It seems odd they can be allowed to combine their calculations—creative mathematics, I guess. I would think they would have to be separate. And look at these grading plans. There's gonna be a lot of land bulldozed to level off many of those building areas. I know there's a ravine that runs almost the whole length of the forest on this southern parcel. It's got to be at least a twenty-five-foot drop in many places. That's a lot of land fill!"

"Did you see the copy of the traffic assessment that was performed last July?" Sarah asked. "It says the new South Campus will be accessed from Route 2 as well as from Baker Street."

"Yeah, Caring Home Services seems to keep ignoring what the ZBA tells them about what they can't do. How convenient for them. And the worse part is the Planning Board doesn't seem to care."

ii.

When the Zoning Board of Appeals met in December, it hadn't snowed yet and the ground remained bare. The public meeting hall was reminiscent of the same stark, barren landscape, and much to Nelson's displeasure, the uncomfortable metal chairs remained.

As Nelson sat down, he grimaced at the first contact of cold, hard metal and the thought of sitting through another public hearing created a sense of despondency. Once a year was more than enough.

Sarah looked at the nameplates on the curved table that

faced the public and noticed most of the names were different from those only the year before. "Looks like all the board members are different this time with the exception of the chairperson," She removed her winter coat and hung it on the back of her chair. "There was an article in the newspaper about new members being elected. I guess a couple resigned and a couple ended their elected tenure."

"Wow. I guess so," said Nelson, surprised. He slowly scanned the slightly skewed nameplates and added, "You're right, they've all changed except for the chairperson. We didn't get out to vote at the last town election 'cause we were both sick that day. I had forgotten about that. So only the chairperson is the same?"

"He's the only one. I'm not sure if that's good or bad."

"I guess we'll find out."

Facing the public from left to right were ZBA board members Rachel Greene, Jane Emery, Peter Bolduc, Michael Grady, and Eleanor Adley. Chairperson Bolduc was the last to take his seat and opened the public hearing with a familiar introduction.

"Caring Home Services is requesting a special exception to terms of Title 10, Section 14.060, Subsection E.1 and E.2 of the Land Use and Development Code Zoning Ordinance to expand the existing CHS facility, zoned as urban residential."

Phil Dwyer took the initiative and quickly rose, addressing the board members with his hoarse, high pitched voice. Nelson recognized him from the previous ZBA meetings as the director of development for CHS.

"CHS started with thirteen apartments on our North Campus. Since then, there have been four expansions, now totaling eighty-six apartments. We completed what is considered the North Campus a few years ago, and last summer we completed Phase One of the South Campus, which is located off of U.S. Route 2, the main highway that runs parallel to our southern parcel.

"The State requires we go to the Department of Environmental Protection for approval and requires a master plan for everything that is planned for the property. We have therefore developed a master plan over the last year, and an application was made to the DEP in early September of this year upon completion of Phase One. We anticipate that part of the approval process will take another six months to complete. We are before the ZBA tonight for a special exception for continued development of our elderly housing. After this, we'll go to the Planning Board for approval of the site details.

"We plan to provide a full range of retired living conditions. The facility will have assisted living at some point with twenty-four hour, seven day a week care, providing meals and some nursing care. If we start construction by next spring for Phase Two, we will complete that phase by the following spring. Phase Two will provide an additional forty-four units, and we plan to continue this expansion into other phases of the development."

Dwyer's voice became increasingly hoarse, almost a wheeze, as he continued his presentation.

"Caring Home Services is a non-profit organization, and as such, does not pay normal property taxes. We do pay a fee, however, at our discretion, in lieu of property taxes to the town. That fee is based upon the existing property mill rate minus the school portion of the town's budget. We deduct the school portion because this facility is not adding any children to the schools. We figure paying a service fee to the town is the least we can do, even though it's not required."

At that point, Dwyer introduced Kurt Tussi of Tussi Engineering and Architecture to the board members.

"I'd like to bring the board members, who have not seen this project, up to date and explain the overall plan," said Kurt. "Caring Home Services consists of two campuses. The North Campus is a twelve and a half-acre site off Logan Road. It started with two expansions to one building for a total of sixty apartments and then two other expansions into a second building. As mentioned earlier, we now have a total of sixty apartments on the North Campus.

"Caring Home Services, Incorporated, which I'll simply call CHS, purchased a thirty-two and a half acre parcel of land located off U.S. Route 2 as a South Campus, and we are requesting a special exception for elderly housing. The entrance to Phase One of the South Campus shares an entrance as a right-of-way off Route 2 with the Alliance Professional Office building. The South Campus plan for Phase One came before the ZBA two years ago for a special exception to construct twenty-six apartments. The additional apartments for which today's special exception is being requested will be located adjacent and slightly north of the Phase One development that we call Phase Two."

As Kurt continued his presentation to the board, he walked over to the easel where two blueprints were exhibited.

"This site plan shown here today illustrates the phasing of this development. The total build-out of Phase Two will consist of forty-four units in five additional buildings. Phase Three will be forty units in nine buildings. Phase Four will be thirty-three units in six buildings, and Phases Five, Six, and Seven will require a large building called the Great Hall with one hundred-eighteen units. That building will consist of fifty-two units in Phase Five, thirty-six units in Phase Six, and thirty units in Phase Seven. There is a storm water management plan required as part of the necessary permit from the Department of Environmental Protection, and the State Office of Inland Fisheries and Wildlife are reviewing the natural aspects of the site. We have not yet filed the site plan amendment with the Planning Board, but we've asked to be placed on their agenda for a sketch plan review before submitting the full application."

With slightly more emphasis in his voice, Kurt continued.

"This board has granted a special exception for this use on previous occasions, so we're hoping you will grant this special exception and grant the project in its entirety this time. It's the same project the DEP is reviewing and the same project to be reviewed by the Planning Board."

Chairperson Bolduc glanced at the board members, then, facing the public, he said, "Thank you, Mr. Tussi, for your presentation. Is there anyone here who would like to speak in favor of the application?" The room was quiet. No one spoke. "Is anyone speaking to oppose this application?"

Nelson, although disliking the idea of public speaking, reluctantly rose, asked to speak, and was recognized by the chairperson.

"What is the total number of *buildings* proposed to be built on the South Campus site?" Nelson asked, even though he knew the answer to his own question. He just wanted the audience to understand the size of the complex being proposed.

"There are a total of twenty-seven buildings," Kurt answered.

"I'm concerned about that many buildings on this site," Nelson said. "It's my understanding that by receiving approval of a special exception from this board, you would be allowed more buildings per acre and therefore many more apartments."

"A special exception is a generally allowed use," interrupted Chairperson Bolduc, "which is subject to certain criteria defined in the town's Land Use Ordinance. If the criteria are met, the use is allowed. The board can't change any rules or waive density or setbacks for a special exception."

"Well, with that many buildings, I'm concerned about fire," said Nelson. "You also need to consider the runoff of water and oil from the parking lots and other pollutants, such as phosphorus, into the wetlands, which I trust the DEP is looking at. Wildlife is also affected in that part of the forest, dramatically, I might add, with that many buildings being proposed."

"I think this special exception allows a density waiver of up to eight apartments per residential acre," said Rachel Greene, "which isn't allowed otherwise."

Allen Treble, the Code Enforcement Officer, rose quickly and added, "The Planning Board will get into the clustered aspect of this development, not the ZBA."

"I just wanted to inform Mr. Quip about the density waiver allowed by a special exception," Rachel continued. "I talked to one of the Planning Board members and asked if there were special things that elderly housing projects would receive and was told they would be allowed to have a higher density."

Phil Dwyer quickly added to the discourse. "Elderly housing is allowed a higher density of people per dwelling than a typical residence. That, of course, means we can have more buildings per acre."

Suddenly, Mary Vaschon forced her chair back as she stood and asked to be recognized, her demeanor stolid but her round face a little flushed with apprehension.

Nelson was pleased to know he was no longer a one-person show with no abutter support.

Mary and her husband, Joe, had lived next door to the Quips for over fifteen years and were good friends. The

Vaschons, in their mid-fifties, had migrated from a farmstead at the northern tip of the state after it became increasingly difficult to make a living on a small farm. Joe was offered a welding position at a ship building company in Laslo and they had decided to move. They liked to hunt and fish and enjoyed the outdoors. They were the kind of individuals who would always pitch in to help anyone who needed assistance.

"You need to understand that there are more wetlands back there than people realize," Mary interjected. "In the middle of summer, you can ride a four-wheeler down into that parcel of land and still get it stuck up to the axle in muck and mire." She turned away from the board members to face Phil Dwyer and continued.

"What you are proposing is encroaching close to those wetland areas. Another thing. I'm tired of living in this town and having people not pay their fair share, like your organization. We've heard a lot about everyone paying their fair share in the last few years, haven't we? But many of us are being taxed right out of our own homes because we're paying for someone else. We would just like you to pay your own share, just like the rest of us." She then sat down with a defiant expression on her face.

With that outburst, Nelson decided to proverbially add more fuel to the fire. He stood up once again to continue the discussion, facing Phil Dwyer. "I believe homeowners in this town should realize that your organization only pays a very small portion of what should be property taxes to this town. Your company calls it a service fee in lieu of actually paying taxes. You justify this by your non-profit tax status even though you make a large profit from the rent you generate from all the apartments. You don't provide charitable services for anyone living in those apartments, that I'm aware of.

"These buildings and tenants may not be a burden on the school department, but they are a burden upon the fire department and other town services. There are a lot of people who don't have children in schools but who still pay that portion of their property tax bill, and that's a large portion of their taxes. Allowing additional structures in your development to be built and not taxed will increase the service costs to the town and its residents. That will result in increasing everyone else's property taxes. Whether or not you're considered non-profit by the IRS, you're still generating profits from your rentals."

It was noticeably clear that Phil Dwyer was irritated by Nelson's comments.

His face was flush, the room—quiet.

iii.

The code enforcement officer, Allen Treble, broke the awkward, tension filled silence.

"Caring Home Services is asking for a phased project, ultimately totaling two-hundred and sixty-one units, with twenty-six units already built on their South Campus property. This development is within the urban residential zone that allows elderly housing as a special exception. Normally, the net maximum density can't exceed three dwelling units per net residential acre. Under our Zoning Code, however, the standards can be increased to eight dwelling units per net residential acre as a special exception for elderly housing. This application is set up as a phased project, which can't be substantially completed within one year so the ZBA may wish to provide additional time for the applicant to complete the entire project."

"Does the total of two-hundred and sixty-one units include the North Campus property?" asked Rachel, as she turned her attention specifically to address Tussi.

"The thirty-two plus acres of the South Campus supports the two-hundred and sixty-one units as a total build-out," Kurt said.

"Is that because elderly housing per the town land use ordinance allows eight units per net residential acre?"

"Yes."

"Since the entire project is owned by the same group," Rachel continued, "the total number of units is actually two-hundred and sixty-one units in the South campus plus the sixty units already built on the North campus. I do have a concern about the tax issue. I think elderly housing is good for the community because you get people to pay taxes, and they are not using the school system. I've already discussed this property tax situation with a few members of the Planning Board. I was told the elderly housing projects get to have a higher density because it doesn't place a large burden on the community. Now I hear that this development will not be bearing the full tax burden. I simply don't see what the economic benefit is to the town. The development itself will not be paying its own share and will actually increase the tax burden on everyone else. It seems strange to me that a certain group can pick and choose whether or not to pay for schools or not. I'm surprised that such a deal was ever made to only have CHS pay a small service fee to the town in lieu of property taxes like everyone else. The size of this development will have a huge impact on town services."

Chairperson Bolduc, seemingly perturbed about the conversation, interjected. "It's my understanding that once the Federal Government has given a non-profit status to an organization, it means you can't make a profit on things like rent, and the town can't tax that entity, period. I don't think this is a town issue. Looking at the criteria in the ordinance, I don't know that this tax issue would fit under any special exception criteria. If it doesn't fit, then I don't think it's something this board is supposed to consider. The abutters may be concerned about it, and it is a political issue, but I don't think it's a town issue."

"That's a problem all by itself," Nelson whispered to Sarah. "He's not thinking about the repercussions. If that company is not making a profit with all that rental income, then where's all the so-called non-profit money going? They'd probably tell me, in a nice way of course, that's it's none of my business if I asked such a question, especially during a zoning board meeting."

"But it makes you wonder, doesn't it?" Sarah whispered back. "Probably just to buy more land and build more apartments which ultimately increases their non-profit income."

Nelson noticed a well placed smirk on Sarah's face after her well placed remark about a non-existent profit.

Turning to face Bolduc, Rachel tersely responded. "My issue is not so much that it is right or wrong for more elderly housing. This is a board that deals with how the town will be developed in the future. It affects how the board looks at large projects like this one. I have to question if such a development is good for the town. Although the application before the board is only for Phase Two, the applicant is asking the board to approve the whole thing—all seven phases. Mr. Tussi stated the application is for the plan in its entirety."

Rachel continued with increased emphasis and zeal to her voice.

"There is no way I could approve of something this size on a five-year plan. There are reasons why there are expiration dates on approvals. It gives abutters another forum in which to respond to further development. I would be more comfortable voting for the forty-four units in five buildings for Phase Two only. I don't see how anyone can foresee all the problems that a project of this size can cause. I believe the board should consider this project one phase at a time, since it appears it will take at least a year to build out each phase."

"In reading page two hundred and thirty-eight of the Land Use Code," Chairperson Bolduc responded, "it can be implied that this kind of clustered housing development is allowed. The Zoning Board doesn't get involved with that decision; the Planning Board does. This board looks at the use of elderly housing, and upon approving that use, it opens the door for the applicant to move forward to the Planning Board process."

Bolduc seemed to think more about Rachel's comment, hesitated with a quizzical look on his face, then turned back to address Kurt Tussi once again. "Why is approval being requested for all phases of this project? If the DEP approves the whole thing and this board grants approval for Phase Two, your client can always go back to the DEP and amend what has been done if there are any changes to the other phases."

"That's at least a fair question to ask," Nelson whispered to Sarah.

"My client is asking for approval of a phased project to be constructed within the time limits that the town ordinance allows," said Kurt. "It's no different than a subdivision that this board would approve to be built in phases."

Nelson noticed Kurt was carefully choosing his words.

"How many years will it be before Phase Seven is completed?" Bolduc asked.

"It would be five years, but that depends upon the demand for apartments."

"That also means it could be fifteen years," replied the

chairperson.

"The town's ordinance won't allow for that," said Kurt. "Subdivisions have to be completed in three years, with extensions up to ten years allowed by the Planning Board."

Treble, who had kept quiet throughout the recent discourse, spoke up with authority. "The Zoning Board approval is good for one year to substantially complete the phase within the year, unless of course, an extension is approved."

"Will Phase Two be done within the year?" Bolduc asked Kurt.

"Yes."

Jane Emery sat just to the right of the chairperson. She was in her early sixties, her pure white hair, which was pulled back into a single braid, swirled as she turned to face Phil Dwyer. Her blue eyes seemed invigorated as she spoke.

"Mr. Dwyer stated that there were other contributions which were agreed to be made in lieu of paying property taxes. Mr. Dwyer said a fee for services is paid and covers everything the development uses, so it's paying its fair share of town costs. He also said the fee is based upon a percentage of the rent and if the rent is increased, so is the fee."

"I agree with Mrs. Greene about not approving all the phases," Chairperson Bolduc interjected, ignoring Jane Emery's comment.

Nelson was surprised by the chairperson's sudden agreement with another board member but wondered why he had dismissed Jane's statement.

Eleanor Adley, younger than Jane with short, straight black hair, a color too dark to be natural, sat to the chairperson's left at the farther end of the curved desk. Her high-pitched voice emanated throughout the room as she spoke for the first time.

"What has the Planning Board done in cases of subdivisions that take longer than one year to complete? And concerning the tax issue, what isn't the town getting from this, other than school fees?"

"I don't remember hearing about any subdivisions since I've been on the board," replied Bolduc.

Michael Grady interrupted. His thin face, exacerbated by his tightly wound hair into what would be called a 'man-bun', appeared drawn and expressionless. Younger than all the other board members, he always seemed to have all the correct answers, even when he was wrong. To Nelson, he was possibly too arrogant to serve on a town board. The noticeable freckles on his face moved as he spoke.

"As a non-profit, this development doesn't have to pay any taxes at all. It's voluntary on the applicant's part."

Nelson whispered once again to Sarah. "I don't think that's true. I think there's more to it than they're leading us to believe."

"This tax issue," Michael continued, "is in regard to the Federal government, and it isn't germane to what this board is doing here tonight. There's nothing this board can do in order to affect that. My concern is with over-building of non-profit sites in town. Deals can be made with the Planning Board on the ordinances of elderly housing for a number of things. If the town commits to a lot of non-profit building, it could be shooting itself in the foot."

Eleanor Adley quickly spoke again. "Mr. Grady, what kind of deals can be made?"

"I'm sure that certain exceptions can be made to elderly housing with the town," was his lackluster and elusive reply.

"A lot of policy decisions are made by the town," said Bolduc. "The town could do something to limit elderly housing, or maybe not. This board has to look at the Land Use criteria regarding a special exception use. I don't see anything here that fixes the tax issue. The fire concern could be an issue, although fire trucks can get in there, and the buildings have sprinklers. But I think that's a Planning Board issue.

"Does the board want to limit its approval to Phase Two only?" Bolduc asked.

"If the approval is open ended, I can't vote in favor," Rachel said.

"Well, the applicant will have to come back anyway," said Bolduc. "As Mr. Tussi already stated, they can't do more than one phase in a year, and that is all the board's approval is good for. What do you think, Mr. Treble?"

"This project would end up going before the Planning Board," Allen said, "therefore the time period before the Planning Board would not be counted as part of the expiration time limit of this board's approval. If it's March before the applicant gets before the Planning Board, this board's one year time period would start in March."

"I could go along with the approval of only Phase Two," said Jane. "I think it's a good use of the area at this point, but the entire project is over three hundred apartments, and I don't think the board should approve that tonight. Phase Two is as far as I would be willing to go. Traffic is also a factor that should be of consideration here. I would like to give the neighbors and the abutters a chance to come back and discuss the possibility of additional phases."

"When I do the math, I come up with a total of two-hundred and sixty-one apartments being allowed," said Rachel as she turned to view her fellow board members. "Mr. Tussi said it's 32.7 acres times eight units per acre. There are a lot of wetlands back there. It looks like there are just over two acres in Phase Two where the wetland setback sweeps up in a curve over designated parking spaces. There are structures that also appear to be extending out over the allowed setbacks."

Phil Dwyer quickly rose from his seat. "Those are decks attached to the buildings."

"Can the decks be closer to the wetlands than the actual buildings?" asked Bolduc.

"It depends upon the size of the wetland and the size of the deck," Treble said. "At most, these decks have a fifty-foot setback from the wetlands. Parking lots would have a seventy-five-foot setback for over a twenty stall parking area."

"Who's overseeing these wetlands?" asked Rachel. "Is the DEP going to confirm that everything is done according to plan? Mr. Treble, will you be checking on this as the town code enforcement officer?"

"There are engineered plans that have been flagged by wetland scientists," Allen said.

"The DEP requires a lesser setback of seventy-five feet," said Kurt, "where the town of Laslo requires a hundred feet from the wetlands. If there is a known habitat in the area, Inland Fisheries and Wildlife requires a hundred-foot setback. When a project has both DEP review and town review, anyone with a concern can call the town or DEP as an enforcement issue."

"I really don't want it to get to that point," said Rachel. "I want to make sure that Phase Two will meet all the wetland setback requirements."

Kurt moved closer to Phil Dwyer, as if to protect his client. "What happens with this project and what has been done in the earlier phases is that a site plan is presented to the Planning Board."

He looked briefly at the public then turned his attention back to the ZBA members. "Mrs. Greene has basically asked if the buildings are set exactly where they are on the plan for this project. They have been. The roads and buildings are established with an instrument and are precisely set as the plan shows. There is very little wiggle room. Sometimes the general contractor sets the buildings and roads, but in this case, I've done it. The DEP reviews the resulting setbacks and any sedimentation going into the wetland during a site visit. The DEP can also ask for a third-party investigator."

Glancing over his shoulder at Nelson, he continued.

"Mr. Quip has previously said that he questions the possible pollution to the wetland from the parking lots. And he indicated that if sediments from erosion travel to a wetland, pollutants can attach to it. The DEP is reviewing that now. The setbacks and buffer areas offer another level of protection and the buffers are deed restricted forever and filed in the County registry of deeds, unless the applicant goes back and asks the DEP to modify the plan."

Rachel turned her attention to Treble. "I know we're here to either approve or disapprove the use of elderly housing for this project, but is the Planning Board supposed to review the specifics of the plan itself?"

"Yes," he responded.

"Then will an overall impact study be performed because of the size of this project?"

"Sometimes the Planning Board does that."

Chairperson Bolduc carefully observed the board members first to his right and then to his left. "Is this board comfortable with approving the use but not approving the cluster type development of eight apartments per acre density?"

"Is Phase Two in this approval?" asked Grady.

"Our vote will just be to approve Phase Two," replied the chairperson. "The applicant is asking for approval of the entire project, but the board's approval only runs for one year, therefore approval is only for Phase Two."

Grady turned to face Phil Dwyer. "Mr. Dwyer, can anything be set up as part of the special exception for town residents having a priority to receive these units?"

Phil Dwyer responded. "I'm not allowed to do that, but most residents are from this town."

Nelson whispered once again to Sarah. "The discussion seems to go from one subject to another. I wish they'd settle upon one topic at a time and finalize at least one of their discussions."

"These are just apartment rents. What does Grady's question have to do with any of this?" Sarah asked in response.

"I have no idea," he replied.

It was at that moment that Michael Grady determined it was time to cease the continued deliberations and made a motion to the board members.

"I move that the application of Caring Home Services requesting a special exception to the terms of Title 10, Section 14.060, Subsection E.1 and E.2 of the Land Use and Development Code Zoning Ordinance be approved to expand the existing CHS facility, Phase Two only, at property located at U.S. Route 2, Map 2, Lot 35, in our town of Laslo, zoned urban residential, be approved. Construction shall be in accordance with the plan submitted and signed and dated by Phil Dwyer of CHS and Mr. Bolduc, chairperson of this board."

Rachel Greene quickly seconded the motion.

There was no further discussion among the board members, and no further discussion was requested of the residents. The motion was unanimously approved by a show of hands.

Nelson noticed a wry smile on Dwyer's face as Peter Bolduc concluded the public hearing. "The applicant will receive written notice confirming this board's decision within one week."

He shook his head as he turned to Sarah, slightly astonished at the curt summation. "That was quickly decided. Looks like we'll have to live with this Phase Two development."

Nelson, Sarah, and a few of their neighbors, somewhat stunned by the abrupt approval, slowly exited the town hall before the next application before the ZBA was discussed. They were done for the evening, exhausted from the random deliberations.

Three days later, abutters received a copy of an approval letter issued to the applicant. Reading it, Nelson wondered what would eventually become of the forest and its inhabitants. The cost of construction was on the rise. The average cost of gasoline had risen to three dollars and fifty cents per gallon, food stamp recipients had risen from approximately twenty-eight million to forty-seven million people, the unemployment rate had practically doubled, and the national debt had increased from eleven trillion dollars to fifteen trillion dollars.

Yet, with a questionable economy, the developer appeared to have plenty of money available.

iv.

It was late morning, the day after the ZBA hearing, when Maxwell arrived back at the lab. He had left at 3 a.m. to get some much-needed sleep at home, and knowing the unconventional hours he kept and the time he had left, his staff was surprised to see him return so soon.

He climbed the steel stairs onto the grated platform and noticed they were all busy at their desks, monitoring the two satellites that had managed to travel toward their somewhat transfigured objectives. After Dora provided her typical good-morning greeting and he was seated behind his desk, he spotted Harold walking toward him with scrolls of paper outputs in hand.

"Dr. Draper, have you been reading the news reports of the negative trends in regard to Iran's nuclear assessment?" Harold asked. "They're a bit disturbing to say the least."

"Yes," said Max. "After you finished tying all the media sources and government agencies into our system, I asked Dora to keep a constant watch on their activities and update me from time to time. I was just reviewing the results of those reports yesterday. I can summarize those events for you if you'd like me too."

"Absolutely," Harold said, with a somewhat worried expression on his face.

"It's a troubled progression that started about nine years ago. I have my notes right here. Back then, there was some

news about the discovery of two nuclear sites under construction. One of them was an enrichment facility in Natanz,
which is partly underground, and the other one was a heavy
water facility in the town of Arak. Since then, there's been a
continued trend in their nuclear proliferation.

"The following year, after those two facilities were discovered, Iran agreed to co-operate with the International
Atomic Energy Agency and suspend its enrichment and re-
processing activities, even though they still imported uranium from China and continued to enrich. Then they reneged
on their promise to permit the IAEA to carry out inspections.
The next year they commenced construction on a heavy water reactor. Two years after that the IAEA reported that Iran
was in non-compliance with its safeguards agreement to the
United Nations Security Council, which demanded that Iran
suspend its nuclear enrichment programs. Two months later,
the President of Iran announced they had successfully enriched uranium to 3.5 percent using over a hundred centrifuges and told everyone they had to be treated as a nuclear
power. Three months after that, the UN Security Council demanded they suspend *all* enrichment and imposed economic
and trade sanctions for non-compliance under a UN Resolution 1737. A year later Iran was still continuing to produce
enriched uranium.

"After that, UN Resolution 1803 was passed extending
sanctions. It was that same year when the IAEA had obtained corroborating information from intelligence agencies of
several countries that pointed to Iran performing sophisticat-
ed research into some key technologies needed to build and
deliver a nuclear bomb. To make matters worse, the IAEA
substantiated the installation of new centrifuges, including
more advanced models. The IAEA's request to access those
sites was refused and that, of course, caused concern regarding possible military dimensions to its nuclear program.
Iran continued to enrich uranium and within the following
year, they had produced over a ton of low enriched uranium.

"It was then that our Secretary of State candidly ruled
out the possibility that we would ever allow Iran to produce
its own nuclear fuel, even under intense international inspection. Two months after that comment was made, Iran informed the IAEA that it was constructing a second enrich-

ment facility at an underground location at Fordow. If you take a close look at that facility, it's obvious that it's too small to be useful for a civilian nuclear program but not too small to produce enough highly-enriched uranium for one nuclear bomb per year. There were also reports that Venezuela was helping Iran to obtain uranium and evade international sanctions.

"That's bothersome," Harold said. "Where are we right now with them?"

"Well, last year the IAEA issued a report scolding Iran for failing to explain purchases of sensitive technology as well as for the conduct of secret tests on high-precision detonators. They noted there were modified designs of missile nose cones to accommodate larger payloads. As a result of those findings, the UN Security Council imposed a complete arms embargo and extended asset freezes. It was also discovered that Iran started using a second set of one hundred and sixty-four centrifuges linked in a string of machines to enrich uranium up to twenty percent at its Natanz pilot fuel enrichment plant. Last month, the IAEA Director stated that evidence gathered by the agency indicated Iran had carried out activities relevant to the development of a nuclear explosive. Officials identified a large explosive containment vessel inside Parchin, a military complex located just south of Tehran. The IAEA requested access and information, and we stated sanctions would be stepped up. As a response, Iran threatened to reduce its cooperation."

"What cooperation?" asked Harold. "That's almost ludicrous."

"Yeah, I agree, but right now, that's where we're at.

"There also appears to be other troublesome events on our own home-front to watch, as well. The data from all those media sources you managed to connect us with implies there's going to be some sort of issue with the Internal Revenue Service. Dora noticed an internal list that keeps appearing with names of conservative organizations associated with requests for tax exemptions relative to 501(c)(4) applications. Apparently, anything related to words like progressive, occupy, patriots, debt, government spending, challenges to the Affordable Care Act, and integrity of federal elections are all being targeted for scrutiny and delay."

"Dr. Draper, have you noticed anything strange with some of the data transmissions from the satellite feeds?"

"You're talking about the Turing-B satellite, aren't you?"

"Yes, in particular the satellite that seems to have inadvertently approached that unforeseen traversable wormhole. The large gravity deflections we've witnessed certainly make its relation to such a location suspect."

"Dora's been trying to help me figure that out," Maxwell added. Some of the radio signals we've transmitted to that satellite from news media appear to be slightly altered when the transmissions are repeated back to us. We're looking at time differences and seem to be receiving information differences as well. Transmissions we've sent regarding events on earth appear to be modified, or you might say enhanced from their original source and time of transmission. Our group is trying to decipher whether or not time is compressed. You could use the term, imaginary time, caused by the extreme force of gravity near an event horizon. We're actually trying to establish the same type of gravity effects on a smaller scale by producing a miniature black hole with the lab's particle accelerator."

Maxwell continued his explanation. "The stronger the force of gravity, the larger the time dilation effect. So, how's that for a simple scientific explanation? Even though we are transmitting news reports directly to the satellite, it's also receiving other radio signals transmitted from earth, sources even *we* haven't linked to. Some of the information we've been receiving from that satellite is information from our local media I wasn't even aware of."

"Let me paraphrase what you're saying about time dilation that seems to be occurring here, so you can validate my understanding," Harold said. "I know that space-time will bend due to differences in either gravity or velocity—each of which affects time in different ways. The faster you travel with respect to someone stationary, the slower your interval of time. If you traveled away from the earth at the speed of light for several years and then returned, you would find the people on earth much older by several decades than you when you returned. The faster the relative velocity, the greater the magnitude of time dilation. I understand that gravitational time dilation, however, has the opposite effect of the relative velocity time dilation. Both velocity and gravity slow down time as they increase in magnitude. As you travel farther away from earth, gravity decreases and speeds up time. In essence, the clock that is closer to the gravitational mass goes more slowly than the clock that is more distant from the mass. So the data that is transmitted from here and arrives at the satellite, where gravity has increased, could arrive earlier than the data re-transmitted from the satellite back to us again at a later time. But I would think that whole scenario might be dependent on the effects of the wormhole."

"The problem is we're just not sure what effects the wormhole has on that transmitted data," said Max, "Do we receive really old news or news we receive from a future transmission? How is that even possible? Why would any of the transmissions be altered in any way? Why would we re-ceive any variations in what was originally sent?"

"Has that actually happened?" Harold asked.

"That's what Dora and the other staff members are trying to figure out. Perhaps what we're receiving has come from sources other than what we have transmitted from our facili-ty. Perhaps the satellite has used its built-in artificial telepresence to determine a trend in information and then re-transmitted an alternate response. But that would be way beyond its design capabilities. I would think it's all about some added transmission sources. That could explain *some* things. I mean, we certainly haven't consolidated the entire number of news media outlets. As you know, a wormhole is fundamentally a shortcut through space-time, and that could also have some effect. In this case, it appears the Turing-B satellite has been caught in a wormhole that can be crossed in both directions, which is only possible if exotic matter with negative energy density could be used to stabilize it. It also makes me wonder if you could create a tiny wormhole and then inflate it to macroscopic size by a negative mass. Could we create something like that here?"

"Sounds like you have some interesting concepts to in-vestigate with our particle accelerator."

"Yeah, I have a few thought-provoking ideas," Max agreed. "Meanwhile, we'll keep reviewing the transmissions we receive. There's been a lot of them."

Year Four

"Why not just tell the truth?"

– Raymond Carver

Chapter Seven

Twisted Truths

i.

It was early morning on a cold rainy day in the first week of March when Mary Vaschon called Sarah. "Did you know there's a Planning Board Meeting about the CHS development next Thursday? There's a notice in today's paper, along with an article about the project."

"I haven't looked at the paper yet," Sarah replied. "Nelson already left for the office. He won't be happy when he hears about another meeting, but at least the article might draw more attention from residents."

"It looks like a meeting's being held just to review their site plan. The notice doesn't provide much information, only that there's a meeting. It's not a public hearing where we can discuss what's being proposed. It's a meeting to inform us of what their intentions are."

"Well, we have a good idea as to what their intentions are. We found that out at last December's ZBA hearing. So now they're at the Planning Board stage with their Phase Two, and we aren't allowed to speak since it's not a public hearing? We can only just listen?" asked Sarah.

"Apparently. But I think at some point there has to be another public hearing."

"I'm afraid there will probably be more than one."

ii.

Nelson and Sarah arrived at the town hall just as the five Planning Board members sat down behind their respective nameplates. From left to right, facing the public, were Elaine Graft, Brett Manley, Chairperson Ralph Tunney, Don Morgan, and Drew Laden.

As Nelson observed each one in succession, he wondered how their distinct personalities might affect their decisions regarding compliance to the town ordinances. The board members hadn't changed from previous meetings he had attended for other projects, and neither had the hard metal chairs.

Members of the public sauntered into the room, causing the meeting to start a few minutes late. Sarah pointed out a reporter she recognized from the Laslo Journal among those arriving late, whose photo had appeared in the newspaper next to the article about the development.

The chairperson interrupted the low toned conversations and asked people for their attention. "The first item on our agenda tonight is the preliminary site plan for a development project by Caring Home Services. Mr. Phil Dwyer represents CHS, and I understand he will be the first to speak."

With that introduction, Dwyer stood and faced the Planning Board members, his back to the audience.

"Thank you, Mr. Tunney. It's urgent that we get these plans approved as soon as possible. This process began quite a while ago, and we already have many applicants waiting for our assisted living housing. Their situations are pressing."

"Mr. Dwyer," Chairperson Tunney said, "this board has decided it needs an independent review of this project to help in the assessment during deliberations so we can properly address concerns regarding the town ordinances and any issues the board members may have. We'll pursue the appropriate process as expeditiously as possible, but it's the board's intention to receive comments from an independent peer review before a public hearing is held."

"I just wanted to remind everyone that we presented the site plan for this project to this board last year, a month after we presented it to the Zoning Board of Appeals for a special exception. Members of this board have already performed a site walk to review parking issues, sidewalks, street width, the number of units proposed, and the filling of wetlands. We also had a traffic study performed by Townsend Engineering. Two off-street parking areas have been added and three buildings have been removed from the plan, reducing the number of apartments by twelve."

"This reduction in the number of buildings," interjected Brett Manley, "is this just for Phase Two or for the entire seven phase project?"

"We're talking about the entire project, not just Phase Two," Kurt Tussi said. He stood and moved next to Phil Dwyer. "We also have shifted areas of landfill away from the wetlands. A storm water management plan has been revised, and we're leaving the steeper grades of the natural land contours and possibly doing less blasting, even though lesser grades would be more desirable."

Elaine Graft appeared anxious. She peered over the thin, metal-rim frame of her glasses and flicked away a few strands of red hair from her forehead. "What about underground parking to decrease the amount of tar and runoff into nearby wetlands?"

"The basement space is already fully used for storage, exercise space, and maintenance areas," replied Dwyer.

"Although I have concerns that this entire project will result in a long term, substantial change to the town," said the chairperson, "I think it'll provide affordable housing for assisted living. This is a complicated project and there are a lot of technical issues, with this being such a dense development."

"I'm having some difficulties particularly with the layout," added Elaine, as she turned to face Ralph Tunney. "Specifically, the access road from the North Campus crossing open water over the wetland area. I understood that CHS couldn't justify the cost of such a bridge previously and had relocated Phase Two for that reason. I simply can't proceed with this plan as it's proposed."

"That access road was designed the way it is due to the direction given by this board during an earlier approval process," Kurt replied, obviously annoyed with Elaine's comment. "CHS is proposing to build that road later in the development process."

"That was a reluctant agreement made by our board, with no vote, and no approval." Tunney quickly responded.

"What exactly does it mean to make an agreement with someone, not vote on it, and not approve it?" Nelson quietly asked Sarah. "By doing that, do you have any agreement at all?"

Sarah just shook her head. "Too bad we can't ask any questions; this is not supposed to be a public hearing," she whispered, reminding Nelson not to speak too loudly.

"At this point, I don't think there's much more to discuss," said Brett. "I therefore motion that the application for Caring Home Services is subsequently complete and is only conditioned upon the submittal of a landscape plan, a receipt of satisfaction from Fire Chief Gerard, and the completion of a peer review."

There was unanimous approval by the board members as they ended the session by calling a ten minute recess before the next applicant.

"When did the discussion about the Fire Chief's review of the plans come up?" Nelson asked Sarah as he donned his coat.

"I don't know. It must have been at another Planning Board meeting we missed earlier or that was held during some behind the scenes discussions with the code enforcement officer."

"Well, this meeting was certainly short and sweet," said Nelson.

iii.

It was June before the Planning Board reconvened and scheduled the first public hearing for Phase Two of CHS's development proposal. Nelson found himself at the town hall once again.

"It seems like we're either attending ZBA or Planning Board hearings all the time lately," Nelson said to Sarah. He looked down at the not so favorite metal chairs then quickly glanced at a copy of the Board's agenda for the evening after he sat. There were two hearings scheduled and CHS was second to be heard.

Time seemed to drag on forever. Although Nelson wiggled in his uncomfortable metal chair, he was relieved it was warmer than it had been when he first sat down.

Distraught with the thought about the effect of a development upon the forest and its wildlife, he was relieved when the chairperson finally announced the application for Caring Home Services would be discussed.

Phil Dwyer made his usual quick introduction to the Board members.

"As I mentioned during the last Planning Board meeting,

we need a decision for the approval of our application as soon as possible. There are many people on our waiting list. Mr. Tussi, the architect for our project, will briefly speak once again about our project."

Kurt Tussi stood, scratched his dark beard, as if to ponder his initial statement, and addressed the board.

"Let me provide a quick summary. As you all know, the North Campus of this development has already been built. This application is for Phase Two, to be located on what is called the South Campus where Phase One is already completed. According to the Town Land Use Code, we've calculated that two hundred and sixty-one units can be built on this site. We are currently proposing an additional two hundred and twenty-three units for Phases Two through Seven, for a total build out of two hundred and forty-nine residential apartments on the 32.7 acres of the South Campus, of which Phase Two consists of forty-two units. I'm here to answer any questions you have for us, Mr. Chairperson?"

"Let's hear what the public has for questions. Are there any members of the public who wish to speak about this development?" asked Ralph Tunney.

Nelson stood, stated his name and address, and was recognized by the board's chairperson to speak.

"I oppose this high-density cluster development. Last December, Caring Home Services requested approval from the Zoning Board of Appeals for all seven phases of their development. After hearing some of the public disapproval, the ZBA only approved Phase Two, with the understanding that CHS would have to return for the approval of additional phases as well as for any additional changes made to any approved plans for Phase Two. At that time CHS stated there were forty-four units in Phase Two. Now they're saying there's forty-two units with the same number of buildings.

"I believe there are many issues that remain to be discussed. They include street access, tax-exemption, an insufficient number of fire hydrants, which according to their site plan shows none for Phases Five and Six, narrow roads, only one entrance into the property, and high-density impact on wildlife and the environment. I have a detailed letter explaining those concerns for your consideration while you continue to review this project."

Nelson handed his letter to the chairperson and then sat down.

"Thank you for your comments, Mr. Quip," said Ralph. He quickly placed the letter underneath his notepad. "We'll note your concerns. Anyone else?"

"My name is Marsha Moran and I live in one of the apartments in Phase One. This type of housing is needed because people are being taxed right out of their homes. Therefore, it's less expensive to rent these apartments."

Joe Vaschon, another attendee clearly a little vexed at Marsha's statement, stood before the board members, his face slightly flushed. "What you're saying is that the rest of the property owners can pay more because *you* rent a place that doesn't pay property taxes. That kind of transfers the burden to others, doesn't it? These high-density clusters simply don't contribute to our tax base, and that's a problem for the rest of us. It's like a redistribution of wealth."

Joe's wife, Mary, stood next to her husband and added, "I'm concerned about water from all the proposed parking lots backing up on the abutters. And I'm also opposed to the tax situation that Caring Home Services has with our town. They should be paying property taxes just like everyone else."

Kyle Doran, another abutter who remained sitting, said, "I agree with Mary Vaschon. There's already an existing water problem in the area. I have standing water on parts of my property for eight or nine months of the year. Runoffs from parking lots will heighten that problem."

Ned Garth volunteered his name to the public and said, "I live in Phase One of the South Campus, and I know that the Town's Comprehensive Plan talks about the necessity of elderly housing. What better use of the forest. Are trees and wetlands more important?"

Sarah turned to Nelson. "Wow, I can't believe anyone would make that sort of statement."

"Yeah," said Nelson, "a little 'only care about me' attitude there. Guess I better get a copy of the town's Comprehensive Plan to see what it says. I've never looked at it, not that I really want to."

"I see at least three problems," Will Penton stated as he stood, not waiting to be recognized by Tunney. "First, there is only one access road being proposed. Second, this development is much too high a density, and third, such a massive development in the back yards of the abutters would lower their property values."

Millie Hodgdon, the petite white haired elderly woman who lived on Baker Street, was then recognized to speak by Tunney.

"I just have a few things to say. I'm one of the abutters, and the size of such a development will greatly affect this area. There's a lot of wildlife in those woods; the habitat for many of those animals will become non-existent. As several of the abutters have mentioned, there's also a great potential for water runoff problems onto many of our properties from the proposed paved parking lots."

Millie Hodgdon's remarks caught Kurt Tussi's attention, causing a quick response. "I have provided a map of the area we're talking about to this board titled Maine Department of Inland Fisheries and Wildlife Report which states, and I quote, *'There are no identified wildlife inhabitants associated with this site'*. I also have a letter from the State of Maine Department of Conservation that states, and I quote, *'There are no rare or botanical features documented specifically within the project area'*. So, according to those agencies, there is no impact to this development site to wildlife or botanical features."

Willa Hunter, another resident of the Phase One apartments, said, "I'm a current resident, and I think the traffic issue will lessen over time once they have group transportation and a van service established."

Sarah turned to Nelson. "Where did that information come from? I've never heard anything about a van service being proposed. Wishful thinking?"

Before he could respond, another resident commented. "My name is Jane Williams, and I think the apartments are wonderful, but I do think the company that owns them should pay taxes and not impact the abutters."

The room became quiet with that last statement, then Chairperson Tunney asked if anyone else had anything to say. No one spoke.

"Since there are no further comments, I am closing the public hearing portion of this discussion. I want everyone to know that the Laslo Conservation Commission has submitted memos about this development to the board. Site walks have been done by some members of the board, but not all, and by the Conservation Commission.

"Comments have now also been received from the peer review performed by Grafton Engineering, and we will need some time to digest those comments. This board will focus on Phase Two of this project. The other phases can be put on a different track with an eye toward future construction. This board does recommend to Mr. Tussi that there appears a need to extend the sidewalks, shift the parking areas so they don't back out into the roads, and extend buffering areas between the buildings and abutting single family homes. Are there any further comments from the board members?"

The other four members exchanged glances with one another, and Brett was the first to speak.

"I motion that we continue the public hearing for Phase Two of Caring Home Services at a future time to be determined by our Town Planner, Mr. Hatch."

The motion was seconded by Drew Laden, the only member of the board who hadn't said anything during the hearing. All board members approved the motion and then adjourned the public hearing.

iv.

As soon as Nelson arrived home, he e-mailed Maxwell and told him the results of the hearing, and of his concerns. It was later that night when he received a reply.

E-mail: June 7
To: NelsonQuip
From: Mdraper
Subject: Your Concerns

Hi, Nelson,
So you've had your first public hearing by the Planning Board for that Phase 2 development. I don't envy you sitting there listening to all of that rhetoric. I was surprised to hear about the no identified wildlife statement made by the developer, and that there would be no impact. If I were you, I'd look into getting a copy of that letter and see what it really says. Statements like that can always come in a variety of

lies, or in today's verbiage—misspoken truths.

Both you and I appear to have conflicting information that needs resolution. I'm getting a lot of satellite feedback from news media on events happening outside our country that could affect all of us. Some of the reports are rather disturbing.

There was an intelligence report just this month reporting recent attacks on one of our compounds in Libya. The report mentioned an expectation of an increased number of terrorists and more attacks occurring in the eastern part of that country.

Additionally, we've been getting a lot of mixed radio transmissions from the satellite that's experiencing increased gravity pull—you know, the one I've mentioned before to you, Turing-B—nearest what we consider to be a black hole.

For instance, there was a satellite transmission about a former military intelligence building in Benghazi being bombed. Yet, I haven't been able to verify the account of such an event. There was also a report about a cable being sent by our Ambassador in Libya to our State Department, raising concerns about the deteriorating security situation and requesting additional security resources. It's odd that I can't locate or verify any such request through our sources.

Turing-B also transmitted a report about Iran more than doubling the number of centrifuges at their underground facility at Fordow from 1,064 to 2,140. There was an AP report about the IAEA receiving intelligence that Iran had performed advanced work on computer modeling for the performance of a nuclear warhead. Their nuclear chief was quoted as saying they had intentionally provided false information about their nuclear program to mislead our intelligence, saying they understated their progress. I can't find anything, anywhere, that confirms these reports even exist—only what we've received from Turing-B.

I'll just have to keep investigating these somewhat confusing news transmissions. As I mentioned, statements can be in a variety of misspoken truths, whether or not they are in regard to local or national issues—make comparisons as you write. Keep in touch.

Best,

–Maxwell

Chapter Eight

Deliberations

i.

The remainder of June and the month of July passed without incident, and the summer remained quiet until the middle of August. That's when abutters received notification from the town once again of another public hearing before the Planning Board. Sarah visited the town hall and obtained copies of the latest CHS site plans as well as a copy of the peer review performed by Grafton Engineering in order to prepare for the meeting.

It was early evening, a week before the public hearing when Nelson and Sarah got together with five of their neighbors at their house to discuss the information Sarah had obtained.

"At least I know why there is a two apartment disparity in the numbers from the discussion at the last public hearing," Nelson said to Donny as he pointed to the site plans. "They've removed one building containing four apartments and changed one of the other buildings that originally had four apartments and increased it to six apartments. Where there once was a building is now actually more tarred parking area making the water runoff even worse."

Donny carefully eyed the two differently dated site plans. "One of the general notes on the plans has been removed. Look at this. The old plan from last year notes a traffic count of 3.48 trips per day for each apartment using a total of 261 units, generating eight hundred and eighty-seven trips for all seven phases of the development." He quickly picked up the small calculator Nelson had been using and typed in a few numbers. "Apparently they rounded the trip count down to 3.4 in order to get the number down to eight hundred and eighty-seven. Even the copy we have of the official traffic engineering study that was performed last winter indicates the traffic count is based upon 3.4 trips. So if 3.48 trips per day are used and the number of units in Phase's One and Two total sixty-eight, then the trip count for both phases would be two hundred and thirty-one, which means they need two access roads. This latest plan doesn't mention the traffic count at all. I wonder why that information was removed?"

"Maybe because the Town Land Use Code specifies that a second access road is required if the trip count is greater than two hundred," Nelson said. "It's as simple as that. The trip count would have to be around 2.8 not 3.48 in order to achieve a trip count less than two hundred and not have to worry about a second access road into the property."

Will Penton had a look of concern on his face. He leaned in to take a closer look at the plans.

"I seem to remember that during the second ZBA discussion for Phase One, Kurt Tussi said the traffic count was less than eighty trips per day. He also mentioned that two means of access are required per town ordinance when the traffic count exceeds two hundred. Since they were talking about twenty-six units for Phase One at the time, doesn't that come out to over eighty-eight, not eighty based upon the twenty-six units already built? So, Mr. Tussi kind of expanded the truth a little bit back then, didn't he? That means it was okay for the first phase to have only one access road. But if you add twenty-six units to an additional forty-two units from the proposed Phase Two, that results in sixty-eight units for a total traffic count of two hundred and thirty-one; you know, sixty-eight times 3.4, if you round the count down to 3.4. Like you said, that should mean the developer is required to have two access roads, not just one."

"Interesting," said both Josh Gosling and Mary Vaschon in unison.

"You've actually been reading that Town Land Use Code document, huh?" Joe Vaschon asked Nelson.

"Yeah. It's pretty dry reading. I also read the Town's Comprehensive Plan, which contradicts the Town Land Use Code Ordinance."

"How's that?" asked Joe.

"The Town's Comprehensive Plan stipulates that cluster

housing developments retaining open space and reflecting village like patterns of development should be allowed a density of up to four units per net residential acre, with no exceptions, not eight units as specified in the Town Land Use Code. It's really important for people to understand that by State law, each town is required to have a Comprehensive Plan for a town's future growth, and it legally takes precedence."

"Doesn't that mean the density calculations should be based upon the four units per acre instead of the eight units per acre, which is what the ZBA and Planning Board are allowing CHS to use?" Mary asked.

"It certainly appears that way," Nelson said. "The Comprehensive Plan also stipulates that the town currently has a sufficient number of elderly housing units. If you add up the number of units currently available, the town is actually forty-three percent over the numbers allocated in the Comprehensive Plan, not including the twenty-six units already built by CHS in Phase One. The additional forty-two units, proposed for Phase Two, would increase that percentage even more."

"So, is that any sort of problem for the developer?" asked Joe.

"No, I suppose not. It just goes to show that our town already has more than what it needs in terms of elderly housing apartments," Nelson replied. "The town is simply not obligated to approve more units as the developer would have you believe. I've also talked to a few real estate agents. I found it interesting to note that rentals in the area of comparable size and amenities are actually less in cost than the average rental apartment on CHS's so-called South Campus. I'm not sure what their benevolence factor is at this point. Just what charitable things do they really do?

"The Comprehensive Plan's mission statement includes the fact that the town should maintain a stable tax rate. So I looked into the property tax requirements of 501(c)(3) companies in our state. The Maine Revenue Services Administration states that under the non-profit Corporation Act, failure to incorporate in the State of Maine prohibits exemption from property tax. I verified that with the Director of the Maine Bureau of Corporations. Caring Home Services is incorporated in New Hampshire, not Maine, and therefore isn't exempt from property taxes in the State of Maine. In addition to that very simple requirement, the State requires that any corporation claiming property tax exemption must be organized and used exclusively for benevolent and charitable purposes. The charitable use of the property is a prerequisite to the tax exemption, as well."

"Even though they're not incorporated in the State, how are they charitable?" asked Will.

"I simply don't know," Nelson answered. "I haven't been able to figure that out yet. There's also another interesting point in the State law."

"What's that?" asked Joe.

"Even if a company has been recognized to be exempt from property taxes, the town's tax assessor's office is supposed to review the exemption status every year to ensure a company qualifies. And that review includes looking at their articles of incorporation, property deed and by-laws, and financial statements."

"Then, if they don't appear to be qualified, which appears to be the case with CHS, what has our tax assessor been doing all this time?" asked Joe.

"Apparently not what he's supposed to be doing," Will replied.

"Well, I believe the trip counts are also important to the development," Josh interjected. "Evidently, trip generation numbers are calculated dependent upon the type of housing being constructed and historical traffic data. I'm finding that all these rules and regulations are sure one long learning process. The official memorandum to the town's Code Enforcement officer from the traffic engineering consultant of Townsend Engineering is a little vague, however, on how the standards are derived."

"Actually, I did a little investigation regarding traffic counts," said Nelson. "I was getting tired of not understanding what they were talking about. The internet can be a very useful tool at times. There's a chart available from the Institute of Transportation Engineers that defines trip generation rates for different types of housing. For elderly housing, the average daily trip rate is specified to be 3.48. If you remember, the original Phase One plans used a trip rate of 3.48. The ITE standard is 5.86 trips per day for a Retirement

Community and 2.02 trips per day for a Congregate Care Facility."

"So, what *is* the actual standard that should be used for this development?" asked Josh.

"I don't see how it can be a Congregate Care Facility," Nelson said.

"Okay, I'll bite. What's defined as a Congregate Care Facility?" asked Mary.

Nelson smiled at Mary's comment. She knew how particular Nelson could be.

"According to the ITE standards, it's defined as an industry segment between independent living and health-related services of an assisted living facility. Congregate Care facilities are supposed to provide social activities, security, meals, housekeeping services, and transportation."

"Caring Home Services certainly doesn't qualify for that," Mary replied. They're just providing rental apartments for people over the age of fifty-five. They don't provide anything to the tenants, not even charitable services."

"I'm sure they'd love to use the 2.02 trip number as a Congregate Care Facility," said Josh. "For sixty-eight apartments, that would give them a traffic count of only around one-hundred and thirty-seven, so they wouldn't need a second access road according to town code. It wouldn't surprise me in the least if they tried to use that number."

"I don't see how they can change the original 3.48 number, since that was the number used previously for their earlier plans," Nelson said. "They just can't keep changing that number to suit their fancy. By the way, Sarah found a copy of the letter from Fire Chief Gerard regarding his comments about the development that the Planning Board members mentioned back last March."

"What did the Fire Chief say?" Will asked.

"He reviewed the plans for Phase Two and said he had no real concerns at that time. He also said he supported the proposed bridge over the wetlands from the North Campus to the South Campus for emergency services. The idea behind such a bridge was addressed in the first notice we received from the town, regarding this project. Then he goes on and kind of contradicts himself saying the size of the development is quickly depleting the current water main capabilities."

"Whoa," Will protested. "First, CHS tried to use Baker Street as an access to their proposed Phase One and that was denied by the ZBA. They were told they couldn't use that street because it was a small substandard dead end road in width that abutted CHS's property, and it would become a dangerous intersection, entering onto Route 2. To extend that road, they would have to cross a small wetland where the road meets the beginning of their property. Then they proposed using an extensive bridge to connect their North and South Campus, and ultimately found that was prohibitively expensive. In addition, I read where the Conservation Commission said they opposed a connecting bridge over all that wetland. I understood that CHS finally settled on accessing the bottom part of their South Campus using a right of way onto Route 2 in order to construct their Phase One. And for some reason we're talking about a bridge again?"

"Yeah, we are—again," Nelson said. "Seems like at one meeting, something is said, and then at another meeting, something else is said, so we're always discussing everything all over again as though we're in a constant state of flux. It's almost like they're trying to confuse the issues, and they seem to be doing a pretty good job of it.

"Kind of sounds like what occurs in everyday politics where a constant state of flux is an avoidance tactic—people forget one issue as another one starts. It appears that very few people or board members are really doing their homework here in town. These are important decisions being made that affects a lot of people."

"What's the peer review say about the project?"

"They bring up some interesting points," Sarah answered. "The peer review was done by Grafton Engineering. I have a copy of it right here. Our town planner, Todd Hatch, was a little disgruntled when I asked for a copy. Then he kind of got even with me when I pressed him for information by charging me twenty-five cents a page. Anyway, their report states that they performed a limited peer review for specific project issues requested by our Laslo Planning Board. The review was limited because of the sparse information provided by Caring Home Services. Not much of a surprise there, huh? Grafton Engineering reported that the application materials didn't provide clear intent or design information for the so-called proposed road crossing the wetland."

Josh interrupted. "Why does the wetland issue keep appearing when the Conservation Commission stated they weren't supposed to cross the wetland with a bridge?"

"Many of the same issues keep reappearing, don't they." stated Joe.

"The Conservation Commission also had other concerns they included in a letter to the Planning Board," replied Josh. "I remember reading about them."

"What were they?" asked Joe.

"They stated that wildlife was a concern because many animals were being forced out of their habitats due to the expansion of this project. They also asked whether or not state and federal wetland permits were considered for impact, whether or not the wetlands have been properly flagged, and whether or not the existence of vernal pools which provide breeding grounds for wildlife have been considered."

Sarah added to the discussion. "The review also stated that the intersection with Route 2 at the southern proposed access point was not evaluated for traffic. There was no information regarding the amount of wetland fill. Onsite soils mapping was not provided, and information and reports were not included describing the value and character of the wetlands. They also mentioned that the area for streets and access were not deducted from the overall acreage in order to determine the number of units per acre that are to be built, which is a requirement."

"So there are no final conclusions from the review?" asked Joe.

"Apparently not, just the details of the review itself. Guess we'll have to go to the public hearing next week and find out where we stand," Sarah said.

ii.

Nelson sat in the same row with several of his neighbors. Joe Vaschon sat to his right and Sarah to his left. Just as Nelson finished looking about the room, trying to recognize additional abutters, he noticed that a woman at the far end of the same row was passing down a letter for everyone to read and sign. He had never seen her before. Sarah read it, signed it, and passed it along to Nelson.

The letter was attached to a petition containing several signatures opposing the CHS development, noting residents' concerns about health and safety issues as well as concerns about excessive parking and water runoff problems into the wetlands. It explained the premise for concerns, and was signed by Emmy Anderson, stating she was an abutter. Nelson reviewed the several signatures on it, added his own in agreement, and handed it to Joe.

Nelson turned to Sarah. "I've never seen her here before. I'm glad other people are starting to take an interest."

The meeting was called to order and Phil Dwyer addressed the board with his usual presentation.

"As previously mentioned, there currently are a total of sixty units on the North Campus and twenty-six units on the South Campus known as Phase One for a total of eighty-six existing apartments. This Phase Two part of our development proposes an additional forty-two units in four buildings. As I stated in the first public hearing, the master plan for the entire South Campus is to establish a total build out of two hundred and forty-nine residential apartments. There's a real need for this elderly housing complex."

"I think there's a real need for them to make money. That's what I think," said Joe, in his usual gruff manner.

Nelson nodded his head in agreement.

Dwyer continued his presentation. "Abutters who spoke at the previous public hearing in June were expressing their concerns about Phase Four of the master plan. That's not what is being applied for at this time."

"I don't remember anything about a discussion of Phase Four, do you?" Joe asked Nelson as he nudged him with his elbow.

"No. I don't know where that came from," he said. And I see no one on the board questioned that comment."

Kurt Tussi took over the presentation and summarized the changes to the site plans, explaining the two-apartment difference in Phase Two from the previous public hearing. "I'll address the lot coverage calculations later with the town planner and also reply to the Peer Review comments at the next meeting."

"Are there any responses from the public?" Chairperson Tunney inquired.

Nelson stood up, addressing the Planning Board. "I've stated several times before, I am opposed to this expansion. I believe there are several violations to the Town Land Use Code, and I've addressed those concerns in a formal letter to this board. As I've mentioned on other occasions, I also believe this project puts an undue tax burden on the residents of this town. According to Maine State Law, Caring Home Services doesn't qualify to be exempt from property taxes."

"Property taxes are not the issue with this board, Mr. Quip."

"What about the trip counts and the requirement for a second access road into the South Campus for Phase One and the proposed Phase Two?" Nelson asked. "Don't they need a second access road based upon a trip count of 3.48?"

"Yes, they'll need a second access road," said the chairperson.

"So you're saying a second access road is required for the Phase Two development?"

Somewhat annoyed at Nelson's repetitive question, Chairperson Tunney replied. "Like I said, a second access road would be required."

"Thank you for the clarification," said Nelson, and then sat down with a slight smile on his face, knowing the chairperson had finally confirmed at least one requirement, or at least so he thought.

Marie Paterson, another abutter, whom Nelson hadn't seen at any previous meeting, stood and addressed the board members. "I agree with Mr. Quip," she stated. "I believe the developer's charitable tax status should be checked in order to understand why they don't pay property taxes. Like many other people, I'm also concerned with the environmental impacts of this development."

"Well I think the contributions to the community goes far beyond dollars and cents," clamored one of the CHS residents.

Emmy Anderson stood to address the board. She was a tall woman, very thin, with graying hair, in her early sixties. Although you could see she was somewhat nervous, she was emotionally charged and made her way to the podium walk-

ing sideways through the narrow rows of chairs. With une-
quivocal clarity, she stated her name before the planning
board.

"I want to go on record that I am an abutter to the property owned by Caring Home Services. I oppose this development and believe they should be paying property taxes
like everyone else. I have a petition signed by many residents opposing this project that I would like the Planning
Board to keep on file. There is also information attached for
our tax assessor, Mr. Simon Duncan, to review. I think he
really needs to read this," she said. She glared at the chairperson and handed him the petition sheets. Then, nice as
pie, she thanked the board members for listening, and returned to her seat.

After watching her take her seat, Chairperson Tunney
asked if anyone else had anything to say at that time. Hearing no further response, he closed the public hearing.

The board members began discussing the locations and
layout of parking, more efficient use of paved areas, the
length of the one access road into the development, items in
the peer review, and the adequacy of lot coverage calculations for housing density. The most disturbing part of their
conversation occurred when the board members referred to
the use of an ITE trip count standard of 1.94.

Wondering where the new number came from. Nelson
raised his hand to ask and was notably ignored by the chairperson. He then stood, "Mr. Chairperson—," but was curtly
interrupted from finishing his question.

"Mr. Quip, please sit down. The public portion of this
meeting has been closed. No further input from the public
can be added during the rest of this meeting. This panel will
continue with our discussions. You will have to bring up other
issues at the next public hearing."

Tunney turned back toward the other board members to
continue their discussion. Nelson sat down, frustrated. After
another hour, the chairperson announced another public
hearing was to be scheduled by the Town Planner when more
information was available.

Overall, three hours had passed and as Nelson stood to
leave, he turned to Sarah, shaking his head. "That was kind
of a waste of time, except for signing that petition. Evidently,

CHS didn't have all their responses ready for this Planning Board meeting and for the most part, all they did was to continue discussions among themselves. I wonder where they got that new trip count number. It doesn't match anything in those ITE standards that I reviewed earlier. They're really trying hard to eliminate the requirement for a second access road, even though the chairperson stated one is required. This is like a bad soap opera."

Nelson e-mailed Maxwell after he arrived home. He told him about the discussion he had at his house with his neighbors, about the Planning Board public hearing that night, and about the twisted truths that continued to bother him. Two days later, Nelson received an e-mail from Max.

iii.

E-mail: Aug 31: 0200
To: NelsonQuip
From: Mdraper
Subject: Strange Data Receipts

Nelson,
The parallels between what you are witnessing locally and what I'm observing nationally concern the obfuscation of information. News reports I've received from one of our satellites which haven't yet occurred actually complicate my understanding of what is true and what isn't. By the way, I received your first two Chapters. The comparative scenarios of your quest and mine may pose an important message to people. We can discuss more of this later as we put this all together.

That report I told you about last June, regarding the bombing of a former military intelligence building in Libya, well that event actually happened the beginning of this month, not in June, which is when we received the satellite transmission about such an incident.

In addition, the cable that was reportedly sent to the State Department in June regarding the request for additional security forces for our embassy—it was also just sent this month, on August 16th, not in June. And there have been several inconsistent radio transmissions received since then.

Of course, the State Department has not reacted on those requests, no matter whether they were sent in June or just now in August.

We also received a garbled radio transmission from Turing-B of an account regarding an attack on the embassy in Benghazi. The transmission indicated that several lives were lost because it was not adequately protected. There was no date in that transmission as to when the attack occurred. And there have been no other reports in any of the news media of such an incident—only that solitary transmission from a radio signal re-transmitted from Turing-B.

It still makes me wonder if the AI aboard that satellite is projecting probable occurrences based upon the information it receives. It still makes no sense to me. I'm still trying to understand what's going on. And those reports of Iran's nuclear program I mentioned in my June 7th e-mail, well those reports were actually issued this month, not in June. We seem to be getting news before it has actually occurred.

It's extremely important that I determine the time rate of receiving transmissions versus the time they were sent. The question—is time compressed as the force of extreme gravity warps the space-time continuum? Some of the radio transmissions Dora has sent out to our satellites seem to be altered upon being retransmitted to us.

As I've mentioned more than once, events appear to be modified from their original times of transmissions. So we're trying to decipher whether or not time is compressed into what we'd term as imaginary time due to extreme forces of gravity. We're also trying to establish gravitational effects by actually producing similarities of a black hole with the particle accelerator in the lab.

As for local and national politics which affects us all—well, there's a new election brewing. We seem to be constantly taking steps backward, and I hope people understand it's time to fix what's being broken. I hope people wake up and realize that things could get worse if they don't pay attention and act accordingly.

—Maxwell

iv.

It was mid-November, one week before Thanksgiving, when the Town Planner scheduled another public hearing for CHS. The only item on the agenda was the continued discussion for the development of Phase Two.

Nelson sat facing the familiar faces of the board members; their orientation to the public hadn't changed. Waiting for the public hearing to begin, Nelson found himself collectively scrutinizing their individual, distinctive physical characteristics.

Elaine Graft resembled a meerkat, having black arches around her eyes, perhaps from dark bluish eye shadow; her metal-framed glasses enhanced the look. Her most interesting feature was her red hair. She wore it straight back with strands resembling cords of rope, wrapped into a bun that looked like some sort of nest. When she turned her head, you could see one thick cord of hair that stood out dead center of the bun—its purpose, unknown.

Brett Manley always seemed to wear dark colored t-shirts, mostly black, no matter the weather. The word 'DON'T' was tattooed just above his left elbow and no matter how hard Nelson looked, he couldn't see if any other word followed.

Ralph Tunney, who was a retired real estate developer, always seemed to be disorganized and in a somewhat constant state of disarray. His loose-fitting clothes seemed to fit his disheveled demeanor, and his large head, round face, and large pair of black, shiny, fishlike eyes made him the perfect center of attention as chairperson.

Don Morgan, on the other hand, seemed to blend into the background with his blond hair slicked back from the front of his head, accompanied by a blond mustache and beard completing his polished look.

Drew Laden was stark in comparison to Don and had a stone-faced look about him with a hooked nose. It appeared as though he was always smelling his upper lip, an effect enhanced by his cookie duster mustache which moved up and down because he was constantly chewing on something—most likely, a wad of gum.

Nelson's attention returned to the chairperson when he peered at the public and started the proceedings.

"Mr. Dwyer, would you care to present the information you have for tonight's public hearing?"

"Thank you, Mr. Tunney. I would like to address only two issues. First, I want to address the board in regard to a petition on file from some of the residents concerning health and safety issues with changes to parking accommodations in our development. I am proposing that the parking layout will remain the same, but we'll install speed bumps with posted speed limit signs."

"Guess they didn't like Emmy Anderson's petition," Sarah whispered to Nelson.

"Second, this review process is taking too long. I'd like the board to consider the expense of these deliberations, and, with that in mind, we're hoping for a final decision at the end of tonight's public hearing."

Will Penton, who sat directly in back of Nelson, tapped him on the shoulder, leaned his head over, and whispered, "Their arrogance amazes me. They're really trying to ignore us and push this thing through, aren't they?"

Mary Vaschon was sitting next to Will and, overhearing his remark to Nelson, added, "You ain't kidding they are."

"Well, we should get on with the public hearing then, shouldn't we?" replied Chairperson Tunney, referring to Dwyer's dry and curt remarks. "The public hearing is now open for discussion."

Almost as if in a staged, rehearsed performance, several members of the public stood and requested to be recognized by the chairperson. Nelson had seen a few of the same people speak before. They were all residents of the Phase One apartments.

Willa Hunter spoke first. "I think this is a wonderful project. The presentation has been clear. How could this board not approve this project?"

Ned Garth stood in support. "Caring Home Services owns this land. Why shouldn't they be allowed to develop it the way they want to?"

"I see this as a high priority for the Planning Board to approve this development," stated Marsha Moran as she quickly stood, spoke, and sat down.

At that point, Nelson decided it was time the public heard what he had to say. He stood to summarize a few of the issues that had been discussed over several of the past Planning Board meetings. As he walked over to the podium to face the board members, he noticed that the number of people attending the hearings seemed to be growing.

Once recognized by Tunney, Nelson began his practiced dissertation. "In December of last year, a Zoning Board of Appeals public hearing was held and Caring Home Services requested that all seven phases of their development project be approved for a total of two hundred and sixty-one units on what they consider their South Campus. Presented with a bit of public disapproval and the idea that CHS wasn't paying any property taxes, the ZBA only approved Phase Two of their project consisting at that time of forty-four apartments in five buildings. They were told they would have to return for approval of additional phases or for any changes made afterward.

"Also, the Land Use Code stipulates that ZBA approval expires if construction hasn't commenced within six months of the date in which the approval is granted or if the work is not substantially completed within one year. Work on Phase Two has not commenced at this point in time, and even if it had, it could not be completed within a one year time frame. Since CHS has not met the time restrictions imposed by the ZBA, the Planning Board shouldn't allow approval of Phase Two. Many of us don't understand why the Planning Board continues to discuss and allow approval.

"During the Planning Board discussions this last August, it was noted that there is only one access road into the South Campus. That may be fine for the twenty-six apartments already there, but the additional forty-two apartments now proposed for Phase Two don't meet Code requirements. Back in January, almost four years ago, the ZBA told Caring Home Services that the town's Land Use Code required two means of access when traffic counts are greater than two hundred trips per day. At that meeting it was noted that there were around eighty trips per day for the Phase One proposal. Simple math ratios using the Information Technology Equipment Safety Standard of 3.48—a number which was used on the original plans for Phase One—show that an additional forty-two apartments in Phase Two would exceed the two hundred trips per day.

"However, during the same Planning Board meeting last August, the trip count somehow was reduced from 3.48 to

1.94, which allows Phase Two to require only one access road. Traffic certainly hasn't been reduced since Phase One was constructed. That ITE number has also mysteriously disappeared from the general notes on the site plans. Somehow, a new trip count number is now being used."

He paused to allow his words to sink in before continuing.

"I'm just saying that the newly configured number of trips appears to have been manipulated in order to meet the continued construction phases of this development without requiring a second access road. Remember, during earlier discussions of this Phase One project, the use of Baker Street as a secondary access was disallowed by the ZBA. The Laslo Conservation Commission also expressed their concern about a bridge being built to connect the North and South Campuses, yet the blueprints for this development still show both campuses connected by a bridge."

Nelson looked at a few note cards he had annotated in order to stay focused, and continued.

"Furthermore, this is a high-density cluster housing development. Fire departments normally recommend fire hydrants every two hundred feet in such a development, and in some cases at least two fire hydrants within three hundred feet of each building. The few hydrants shown on the site plans are spaced three to four hundred feet apart, and none appear on the Phase Two portion of this development. There may be sprinklers in the proposed buildings, but abutters are concerned about exterior fires, as well. There's also over two and a half acres of parking lots proposed, and we're concerned about water, oil, and other fluid runoffs into the wetlands and onto adjacent properties."

Ralph Tunney interrupted Nelson as he spoke. "Mr. Quip, you only have three minutes for your comments in this public hearing. Please remember that. Each person has three minutes to speak. You've already had well over that."

"I'm sure several people in the audience will remit their three minutes to me so I can complete my statements," said Nelson. He looked around at several of his neighbors, who all nodded their heads in approval. Nelson figured that many of them would rather have someone else stand up and address the Planning Board members than facing the panel themselves.

Tunney, exasperated with the noticeable response from the public, threw his hands up in a sign of exasperation. He reluctantly replied, "Go on, Mr. Quip, go on. Continue."

"About a year ago, during a ZBA hearing, members of the public discussed the fact that CHS pays no property taxes to this town. CHS is listed as a non-profit organization and is exempt from federal and state taxes. They accept donations as a charity but don't subsidize their tenants in any way. They don't provide medical services, transportation, food services, cleaning services, or any other special services. Therefore, they operate like any other landlord renting apartments.

"Reviewing public records, I found that CHS believes it pays its fair share by donating two percent of the rent they collect. That means for every one thousand dollars collected for rent, they pay twenty dollars to the town. Because it's a donation, it could actually be withheld from the town at any time.

"As residents, we pay property taxes based upon the valuation of our property. We can't just *not* pay it if we don't want to. According to their rental prices, therefore, CHS donates about six thousand dollars to the town based upon approximately three hundred thousand dollars of the rents received from their twenty-six apartments in Phase One.

"In many instances, one property owner alone in this town pays what CHS pays for all their buildings and apartments on their entire South Campus. This type of high-density cluster housing doesn't contribute to our tax base. Such housing will actually increase the costs of services by the town, including additional costs when the sewer treatment plant has to be expanded.

"In addition, I've reviewed the town's Comprehensive Plan which, by State law, takes precedence over the town's Land Use Code. Page 210 of our Comprehensive Plan indicates that their North Campus, consisting of sixty apartments, substantially meets the estimated current needs of senior housing. There is no mandate that says the town has to add more units. Most importantly, the Comprehensive Plan stipulates that cluster housing developments retaining open space and reflecting village like patterns of development, such as this type of development, are allowed a density of up

to four units per net residential acre, not eight units as specified in the Town's Land Use Code.

"I don't believe the continued expansion of CHS conforms
to the town of Laslo's Comprehensive Plan. This high-density
cluster type of development provides no tax revenue. As a
taxpayer and abutter to this development, I oppose the continued expansion and request the Planning Board to disapprove the proposed Phase Two of this project. I have a petition with seventy-two signatures from abutters agreeing with
these comments, and I would like it to be placed on file with
the minutes of this public hearing."

Nelson handed the six-page document to Tunney, walked
back to his seat, and sat down, relieved he had completed
his message.

"Thank you, Mr. Quip," the chairperson said. "Are there
any other members of the public who wish to speak?"

With that invitation, Gina Taylor, a resident of Phase One
stood. "Since Caring Home Services already owns this land,
they should be allowed to build upon it. These tax issues
don't belong in a conversation before the Planning Board."

Mary Vaschon quickly responded. "I oppose this project
as a taxpayer and resident. If the Planning Board doesn't
want to discuss the property tax issue, then whose concern
is the taxes anyway?"

Another woman stood up and addressed the Planning
Board. "My name is Ann Reynolds, and several years ago I
used to be a member of the Planning Board. I'm opposed to
this type of development. There *is* a tax issue that needs to
be discussed. I received information from a resident with
some valid points that need to be addressed by our town Tax
Assessor, Mr. Duncan. I'll give the board members a copy of
the information I have which cites various State of Maine
laws.

"In order to be exempted from property taxes, ownership
of a tax-exempt benevolent or charitable institution must be
incorporated in the state. I understand that Caring Home
Services is not incorporated in this state. A charitable corporation must also occupy and use the property exclusively for
benevolent or charitable purposes. In this particular instance,
the property is rented out to the general public. Because the
property is rented, it doesn't qualify for the exemption under

occupancy.

"As for the Department of Environmental Protection approval of this project—what is considered significant for the community may be different than what is significant to the state. This is not a matter against CHS itself or seniors, only that there should be fair and equal taxes for everyone."

Ann thanked the board members for listening then walked over to Tunney and handed him a packet of information for the Planning Board to review.

Upon hearing Ann's statement, a well-dressed man slowly stood and asked to be recognized to speak. Nelson observed his light blue tie, dark blue dress shirt, and dark gray suit coat was a glaring contrast to everyone else in the audience. He was smartly dressed, as if he were attending an important business meeting, unlike most of the residents who wore their casual jeans, khaki pants, sport shirts, and everyday jackets. His well-trimmed, thin mustache moved slightly as he quietly spoke.

"My name is Stanley Sloan. I'm on the board of directors for Caring Home Services as well as on the board of directors for the Salvation for the Society of Churches. I want to tell all of you that Caring Home Services is a benevolent and charitable organization. We bring stability and integrity to a community with a senior population. We are a nondenominational organization and have a pastor who resides on the premises who is available to the residents. I just want to say that making room for seniors is not a liability. The people opposing this project should take that into account with these discussions."

A woman in the audience stood as Stanley Sloan returned to his seat. It was the blue and red striped bandana tied around her forehead that caught Nelson's attention. She was sitting several rows toward the back of the room. Her curly brown hair had a slight frizzy look to it and a single string of pink beads hung down around her neck accentuating a noticeable contrast to her purple blouse.

"Hi, I'm Nikki Williams. I own land abutting this development. I don't remember anyone here ever saying that seniors are a liability. We're all gonna be one someday, if we live that long. So that would make us all liabilities, wouldn't it? I think what we're all concerned about here is the wildlife in that forest being replaced by this new city of Queens. I mean—jeez—there's a ton of buildings proposed to be built out there in the woods. I've walked the property, and there's a lot of wetland and deep ravines on that land. They're gonna fill in those areas just to put all kinds of apartments up and then not pay taxes to boot? I don't think this whole discussion's got anything to do with seniors. I think it's all about a company trying to over-develop the land just to make some money."

"Well, she sure says it like it is, doesn't she? Even her name seemed to match her hippy-like appearance," Sarah whispered to Nelson. He was stunned by the unexpected outburst by someone he had never seen before.

"That's all I have to say at the moment," she said, "but I'm sure I'll have more to say later." And then as abruptly as she had appeared, she sat down with an energetic thump onto her chair.

As she sat down, she tapped the shoulder of the woman sitting next to her, who then stood and addressed the Planning Board.

"My name is Marie Paterson. I live next door to Nikki, and I also own property that abuts this proposed development. Nikki is right to have concerns about our taxes. She's been a neighbor of mine for several years. This project shouldn't be built in a residential zone. It's too commercial a use of the land and doesn't belong in this part of the town."

Nelson watched as Marie Paterson sat down and noticed the scowl on Stanley Sloan's face. His pursed lips exhibited a sign of anger at the remark. *Not a good look for such a benevolent man,* Nelson thought to himself.

The room turned silent until Tunney looked at a woman in the audience and asked, "Does Joan Landers of the Conservation Commission have any information for us?"

"Yes," she said, still sitting. "I have previously submitted a letter to the members of the Planning Board, regarding several inconsistencies with the information the applicant has submitted. You should all have that information in your pre-meeting packets."

"Yeah, if any of them have taken the time to read the stuff," Joe Vaschon whispered sarcastically for anyone close to hear.

"On more than one occasion now, we have asked the developer to remove the mention of a bridge across the wetland connecting their two separate properties. They continue to leave those notes on their site plans, ignoring our request. The significant wetland on this property should not be crossed or impacted since it drains into a pond located outside this property, which is recognized as a vernal pool. We've also requested that the Planning Board require underground parking for the CHS apartments. That would reduce paved areas and contaminated water runoffs into the wetlands. Mr. Dwyer has repeatedly stated that such parking would drive up their costs, so nothing has been changed. We've also requested that their plans show the trees being retained on the property just as other applicants are required to do. The current plans show no trees will be retained. There are other issues brought up in our letter to the board members and those concerns should be discussed among yourselves."

Nelson turned to Sarah. "Evidently they don't share all of that info with the public. I'd really like to read *all* of their concerns."

Joe Vaschon overheard Nelson's comment and whispered, "Beyond our pay grade, buddy." He chuckled at his own remark.

"Is there anyone else who would care to speak for or against this project?" Chairperson Tunney asked.

Everyone looked around to see if anyone else would respond. No one spoke.

"Since there are no further comments, I am closing this public hearing regarding the development of Phase Two as proposed by Caring Home Services."

The town planner, Todd Hatch, stood to address the Planning Board members. "I just want this board to understand that even though the applicant's Zoning Board of Appeals special exception has expired, it's not a basis for denying this project. The Town Land Use Ordinance Code allows the Planning Board to approve the plans separate from any ZBA approval. Therefore, we can and should proceed with approving this project."

"We certainly should continue with this process," replied Tunney. "There are several open issues we do need to deliberate upon, however. There's a question about the amount of fill being used, a verification of the number of trips per day, where the connecting bridge should be located, parking issues, secondary road access, and the question about ZBA approval."

"Why does it always appear that everyone is trying to move this project forward as a done deal and ignoring things they don't want to hear?" Nelson whispered to Sarah, exasperated by the chairperson's remarks. "And they keep mentioning the use of a bridge. Are they tone deaf? I feel like we're in some sort of governmental, bureaucratic policy debate where there's all this rhetoric and the real issues keep getting ignored."

"It's getting very late and there's a lot more to discuss here," Drew Laden said. I make the motion that we continue the public hearing on another day and have it rescheduled by Mr. Hatch."

"I second that motion," said Elaine Graft as she pulled the cord of hair that had dipped down below the base of her shoulders.

"Before I adjourn this meeting," Chairperson Tunney said, "you should all note that the public hearing portion has been closed. Anyone having further information or comments on this application must submit it in writing prior to the next meeting. Since the motion to adjourn has been seconded, our board deliberations shall continue at the next scheduled meeting."

V.

Will Penton, and Mary and Joe Vaschon approached Nelson and Sarah when the other members of the public got up to leave. Joe was the first to comment.

"Well at least they didn't get to a final decision tonight as they requested."

"Did you notice they looked a little concerned about these discussions," said Will. "I think that holier-than-thou guy with the nice suit was sent by the Board of Directors for CHS to watch the proceedings and help defend Phil Dwyer."

"Yeah, he's over there right now on the other side of the room talking to his buddy Phil about something," Mary motioned with a nod of her head in their direction.

They started to walk up the aisle toward the exit when Emmy Anderson approached. Nelson recognized her from the Planning Board meeting held in August when she requested signatures on a petition opposing the development. The red frame of her glasses was a noticeable feature, casting a contrast to her light blue eyes.

"Hi, Mr. Quip. I'm Emmy Anderson."

"Yes. Nice to meet you. You're the person who sent a petition around opposing this project. Thanks for the support."

"Well, I heard you were a CPA and thought maybe you could help me out a little by finding out more about our opponents' non-payment of property taxes and how they get away with it."

"I've been so busy lately I haven't had a chance to pursue that issue," Nelson replied, "but that's not a bad idea."

"I teach at a community college and I have next week off, so I will have a little time available in order to have a discussion with our town tax assessor about the property taxes not being paid by these people."

"I might be able to arrange a meeting with an IRS agent so we could discuss the federal tax requirements and perhaps shed some light on the state and town requirements," said Nelson. "I know a guy in the fraud, waste, and abuse section who might be willing to discuss the non-profit tax requirements. We've worked together on several issues in the past. I'll email him and request his assistance."

"That'd be great. Here's my phone number so we can keep in touch. I think we need to support each other in this matter. One person can't do it all."

"That's for sure. I'll see what I can do. I'll call you if I can arrange something soon. Thanks."

"She'd be a big help in discussing taxes," Will said after Emmy left and they all continued up the aisle toward the exit.

Just as the five of them reached the back of the meeting room, Nelson noticed one of the town residents who had spoken to oppose the development was red-faced, dabbing a tissue to her face, attempting to hide tears. She was standing beside another woman he remembered seeing previously. He tried to remember what the upset woman's name was: *Mary, Maria, no, it's Marie. Marie Patterson.*

"I wonder why she's crying?" asked Mary.

"Don't know. Maybe we should inquire." When they reached the woman, Nelson asked, "What happened?"

"They threw Charley out," she said. "I'm sorry. I didn't mean to get emotional about this, and it's a little embarrassing." She wiped at her cheeks as she spoke.

"Who is they and who is Charley," Mary questioned.

"Charley's an elderly friend of our family. He was living in an apartment on the South Campus."

"And they just evicted him?" asked Nelson.

"Yes."

"Why?"

"They said he was too old to remain living there, that he should be living in an assisted living center. They have coin-operated washing machines and dryers in the apartment building where he was living. Evidently, he was accused of adding powdered laundry detergent into one of their dryers instead of into a washing machine, causing it to seize up. I guess it ruined the dryer. He's eighty years old and still pretty acute in his thinking, but evidently not astute in doing laundry." She smiled at her remark, and continued.

"He really has no issues with dementia and is able to live without any assistance. I just don't see how that man from Caring Home Services could stand up and say how they are so benevolent and that they bring stability and integrity to a community. There's no integrity in what they did to Charley. I'm sorry. I'm just upset over this," she said, and again cleared her eyes with a tissue before introducing herself.

"I'm Marie Paterson and this is my next-door neighbor, Nikki."

"I remember you from a past meeting," Nelson acknowledged. "I'm Nelson. This is my wife, Sarah, our neighbors, Joe and Mary Vaschon, and Will Penton."

Marie nodded to each person, then blurted, "I just don't think it's very Christian-like for an organization that is supposed to care for elderly people to simply evict Charley! They said he couldn't manage his own everyday needs. They have to be lying about what he did. I've helped him to buy groceries, and he purchases a liquid laundry detergent, not a powder. He couldn't have used a powdered detergent. He didn't have any! I think it was just an excuse to move him out of their apartments."

"How long had he lived there?" asked Joe.

"Less than a year," Marie said. "He used to own a good portion of property that bordered their North Campus. They wanted his land in order to enhance their density calculations, so they offered to rent him an apartment in their new complex for as long as he would like at a reduced rate if he'd sell them his land. Once they got what they wanted, I guess they didn't really care much about him. Now they just don't want him living there at all because he's getting older and they don't offer any type of services."

"Don't sound none too charitable to me," said Joe.

"Doesn't surprise me much," Will agreed. "But I thought Phil Dwyer said they had people waiting to get into their assisted housing."

"There's nothing on their site plans about that type of housing, only more apartments," Nelson reminded the group.

"They have no such facility," Marie reiterated. "And Charley had no place else to go. I took him in for a few nights until he was finally able to contact his daughter and move in with her. I'm really upset over all this. Guess you can tell that, huh? People just don't realize what's going on here. Anyway, I just get too emotional to talk to other residents about this. You can tell why I can't speak about this in these public forums."

"Unfortunately most residents in this town just aren't paying attention to what's happening around them," Mary said.

"It's not just local issues people aren't paying attention to," Nelson replied, thinking about Maxwell's earlier emails. "There's a *lot* of things people aren't paying attention to."

Chapter Nine

Interrogation

L

Only four days had passed since the Planning Board meeting. Emmy Anderson, Nelson, and Kevin Randall, an Internal Revenue Service agent, sat around a small circular oak table in Nelson's office. It was early morning, and the three steaming cups of coffee on the table left just enough space so the agent could open the file folders he had brought with him for their discussion.

Emmy's presence seemed to infuse the room with vitality and energy. Nelson recalled she was an art teacher with a vast knowledge of materials and techniques, and had the ability to encourage her students to push their creative ideas, allowing them to express their thoughts and opinions. He felt her energy, knowing she would listen and formulate her opinions based on the mornings' discussion. That inherent ability would allow her to pursue the property tax issues in question with town officials.

"Very nice to meet you, Ms. Anderson, and good morning, Nelson." Kevin Randall initiated the conversation. "I received your e-mail a few days ago, and I've taken some time to review the tax exemption status of Caring Home Services. Since they're filed as a 501(c)(3) corporation, they're open for public review."

"Thanks for meeting with us, Kevin," Nelson said. "As I mentioned in my e-mail to you, Emmy wants to discuss the tax exemptions with our town tax assessor. She has a meeting with him tomorrow and needs to know if the federal tax exemption filing has any relevance to the taxation of their property by our town."

"I'm not entirely convinced our tax assessor has reviewed the property tax issue with this organization," Emmy quickly interjected. "That's why we wanted to talk with you. We really appreciate you taking the time to discuss this with us."

"I saw you were both fairly thorough with the information you requested when I responded to your emails," Kevin replied. "I will do what I can to clear up a few of your questions." He glanced over to Nelson. "Nelson, you've always been very helpful in clearing up matters with your clients with us. Since I had time in my schedule to meet with the both of you, I thought I could at least provide you with the public records and discuss their link to the charitable exemptions claimed. Let's get down to specifics." Kevin returned his attention to the file folders before him.

"Caring Home Services Incorporated filed a Form 1023 as a charitable corporation over fifteen years ago and stated that their plans called for the construction of a continuing care retirement community."

Emmy had a quizzical expression, and asked, "What's a 1023?"

"Form 1023 is the application for recognition of Exemption from paying Federal Income Taxes under Section 501(c)(3) of the Internal Revenue Code," Kevin answered. "In that application, they stipulated they would offer apartment-style quarters and would provide short-term skilled care. They also stipulated the community residents would have the use of an on-site nursing home. The form asks if the organization or any part of it is a home for the aged or handicapped. Caring Home Services answered 'yes' to that question. Now this is where it gets more interesting." He leaned in to emphasize his message. "They include the fact that there will be charges for rentals as well as meals, and they indicated the facilities would be designed to address the health needs of the aged with the exception of hospitalization. From what you've told me, their organization hasn't followed through on any of those requirements."

"From the information presented to the public and the information I've read," said Nelson, "Caring Home Services only rents apartments to persons over fifty-five years old, which, in my opinion, really doesn't qualify them under the federal 501(c)(3) regulations."

"Let's get right down to the IRS requirements," Kevin said, looking first at Nelson then at Emmy. "There's a statute under section 601.201 of the IRS rules that says a ruling recognizing an exemption may not be relied upon if there is a material change inconsistent with the exemption in character, purpose, or the method of operation of an organization. That's a direct quote from that section. Since they haven't corrected their Form 1023 to reflect their current operation, they could be reviewed to see if they still qualify for a federal tax exemption. That's not the department I work in, but I'll give you the address so you can contact that section and ask if they'll do a review.

"You should also review their Form 990, which is the 'Return of Organization Exempt From Income Tax' form. I didn't have a chance to get a copy of that for you. It's supposed to be filed much like an individual income tax form 1040, with which I'm sure Ms. Anderson is familiar. You might find some sort of disparity there as well."

"What we were most interested in at this point is the effect of their exemption in regard to paying property taxes to our town," said Nelson.

"I can help you out there." Kevin focused on Emmy. "Ms. Anderson, in your e-mail, you mentioned that during the last Planning Board meeting, a person by the name of Ann Reynolds sited various laws in the state regarding property tax exemptions. I looked into that a bit and from what I can discern from the Maine Revenue Services Property Tax Bulletins, Caring Home Services is not exempt from property taxes. They may be exempt from federal taxes if they still qualify under Form 1023, but not from the town of Laslo for property taxes."

"What are the requirements in this state?" asked Emmy.

"There are a couple of items that are addressed in the MRSP Bulletin 5, Section 652 regarding property of organizations and property taxation. Ms. Reynolds' statement at the public hearing was correct. There are ownership and occupancy and use requirements. I'll explain."

"Yes, by all means," Emmy encouraged.

"Ownership must be by benevolent and charitable organizations incorporated in the state. The company you are opposing is a New Hampshire based corporation with the ability to do business in Maine. Therefore, under state law, failure to incorporate within the state prohibits exemption from the property tax. In addition, the corporation must be used solely for benevolent and charitable purposes. The organization must be exclusively charitable, by statute. In this instance, apartments are rented out to the general public and because of that, they don't qualify for exemption under the term occupancy."

"So it appears CHS should have been paying property taxes all these years?" asked Emmy.

"I'd say you should have that discussion with your town tax assessor," Kevin answered. "Even if CHS doesn't qualify for property tax exemption, they could still qualify for a federal tax exemption. If CHS has any other developments under their umbrella somewhere else that comply with the charitable purpose they applied for in their original Form 1023, they could still qualify as charitable under 501(c)(3) rules. But that requirement has nothing to do with the property tax exemption issue in your town. I'll leave copies of these forms with both of you so you can review and discuss them with your town tax assessor." He gave both Nelson and Emmy the forms before closing the folders. "I hope I've been of some help in answering your questions."

Nelson and Emmy looked at each other and nodded their approval. He reached across the table and shook Kevin's hand when the man rose to leave. Both thanked Kevin for his time and his assistance.

ii.

It was late the following morning when Emmy met Simon Duncan, the town tax assessor, for the first time.

"Good morning, Mr. Duncan. Thanks for meeting me this morning," she said after taking a seat.

Simon Duncan's response was curt and gruff, but also polite in an off-handed way. "What can I help you with? I understand there's been some discussion about Caring Home Services not having to pay property taxes."

"That's right, Mr. Duncan. Last August, I presented a petition to the Planning Board containing almost two hundred signatures from residents requesting you re-assess and tax the property owned by CHS at the fair market value. I also provided a packet of state requirements for your review. Yesterday, I substantiated my review with Mr. Kevin Randall of the Internal Revenue Service."

"I looked at the state of Maine requirements you gave me, but you had nothing in that packet about their IRS forms," said Simon.

"Since I sent those to you, I emailed a letter to CHS and asked them for copies of their IRS Forms 1023 and 990 . In response to my letter, their attorney informed me that as an abutter to their property, I was not entitled to that information. That's why the forms weren't in that packet of information."

"Then you can't really examine their tax exemption status, can you?" asked Simon.

"First of all, it's not my job to examine their status at all. It's your job. According to the town charter's list of responsibilities, your job requires that *you* assess the property tax requirements of companies in this town once a year, not me. In addition, you're supposed to review the articles of incorporation, property deeds and by-laws, financial statements, and the building values. Have you done all those things?"

"No—I haven't," Simon said, his facial expression showing he was stunned by Emmy's eloquent, yet harsh delivery.

"Evidently then, you haven't been doing your job, at least not in this case," she stated matter-of-fact. "I decided to visit CHS last week and posed as a perspective tenant, to find out what their rent was; just to see what I'd get for my money. I made an appointment to meet with a representative at their church on what they call their South Campus. I met a very friendly woman just inside the single large central front door. She showed me around. The first stop was at a small special room right inside the door, off to the right of the entrance. The ten by ten foot carpeted room contained a few folding chairs facing a brown wooden podium at one end of the small room. It wasn't much bigger than a small storage room. She explained to me that the room was devoted to the tenants and their need for prayer. I asked her if that was their only 'chapel'. She told me it was, and that the rest of the rooms were all apartments within the church. Have you ever known of a church that includes apartments for rent? And have you ever inspected or looked at the property?"

"No I haven't. I always assumed that building was exclusively a church," said Simon. He looked away, unable to meet her stare.

"Well, Mr. Duncan, you know what they say about the word assume, don't you? It *ain't* exclusively a church, I can tell you that much. I also want to point out those IRS forms CHS doesn't want us to see are legally available for public review because of their federal tax exemption status. Their attorney either doesn't know what the hell he's talking about, or worse yet, he thinks we're stupid. In my opinion, it's probably a combination of both.

"From all this information, it appears that CHS doesn't meet the state's definition of a benevolent or charitable organization. If tenants can't pay their rent, CHS doesn't subsidize those people, and they have to move out. They offer no assisted living, no dining services, no transportation, act like any other landlord, and they charge full market rental rates. It also appears that at zoning and planning board hearings, they change their facts depending on which town code they're trying to meet, or perhaps I should say, circumvent."

"You're being awfully negative, Ms. Anderson. What do you mean about changing the facts?" Simon demanded, obviously irritated at the elevated tone of Emmy's voice and the accusations of him not doing his job properly.

"I'll give you an example. The number of trips per day annotated on their site plan has changed four times. They describe themselves on their website as a 'retirement community'. At a zoning board hearing they changed that description and called themselves a 'congregate care' facility, which by definition means they provide meal assistance, housework, healthcare, and shopping. They really don't offer any of those amenities, by the way. Then they changed that term by saying they were an 'elderly housing' facility. And then to top things off, a firm doing their graphic design work described them as a 'real estate developer'." She double-quoted her fingers in the air with each description to emphasize her point. "Each one of those criteria changes the necessary International Traffic Engineer standards, which in turn determines whether or not another access road is required based on the number of trips per day—a rather important issue. If there's ever a fire, it could be a disaster."

"So why does a property tax exemption issue get brought

up in a public hearing before the Planning Board? It's got nothing to do with the proposal for their development."

I guess I'll have to explain that to you as well, Emmy thought to herself as she felt her frustration level rising within her normally mild demeanor. She suspected the red frame of her glasses became a close match to the color in her cheeks.

"Expanding such a development without compensating for the cost of additional town services affects all of the residents of this town. There are several statutes in our town's Land Use and Development Code Zoning Ordinance that apply to this issue. They're all from Title 10, Section 14 and can all be linked to the importance of having a secondary access road which is based upon daily trip counts."

Emmy opened her copy of the town's ordinance codes she had brought to the meeting, just in case she needed to refer to it, and read them to Simon. "What I'm trying to tell you, Mr. Duncan, is there are unintentional consequences to intentional changes, and that's what happens when the Planning and Zoning boards don't consider the property tax exemption. It's a separate issue that should be reviewed by your office."

"Why should I review and re-assess the opinion of the previous town tax assessor who provided the original exemption to their property taxes?"

Emmy smirked with a perceptible sneer before replying to Simon's question. She had expected such a question from him.

"You need to consider the fact that the previous tax assessor went to prison because of illegal deals he made for property tax fixing. A review of all exemptions should have been performed, knowing there could be some outstanding issues. It would be a good idea if you inspected the church on their South Campus for what it really is." She paused to let her statement sink in.

"Look," she added, "Phil Dwyer, the spokesman for CHS, believes they pay their fair share by donating two percent of the rent they receive. That means for every one thousand dollars collected in rent, they donate twenty bucks to the town. Based upon their advertised rental rates, Phase One of their South Campus currently collects more than three hun-

dred thousand dollars per year from their twenty-six apartments. That means they donate about six thousand dollars to
the town. Since all of us pay property taxes based on the
valuation of our property, do you really believe that's a fair
share? We appear to be paying their fair share *for them*."

Without waiting for a response, Emmy continued. "In
many situations, one property owner alone pays the amount
that CHS pays for all their apartments on their entire South
Campus. It's not fair for other landlords who do pay property
taxes that have to compete with this rental agency. Nor is it
fair for elderly people who own their own homes and live on
fixed incomes to have to pay increased property taxes, because the town service costs for fire, police, emergency, water, and sewer are increased due to such developments that
don't *pay* taxes. You have to understand that Caring Home
Services is probably the most profitable rental agency in the
town of Laslo. I and all those people who signed the petition
I presented several months ago would like you to investigate
this issue and reevaluate this property tax exemption issue."

"I want to let you know that I will be looking into this issue," Simon said, finally able to get in a word when she qui-
eted down. "I will be asking CHS's attorney several questions
regarding their position as to why they expect an exemption
from property taxes. I'll be discussing their response with the
town manager."

"I certainly hope so, because I'm sure you'll hear more
about it during future planning and zoning board public hearings."

"I'll even give you a copy of their responses just so you'll
be up to date on our review of the situation," replied Simon.

His facial expression showed her he was hoping his response would end their conversation and her lecture on the
requirements of his job.

Emmy graciously accepted Simon's courteous response.
"Thank you, Mr. Duncan," and she departed.

Year Five

*"Alone we can do so little;
together we can do so much."*

– Helen Keller

Chapter Ten

Counting

i.

Cold rain sifted down from a platinum colored sky, each drop more frequent than the last as it dribbled down the windshield of Marie Paterson's ten-year-old Chevy truck. The windshield wipers were set to low, just sufficient enough to clear the continuous drizzle so the passing cars on Route 2 could be observed.

It was mid-January, and although there had already been a few days of snow flurries, it was only a mist-like rain that threatened the day. She knew snow would be sure to follow in the days ahead.

If only the snow would hold off a bit longer, thought Sarah, as she snuggled into her winter coat, avoiding the chilled morning air. She sat as close to the old truck's heater as she could manage.

The grayness of the day was as depressing as the number of extended public hearings she had attended. There seemed to be no end to them—one after another. And at every hearing, people learned something new about the proposed development—something either not mentioned before, perhaps purposely left out, or something that somehow had been changed.

Marie and Sarah were the early morning shift, taking turns watching the only entrance into the South Campus of the CHS property. They sat in the old truck with the heater blasting, clipboard in hand, recording the number of cars accessing and exiting the South Campus facility. It was 6:15 a.m. and Marie was still yawning from her early morning start.

"I'm not used to getting up this early," Marie said. "I should have brought some coffee for us."

"I already had two cups before you picked me up this

morning," said Sarah, "so I never thought to bring some. Besides, if I drank more, I'd have to...;" Sarah hesitated, then smiled at Marie, "take a pee." She continued. "I had to wake Nelson up before I left. Otherwise, he would have probably overslept and gotten into his office late. Guess I'm the alarm clock for him and the kids."

"Did you hear about Emmy Anderson's discussion on property taxes with Simon Duncan?" Marie asked. "I guess she basically told him how he should be doing his job."

"Yeah, I heard. She e-mailed Nelson and said the town was supposed to be looking into the matter. She sent him a fairly detailed summary of her conversation with Mr. Duncan and said it was hard to believe he had never checked about CHS paying property taxes. She ended her e-mail by stating she thought he was an asshole."

"Those are strong words coming from someone the likes of Emmy. I'd like to have been a mouse in a corner of his office during that conversation." She changed the subject, still yawning. "So, when's the next public hearing with the Planning Board? I wouldn't be surprised that in another week or so we'll be right back at it again. What I'd like to know is how come these guys get to be placed on the Planning Board hearing agenda so quickly. All the other developments have to get back in line to be put into their public hearing schedules, but not them."

"I don't know," said Sarah. "I'm not sure why we're sitting here continuing to count cars either, even though it was my idea to begin with. Are we just wasting our time? Nelson doesn't believe there's enough traffic into and out of Phase One to give us a good indication of how much traffic will really be generated with the addition of Phase Two. I bet he probably thought I was nuts for suggesting it."

"We all agreed to do this. Will and Emmy are supposed to meet us here and continue the count." Marie noticeably shivered, and added, "This old truck of mine doesn't have a very good heater, does it?"

"At least it puts out *some* heat," Sarah commented, holding her hands up to the air vent to warm them. "Does Emmy and Will know where we're watching this entrance?"

"Yep, I told her we'd be in this parking lot across the street from the entrance to the South Campus. Luckily, the market here doesn't open till 10 a.m. so we won't be block-ing any of their customers. That way we can face the en-trance and count the number of cars entering and exiting, as well the number of cars traveling north and south past the entrance."

They both sat and watched, recording the results of the traffic flow. The cold drizzle finally stopped by the end of their designated shift.

The total count was twenty-six cars entering and exiting, three hundred and thirty-six cars traveling northbound, and two hundred and eighty-four cars traveling southbound.

Still chilled from the early morning air, they were relieved when Emmy and Will arrived right on time to start their shift and count the traffic until 9:30 a.m. They couldn't stay any longer than that, because Will had to be at a job site at 10 a.m. with a bucket crane to remove dead limbs from a few oak trees.

Will sent a text a few hours later. By the end of their shift, Will and Emmy had witnessed an additional forty-seven cars entering and exiting, two hundred-sixty-one cars travel-ing northbound, and four hundred and eleven cars traveling southbound.

ii.

After Nelson arrived home from work that night, Sarah handed him the clipboard with the results of their combined surveillance.

"Wow, I'm surprised at these numbers," he said. "I never thought they would be as high as they are for just Phase One of their development. I actually thought there would be an insufficient number of trips, thus removing our argument re-garding the necessity of a second access road. Guess you were right and I was wrong about doing this car count. I re-ally didn't think it would amount to anything worthwhile."

Hearing the remark, a slight grin appeared on Sarah's face. It wasn't often Nelson admitted he was wrong. About anything.

"At least we had some help doing this. I just figured it was something that needed to be done—just trying to be honest, one way or another."

"Unlike other people." Nelson quipped. He returned his gaze to the results. "This shows that for morning traffic on a typical mid-day, there were a total of seventy-three trips counted for entering and exiting Phase One, which contains only twenty-six apartments."

"So what do we derive from this information that can be useful?" Sarah questioned.

"Let's go figure that out." Nelson moved away from the kitchen counter he was leaning against to the table, with pen, paper, and calculator in hand. "If an additional forty-two apartments are built in Phase Two, that would result in a total of sixty-eight apartments. If you proposed a simple math ratio based upon twenty-six apartments per the seventy-three trips you counted, then wanted to know the relative number of trips based upon sixty-eight apartments, the equivalent ratio would yield the total number of trips to be one hundred and ninety-one."

"So what you're saying is for this three hour count we performed this morning, an estimated one hundred and ninety-one trips would be made if another forty-two apartments were added as Phase Two?"

"Yes, exactly," Nelson said. "Remember, you guys did this count for only three to four hours. Within a twenty-four-hour time period, those numbers would easily translate to more than two hundred trips per day. In fact, if you think only about the fact that Phase One had seventy-three trips in that short time period, those twenty-six apartments actually translate to more than two hundred trips all by themselves."

"I believe there's another Planning Board meeting in another week or so," said Sarah, interrupting Nelson's thoughts about organizing the trip count results.

"Terrific," he sighed. "I look forward to another hearing of disoriented rhetoric. At least we've information on an actual traffic count, more than what the developer has done. Guess it's time to write a quick e-mail to Maxwell. It'll help me vent."

iii.

E-mail: Jan 15
To: Mdraper

From: NelsonQuip
Subject: More Public Hearings

Hi, Max,
Just thought I'd vent a bit about the continuing saga of our fight regarding the proposed development in our town. One of the abutters, Emmy Anderson, and myself had a meeting with an IRS agent whom I know. We discussed the property tax exemption that Caring Home Services gets with our town. Apparently, by law, they shouldn't be getting any property tax exemption. They don't meet the exclusive charitable and benevolent purposes, and they aren't incorporated within the state.

I understand the town's tax assessor is supposed to be reviewing the situation. I also question their federal tax exemption regarding the 501(c)(3) status. There should be another planning board meeting soon. Can't wait (note my sarcasm). They don't seem to want to talk about this issue, even though these meetings seem to occur one right after another.

Emmy also had a meeting with our town tax assessor, Simon Duncan. She kind of read him the riot act on how to do his job. I've attached a summary of the conversation she had with Simon. She wrote down what she could remember about it in order to keep a record of things. She's pretty thorough. Thought you'd find it interesting. Hard to believe this is all happening.
Later
–Nelson

It was the following day when Nelson received a reply.

E-mail: Jan 16
To: NelsonQuip
From: Mdraper
Subject: More Public Hearings

Always nice hearing from you, Nelson. Keep taking notes about what's happening with your residential protesting. Your forest development issue has many parallels with national political events happening across the country.

You've mentioned local issues with 501(c)(3) exemptions. Well, there's recently been a lot of static about IRS 501(c)(4) exemptions on a national level. Those types of exemptions apply to organizations that engage in political activity, endorse or oppose political candidates, or donate money or time to political campaigns—a little different from your religious/benevolent exemptions.

There are so-called 'tea party' or 'patriot' organizations that have been applying for tax exemption status. Keep in mind these have to be approved before they can be exempt and considered to be non-profit. Until then, those organizations are not tax exempt. But I don't see a lot of those requests being approved, particularly any of them that appear to focus on federal debt, spending, and taxes.

News broadcasts from Turing-B indicate the IRS is targeting some of these more conservative type of organizations, delaying their approval on purpose. Any group with political theme names like 'We The People' and 'Take the Country Back' and words like 'tea party' and 'patriots' appear to be flagged. On the other hand, more liberal type groups don't appear to be targeted.

Dora (you remember—my assistant) has been constantly receiving and reviewing data at my request from a ton of resources lately, looking at anything that could lead to governmental changes and partisan influences. According to our foretelling satellite, you'll see this targeting exposed later on. You can expect members of Congress to grill the Director of the Cincinnati Office of the IRS, but they'll just say they know nothing about it. I wouldn't be surprised if they also can't recover the thousands of e-mails involved with this as well.

Investigation in this instance will only reveal the IRS to be a mismanaged bureaucracy, enforcing rules that they'll say personnel did not fully understand. Think about it; these two types of tax exemptions coincidentally have local and national parallels.

And mentioning coincidences; go back and read that e-mail I sent you last August 31st. That garbled radio transmission we received about the embassy in Benghazi being attacked. You'll recall that actually happened the following month.

More troubling is the fact that the Secretary of State said she never saw a cable warning about the consulate not being able to sustain a coordinated attack, and they weren't aware of security problems. Yet the outgoing Defense Secretary and the Joint Chiefs Chairperson said they knew about the warning.

They were also aware of two IED attacks on the consulate in the months leading up to the September 11th attack. The June attacks blew a hole in the wall of the compound and were part of dozens of incidents in the region that should have been considered as warning signs.

That forecast of events has caused me to keep a closer eye on anything to do with Iran, concerning my worst fears. Back last November an IAEA report stated they had produced over 500 pounds of near 20% enriched uranium and they continue to deny access to the Parchin military base. It was also reported that 2,255 centrifuges have been installed at Natanz. What's disturbing is that a 154-page report just issued by the Institute for Science and International Security states that Iran could produce enough weapon-grade uranium for a bomb within the next few years. That's a scary thought.

Before I forget, one other thing about Natanz— We did receive a radio transmission from Turing-B that 12,699 centrifuges had been installed. That's a large disparity from the confirmed numbers we previously had from the media. But I haven't been able to confirm that source from anywhere. I wonder if that's true now or will those numbers show up a month from now?

I found the summary you attached of the conversation Ms. Anderson had with Mr. Duncan to be worrisome. Although she was discussing local issues, she also pointed out two very disturbing insights relative to the national scene. She mentioned the idea of paying a fair share and insinuated that individual property owners have been put in a position of paying for others. We continue to witness the same scenario for the redistribution of wealth on a national level lately.

The other astute observation she made was 'that there are unintentional consequences to intentional changes'. I also see that as a disturbing trend in our national policies, as well. Interesting how these relationships are relative to one another.

So, how are you doing on combining your issues with mine and writing more chapters? After reading those first two chapters, I believe 'joe citizen' might read what you've written and find the parallels disturbing, to say the least. Perhaps they'd possibly pay attention to such analogies. Just a nudge for more material...
Take care
—Max

"You haven't sent Maxwell any more of the Chapters you've written lately, have you?" Sarah asked, after she finished reading the e-mail Nelson showed her.

"Not yet, even though I have quite a few more Chapters written. I guess I kinda should send more to him soon. I've starting writing down additional sequences of events from those we've witnessed locally, and I've included Maxwell's radio satellite transmissions and observations, as well. He has a point. It's hard to imagine this sort of shit can happen—to anyone—to everyone."

Chapter Eleven

Obfuscation

L

It was unusual for Donny, Nelson, and I to take an early morning walk in the forest at the same time, particularly in January. Normally, it was only Donny and myself, and not so late into the winter season.

On that particular day, I saw Nelson as he walked along a pathway that paralleled the edge of his property line, talking to Donny. Several inches of heavy snow had all but disappeared due to an unusually early January thaw, reducing the well-worn path from a snow trail to a muddy walkway.

I attempted to catch up to them and provide a casual good-morning greeting, but then decided not to interfere when I saw it was a somber conversation.

"We just got a notice of another Planning Board hearing," Nelson said to Donny as the three of us tried to avoid the embankments of snow left alongside the trail.

"Didn't you just attend one in November?" Donny asked.

"Yep, and we just got another letter from the town about three days ago," Nelson answered. He pulled a folded letter from his shirt pocket. "You got a notice, didn't you?"

"Yeah, I'm pretty sure I did, but I didn't pay much attention to it. You've been handling the meetings pretty well, so I figured you'd keep me posted."

"Well, they're going to discuss the expansion of their Phase Two project again next week."

"I haven't been feeling well lately, so I won't be going to the meeting," said Donny. "It's just too late at night for me to sit through the anguish of listening to all the rhetoric. They never seem to resolve any one issue."

"I understand. I'll let you know what happens."

"Thanks. Just remember, I'm available for discussions

with the rest of the neighbors. I might be able to contribute additional insight."

We continued on the old trail until it split into two paths. I decided to follow the lesser-defined trail. I wished I could have been more help, but I had my own reasons for not attending town meetings. They were not for health reasons, unlike Donny.

ii.

Nelson looked around as he sat down and noticed there were a few more people attending the public hearing than he had seen at previous meetings. He attributed the increase to the several articles that had appeared in their local newspaper. They'd mostly regarded the property tax concerns he and other residents had raised. He also noted the same reporter was there again. With two other agenda items to be discussed that night, it was later in the evening before the Planning Board finally opened the public hearing for the CHS proposal.

Kurt Tussi of Tussi Engineering and Architecture was the first one to speak.

"Phil Dwyer is here tonight to answer any questions the board members may have. We have submitted revised plans to include issues mentioned at the last public hearing. We've worked with the town's code enforcement officer, Todd Hatch, in order to provide some changes requested. Landscaping is now shown around the apartments on the grading plan. We have enlarged the entrance into the development for a right-hand turn lane that we agree to construct. We've also provided a municipal impact statement.

"Caring Home Services currently pays somewhere around seventeen thousand dollars as a service fee to the town for the North and South Campus. Based upon proposed rental income, the Phase Two project would increase that amount and pay a fee of about twenty-seven thousand dollars. There are no impacts on the schools, and Fire Chief Gerard figured that the Laslo Fire Department only makes about two to three visits per year, so it costs between six hundred to nine hundred dollars per year for firefighting. There are less than thirty calls per year to police, and these are for an ambulance and unintended death. We've also talked with Joan Landers of the Conservation Commission and have provided buffers to the wetland areas."

Nelson did a quick calculation in his head. Turning to Sarah, he whispered, "If their service fee increases by ten thousand dollars for an additional forty-two apartments, that means they're making half a million dollars in rents. The average rent for those small apartments is therefore at least a thousand dollars a month. That's not a great deal of savings for this area, not for a small apartment."

Nelson's train of thought was interrupted by Kurt's placation to the board members.

"We've been coming before this board for over a year. Mr. Dwyer has enjoyed meeting with the members of this board."

"Yeah, I'll bet he has," whispered Sarah.

"There have been a lot of articles in the newspaper regarding the nonprofit status of Caring Home Services. We've been doing charitable work in this town for ten years now."

Joe Vaschon was sitting with his wife directly behind Nelson and Sarah. They overheard him comment to Mary quietly, "What charitable work? Renting apartments?"

He smiled at Joe's comment then promptly returned his attention to Kurt's spiel.

"Every contract our firm has with CHS is based upon an hourly rate, and we give them the ten percent discount we normally give to the municipality. That is meant to help CHS keep their rentals affordable. We're not putting anything in front of you that doesn't agree with site plans and approvals that CHS has had in its past phases.

Kurt thanked the members for listening and sat down.

"Is there any public comment to be made on this development?" Tunney asked. He fixed his look directly at Nelson. "I would like to stick to new things and not dwell on past comments."

Nelson decided that was a good enough invitation and stood to address the board.

"There are a lot of unresolved issues regarding this development as well as a lot of opposition from abutters and other residents. For instance, I simply don't understand how the number of trips per day has been so drastically reduced.

In previous hearings, this Planning Board has stated that a second access road was required for Phase Two. There is no emergency access. If there's ever a fire, it could be a real problem. I also know that some people have requested public files for review and have not been able to find documents that should have been available from the town, including federal tax forms. Furthermore, the tax assessor hasn't performed a review of the exemption status to make sure that Caring Home Services even qualifies for a property tax exemption—that's still questionable.

"I am also very concerned about the amount of salt and sand being dumped in wetland areas from the massive number of parking areas and roads throughout the proposed complex, especially during winter. One of those roads is still shown to extend onto Baker Street as well as another road that connects their two lots of land by a bridge crossing a large wetland area. CHS has been told in the past that neither of those accesses can be used, yet they still show them on their site plans and the Planning Board keeps approving them."

"Look," said Tunney, "there is a line on their site plan showing what is considered as Phase Two. That's what we're discussing, not the entire build-out of the development."

"But even at this stage," Nelson countered, "we need to look at the issue of a second access road. Because there have been changes made to the plan. I don't think the Planning Board should make a decision until the ZBA looks at the second phase of the development again. I'm not convinced the ZBA will re-approve this second phase of development. I also believe this project is damaging to the town's infrastructure."

"Thank you, Mr. Quip. You have been most informative."

Nelson sat down, discouraged from being somewhat dismissed, and another abutter stood to speak. Nelson recognized him as a neighbor who lived next door to Marie Paterson. He was a large fellow and seemed almost as wide as he was tall. The color of his heavy blue winter jacket and blue jeans offset the contrast to his full gray beard, thick black-framed glasses, and round face.

"My name is Kevin Sparks. I want to address my concerns about the wetlands. I work with Will Penton, who has previously addressed this board. I'm a certified arborist and provide landscaping services in Laslo. I know you're only looking at this Phase Two right now. You don't have to re-mind me of that. But the other phases have to be considered before you proceed with approvals. You just can't ignore them as you suggested to Mr. Quip. I've been looking for a copy of those wetland permits as well as information on how they came up with their studies. I've also been looking for the flagging of the wetlands, which is required. If they *were* flagged, they certainly aren't now. When I walked the land they propose to build upon, I wasn't able to find anything that resembled any type of markings denoting their surveys. Perhaps it's been too long since they did the surveys. My brother-in-law went with me and he knows about wetlands. He sits on an ecological board for the state."

"We're considering what the development has provided this board tonight," said the chairperson.

"Well, I may have to live with that, but I'm telling you that the delineation of the wetlands has not been done. There's also no information on file regarding the vernal pools that could exist on this property. I came to this town office and looked at Mr. Todd's code enforcement files, with his permission of course, and the files are incomplete regarding vernal pools. I'm one of those people Mr. Quip mentioned who couldn't locate documentation that should be available. The possibility of vernal pools should seriously be reviewed. I don't think you should approve this project."

"I just want you to know that we have had three site walks," said Chairperson Tunney, "and some of us have even done self-guided walks on the property. I'm telling you there was a time when things were marked out."

"I've never seen any flagging, and I've lived near that property for many years."

"I feel that the applicant has generally responded to what the board has asked for," defended Tunney.

"I disagree," Kevin adamantly said. "I still think the de-lineation of the wetlands for the Phase Two of the South Campus is in question. Just look at Section 14.28.390.B of the Land Use Code. It states that 'if there is a dispute regard-ing the existence of boundaries of the wetlands, the bounda-ries shall be determined at the expense of the applicant, by a qualified wetlands scientist or a qualified state certified soils scientist agreeable to both the Planning Board and the applicant'. Mr. Kurt Tussi stated he was licensed in New Hampshire but never mentioned he was qualified to determine wetland delineation within the state of Maine."

"But I personally marked the areas myself," said Kurt.

"Well there appear to be discrepancies on the site plan, and there are also blatant omissions about vernal pools. There has been misleading information provided by you from the Maine Department of Inland Fisheries and Wildlife Report. I had a discussion last week with Mr. Scott Peterson from the State of Maine Department of Conservation. I have a copy of the letter he wrote to you. You read a portion of that letter to this board concerning the confirmation of botanical features of the land in question for development."

Kevin pulled a paper out of his pocket. Unfolding it so he could read from it, he continued.

"The sentence you quoted which states *'There are no rare or botanical features documented specifically within the project area'* is followed by another sentence which you left out of the information you provided. That sentence continues the discussion, and I quote, *'This lack of data may indicate minimal survey efforts rather than confirms the absence of rare botanical features'*. The letter further states, *'You may want to have the site inventoried by a qualified field biologist to ensure that no undocumented rare features are inadvertently harmed'*. And that same letter continues by stating, *'In the absence of a specific field investigation, the Maine Natural Areas Program cannot provide a definitive statement on the presence or absence of unusual natural features at this site'*."

"We simply didn't think a site survey was necessary."

"But the information you provided is misleading, particularly how you presented it to this board."

"I don't believe it was."

"I have one other important thing to say about information provided to this board regarding this development site. Mr. Tussi actually told this board that the Maine Department of Inland Fisheries and Wildlife Report mentioned there was no identified wildlife inhabitants on a map associated with this site. He stated, and I quote, 'the Maine Department of Inland Fisheries and Wildlife found no records of any essential or significant wildlife inhabitants of special concern associated with the site'. When I reviewed the paperwork submitted by the developer, I found a statement that says the applicant had made adequate provisions for the protection of wildlife and fisheries. Mr. Peterson told me that a physical review of the site for CHS was never performed, and that the information used by the developer was taken from an old database. He mentioned that the map was inconclusive by itself and not conclusive of any on-site review findings. The residents surrounding this area have seen wildlife such as gray and red fox, raccoons, deer herds, coyote, opossum, moose, snowy owls, turkey vultures, wild turkeys, red-tail hawks, spotted salamanders, turtles, and others. Some of that wildlife may be of concern to the state of Maine."

"There simply are no significant species in this area," said Kurt.

"I think the state should make that decision, not you. I just wanted to raise these issues with this board," said Kevin. He folded the paper and returned it to his pocket before sitting down, frowning.

Mary Vaschon stood. "To me it sounds like this board is simply going to allow these types of projects by tax free exempt corporations to go ahead and build whatever they want to build, and we're all going to have to pay for it."

"Mrs. Vaschon," said Tunney, "specific points have been raised as to traffic counts, tax exemptions, and wetlands staking. Our town planner, Todd Hatch, has told me that our town tax assessor, Mr. Duncan, and our town attorney are meeting to discuss the property tax exemption later this month. They will be reviewing the issue, not us."

"That leaves us with traffic counts and wetlands staking," board member Drew Laden stated.

"It's my understanding, that the traffic count was a borderline issue and the applicant understood it would have to be addressed in the future," Tunney commented.

Nelson looked up as Brett Manley addressed the audience. He appeared to be the youngest board member, in his late thirties. Nelson wasn't sure what his background was. The tattooed word DON'T flexed on his arm as he rested his elbows on the desk.

"There's a traffic engineering report available regarding the trip counts. Three pages from the back of the report is a table that shows the daily trips at 2.5. I'd like to know if that is the number being used to determine the traffic count. The report denotes that the number used is based upon the ITE Standard for Congregate Care."

"Yes, I believe that the ITE standard used may be a little more than two per day," said Kurt. "The Director of Public Works for Laslo is in agreement with that number, and he doesn't think a second access road is required."

"Nevertheless, I'd like a definition of Congregate Care so I can understand the ITE Standard in determining the traffic count."

"Congregate Care," Kurt explained, "includes elderly residents, most over fifty-five, who tend to travel less than normal than those who live in condominium units."

"I'd like to see the actual definition in writing. I believe your traffic count is awfully low. People live longer and are more active. Are there functions where a good portion of those people will be going out more than others? I'm just trying to figure out if this project is what the applicant is calling it," questioned Brett.

"The traffic engineering report you have," said Kurt, "uses the 2.5 standard. The Director of Public Works went through that report with us and is in agreement. He actually suggested using a trip count of 2.15 versus 2.5 to the members of your board."

"At 2.15 trips per day," said Brett, "does that include any employees driving back and forth?"

"Yes," said Kurt.

"Does that include guests as well?" asked Drew.

"Yes."

Brett reacted with an inconsequential look, accepted Kurt's response, then changed the subject.

"We also need to review the length of the proposed access road from Route 2 into Phase One that continues into Phase Two. The Land Use Code only allows the length of a dead end road to be one thousand-two hundred feet in length. This road is over thirteen-hundred feet in length. So, there may be a need to provide a waiver to approve the total length."

"Looking at it from a safety point of view," interjected the chairperson, "I don't believe they need a secondary access road."

Ignoring Tunney's remark, Brett repeated his statement. "Looking at the length of the road to the end of the proposed Phase Two, we may need to have a waiver."

"I wish they'd settle on one issue at a time," whispered Nelson to Sarah, getting a little frustrated with the panel's discussion. "They keep going from one subject to another, never reaching any conclusions. Besides, the chairperson has contradicted his previous admission about requiring a second access road."

Chairperson Tunney said, "The applicant will need to add that waiver to their package."

Drew Laden said, "They can't just simply add the waiver onto their site plan. We need to act on that waiver first and vote on whether or not we approve it."

"I still have trouble with the parking," said Brett.

Tunney responded. "I'm satisfied with the integration of the parking in the next stage."

"What happens if the development stops at Phase Two?" asked Brett. "We wouldn't approve it without a sidewalk, particularly if there would be more development within the woodland corridor. We are beyond Phase One at that point. We still have a fairly good-sized project with parking that could be put somewhere else. I understand that it could be an inconvenience to some of the people living in those units, but I think that having no parking under the larger twenty-six unit building is also an inconvenience. I can see where they are going with it and the reasoning they don't want to make the change now, but what if there never is a Phase Three and Phase Four and so on?"

"I think the rationale is that the amount of traffic is acceptable until we increase the traffic at the next phase," Chairperson Tunney said.

"I would like to see a more permanent sidewalk area," said Brett.

"I'm inclined to accept it as presented," Tunney countered.

"That statement seems to be more obvious than ever," Sarah commented to Nelson.

"The last item we need to discuss is the wetlands delineation," said Drew.

"We already did that," Kurt said. "Everyone has walked it. The DEP found flagging delineation acceptable and issued the permit."

"The bigger issue for me is the fact that we are coming up with requirements in future phases that other boards will need to know about," said Elaine Graft. "How do we make sure they know what those requirements are and make it so other boards know we've looked at them?"

Sitting behind him, Joe tapped Nelson on the shoulder and whispered, "I thought the chairperson said that they were only discussing Phase Two, not the entire built-out development."

"Yeah, so did I," said Nelson.

"We have the minutes of our meetings and the information that our Director of Public Works has provided to us. If future phases are approved and built, then improvements will be made in accordance with the plan. We can add that information as a note on the site plan," Tunney replied.

"I agree," Drew Laden said. "I think the site plan is the most reliable place to have a message. Any other piece of paper is bound to be lost."

"They're going to have to go back again to the ZBA for Phase Two approval," said Elaine. "They need to know we have reviewed this. It's confusing. Look at how long we've deliberated."

"I believe that some of the buffers to the wetlands have been recorded," said Tunney.

"Yes. The buffers have been recorded," Kurt agreed.

Brett Manley was quick with his next comment. "This development falls under the cluster development ordinance."

"The wetland buffers are required by the DEP," said Kurt. "They are shown on the plan. We have provided the recorded declaration of those buffers."

Elaine Graft was next to speak up. "We've been talking cluster development the whole time."

"I don't know that we've been talking cluster," said Kurt.

"It's a cluster," said Elaine.

"Yeah, it sure is," whispered Joe in Nelson's ear.

"Do we need to designate areas of open space, which is one of the things that we have to do in a cluster development?" asked Brett. "I think we may need that shown on the plan as well."

"The question appears to be whether this project falls under cluster housing or whether or not it needs to meet cluster housing requirements," said Kurt.

"Mr. Tussi, have you used eight units per net residential acre?" asked Brett.

"Yes."

"The cluster ordinance is on page 229 of the Land Use Code. It says that the standards can be modified," Brett said.

"Brett, you're actually talking about the density of the housing," said Tunney.

"I'm using the density for elderly housing," said Brett. "The way I read the ordinance, elderly density is cluster housing."

Drew Laden spoke up in Brett's defense. "I read the ordinance the same way Brett reads it."

"The reason for the ordinance is to allow flexibility for design," Elaine said.

"It makes sense for the elderly because they will want things closer," said Brett. "I'm not sure why we didn't talk about this before."

Chairperson Tunney was quick with an answer. "We did talk about this before, but we got away from it. We need to determine whether this works as a cluster development, since that is what it is. I think we are to only look at Phase Two at this time, though. Mr. Tussi, the applicant needs a waiver application for road length from Route 2 to the end of Phase Two. The application also needs an added note that sidewalks will be added within five years if there are no further phases. The cluster housing issues will need to be addressed. There is a conservation easement issue that is ongoing at this point as well."

"We're about to run out of time and exceed the 10 p.m. limit of this meeting," Don Morgan reminded the other board members. "I believe there is still some confusion or disbelief about the number of trips in and out. Could a traffic count in an existing subdivision be performed in order to determine what the trips are per day?"

"I'm not ready to require a traffic count," said Tunney.

"But it's too easy to manipulate," said Brett. "I'd like more information."

"I think it's based upon a set of standards," said Drew.

Nelson slapped the palm of his hand to his forehead in response to Drew's comment. He turned to Sarah and whispered, "The chairperson himself talked about the ITE stand-ards that are used to figure the requirements for a second access road. That's been discussed more than once. Didn't Brett bring that topic up earlier? Where's Laden been any-way—sleeping?"

"There's a lot to discuss here," said Brett. "I think we should continue the public hearing for CHS at the next avail-able meeting date scheduled by our Town Planner."

Chairperson Tunney said, "I don't think we should put this off. I think we need to get it done as soon as possible. I think we need to extend the meeting for a few more minutes and then schedule another public hearing."

"Mr. Tussi," said Brett, "are you familiar with the cluster provision? Is it within our ordinance?"

"Yes. It's in the ordinance."

"I have a concern about the parking in the proposed ex-pansion," said Elaine. "You don't have any handicapped park-ing in front of or near the buildings. Although there is handi-capped parking, I'd like to see them closer to the apartments. The first plan was actually better than your sec-ond redrawn plan. Could you find a way for each apartment to get a spot in front of the unit, not backing out into the driveway?

"What about the road length waiver we discussed earlier," asked Drew. "We haven't finished discussing that."

"From what I'm hearing," whispered Joe to his wife, "they haven't finished discussing anything. They keep flitting from one subject to another. Even I'm having a hard time trying to figure out what the hell they're talking about."

"The waiver will be considered first," said Tunney, "but we'll have to adjourn for the night. We have exceeded our time."

The cold night air greeted Nelson when he left the Town Hall. He turned to Sarah and his next-door neighbors, Joe and Mary, and asked, "Did they come to any conclusions about this Phase Two development? They jumped from one subject to another, never resolving anything. I'm not even sure where we are at the moment."

"It seems to me," said Mary, "the Planning Board would just as soon give them waivers for anything, just to meet ordinance requirements."

Will Penton sauntered over to the group, along with Marie Paterson and Nikki Williams. Sarah turned to face everyone. "I wonder how many more hearings they're going to have before we know what's going to happen."

They talked briefly among themselves until a cold wind from the east removed the clouds from a crisp wintry moon. The casting shadows reminded Nelson it was late and time to disband. They were all tired, frustrated, and at the same time irritated at the consistent redirection of discussions.

iii.

When Nelson arrived home, he checked his e-mail and found a condemnation of other matters from Maxwell.

E-mail: Jan 23
To: NelsonQuip
From: Mdraper
Subject: Disturbing Changes

Hey, Nelson,
Got the additional chapters you sent; guess they've prompted the following rant.
Ever since I've become more obsessed with reviewing news reports and differences from one source to another, I've been looking over the many changes happening in the country. Unfortunately, they are not all positive.
Did you know that over the last five years food-stamp rolls have gone from 28 million to almost 48 million people, about a 70 percent increase? The pool of potential candidates for assistance has been increased due to the encouragement by the federal government to allow people into the program with relatively higher incomes. The goal of this program was to help people with government aid before their savings were wiped out. It was to make sure the unemployed had enough money to pay for gasoline and phone bills. Changes to increase the eligibility encouraged many people to expect continuous handouts, losing their motivation to improve their status quo.
The average cost of gasoline used to be $1.79; now is $3.89 per gallon and quickly increasing. With production of

oil from fracking in our own country and differing issues in the mid-east, I expect you'll see fluctuations—both up and down for several years.

There are also more people unemployed than what is being reported. A lot of people aren't even trying to find employment. So the percentages being reported are probably half of what they really are. Amazing how people can swallow the misaligned and fabricated facts they're given. (I don't have to tell you much about misaligned facts though, do I?) And think about it—only a few years ago the national debt was at 10.6 trillion dollars and now it is approaching 18 trillion dollars. Eventually it will rise to over 20 trillion. Scary to see what's happening in such a relatively short period of time.

Again, sorry about the venting. I've kept it short though. I guess we're both frustrated about different, yet the same type of situations—where it seems like we can't do anything about them. I'll get back to you with comments on the chapters you sent, shortly—that's really why I'm e-mailing you. Keep in touch.

–Max

Chapter Twelve

Win Some Lose Some

i.

The month of January continued to be no colder than others in past years, but the consistent snowfall had already made the winter seem longer than usual. A January thaw had come and gone, and within only two weeks was replaced by several feet of snow. Attending nightly public hearings didn't help the winter doldrums either, adding frustration for the many trips to the town hall after work. Three weeks after the last Planning Board hearing, Nelson, Sarah, and their neighbors received two more notices regarding additional public hearings.

It was late Friday afternoon when Sarah handed Nelson the mail with that certain look of hers. He knew something was up.

"You're kidding," he said as he read the form letter. "It's bad enough when there's a ZBA and Planning Board meeting in the same month. This time we're having two public hearings in the same week?"

"Looks like that third week in February is going to be a long one. Kurt is really pushing to get this Phase Two approved."

"If they'd fix the problems instead of circumventing them, perhaps they would. I think we've got more research, organizing, and writing to do. We'll need to call Nikki, Marie, Joe, Mary, Will, Emmy, and whoever else we can get to start canvassing for more signatures in an opposition letter regarding this expanding mess. I'm not giving up."

Sarah just smiled and curtly added, "Didn't think you would."

ii.

Will Penton approached Nelson and Sarah as they stepped from their car. It was a typical cold February night, already pitch black outside, thanks to daylight savings. "I barely gathered up enough courage to attend this hearing tonight," he uttered. "Do you realize it's been about two years since we've had to attend a Zoning Board of Appeals public hearing for this project?"

Joe Vaschon, who had just arrived, overheard Will's comment as he approached. "I guess it's been the number of Planning Board hearings we've attended that has made this process seem so long."

With that comment, they entered the public hearing room and sat down in unison, trying to make themselves as comfortable as possible. *How I hate metal chairs*, thought Nelson, as he noted that even Josh Gosling, who hadn't attended any of the Planning Board meetings, was attending the ZBA public hearing. Marie Paterson, Emmy Anderson, Nikki Williams, Joe and Mary Vaschon—they were all there. Nelson smiled when he noticed that Nikki and Marie sat directly behind him, remembering that Nikki always shared a whispered comment or two during the hearings.

The five ZBA board members and their positions facing the public hadn't changed, and Chairperson Bolduc read the familiar application to the audience in a monotone voice.

The CHS representative, Phil Dwyer, stood by his chair and was the first person recognized to speak.

"I'm here to ask this board once again to approve an expansion that was granted over two years ago last December. This board granted approval for forty-four apartments, and we are now requesting approval to build only forty-two. I think there is a great need for what we are planning to build here. We have one hundred percent occupancy all the time, and there is a waiting list of people now. If construction on Phase Two is started in a couple of months, which I hope will happen, it will take a year to complete, and during that time, the waiting list will continue to grow. We had hoped to start this project last spring, but the Planning Board process is still ongoing. This development is on the Planning Board's agenda again this week, and I expect to receive approval then."

"How's that saying go?" Nikki whispered to Joe. "Wish in

one hand, and shit in the other. In his case, I hope he does both in the same hand."

Joe smirked at her tasteless, although fitting, comment.

"Timing of construction is important," Dwyer continued. "As a non-profit organization, we try to keep the rental rates down. Because of our non-profit status with the IRS, our housing development does not pay property taxes, allowing us to charge less. The cost of construction material, such as steel, sheet rock, and plywood, has gone up and are adding to the cost of this project, which is negating this benefit. This is of concern because this is a facility for people of modest means. I trust this board will take all this into consideration and grant the renewal of the special exception approval. Thank you once again for listening." Phil returned to his seat.

Kurt Tussi promptly stood and paced the floor as if on cue to address the five ZBA members.

"As you know, we've completed Phase One, including five buildings and a church. As Mr. Dwyer mentioned, Phase Two of this project was proposed to this board over two years ago, and the board granted a special exception at that time. I told this board that the project required approval from the Department of Environmental Protection and the Planning Board. The DEP approval was received last October, but we're still going through the Planning Board process. Portions of the project have been redesigned, and, as I mentioned, we are meeting with them again this week. I'm pretty sure Phase Two will receive approval on that night, as stated by Mr. Dwyer, since we've worked out a lot of the details with the Planning Board.

"When this project was previously before you, this board approved the Phase Two plan consisting of forty-four units in five buildings. What is now before the Planning Board is a different configuration for Phase Two, which is for forty-two apartments in four buildings. This plan is very similar in location to what it was last time, and the parking lot layout is only a little different. There's really nothing more I can add, but I'll answer any questions you might have."

Chairperson Bolduc spoke. "The procedure tonight will be that the board will first hear from members of the public who wish to speak in favor of the application, then those in opposition, and then those who wish to speak about the application. A lot of people are here tonight, so I'd like to go through a couple of things. The board is interested in the criteria for a special exception, and we would ask that people address those criteria. There's been a lot of discussion about how this development will impact people tax-wise, but that isn't anything this board can get into. The ZBA will not make a legislative decision if this project is good or bad; the board will just be following the law before them.

"I am asking that people who wish to speak about this project, please state your name and where you reside. If a speaker wants to talk about something that another person has already said, the speaker can refer to that, rather than say it all over again. It's important to try not to be repetitive but rather stay on the issue so the board can make a decision. If anyone gets too far afield from the topic or it is something that the board isn't going to consider, I may have to cut people off from speaking."

Nelson recognized the town's Code Enforcement Officer, Allen Treble, as he stood and addressed the ZBA chairperson. "This may be out of turn, but when the applicant submitted the application for the board to rehear because their approval had expired, I was unaware that the applicant had been going through the DEP and Planning Board process throughout this whole time. Section 14.22 of the town's Land Use Ordinance Code states that while a project is undergoing DEP and Planning Board review, time basically stops until the review period is over, so this application may not need to be heard again tonight."

Nelson looked about the room at his neighbors' reactions to Treble's remark. The looks of surprise and frustration were noticeable. *This might end everything right here*, he thought.

"This plan is different than what was first approved," Treble continued, "therefore, the board may not want to look at this as a plan that has expired and is being reapplied for, but as a different plan."

Nelson felt a sigh of relief upon understanding that public input to the discussion still might continue.

Eleanor Adley was quick to react. Her short, cropped black hair, made little movement as she quickly faced Treble and replied, "The use is still the same."

"Yes it is," said Treble. "I think that was already stated

earlier. But if there are any changes to the plan, the project has to come back before this board for approval."

"Bless his sweet little heart," Nelson overheard Nikki whisper.

"I think the perspective of this board is that it not operate in a vacuum," said Bolduc. "I think if anything has changed, the board should hear it."

"Will the board assess issues like parking?" Eleanor questioned.

"The board will need to assess whatever standards it is supposed to use under the town's Land Use Code," Bolduc answered.

"Then, according to Mr. Treble," Eleanor said, "their approval has not expired. The board will therefore vote on something different tonight, because the plan has changed. Will the board be hearing this de novo?"

Joe turned to his wife and Nelson overhead him say, "What the crap does that mean?"

Sarah turned around, trying not to raise any attention. "I think it's a Latin phrase meaning 'from the beginning'".

"Why didn't she just say so?" Joe grumbled.

"Yes," said Bolduc. "If the applicant wants to go back to the plan that the board previously approved, the board may not have to hear this, but if anything has changed, the board needs to discuss it."

"There are minor changes to the plan before the board tonight," said Kurt Tussi.

"So, we'll begin our new approval process," said Bolduc. "Would anyone like to speak in favor of this Phase Two project?"

Nelson quickly looked around the room and noticed a large group of people sitting in one area toward the front of the room, next to Phil Dwyer. He recognized the same group of residents from the Phase One apartments. Apparently, they had been asked to participate in the ZBA public hearing; like stuffing a ballot box for a particular outcome.

The first person to stand was Franklin Howall. "I was born in Laslo eighty-four years ago and have been living at the South Campus of Caring Home Services for four years. I searched diligently for a place to live that was peaceful and quiet but didn't find anything else in the surrounding towns.

CHS, which is a non-profit organization, is what I was looking for. I don't believe that this kind of project will have an immense impact on the town. I think it will have some impact, but to say it is immense means to me that it is huge, large and colossal, and it is none of those things. Mr. Dwyer, who is the director, ably manages this facility. I don't have a lot of facts and figures to give, but I think the elderly sitting here today will join me in saying it is a gall darn good place to live. Beyond that, I'd be willing to say this development is a great asset to the town of Laslo."

Howall sat down and was immediately replaced by another person.

"My name is April Johnson, and I've been living at the Northern Campus of CHS for about nine years. I just want the residents to know that I feel very fortunate to have a place to live during my so-called Golden Years. I wasn't able to maintain my private home any longer, and these apartments are a Godsend. I hope the board will approve Phase Two."

The procession of people sitting and standing continued.

"I'm Zack Donaldson, and I agree with everything that has been said about what a great place CHS is. If this project was approved a while back and it hasn't changed, except for minor details, as far as zoning is concerned, then it should simply be a matter of saying it's the same project and why not approve it."

"I'm Mabel Sarti. My husband and I live in this community complex. I think there's a real need for such living spaces, and I'm sure my peers will agree with me."

The room was suddenly quiet after the last statement. No one else spoke in favor of the application.

"That outburst looked like it was fairly well rehearsed," whispered Joe.

Chairperson Bolduc asked, "Can I have a show of hands for those present who aren't in favor?"

iii.

Several hands went up, and Nelson was the first person recognized by the chairperson to speak. He stood, cleared his throat, and began.

"As many of you know by now, I am opposed to a special exception for Phase Two. Many residents of Laslo are requesting that the Zoning Board of Appeals *deny* the request for a special exception for this oversized elderly housing complex.

"The ZBA previously approved this special exception to Zoning for Phase Two over two years ago. At *that* time, approval for all seven phases was requested, but the ZBA was wise in approving only Phase Two based upon the relatively little information available during the hearing. There is now much more information available than there was back then. I provided a summary packet to each board member for tonight's public hearing several days ago. I trust you've taken the time to look it over. The residents and abutters would greatly appreciate your earnest consideration of the many issues with this development and their negative affect on our town prior to your final decision.

"There are also two separate petitions in that summary packet. The first petition opposes this development and is signed by over seventy abutters and people living in the vicinity of this project. They oppose this project because of the adverse impact to the wildlife, the number of units proposed, the inconsistent calculations used, the effect on the visual aspects of this high density cluster housing development, wetlands issues including exclusion of vernal pools, the amount of pavement, drainage/erosion concerns, fire hazards, inadequate access/egress to the proposed Phase Two, the excessive length of a dead end road to Phase Two, the large extent of fill in the amount of twelve to fifteen feet for Phase Two, the non-deduction of land not suitable for use in residential use calculations, and many other concerns addressed throughout the packet.

"In addition, a second petition is included and signed by approximately two hundred residents requesting the town to fully assess and tax the property owned by Caring Home Services. The information contained in your packets was derived from such documents as The Land Use and Development Code Zoning Ordinance, the Peer Review performed by Grafton Engineering, the Laslo Comprehensive Plan, the Laslo Conservation Commission Report, Title 36, Section 652 of the Maine Revenue Services Administration, and Title 13B of the Maine Nonprofit Corporation Act. As you know, there are sixteen individual Criteria Factors of the Land Use Code from Section 14.21.050B1 through B16, and I've addressed those in my summary."

Nelson paused only long enough to give the audience a short break to reflect upon what he was trying to convey, then continued.

"I also want to point out that there are several aspects of this proposed development that are not in compliance with the Laslo Comprehensive Plan. Maine State law requires that the town's zoning ordinance must be consistent with the town's Comprehensive Plan.

"First—Our Comprehensive Plan's mission statement includes the fact that the town should maintain a stable tax rate. Caring Home Services pays no property taxes. MSRA statutes indicate CHS is not exempt from property taxes in the state of Maine, but only from federal income taxes through their current 501(c)(3) status.

"Second—According to the town's comprehensive plan, Laslo already has sufficient numbers of elderly housing units. In fact, the current status of CHS has our town over forty-three percent of the numbers already allocated, including the twenty-six units previously built in Phase One. An additional forty-two units for Phase Two would increase that number in further excess. In addition, current rental units in this area of comparable size and amenities are less in cost than the average rental on CHS's South Campus.

"Third—The Comprehensive Plan stipulates that "cluster developments which retain significant open space, reflecting village patterns of development" should be allowed a density up to *four* units per net residential acre. The current site plans are designed with *eight* units per residential acre, not *four* units.

"The continued expansion of CHS simply doesn't conform to the Town of Laslo's Comprehensive Plan, nor does it satisfy the requirements for a special exception to Urban Residential Zoning. The abutters and taxpayers, therefore, oppose this special exception for zoning. The Zoning Board has the ability to stop this adverse impact to our town. As concerned residents, many of us have extended a lot of effort to point out the irreparable impact and adverse effects of this development to the town, its abutters, and its taxpayers that the approval of Phase Two will cause.

"This cluster housing development will become a congestion of parking lots, paved roadways, and multiple complexes with an inner-city appearance that the abutters and people living in the area will have to view. When you start adding fifteen feet of fill in order to place a building, you are simply not working with the land but against it. There are hundreds of residents now opposing this Phase Two expansion. Maintaining Laslo as a nice New England town in which to live does not conform with this high-density cluster type of development. A decision to approve will affect not only the abutters but also the other residents who already pay high property taxes. We are urging the Laslo Zoning Board of Appeals to *deny* a special exception to Phase Two of this project."

Nelson thanked the board members for listening and sat down, relieved he had managed to get through his oratory without interruption.

For several seconds the board members just sat looking at their audience and then at one another. Chairperson Bolduc finally broke the silence.

"Are there any other members of the public who wish to speak against this proposed project?"

Marie Paterson raised her hand and was recognized by the chairperson.

"My concern is that CHS has labeled this expansion as elderly housing when it's actually a high-density development," she exclaimed. "A high-density cluster permit allows for four units per acre and elderly housing allows eight units per acre. Because CHS has combined the North and South campuses for total acreage considerations, they have added the four additional units to the South Campus. In other words, there's some magic math being done. And they are trying to continue to purchase property adjacent to this land. I believe this is not elderly housing but rather high-density, urban cluster housing. I would like this Board to please recognize this for what it is and not under the guise it has donned."

"Some of the land in question used to belong to my family years ago," Joe Vaschon said after Marie sat down. "One of the reasons I moved back here was to be near family. I know this area well, and I've reviewed the plans for this facility.

The site plan shows an existing ten-foot drop in one area that travels along a ravine extending the length of the property, but I can guarantee that it's actually a thirty-foot drop. That area is all wetland, but the developer isn't counting that area as wetlands when they calculate their available land for building. If anyone from the ZBA wants to walk the area with me, you should bring your hip boots."

The visualization of any board members walking in waist high, muddy water in their hip boots brought chuckles from the audience.

Joe waited for the room to quiet, then continued. "This development will add water runoff onto other properties. The developer knows there's a lot of water out there. There's one pond on the property that has drainage outlets, but it's not considered as wetland. They're really using a lot of land that shouldn't be used, but it's being used to justify the number of units they want to build. They're calling it buildable land, but it really isn't. Knowing the contour of this property and the amount of fill proposed, the developers are not working with the land."

"I'm not totally opposed to this project," Nelson heard Will Penton's slight groan as Kevin Sparks appeared to side with the opposition, but then Kevin added, "It's just that the magnitude of such a development can have a terrible impact on this town. My brother-in-law works as a wildlife biologist and is on a state committee to better evaluate Maine's conservation efforts. He's reaffirmed the fact that there are vernal pools on the property. We walked throughout the area last spring where Phase Two is proposed, and he identified three possible vernal pools that serve as breeding grounds for wildlife. I understand the Planning Board members have recently done a walk also, but the vernal pools can't be determined until spring. That's the best time to observe and identify species in those habitats, as winter is a period of hibernation.

"I've gone through all the paperwork I could manage to find regarding this project, and I couldn't find any studies of the vernal pools and associated field-work data that were done on site in many, many years. I found nothing in the town Planner's Office. The identification and delineation of these fields have not been done, but the applicant claims to have such surveys. Since these discussions have started, I've

walked through the area on a regular basis, and the proposed land-fill comes very close to one of those vernal pools.
Of course it's easier to fill in areas than to worry about con-
forming with the contours of the land. I think the developers
want to get the most they can on this property, and that's
bad for the land. I still maintain the fact that the land has not
been flagged, and I haven't seen any data on how they came
up with the marking of their delineations.

"I also want to let this board know that I talked with the
State of Maine Wildlife Commission. There seems to be a lot
of misinformation that's been presented here, and I think the
residents and abutters have done an extensive amount of
work to bring out these points for this board. People are here
tonight because they care about the town and its future."

"That came out a little better than I thought it was going
to," Sarah whispered to Nelson as Kevin sat down. Emmy
Anderson was the next person recognized to speak. "Go,
girl," Sarah mumbled to herself.

Emmy slowly walked over to the podium to address the
board.

"I realize the chairperson has requested that we not discuss tax issues, however, as you know, the tax status of Caring Home Services has finally come under review by our
town tax assessor and the town's attorney. Many residents
have asked the town to reassess and tax Caring Home Services at the fair market value of their property. It appears
that CHS doesn't meet any of the criteria for tax exemption
here. While they might meet federal tax exemptions, the
state property law does not constitute exemption from property taxes within the town of Laslo. I believe that the welfare
of senior citizens and all persons on fixed incomes would be
jeopardized financially by adding several hundred more
apartments to the already existing eighty-six apartments on
their North and South Campuses. The town grants no
abatements to homeowners over fifty-five years of age, so
why should CHS be exempted? By avoiding property taxes,
CHS places a huge tax burden on independent older home
owners in Laslo."

Emmy's voice became dry, but more emphatic in her delivery. Her emotions were beginning to show.

"This project appears to exploit senior property owners

who want and need to remain in their own homes. The addition of hundreds of neighbors who can vote in this municipality, with no responsibility for payments of services does not satisfy equal treatment under the town ordinances. This situation provides an opportunity for those neighbors voting as a block to pass any type of bond issue, burdening the current taxpayers. I am asking on behalf of the welfare of all Laslo seniors and people on fixed incomes that you deny Caring Home Services their zoning appeal. At the least, this appeal should be tabled until the tax question has been resolved and CHS agrees to support our community with everyone's welfare in mind, not just their profits. Also keep in mind that the Laslo Fire Department is already stretched to the limit."

As Emmy returned to her seat, Ann Reynolds, who Nelson recognized had previously spoken to the Planning Board, asked the board members for recognition to address her concerns.

"Many of you know me. I'm a teacher in our school system. I've reviewed the sixteen criteria under Section 14.21.050 of the town's Land Use Land Code that the ZBA is considering tonight. I want to remind you that I am opposed to this expansion. Caring Home Services is already occupying a large amount of land in their North and South Campuses, and what remains is beautiful open space with a lot of wetland. I am concerned about the density bonus that is allowed for elderly housing. The added four units per acre bonus will result in an intense development of this land. It will therefore allow a greater impact on the open space, with its wildlife habitat and wetlands, rather than if it was being developed under the standard urban residence zone criteria of four units rather than eight units per acre.

"If this expansion was an appropriate use, then I don't believe there would be such a major outcry from abutters and neighbors. I believe what these abutters are saying is that they bought land in an urban residential area, but the expansion of this special exception use is going to change the character of their area and possibly their property values. I think the board should pay particular attention to the criteria addressed in the Land Use Codes during deliberations. Section 14.21.050.B10 addresses the use and the overcrowding of land, which is what I believe would occur. The eight units per acre density bonus will cause overcrowding of the land and an undue concentration of population.

"I'm also puzzled by what seems to be a contradiction on page 124 in the Comprehensive Plan Update, which states that the town already has a sufficient number of elderly housing units for the people of Laslo. I've heard from the developer that there is a need for this project. I'd like the board to ask the director of this project, Mr. Dwyer, what percentage of the people who currently reside at CHS had a Laslo address before moving here, as well as how many people on the current waiting list have Laslo addresses. I think this town wants to do its fair share for the elderly, but since the Comprehensive Plan Update found that Laslo already has enough elderly housing units, I don't think it's right to be using up open space with a more intense special exception use."

"Thank you, Mrs. Reynolds, for your comments," said Chairperson Bolduc.

As Ann returned to her seat, Nikki Williams reluctantly stood and walked over to the podium to address the board members.

"Hi. I'm Nikki Williams. I've spoken to you before in reference to the proposed expansion. I am one of the largest abutters to the CHS property on their North Campus. If the expansion is allowed to continue, the South Campus would also be built right up to the other side of my property line. I would like to discuss a few issues tonight that include the road access for the fire department, the length of the road onto the South Campus, and the effect of this project on property values.

"With all the rearranging of trip numbers per day into and out of the South Campus, there is speculation as to the latest ITE figures used, determining there is no need for a second access road. Of course, the ITE standards used to determine those numbers keep changing. I believe there *is* a need for a secondary access road if this expansion is allowed. Even for Phase One, there is speculation that the road into the current South Campus is not suitable for so much traffic. In addition, the Land Use and Development Code Zoning Ordinance Code states that a dead end road can be extended to a maximum of one thousand-two hundred feet without a waiver. The road into Phase Two will need to be over one thousand-three hundred feet. That, in itself, will require CHS to obtain a waiver to allow the extension. How many waivers and special permits should one project be granted, especially one which has proven to be so controversial to the town? Driving into the South Campus with a regular vehicle on the proposed narrow road for Phase Two could be difficult. It will be practically impossible for a large emergency vehicle to turn around unless they back up all the way from the main road, Route 2."

Nikki paused, shifting her weight from one foot to another, and then continued.

"I want this board to know that I discussed the impact of this project on abutter's property values with a real estate company. I have a letter from Mr. Albert Diamond from Coastal Realty here in Laslo. I'd like to read it to the residents."

She held up a paper she had brought with her and started to read from it.

"In my opinion, a property that abuts a wooded open space would be more valuable than the same property abutting multi-unit housing. This is commonly a reason for zoning to maintain the character of, and subsequently preserving the value of like property. The value of single family housing is highest when surrounded by other single-family housing or by open space. This project you're talking about is not only dense multi-unit housing, but it's housing at which the residents are not always home. The residents and visitors are always coming and going all day long unlike a non-retirement complex where most residents are at work for long periods of time. This constant activity of people coming and going would certainly be a negative factor that any buyer would be likely to consider."

She looked up at each member of the board before lowering the paper to the podium.

"I have copies of this letter for the board members. I'm also making the same comment that Mrs. Reynolds did, about how Mr. Dwyer brought up the fact that there's a waiting list for CHS. I'd like to know how many of those people are Laslo residents. That's all I have to say, for now. Thanks for listening."

Just as Nikki retreated from the podium, Josh Gosling stood by his chair and addressed the board members.

"I own property that abuts the land purchased by Caring Home Services. I know several people who spoke tonight live in Phase One of CHS, and I can sympathize with them; as they suggested, it's a wonderful place. I am, however, opposed to this new expansion for an additional Phase Two. The current facility may have wonderful apartments, but I think this town has already done its job in providing more elderly housing for this area. Many people my age have elderly parents. My mother is trying to stay in her home but has to pay high taxes in order to be able to remain. If my mother had to move, CHS might be a nice place for her to go, but she doesn't want to leave, and she also doesn't want to pay taxes for everyone else who's not and *should be*. I like supporting the elderly, but I also want the tax base in our town to be supported, as well.

"Someone previously commented that if there have been minor changes to the plan, the board should just make it happen. This process started several years ago, and it has been before various boards on numerous occasions. I think that means it has been poorly planned with things that are overlooked, causing problems for the board members and confusion because of the continuous changes. I think CHS should stay the way it is and that the board shouldn't approve any further phases."

"I want this board to know that I own rental property on Baker Street," said Ned Bracken as he stood after Josh finished. Nelson remembered he was up in years, in his eighties. "Mr. Quip has previously talked about a second access road being required for Phase Two. I want you board members to know that Caring Home Services has already put a newsletter out to their residents stating that when this Phase Two expansion is approved, Baker Street will be used as a means for a second access road. Can you believe the kahunas these people have?"

Ned's voice rose with the last question, showing his frustration with the situation and CHS. He paused to regroup then continued.

"The ZBA should keep in mind that the request to use Baker Street was previously turned down twice by this board. Baker Street is a sub-standard street and would have to be rebuilt and widened significantly to accommodate the extra traffic. And Baker Street can't be rebuilt without taking land by eminent domain. I don't think the Planning Board has the authority to approve any project that would require the taking of land by eminent domain. I definitely think this project should be denied."

"I live on Baker Street!" a loud voice called out from the back of the room. A very petit woman stood, her posture showing her determination to speak her mind. "I'm Millie Hodgdon, and I'm opposed to this project. I don't go along with the decision for allowing these units to be built. I've lived here for over fifty years. When I bought my house, it was in an urban area. During that time, I've had wild animals like deer and foxes visit my property. Since Phase One was built, I've seen fewer animals than I used to."

After hearing Millie's unexpected outburst, Joe Vaschon decided to speak his mind.

"There's a proposed road on the site plan that goes through the entire South Campus property and meets up with their North Campus over a bridge. Our Conservation Commission has asked Mr. Tussi several times to remove it from the plans because it goes right through a wetland, and they still haven't removed it. Many of the issues brought up at these public hearings have simply been ignored."

Joe's statement prompted Joan Landers of the Laslo Conservation Commission to respond.

"I can see that people opposed to this project have done a great deal of work, and I want to thank them for their input. The town has a Land Use Code Ordinance for a reason, and the Commission would like the site plan to adhere to the ordinance requirements. The town attorney has provided the board members with advice regarding variances from wetland setbacks. From the site plans I've reviewed, I can see the developers have not come up with a plan that adequately shows all the wetlands. The landscaping plan is also pathetic, which shows these things are a low priority for the developer. I'd like the things that have not been adequately addressed to be a high priority. It's not so much that the Commission is opposed, but we'd like to see the information and changes that we've asked for incorporated in the plans and not ignored."

Jean Abbot, a former member of the Town Council who sat several rows in front of Nelson, asked, "What about the

Baker Street issue?"

"A number of years ago," said Bolduc, "this board said Baker Street could not be used, even before the Planning Board had seen the plans. Baker Street is a substandard road. That discussion is not a subject for the board tonight." He looked around the room, then added, "Since there appears to be no more comments from the people present, this hearing is now closed for public discussion. We will take a fifteen minute break before this board discusses these issues among ourselves."

iv.

Nelson laughed as Millie Hodgdon quickly jumped up from her chair, causing it to screech backward across the floor, and exclaimed loud enough for those close to hear, "Good thing. I've got to go to the bathroom."

Several heads turned with understanding nods of agreement.

Nelson watched people throughout the room stand to stretch their legs and talk among themselves. Nikki Williams approached him, and asked, "Did you know that CHS has retained an attorney for tonight's public hearing? He's right over there!" She motioned in the man's direction with a nod of her head. "He's sitting next to Phil Dwyer—the guy in the suit and tie."

"If that's the case, I think we're gonna be outgunned," said Joe, overhearing her remark.

Sarah turned to face Joe. "You're right. They're going to try and shove this whole thing right down our throats."

"Or up somewhere else," Nikki added.

"This is a little depressing," replied Nelson, finding it difficult to ignore the humor behind her remark. He looked across the meeting hall and watched the two men conversing with each other.

While looking in their direction, Nelson saw Millie head straight for the bathrooms located down the hall and in back of the public hearing room. He turned and noticed that Eleanor Adley and Jane Emery had also left their respective positions from the panel, following Millie out of the room.

It was a good ten minutes before she returned. "Unbelievable," Nelson heard her say after she sat down. Jane had returned to her seat as well, but Eleanor was nowhere to be seen.

It was obvious Millie was excited about something, and Nelson couldn't resist. Walking back three rows, he asked, "What happened?"

"You won't believe this," exclaimed Millie, almost out of breath. She appeared to be elated someone was interested in what she had to say. "I was in one of the bathroom stalls when I heard old helmet hair out by the lavatories weeping and carrying on to Jane Emery."

"Who's old helmet hair?"

"Eleanor Adley, of course," she said, as if Nelson should have known. Millie's exuberance was just beaming. "Doesn't that short-cropped black hair with bangs across the front and straight back cut above the ears look like a football helmet to you?"

"Perhaps," Nelson pondered. "I never thought about it that way."

"Well, Eleanor was all upset, saying she couldn't continue to participate as a board member tonight 'cause everyone was being so mean to all those elderly people and their housing project. She was crying and saying all kinds of things about how cruel the abutters were, about the fact that there just shouldn't be any opposition to this whole thing. She thought all of us should be ashamed of ourselves, and said she just couldn't stand to listen to any more of it and had to leave the proceedings."

Upon hearing about Eleanor's outburst and trying to understand the significance, Nelson muttered the same word, "Unbelievable." He thanked Millie for the update then returned to his chair.

Sarah was waiting with a quizzical look on her face. Just as Nelson finished repeating Millie's story to her, Chairperson Bolduc started the public hearing once again.

"We'll be starting this portion of the hearing with one less board member this evening. Eleanor Adley had to recuse herself for personal reasons. On another note, while we were on break, Michael Grady has asked why this project is a special exception. Let me explain. There are uses that are and are not permitted under zoning. Special exceptions are usually favored by the law but have to meet certain criteria in order to be approved, and they can be approved with conditions and limitations."

Chairperson Bolduc looked directly at Nelson and continued. "Some people have already cited the Factors for Consideration, items 1 through 16 on pages 178 and 179 of the Land Use Code that the board will discuss."

"Does the granting of the special exception have anything to do with the fact that this is a request for elderly housing, not the fact that this is high density housing?" asked Rachel Greene.

"The board is here to see if elderly housing is okay or not okay," Bolduc answered.

Her questioning continued. "Does the tax issue have anything to do with granting the special exception? Does the board have to make sure the tax issue is divorced from the fact that this is a request for elderly housing?"

"My understanding is because it's a non-profit organization, it is not subject to municipal taxes," said Bolduc. "The tax issue isn't specific to this being elderly housing."

The Code Enforcement Officer, Allen Treble, interjected. "That's correct. There are other senior housing projects in Laslo that are for profit and do pay taxes."

"I don't want to discuss the property tax issue at this time," said Bolduc. "As for the special exception, let me clarify once again. In the case of elderly housing, the standards can be modified from three dwelling units per acre to eight dwelling units. And if the elderly housing proposal is considered as clustered housing, the standard can be modified from four units instead of three to eight dwelling units per acre".

"The standard for elderly housing in the urban residence zone is stated on page 128 of the Land Use Code," said Michael Grady. "Let's review Section 14.21.050, which addresses Criteria Factors for Consideration. A few of the residents in the audience have already addressed several of those criteria."

Before he could go further with the review, Rachael interrupted, "Does the First Criteria Factor mean that the character of the development should be in line with the appearance of the neighborhood?"

"Yes," said Bolduc, "for the use of elderly housing."

"Does this development fit within the neighborhood or does it stick out like a sore thumb?"

"I feel this elderly housing use does fit, as there is elderly housing and other residential uses around it," said Bolduc.

"I simply don't see how the scale of the project can be divorced from this," Rachel stated, her voice firm. "The size of this project might fit with the character of the neighborhood for twenty, fifty, or a hundred apartments, but certainly not over two hundred. I have to look at this whole project as a two hundred plus development and ask myself if it fits with the character of the neighborhood. And the answer is—absolutely not."

"I agree with Rachel," said Jane Emery. "I drove around the Phase One property on the South Campus. In its present state, it's lovely and well kept, but as Mrs. Greene stated, what is further proposed will change the whole character of the neighborhood."

"If there aren't three votes for the special exception, it fails," Chairperson Bolduc said, glancing around the room. "If three board members don't think Phase Two meets the First Criteria Factor, it won't pass. The board should address each of the Criteria Factors to see if there are any other issues."

"I have a major concern with the Second Criteria Factor listed for this development since it requires the use of land fill," said Rachel. "I don't see how that's an appropriate use of the land."

"Are there any other board members who find this criterion not to be met?" asked Bolduc.

"Several of the abutters have purchased their land back over fifty years ago, and now this monster is taking over," Michael Grady said. "My own house is situated on a fairly secluded piece of land. I would be concerned if things started closing in around me. I also don't want to proverbially beat a dead horse, but the town's tax rate is ridiculous. Mine has doubled since I built my house over ten years ago. People will come in and see this development, which could affect their outlook for the rest of the town. I think anyone looking at purchasing property looks at the town's taxes. If a large area of property is not keeping up with their end of the bargain, that means the rest of the town will be picking up the added tax burden. I don't believe this meets the Second Criteria."

Just as Michael Grady finished stating he didn't believe the development met the Second Criteria, the tall, slender man sitting next to Phil Dwyer stood. His full white beard, neatly trimmed, gave him a distinguished appearance. And his well-tailored suit added an air of success and resolve to his presence.

"My name is Stanley Dumas. I'm an attorney representing Caring Home Services. I'd like to ask a procedural question."

"By all means, Mr. Dumas. Go right ahead," said Bolduc.

"During the break, I saw Mrs. Adley in the hallway in tears."

"Mrs. Adley has recused herself."

"I heard Mrs. Adley say that this was a mean-spirited proceeding before she left the premises. I am wondering what she meant by that."

"As I just stated," reiterated Bolduc, "Mrs. Adley has recused herself. Any member of the board can do that for any reason."

"It's bizarre to see someone leave during the middle of a meeting."

"Her reasons are her own, Mr. Dumas. Although it does put the board in a bad position, because three like votes are needed for approval," said Bolduc.

"It's obvious that her recusal presents an equivalent of a "no" vote," said Dumas, "and that can affect the outcome of the board's decision. The scope of this project has already been approved by this ZBA board. This request for approval is coming back with only minor changes. I think the focus should be exclusively on the changes, as the board has previously decided the applicability of the Criteria Factors. I believe the applicant has already met the burden of proof. Tonight is about the changes, not the whole subject matter."

"You would have to point to a provision in the Land Use Code ordinance stating that," said Bolduc. "The board has always said if anything changes on a plan, the board has to see it again."

"Your Code Enforcement Officer, Allen Treble, previously talked about the provision in the ordinance, that when a plan goes before the Department of Environmental Protection, there is a time out. This is essentially the same application with some tweaking. With the ZBA deliberating this whole thing, and a board member walking out, I can feel where this is going. This new board meeting is setting aside what a prior board meeting has already done over what are minor changes."

The attorneys' words resulted in an eruption of low volume chatter throughout the meeting room, like a disturbed nest of bees. Nelson watched Chairperson Bolduc respond by asking people to be respectful.

Will Penton spoke up, asking, "Why is Mr. Dumas speaking for the developer? I thought the public hearing was closed to this audience."

"Attorney Dumas asked about a procedural issue, and he is allowed to ask for that," Chairperson Bolduc answered. "The board is not open to comments from the public. If things get out of hand, I'll shut the hearing down, and that will be it." He looked around the room to emphasize his point. "I understand Attorney Dumas' comment, and it is on record. I would like to return to the board for comments regarding the Third Criteria in Section 14.21.050.B."

"It's been brought to my attention that the number of trips per day has changed," said Jane Emery. "It was first stated as being 3.4 trips per day per apartment. Last August, the Planning Board Chairperson stated that a second access road would be required for Phase Two because there were greater than 200 trips per day. Then last November, the developers came back and stated the trip count had changed to 1.94 trips per day and the general note on the plan was removed."

"Why did that number change?" asked Rachel Greene. "It's awful suspicious that the number works out to be just under 200 trips which is a requirement for a second access road."

Kurt Tussi spoke up. "There have been a number of technical issues raised. Those were the numbers used for the North Campus development. The numbers we used to determine trip development were also used by another similar project in Laslo. I asked Mr. Peter Townsend, a traffic engineer, of Townsend Engineering to do a traffic assessment. Mr. Townsend's assessment came out to the lower number using *senior congregate care* housing. That's why the number was removed and the lower number was used. The Planning Board has concurred with that figure."

"That's not entirely true," said Rachel. "I actually read the minutes of that meeting. The Planning Board stated that they didn't necessarily agree with that number because it is not their specialty."

"Well, your Director of Public Works has sent a letter to the Planning Board saying he agrees with that number," said Tussi. "My recollection is that the Planning Board agreed with it."

"Is there a standard used in determining this?" asked Rachel.

"Yes. It's called the Information Technology Equipment Safety Standard, referred to as an ITE standard," Tussi replied. "Which is where the senior Congregate Care definition comes from."

"I'm uncomfortable with using two different reasonings. Is there a different standard for elderly housing?" asked Rachel.

"There are different categories for the ITE Standards, and the traffic engineer thought the senior Congregate Care category fit this development," said Tussi. "When we included the note for the North Campus development, we didn't pick a category but used a similar development."

"Unless someone wants to get an engineer to come in and say this figure isn't correct, I feel it is outside this board's realm," said Bolduc. "This is usually dealt with by the Planning Board."

"I think there should be some common sense involved with this," said Jane Emery. "The developer is now using 1.94 trips per day. That basically says that everyone living on their Campus stays in their house almost all the time. I have a ninety-six-year-old mother, and when she was driving and living in Carson City, Nevada, she wasn't in her house all the time. It's a little difficult for me to understand where the 1.94 trips per day figure comes from based on my experience. These people may have white hair, but I don't believe they stay home all day. The trip count for the North campus as well as Phase One for the South Campus used a number at 3.4 trips a day. Now, all of a sudden things have changed because if they don't lower that number, there's a requirement for a second access road."

"There are a number of technical issues that have come up tonight," said Tussi. "Some of those are revisiting the issues that the Planning Board has already dealt with. I don't doubt this board's responsibility, but the Planning Board may want to provide us with a list of questions."

"If the board wants to do that, it can," said Bolduc. "I understand your concerns, Mr. Tussi, but other than going through these Criteria, I don't know what else this board can do. Does the 1.94 trip count mean it's one trip out and not back?"

"That's just one way," said Kurt Tussi.

Nelson quickly turned to Sarah, who had an astonished look on her face. They had both assumed the trip count meant a round trip since Tussi had previously agreed the trips were back and forth, not a one-way trip. Discussions continued for Criteria Factors Four, Five, and Six with no further rebuke. And after Rachel Green challenged Criteria Factors Seven and Eight, Kurt Tussi managed to provide sufficient clarification. Rachel Green continued to pursue the remainder of the sixteen Criteria Factors.

"I have concern about the Ninth Criteria Factor," she said. "It addresses the inaccessibility of the property. Let me read that Criteria Factor to everyone. It states: '*Whether a hazard to life, or property because of fire, flood, erosion, or panic may be created by reason or as a result of the use, or by the structures to be used, or by the inaccessibility of the property or structures thereon for the convenient entry and operation of fire and other emergency apparatus, or by the undue concentration or assemblage of people upon such plot of land*'. That's quite a statement and as a result of looking this over, I have concerns that there is only one access road for Phase Two. There is no emergency access road that meets this criterion."

"Neither the Planning Board, the Director of Public Works, the Police Chief, or the Fire Chief found that a second access road is needed," said Tussi. "If and when one is needed, I think Baker Street could be used as an emergency access. That request isn't before this board, and I don't believe there is anything in the application referring to a secondary access."

"Is your proposal to have an emergency entrance connected to Baker Street?" asked Rachel.

"There are two possible connections," said Tussi. "An emergency road could be on Baker Street. Your Director of Public Works wanted Caring Home Services to convey some property to the town so there would be room for a cul-de-sac at the end of Baker Street. The other means of secondary access is the wetland crossing to the North Campus property. At this point, however, the Planning Board didn't feel that a secondary means of access is required, so there is not one in front of the board. The reason for having that option on the plan, even though the applicant is only asking for Phase Two approval, is because the Planning Board decided that even though they were only looking at Phase Two, they wanted to see the final layout of the entire project."

"Does the Planning Board feel that even with the completion of Phase Two, there only needs to be one road into the development and that there is no need for an emergency access?" asked Rachel.

"That's correct."

"I actually disagree with that," said Rachel.

"Two years ago when we came before the ZBA, we had two more apartments and this board didn't require a second means of access at that time," said Tussi. "If we had known the board wanted one then, I don't think the applicant would have had a problem with putting a second access on the plan for the board to consider."

"What a bunch of bunk that is," mumbled Nikki.

"The board has a lot more information on this project now," Rachel countered. "It's been stated that the changes to the site plans are minor. I've reviewed the changes. There are a lot of things presented here now that I didn't know about before concerning this project. It's the new information I'm considering as I vote on this project. I wouldn't be doing my job if I didn't consider what I have for review."

"Well said," whispered Sarah. "About time at least some of the board members are reading the information given them."

"I thought the information you're talking about is gathered through the public hearing process," said Dumas. "Did the board acquire this new information outside of the public hearing process?"

"The information was received by the town in late January," said Chairperson Bolduc. "It was also mailed directly to board members, which shouldn't have been done. The town's Code Enforcement Officer told the residents it was inappropriate to mail the information directly to the board members and that it had to be submitted properly through the Town Office. But that was after the fact."

"Mrs. Greene is saying that she is relying on this new information," said Dumas. "The Planning Board is not making the applicant go back to square one, but this board is. I think the board should ask the Town Attorney if it's correct to take in new information after the fact."

"The board doesn't take information just from the people doing the project; they also take information from others," said Rachel.

"This information was submitted without copies to everyone?" Dumas questioned.

"As I mentioned previously," said Bolduc, "the information was submitted to the town on the latter part of January and mailed to board members at the same time, when it shouldn't have been. But it was also presented in a public forum through the town, so it was available to anyone."

"Any information provided by someone other than the applicant," interjected the Code Enforcement Officer, "can be submitted five days prior to the meeting. Those are the rules. Mr. Tussi knows that."

"If an applicant wants to rely on the exact same application, you can go by the rules in the ordinance, but if you change anything, you are back to square one," said Bolduc.

Attorney Dumas was quick to respond. "The Planning Board doesn't go back to square one."

"It doesn't matter what the Planning Board does," said Bolduc.

"Returning to my question concerning Criteria Factor Nine," said Rachel, "which addresses the inaccessibility of the property. I want to reiterate that I have concerns about emergency access and also about the parking. For the second phase, the pedestrians would be walking right on the road, and there is no pedestrian connector. For the people driving into the complex and walking to their apartments, there is no connecting pedestrian walkway."

"There is a sidewalk shown on the plan," said Tussi.

"What about parking?" asked Rachel. "Are cars pulling directly into the road?"

"No. There are no parking spaces that back out into the

road."

"There apparently are two board members who believe the Ninth Criteria has not been met," said Bolduc. "I believe we've discussed the Ninth Criteria Factor enough, for now. Let's move onto the Tenth Criteria Factor as our time is limited. It states that consideration must be given to whether the use or structures to be used will cause an overcrowding of land or undue concentration of population. Several residents have said they feel this development will cause overcrowding and overuse of the property, and two board members have also said the same thing."

"I've noted wetland that is unbuildable has been included in the equation to get the eight units per acre," said Rachel.

"That is typically something that the Planning Board looks at," Allen Treble replied, "not the Zoning Board. Developers are required to provide the calculations of the entire land area and then are supposed to deduct the wetland area."

"That was done and reviewed by the Planning Board and is noted on the site plan," said Tussi. "I'm a wetland scientist licensed in the state of New Hampshire, and I've been recognized by the Army Corps of Engineers and the DEP since the early 90's. I surveyed and flagged the wetlands myself. I can't say all the blue flags I placed are still there, but when I located the wetlands and picked them up with a survey instrument, some of the flags were still there."

"Has the amount of unbuildable land been calculated and deducted from the acreage of the entire project?" Rachel questioned.

"Yes."

"Mr. Quip. Do you agree that it's been done?" asked Rachel, turning her head to look at Nelson.

Surprised that he was suddenly included in the conversation, Nelson said, "I believe the issue is still being discussed. The Planning Board was concerned about the amount of land-fill being used, and if that area was actually deducted from the calculations. So no, I don't think that's been done."

"Yes, it has," Kurt said, somewhat defiant and quick to respond. "The ordinance addresses the subject of 'fill being placed in the wetland'. We don't have that situation. Wetlands that have to be filled or drained to be built upon are not part of Phase Two."

"I asked you, Mr. Tussi, if *all* the unbuildable land has been deducted." Rachel directed her attention and strong reply to the man who spoke.

"The whole plan for the two parcels, North and South Campuses, minus the area not suitable for development, is two hundred and eight units, and the applicant is asking for approval of only forty-two units," said Kurt.

"That may be true," responded Rachel, "but eventually the developer will want to go to the entire two hundred and eight units."

"Yes, eventually."

Chairperson Bolduc spoke up. "Criteria Factor Eleven states that consideration must be given to whether the plot area is sufficient, appropriate, and adequate for the use, and reasonably anticipated for operation and expansion. This factor seems to be stating the same thing as Criteria Factor Ten, regarding crowding."

"The board has to be careful," said Michael Grady. "We're only supposed to be talking about Phase Two here. There's been discussion about the character of the land and taking the whole project into consideration."

"It's hard for me to divorce myself from the full scale of this project," said Rachel. "I know the board is only ruling on Phase Two. When the applicant first came before the board, they wanted approval for the whole thing. This board is supposed to be looking out for the good of the town as an end result of this project."

"This project is being done in increments," said Chairperson Bolduc, "so the board can allow a certain number and then stop it there. I don't have an issue with most of these criteria. The board has to decide if it's okay with these two phases or if it's overbuilt at that point. The board can't assume the applicant will get approvals for the remaining phases.

"Let's move on to the next factor, which is Criteria Factor Twelve. That factor states consideration is given to whether the proposed use will be adequately screened and buffered from contiguous properties. That isn't an issue at this point. Criteria Factor Thirteen discusses the assurance of adequate landscaping, grading, and provisions for natural drainage."

"I have a problem with that criteria," said Rachel.

"There's a lot of wetland on the property I'm concerned about, not only for Phase Two but for the additional phases as well. Mr. Tussi previously said that any development will take pervious soil and make it impervious with parking lots and buildings. Mr. Tussi also said a site like this is somewhat impervious on its own and when development takes place, the soil analysis numbers change."

"What are you getting at with this information?" asked Bolduc.

"The board is only looking at Phase Two," said Rachel, "and a lot of what is shown is getting into other phases which shouldn't be under consideration at this point. During public comments, Mr. Vaschon said the area for Phase Two construction is presently partial wetland; yet, it is not shown on the drawing as being a wetland. Mr. Tussi said it isn't true. He said taking a walk through there is not the only way to determine a wetland. He said it's based on hydric soil, vegetation, and wetland hydrology according to the ordinance. He also said the applicant is not proposing any impacts to the wetland, to include parking lots or buildings, and is not asking for a variance for setbacks."

"Are the future buildings going to be built on landfill?" asked Jane Emery.

"Yes," said Tussi.

"How many?"

"When this plan was previously discussed, the board granted this area to be built upon. The Planning Board suggested maintaining the natural ledge outcrop, so that's being done. Some of the parking lots and most of these buildings will be built on land removed or landfill added."

"Having read the Peer Review, I didn't think it was very flattering regarding this project," Rachel commented. "I wrote some notes, and it seems there was concern about the amount of landfill required, the setbacks from the wetlands not being met, and the wetland crossing. During which Phase is the wetland crossing being proposed to be done?"

"It's not part of Phase Two," said Tussi. "That crossing connects the North and South Campuses."

"I thought the town's Conservation Board told them to remove that option of constructing a bridge?" Sarah quietly asked Nelson.

"So did I," Nelson responded, shaking his head in disbelief from Kurt's announcement.

"What about the setbacks from wetlands not being met," asked Rachel. "It's only thirty feet in some cases versus the required one hundred feet."

"I believe all the setbacks have been met," Tussi answered.

"It seems as though these issues were brought up once before and then later addressed by the developer," said Rachel.

"Yes," said Kurt Tussi. "Some of the peer reviewers didn't understand the proposed decks were less than five hundred square feet and required a lesser setback. The issue with the wetland crossing was resolved. I've met with the Town Planner, Todd Hatch, on occasion in preparing for Planning Board meetings, and he said that the Peer Review Report didn't find one thing contrary to the project in terms of the zoning requirements, with the exception of the deduction of the nonbuildable area."

"Let's move on," said Bolduc. "I don't see where this board would have any issue with Criteria Factors Fourteen or Sixteen. Criteria Fourteen involves pedestrian circulation and Sixteen involves compliance with building performance standards. Criteria Factor Fifteen, however, states that consideration must be given as to whether the proposed use anticipates and eliminates potential nuisances created by a project's location."

"It appears there have been many issues that have not been anticipated," said Rachel, the tone of her voice noticeably heightened with emotion. "I understand *this* is a big project and there are a lot of back and forth discussions. I think we *all* agree that Factors Fourteen and Sixteen aren't relevant, but I don't feel Criteria Factor Fifteen has been met."

"*I agree*," Jane Emery emphasized.

"I understand what Mrs. Greene is saying, but I *don't* agree," Grady countered.

"I think we've discussed these Criteria Factors sufficient for a vote by this Board, said Bolduc, interrupting the Board members debate. You all appear to have already made some sort of decision on this matter. Let's vote."

V.

"Let me say one thing before this board votes," said Michael Grady. "If anyone came here tonight thinking this wasn't a hot topic, then they haven't been paying attention. Like everyone else in Laslo, I too have a strong opinion on whether I feel this development should be paying taxes, but that's not what the board is here to discuss. I have a strong opinion as to whether this should be classified as a non-profit, but that's not what the board is here for. I have a strong opinion on this entire project and whether I think it should be done or not, but that's not what the board is here for either. The board is here to approve Phase Two only. All that I ask of board members who are getting ready to vote is that they vote based upon these Sixteen Criteria Factors from the Land Use Ordinance Code and all that has been discussed tonight. In my opinion, the issues not affected by Phase Two should be forgotten at this point. I'm not even going to consider Phases Three, Four, Five, Six, or Seven, or that there is a twenty or thirty foot drop off in sections of the property requiring massive amounts of fill. The board can't overstep its bounds and not allow Phase Two to be built because Phase Seven doesn't look good. The board should only be looking at this smaller portion of this huge project. That's the board's job.

"With Mr. Grady's added summation, I believe it's time to vote upon this application," stated Bolduc once again. "Is there a motion from a board member?"

"I agree. I think we all have a definite idea as to how we should vote," said Rachel Greene. "Therefore, I move that the application from Caring Home Services requesting a special exception to the terms of Title 10, Section 14.060, Subsections E1 and E2 be approved for voting on Phase Two. That portion of the development includes forty-two units in four buildings: one large multiplex twenty-six unit building, two six-plex buildings consisting of twelve units and one four-plex building consisting of four units, accessed off Route 2, Map 2, Lot 35, in our town of Laslo, zoned as urban residence. If approval occurs, Construction shall be in accordance with the plan submitted and signed and dated by Caring Home Services, Incorporated and the ZBA Chairperson, Peter

Bolduc."

Michael Grady seconded the motion, and there was no further discussion. Nelson nervously watched the faces of each of the board members as they prepared to vote.

Bolduc raised his voice so the public in attendance could hear his statement to the board members. "All those *not* in favor of approving this special exception, please raise your hands."

Rachel Greene, Jane Emery, and Michael Grady all raised their hands in opposition to the special exception. Only Chairperson Bolduc raised his hand when he asked who was in favor.

Nelson witnessed Bolduc appearing surprised at the outcome of the vote and summarized the denial of the application with one curt statement.

"The applicant will receive written notice confirming the board's decision within one week. Note that the applicant or any interested party withstanding may appeal the decision of this board within forty-five days in Superior Court."

Attorney Dumas stood to face the board members. His face appeared flush in contrast to his black conservative suit, tie, and white beard.

"I believe this procedure was totally inappropriate under Maine law. Those Criteria Factors from Section 14.21.050 of the town's Land Use Ordinance Code should have been addressed and voted on individually before making a blanket vote. Case law is clear on that. I am asking that the board reconsider its vote until getting an opinion from the Town Attorney because the stakes are high in this matter."

Chairperson Bolduc appeared to be uninfluenced from the somewhat innocuous statement from Dumas, not bothering to provide a change to the decision.

"As I've already said, the applicant will receive the board's Findings of Fact statement regarding the results of this hearing within a week. The applicant, however, may stay until the end of the remaining public hearings when the board will assimilate its findings over each of the Criteria Factors. We will take another short recess and continue on to the next applicant. It's getting very late."

"Well, that went better than I thought it would, considering all the discussions," Nelson said to Sarah. He stood and donned his coat. "Even if Eleanor Adley had stayed and voted in favor, the board's vote would still have been three to two in opposition."

Joe Vaschon joined Nelson and Sarah as they left the meeting hall.

"I wonder what the Planning Board will do, now that the special exception for eight units per acre has essentially been reduced to four units per acre. The Zoning Board has basically denied them approval to build the number of units they want. There's still a Planning Board meeting scheduled for this week, and I'm not sure whether or not they're going to have an open meeting up for public discussion."

"Yeah, I know," said Nelson. "I'm not looking forward to another night of listening to scattered topic discussions."

"Did we win tonight?" asked Sarah.

"I'm not sure," Nelson answered.

It was late when they arrived home. Nelson moved over to the computer and turned it on while Sarah paid the sitter. She made sure the girl reached her car before closing the front door then looked over at him.

"What are you doing on the computer so late?"

"Thought I'd e-mail Maxwell and complete another chapter of the book. I just wanted to write down a bit about tonight's outcome while it's still fresh on my mind."

E-mail: Feb. 21
To: Mdraper
From: NelsonQuip
Subject: Zoning Board Hearing This Time

Max,

I've got a little more of our story put together. I'll include tonight's hearing as a chapter and send it to you in the regular mail. Perhaps you can mark it up with any comments you might have.

I was somewhat surprised about the information you previously e-mailed me, about the increase in centrifuges at Natanz. That news story was actually confirmed this month. I read about it in the New York Times. Kind of weird that you mentioned it in your e-mail of Jan 16th, last month, before I ever saw it in the news. This nuclear program itch that Iran wants to scratch is somewhat troubling.

The ZBA has denied the developer a special exception, but there's still a Planning Board hearing scheduled in a couple of days. You'll read about it in the chapter I'll be sending. Right now, I'm not exactly sure where we stand on this.

My best,
–Nelson.

vi.

Nelson stepped out of his car and twisted his face away from the caustic, biting wind of a cold February night. As he did so, he caught Nikki Williams' conversation with Joe and Mary Vaschon as they stood at the front entrance to the town hall.

"What in the hell are we doing here tonight for another Planning Board hearing?" she asked as he approached. Nelson could tell she was apparently and justifiably frustrated with the never-ending public hearings. "I thought the ZBA already denied the application for these guys."

She wasn't the only one, Nelson thought to himself.

"So did I," Joe said as he lowered his head to rebuff the cold winter wind. "I thought we'd be done with this. If they can't build eight units per acre by getting an exclusion from the ZBA, then I would assume that changes everything they're proposing. In other words, it will cost them more per apartment. I haven't got a clue as to why they're still proceeding with the Planning Board."

"Neither does the Planning Board," added Mary in a sarcastic tone. "Even though this meeting was scheduled the same week of the ZBA hearing, I thought it would have been canceled."

"Is this an open public hearing tonight?" asked Joe.

"How the hell would we know," replied Nikki. "We're only the abutters. They don't tell us anything, and besides, I don't think they know themselves."

"I'm hoping they'll allow some public discourse," commented Nelson. "Either way, we need to find out what's being said tonight."

Same old uncomfortable metal chairs, Nelson thought to

himself as he entered the public hearing room and felt the outside chill dissolve into the crowded room. Once everyone was in their perspective seats, the chairperson called the meeting to order.

"There will be no open public discussion tonight," stated the Chairperson, "only open dialogue with the applicant."

With an agreeable nod from the chairperson, Kurt Tussi was the first to address the board members.

"I was hoping to come before this Planning Board tonight, seeking final approval after having achieved approval for the special exception from the Zoning Board of Appeals. Unfortunately, that did not occur, as I'm sure you all know by now. I think this board, however, should still consider approving this plan. The original approval from the ZBA two years ago from this past December still stands. We've been caught in a little bit of a bind where the ZBA approved one plan, and that plan evolved into a slightly different one. Please note that I've made the changes this board has requested after your approval, and would be glad to go through the changes with this board."

"The board needs to discuss the procedural issue first, Mr. Tussi," said Chairperson Tunney, "before getting into the nitty-gritty. Is the plan before us tonight also the one that was before the ZBA this week?"

"It's very similar. The ZBA plan had the same layout, but didn't have corrections to the site plan's notes on it."

"Are the number of buildings and units the same?"

"The ZBA has what this board saw a month ago."

"Mr. Tussi was before the Zoning Board of Appeals to get approval on the changes," said Todd Hatch.

"Let me clarify that," said Kurt. "The plan the ZBA initially approved had forty-four units in five buildings. The Plan in front of them earlier this week had forty-two units in four buildings, which is the same one that has been before *this* board for a while now."

"This board doesn't have the benefit of the Findings of Fact statement from that ZBA meeting, so we're at a bit of a disadvantage," said Todd.

"What issues were raised at that meeting?" asked Drew Laden, his mouth chewing his gum at a fervent pace, augmented by a constantly moving mustache.

"We don't redo what another board does," Tunney declared.

"We don't know *what* they did?" countered Drew.

Brett Manley said, "It would be nice to know what they did. If they didn't like something, then we could ask to change that. It's hard to go forward with this meeting without reading the minutes of the ZBA hearing."

"I think they talked about it for an hour or more with no decision," Tunney replied.

Nikki was sitting directly in back of Nelson and Sarah, and in an underlying breath, asked, "Where did he dig that out of, his ass?"

Joe, sitting next to Nikki, tapped Nelson on the shoulder and asked, "Don't these people read the newspaper or talk with other board members before they attend their meetings? This has got to be the most disjointed group I've ever listened to."

Don Morgan slicked his hair back with one hand as he spoke. "Mr. Tunney, in all due respect, based on the local newspaper report, which I read, there *was* a decision. They didn't approve it."

"I guess that doesn't make any difference," said Tunney. "The applicant is still asking us to deliberate and move ahead with the process. Where there has been a denial of the special exception, there is an approval from the year before. Mr. Tussi says the approval is still good. Is he right about that?"

"This board, as well as the Department of Environmental Protection, has asked for changes to their plans," said Brett. "Mr. Tussi thinks the time clock stopped while he was waiting for answers from the DEP."

"I'd like to know if Mr. Tussi actually had to go back to the ZBA at all," said Chairperson Tunney. "If he had already been before them and received a special exception, was he back before them because we told him to do so?"

"I was under the impression from the ZBA that we had to go back because of changes to the plan," said Kurt. "We've gone through this whole process, and my client has spent a couple hundred thousand dollars doing that. It's a tough and unusual process. It is not something I've been through with other towns. All plans change. It's tough to believe that the ZBA gets two cracks at it, and the applicant can end up walking away with nothing."

"Is there legally an outstanding issue at this time for the applicant?" asked Elaine Graft.

Chairperson Tunney said, "Right now there is."

"The Land Use Code Ordinance states that the ZBA rules first," said Don. "Originally, we've said among ourselves that this project was likely to be approved by the ZBA. Now we've learned something different. I think it changes the basis upon which we look at it. I don't see how we can do any more on this right now."

"I think one of the reasons that people on the Zoning Board of Appeals ruled against it was because of the property tax issue," said Brett. "And we can't resolve that. I also think the ZBA matter has to be resolved before we can go on."

"The applicant is entitled to have a decision. If the applicant is asking us to proceed, do we have the grounds to say we are not going to?" asked Chairperson Tunney.

"I don't think we can discuss this issue tonight, because I would like to see what the ZBA did," Brett stated. "The applicant can ask us to move forward, but I want to look at the ZBA minutes and see if there is anything in there that affects our decision. I agree with the applicant that this has been difficult. I'm just not ready to do anything tonight."

"I'm here to represent the applicant." Attorney Dumas stood and thoughtfully stroked his white beard, somewhat defiantly. He paused to consider his next words. "This is an eventful, very emotional issue. For instance, the tax exempt status of this project is irrelevant to both boards. I can understand why Mr. Manley wants to read a copy of the ZBA minutes. However, the basic legal point is that the positions of the Zoning Board and Planning Board are not linked. Obviously, this board has the right to review those minutes. It was about traffic and being too dense. If there was a consensus that this board could move forward subject to getting the ZBA minutes, that would be acceptable."

"I think we need the ZBA minutes and the time to review them," Drew reaffirmed.

"Waivers for sidewalk completion extend back several years and are temporarily in place for the purpose of the original Phase One South Campus development," said Elaine. I think sidewalks are supposed to be completed. Would we need to have another sidewalk waiver?"

Nelson quickly looked at Sarah with disbelief at the abrupt change in the discussion and shook his head. *More disjointed ramblings*, he thought.

Chairperson Tunney said, "Waivers were allowed, but should we be allowing waivers at this juncture?"

"Well, because they were temporary waivers, I thought that they were to be provided now," said Elaine. "What do you think, Mr. Tussi?"

"I don't know," said Kurt. "I thought that sidewalks were to be completed during Phase Two. When we proceed beyond deliberation, the first thing to look at are the waivers."

"Does this board think that time should be devoted tonight to go over the changes?" asked Tunney. "If we don't stay up to speed, I think it will be much more difficult to be sure we cover everything."

Nelson could hear Nikki as she muttered to Joe. "I don't think this board is thinking at all!"

"We need a clear list of items to review the next time we meet," said Drew. "Then we can check off the items as they're discussed and approved."

"We already have waivers for erosion control and road length," said Tunney. "We need an additional one for a revised grading and site plan and entrance plan. There is also a package from Mr. Nelson Quip in our discussion packets that addresses several issues. Has the town planner provided Mr. Tussi with that package?"

"Yes, I have, Mr. Tunney, and Mr. Tussi has given a copy of that package to their attorney, Mr. Dumas."

"It looks to me like the cluster development calculations are correct," said Tunney.

"Absolutely, Mr. Chairperson. They're right on," said Tussi.

"I agree with that assessment," said Todd Hatch.

"Mr. Tussi," said Brett, "would you change the name of the site plan from 'Phase Two' to 'Current Expansion'?

"I'll do whatever the board's pleasure is."

"Yeah, I bet he will," muttered Nikki from the back of the room, just loud enough for Nelson to hear.

"I'm not sure I want you to do that," said Tunney.

"Future expansions could be labeled as such," said Drew. "It is less clear when they are called different phases."

"Then what do we do about the notes on the plans that repeatedly refer to phases?" asked Elaine.

"I think it's clear that we are not approving anything other than Phase Two," said Tunney.

"I think we may want to add in the notes that this is not a phased project as defined by the Laslo Land Use Code," Brett added.

"I'll put that on the site plan as a note," Tussi responded.

"I'm not sure it's important that we say how the project will develop," said Drew. "We could just say that expansions are anticipated on the plan."

"Well, I think that we want specifics on the plan," said Brett.

"I want to get rid of the specifics and terminology phases," said Drew.

Brett countered. "I would like to see the details as to what they are actually proposing."

"So would I," Sarah whispered to Nelson. "I also wish they'd stick to one subject at a time," she added. "Perhaps it's just a tactic in keeping us confused."

"If that's what they're trying to do," replied Nelson, "then I think it might be working."

"If the applicant moves ahead with this in the future, I think there are things that may affect the future plans, such as traffic counts," said Tunney. "Does the board want to address this at all? I know we have addressed it before, and it was raised before the ZBA."

"I think the last time we concluded the traffic count issue was a matter of design standards," said Drew. "We as a board do not have an issue about the traffic count being used. There was a side discussion on this."

"I want to know if those counts are really reflective of this type of retirement community," said Brett.

Don Morgan added to Brett's comment. "I'd like to review the document upon which Mr. Tussi relies."

"The latest edition of the ITE standards reduced that traffic count number somewhat," said Tussi.

"Do you have the exact table of the traffic impact study?" asked Don. "I'd like to review the ITE definitions and understand the associated charts in order to make a decision. We don't currently have that information."

"If we agree with that number, then they don't need a second entrance at this juncture," said Drew.

"The limit is over two hundred trips per day," said Don.

"Does the facility have a van?" asked Chairperson Tunney.

Kurt Tussi glanced over to Phil Dwyer. He quickly and softly replied, "No. We use the Oxford County Van Service."

"We need several pieces of information for discussion," said Tunney. "They include the minutes from the ZBA, the waiver for sidewalks, and the ITE standards chart. I think Mr. Quip has summarized his points very well in the information package he provided to this board."

"The applicant may want to elaborate on the cluster stuff and on what will be left as open space," said Brett. "We've exceeded our time for this evening. Therefore, I make a motion to continue a public hearing for Caring Home Services at another date scheduled by the Town Planner."

Don said, "I second that motion."

"All in favor?" asked Tunney.

The vote was unanimous and the meeting was abruptly adjourned.

"So where do we stand now?" Sarah asked as they left the town hall.

"I have no idea," replied Nelson. "I have no idea."

Chapter Thirteen

Area 52

L

It was just before midnight when Maxwell arrived home. An old faded tan and maroon Ford Bronco sat in the driveway. Alex had arrived home for a one-week semester break from a college in Boston. It was mid-March.

As Max drove up the driveway, he noticed the lights were still on in the house. He was glad he would have the chance to welcome his son home for a few days, and sorry he couldn't have gotten home sooner to provide a warmer welcome.

"Hi, Prof," Alex exuberantly exclaimed when Max walked into the house. Prof was his son's short rendition for Dad he used periodically, and to show his esteem for his father's academics. They were very much alike and very close to each other, especially since Alex's mother had died when he was barely in his teens. His son always had an active interest in what he did and became quite skilled in mathematics and electronics—probably because Max always involved Alex with projects that challenged him.

Their largest combined effort was the construction of a thirty by sixty-foot metal arched building that looked very much like a Quonset hut. They jokingly called it Area 52, because it looked like something out of a science-fiction movie. It was the five-meter satellite dish they had converted into a radio telescope antenna that made the outside of the building stand out from the surrounding trees.

Together they had also assembled a radio transmitter and a receiver, tuned to the 1420 megacycle bandwidth so they could listen to the constant radio signals from space. Alex called their combined efforts a 'geek' sort of thing, listening for ET.

"Sorry I'm so late in getting home. Slow progress at the lab today."

"I figured that. I know you've been immersed in your work lately. I do read all those e-mails you send to me."

"How's your graduate program going?"

"Busy—just like you. But I try to get out and do some other things besides bookwork. I've been running early mornings. It helps with both the mental and physical cobwebs. Did you know the Boston Marathon is next month? I'm actually thinking about participating."

"I'm not sure if that's a good idea, Alex. There's been an increasing amount of media news and e-mail traffic regarding terrorist groups overseas. We also received a disturbing radio broadcast from one our lab's satellites about a terrorist attack in Boston. There was no date mentioned, and I haven't been able to substantiate that report with any news outlets. We can talk about some of the things I've been experimenting with tomorrow.

"While I'm at work, check out the extra communication lines I've added to Area 52. I'll do my best to come home earlier than this. I want to show you some of the things I've been working on as well as the communication signals I've been tracking and documenting. Results are a bit puzzling, or perhaps I should say disturbing. Meanwhile, we better get some rest."

ii.

It was mid-afternoon when Maxwell arrived home; earlier than the day before, as he had promised. He found Alex in Area 52, standing at the workbench against the far back wall, hovering over three computer servers. Alex paused from reading a fist full of news reports and turned to face him, a troubled look on his face.

"Dad, what are all these printouts about?"

"Those are what I wanted to discuss with you. Most of what you're holding was obtained directly from newspaper articles. Some were obtained from other sources, like the internet. And several of them were received from retransmitted radio broadcasts from one of our satellites, Turing-B. Those printouts from the satellite contain the disturbing events I mentioned yesterday—information slightly different from what was originally transmitted—information about events that haven't yet occurred. To try and help us understand the information we received, Dora categorized, correlated, and sequenced events by date and time. It seems as if the satellite keyed on certain words in a radio broadcast sent to it then transmitted a later and updated version."

"That's interesting. How does Dora explain the broadcast differences?" asked Alex.

"She hasn't been able to," Maxwell replied. "It's the first time I've ever seen her stymied, almost perplexed."

"Sounds like you're working her too hard these days. How *is* she?" asked Alex.

"Except for not understanding this time paradox issue, she's doing just fine; always such a huge help at the lab. We couldn't operate without her. *You* know *that*. But getting back to those reports you're holding. There are a lot of things people simply don't know about. Many of the major national news outlets either miss important stories, simply ignore them, or just don't pursue them in great enough detail. I don't understand why—well, perhaps I do. In many instances issues aren't covered very well, simply because of partisan politics."

"What do you mean by that, Dad?"

"Well, as an example, did you know our Secretary of State allowed the approval of the sale of a Canadian company that controls about twenty percent of the uranium mines' operational reserve capacities in the United States to be sold to Russia? There is at least a connection between certain donations, I don't need to say where, and resultant official actions that allowed the deal to occur. The Russians gradually assumed control of a company called Uranium One in three separate transactions over a period of about five years. The mined ore is processed to leach out the uranium, which is a first step toward the enrichment process, and the yellow cake produced by the process is exported out of the country to who knows where; probably being sold as future nuclear reactor material to Iran. The Secretary of State helped such a deal by not opposing it. There were insinuations of wrongdoing and quid-pro-quo situations with her political foundation funding. Major news reports, however, didn't spend a lot of time discussing either of those issues. Of course, there were other agencies involved with the Uranium One sale, as well, like the Secretary of Defense and the Secretary of the Treasury. And now that we have a new Secretary of State, there are foreboding rumblings of a so-called nuclear deal with Iran called the Joint Comprehensive Plan of Action. It's just one of many things that I fear will lead to unanticipated problems."

"Prof, is any of this stuff considered classified?"

"Apparently not, since it appears some of Dora's past information came from the former Secretary of State's own home server. Dora's never been sure that such information is entirely legal, particularly the 'Select Access Program' e-mails. Those e-mails on that home server had a higher classification than Top Secret, and Dora hasn't been able to gain direct access to that type of classified material from any other government agencies. But even though we were previously allowed access, which we aren't anymore, it appears there still may have been negligent treatment of national security information.

"I had a Secret clearance when I worked directly for the Department of Defense many years ago. We weren't allowed to work at home on lesser classified material, let alone SAP material. I would have been behind bars for doing something like that. Even though it's in direct violation of government regulations, I guess it depends on who you are. It makes me worry though about how many entities have had access to such classified material. I assure you that any FBI investigation will conclude it was only careless handling of information, disallowing any legal charges or concern of material content. There may be no proof as to the intent to subvert, but such actions are still gross negligence and therefore should be accountable to the requisite requirements and statute of the law.

"Keep in mind, the messages we've received from Turing-B seem to be more time sensitive than the events mentioned in those SAP e-mails. I refer to them as time-dilated events that have been consolidated from the results of our own data analysis. And I've been reviewing the metadata linked from the lab at work using the servers which you and I had previously connected here in Area 52."

"So, what's the story on that wayward satellite of yours?" Alex asked. He looked at the framed image of the earth taken by the Voyager One spacecraft hanging on the opposite wall, entitled The Pale Blue Dot of Earth.

"Let me give you a little summary background on what we've been working on at the lab," said Maxwell. "Some of this, you may already know. Over the last two decades we've been building a particle accelerator similar to the Large Hadron Collider, only much larger, more than double the size, in order to produce new particles of greater mass. One of our experiments is similar to the ATLAS program, which stands for 'A Toroidal LHC ApparatuS'. It's designed to be a general-purpose detector in order to observe phenomena that involve highly massive particles. As a reminder, our detector is much larger than the one at CERN. The accelerator collides two beams of protons together, each carrying enough energy to produce particles with more mass. The large detector detects those particles, their masses, their energies, and other data. When proton beams produced by the accelerator interact in the center of the detector, a broad range of energies are produced by different particles."

"What would happen if you had multiple beams? I mean like around two thousand or so. If they were just under a millimeter in diameter, the number of those beams could cover a five foot circular area of the detector. What would happen if all those beams came together at the same time?"

"It would take an enormous amount of energy, and the collisions would have to occur at the same time," said Maxwell.

"What if each one of those collisions caused a miniature black hole? What would happen collectively or if you were to put your hand into such a collection of beams?"

"Good questions, Alex, ones I can't answer. Are you alluding to creating a wormhole at the detector end? If so, that could be catastrophic. There would be no way to control the massive gravity effects—like putting a black hole into your living room. But let's get back to your question about our wayward satellite.

"Two satellites were sent out several years ago before I began to work at the lab: Sagittarius-A and Turing-B. They were sent toward what we believe is a supermassive black hole in the middle of our galaxy. Sagittarius-A is on its projected course. Turing-B, however, somehow strayed far from its original course. It appears it was captured by the intense gravity of what we believe to be another black hole; one we weren't aware of. The event horizon it approaches might be considered as a traversable wormhole. I don't believe there is any other explanation for the immense gravity deflections we are detecting. We're studying the time dilation affect. As gravity increases, we are observing differences in original radio broadcast transmissions. That's the information I've been gathering in those reports you're reading. I've been sending a lot of that information with my comments to Nelson Quip. You remember him, don't you?"

"Yeah, he's been a great friend over the years. Was at Mom's funeral. That's when I first met him. He even came up to help us build this complex, metal arches and all."

"We've been kind of writing a book together about people's inattention to events that happen around them. He has been trying to save a forest from being overdeveloped and has been attending public hearings. By doing so, he's found that people don't always understand or confront the consequences of inveterate lies. What he has encountered is similar to the deliberate obfuscation of national policy information to the general public I have observed from news media outlets and from comparing satellite radio transmissions. There are definite analogies to what Nelson and I have both been experiencing. Once he completes his manuscript, I'll direct him to a publisher who I believe will be interested."

Chapter Fourteen

Reconsideration and Retrial

L

Nelson stepped out of his car into the blustery blast of cold, frigid March night air. The scattered snow showers dispatched heavy wet flakes that settled on the top of his thinning hair and added to his awareness of the damp chilled night.

"What a night to have to attend another one of these meetings," he mumbled to Sarah. "I'm glad you saw the notice in the newspaper about a Zoning Board of Appeals meeting tonight," he added. "Otherwise, we wouldn't have known. They never bothered sending us a notice. We got their conclusions from the last meeting so I figured, or should I say hoped, there wouldn't be another meeting on this."

"Someone must have pressured the ZBA into having an additional meeting," she said.

Concentrating on the black ice beneath his feet, Nelson glanced up barely in time to see a person frantically running toward him. The reduced lighting made it difficult at first for him to recognize who it was. He watched Eleanor Adley approach, running, slipping, sliding, and bending forward, quickly stepping from side to side as if trying to avoid the cascading snowflakes. It was then he realized she was chasing a wig, her helmet hair, a name conferred by Millie Hodgdon, the sweet old boisterous lady who lived on Baker Street. An unexpected gust of the night's turbulent weather must have removed her helmet before she could enter the town hall. With a modicum of indifference, Nelson tried to retain his composure as her wig came spindling and trundling past him, as if a small mad dog had gotten away from its owner. He tried to snatch it from the slushy ground, but was too late. On it went, carried by an indifferent wind.

Eleanor sped past him with a surprising sprint of rapaciousness, finally stopping the furry escapee by grasping a few of the longer strands of hair caught by the cold dense slush. It was an interesting start to the evening, and Nelson wondered if further surprises were to follow. *That is probably going to be the best part of my evening,* he thought. With a smirk, he entered the town hall and sat down just as the hearing was called to order by Chairperson Bolduc.

"We're here tonight because I've received a letter from Attorney Dumas who represents Caring Home Services. He has requested a motion for reconsideration regarding our previous decision to deny their request for a special exception in terms of Title 10, Section 14.060, Subsections E.1 and E.2.

"I want everyone to know that the only people who can vote on this reconsideration are those who voted upon it at the last meeting when it was denied."

The chairperson looked toward his left, directly at Eleanor Adley, who had just managed to arrive at her seat, and added, "That means, Mrs. Adley, you cannot vote on this tonight."

Nelson looked at the chairperson and smiled slightly upon hearing his comment to Mrs. Adley, satisfied she wouldn't be voting. His smile broadened upon noticing her hair was slightly askew to one side before she quickly straightened it.

"A reconsideration is usually requested by a board member who voted against an appeal and has had a change of heart," continued the chairperson. "In this case, the applicant requesting the reconsideration has to present new evidence that couldn't have been presented before the vote was made, for whatever reason."

"I didn't vote on this application," said Eleanor as she swabbed her wet helmet hair with a scarf, "but I'd like to make comments whenever it's appropriate."

"Is this board being asked to approve this project tonight or just if we'll reconsider a vote?" asked Michael Grady.

"In the past," said Bolduc, "this board's procedure has been not to spend the time at a hearing unless one board member moves to have a reconsideration because of new evidence. I'd like to know if any board members who voted in the negative want to do this. I don't believe there is any sense in scheduling this hearing again and spending hours on it unless there is something new that couldn't have been submitted the first time."

"Has someone asked for this to be reheard?" asked Rachel Greene.

"Yes," Bolduc answered. "As I've already stated, the reason for reconsideration tonight was contained in a request submitted by CHS's attorney.

"Can this be done if the plan changes?" Rachel questioned.

"A developer can come back to the board with a changed plan, but it wouldn't be heard as a reconsideration," said Bolduc. "The board needs to determine what process it wants to follow. Whether they want to ask questions tonight or read the application that has been resubmitted and decide if they will hear this at the next meeting. The board can ask questions tonight to help determine what the new evidence or argument is that wasn't presented before and why it wasn't presented. If there is nothing new that couldn't have been presented the first time, then I don't want to spend hours hearing it."

Nelson watched a smartly dressed woman sitting next to Phil Dwyer stand. With a soft, melodic voice she announced, "I'm Nancy Stacy, Mr. Chairperson. I'm an attorney and will be filling in for Mr. Dumas who couldn't be here tonight. I'll be speaking on behalf of Caring Home Services. As a point of order, it has been stated that only those who voted at the February meeting can vote on a motion to entertain a reconsideration. I would ask that everyone be allowed to vote on whether or not to entertain the motion for reconsideration. The discussion will be stacked against my client if not everyone votes on the motion."

"Mrs. Adley recused herself from that hearing," said Bolduc. "You can't have someone who didn't decide on the previous merits become involved with the reconsideration issue. Section 16.46.080 involving review procedures stipulates that the rulings by the chairperson shall prevail in such instances. Since Mrs. Adley recused herself from the vote in February, she cannot reconsider a vote she never made."

"If there is a rehearing, the entire board should participate," said Eleanor.

"If the board decides to reconsider a hearing and we vote

upon conducting a new hearing, you will be able to vote at that time," replied Bolduc.

"There was also some discussion as to whether the board should even entertain this," said Stacy "Have the board members had the opportunity to review Attorney Dumas' letter?"

"The *voting* board members have received it," Bolduc replied.

"It's not in my packet," declared Eleanor.

"The point is there's a threshold that has to be met before the board can have another hearing," said Bolduc, shaking his head in frustration and ignoring Adley's comment. "There has to be something new to get to that point."

"Those reasons are outlined in Mr. Dumas' letter," said Stacy. "I would welcome the opportunity to make my points."

Bolduc looked at the other board members. When no objections were heard, he said, "Proceed."

She moved to the podium to address the board members directly.

"My first point is that in the board's denial, the members did not, as required by the Land Use Code ordinance, specifically Section 14.21.050, vote upon each of the sixteen Factor Criteria that should be considered," said Stacy. "There was limited discussion and case law says that each and every criterion should be considered."

"It seems clear to me that if the board was wrong on those points, the State of Maine superior court would rehear it as an appeal," said Bolduc. "That's not a basis for a new hearing, but it could be for a reconsideration in order to confirm a decision."

"My second point is that a special exception was granted for Phase Two in December, two years ago," said Stacy. "It's my position that the special exception was granted and that the board should not have undertaken a new review. Any review on the second application should have been limited to those minor changes that the Planning Board made to the application. I am raising the issue of whether there was a requirement for Caring Home Services to come back before this board the second time around. The ordinance states that once a special exception has been granted, it expires within six months if work hasn't started and that work must be substantially completed within one year. There's a provision in

Section 14.21.040.K which holds that expiration period pending DEP and Planning Board review."

"That issue was addressed at the last meeting," said Bolduc. "The site plan itself changed and that's why it needed to come back to the board for review."

"Where is that stated in the board's findings and conclusions?" asked Eleanor. "The findings of fact and conclusions from that hearing are inadequate. The findings are connected in no way, shape, or form to the conclusions. The conclusions aren't supported by the findings. Every finding has to be related to a conclusion and vice versa."

"She sounds like one of their attorneys," Sarah whispered to Nelson.

"The board's decision can be appealed and we can go through that rigmarole, but the point of this motion is to reconsider and prevent all that," said Stacy.

"Sounds like the board's being threatened with legal action if they don't approve everything," Nelson said to Sarah's comment.

"The new evidence is that in addition to the procedural things I've mentioned, there are substantive issues that need to be addressed. The applicant made its case and people had the opportunity to speak in opposition, but there was no opportunity to rebut those objections. In conjunction with the motion to reconsider were two documents submitted by Mr. Tussi of Tussi Engineering and Architecture in response to the concerns raised. The applicant didn't have the opportunity to respond with respect to traffic and decreased property values. The applicant would like to be able to address those substantive issues. I know that tonight's hearing is not the proper form in which to do that. This meeting is just for the board to decide whether or not to entertain a motion for reconsideration. Mr. Tussi can give the board a recap of the material submitted with this request."

As CHS's attorney returned to her seat, Kurt Tussi stood and addressed the board members. "This project has had six special exceptions approved by the board over the last ten years for both the North and South campuses. I don't believe the applicant is asking the board to approve something so completely farfetched that it doesn't qualify for a special exception. You must remember this development has been approved by the ZBA several times in the past.

"Mrs. Greene was emphatic that the reason she didn't feel she should approve the special exception was because she had all this new information from the abutters. I hadn't provided a response to that information. In retrospect, if I had it to do over again, I would have addressed all of Mrs. Greene's concerns brought up by the abutters and would have gone through the sixteen Criteria Factors. I felt this application was the same as the others, so I didn't do that.

"My recent letter to this board answers every one of the points brought up by the abutters. I believe this is new information for the board to consider. I have presented documents that have been prepared by professionals. They include comments from the DEP, the Maine Historical Preservation, and a traffic report from a traffic engineer. I think the board has to give that information more consideration than that supplied by the abutters, since that is what these professionals do for a living."

"And we're just 'chopped liver' I suppose," mumbled Nikki sitting directly behind Nelson.

"If the board wants to take a site walk," Kurt continued, "I would be glad to do that. I think the board needs to reconsider this information and hear every one of the technical issues from the applicant as well as the abutters and then make a decision."

"I keep hearing about what this board has approved," responded Michael Grady. "I haven't approved anything. The last time this issue was before this board was the first time I heard an appeal for this project. I don't care what the board did before that. I take extreme exception to some of the wording in your letter, Mr. Tussi, such as 'hurried discussion' and 'never discussed different parts of this'. During these deliberations, this board has had to extend the discussions several times. On those nights, it seemed like we were here forever. I've taken notes in my journal for every single point discussed the night we made our last decision. The board talked it into the ground, and if someone says the board didn't talk about it, they weren't here. Someone may not agree with what the board did, but they aren't right to say the board brushed over anything.

"Your letter also talks about ex-parte contact having occurred. You know, the idea of talking to outside interested parties. Everyone talks to everyone about everything all the time no matter what, and you don't say to someone, leave me alone, don't talk to me. People will come up to board members and give us their opinion on what should happen. I have heard from abutters that this is the worst thing to happen to our town, and I have also heard from people wondering where their parents might go to live. I don't think your statement about talking to other people has any merit with our decision on this.

"You also have a paragraph in your letter about Mrs. Adley leaving the hearing and saying it was a mean-spirited proceeding. The board hadn't even really started deliberations when she left. At that point, the board was just listening to what was going on. Discussion was very spirited on both sides, with the abutters not wanting this, and with the people living in the apartments of CHS wanting it. Since the board hadn't even started discussions at that point, I don't know what was mean-spirited.

"I do agree with Chairperson Bolduc about new evidence. The abutters brought up a lot of issues, and the people from Tussi Engineering, as well as Caring Home Services, were blind-sided by the volume of information presented. Your letter addresses those concerns, and perhaps that's sufficient justification to re-look at this. There are a lot of questions but not answers, such as the access road and why the trip counts kept being changed. If the applicant has a real answer that it didn't have at the last meeting, then maybe this is worth looking at. I didn't vote for this project because there were too many questions that weren't answered."

"From what I am hearing, Mr. Tussi is saying that from his perspective, there is a process that must be followed," said Rachel. "For the most part, the professionals who propose these developments have an advantage. Mr. Tussi said this project has previously received several approvals. However, the opponents of this development were well organized at the last meeting. There was a lot of emotion, and there were issues the applicant didn't fully address. Professionals can attempt to provide explanations, but where does the truth lie? It depends. I don't have a lot of sympathy for a developer who hasn't provided sufficient responses in order to receive approval for additional changes. They have resources such as time, money, and lawyers that give them the upper hand. It was the people in the neighborhood who got organized and worked hard. For once, I question the fairness of the strongest team losing and now saying it isn't fair; they want a chance to answer everything their opponents brought up. I disagree with Mr. Grady that it's fair for the developer to get another chance. There are a lot of unanswered questions. There was a lot of emotion and people maybe saying things that weren't true because they were talking about what's going on in their backyard, but you can't ignore the momentum of so many people coming together. The developer had its chance."

"It's difficult to answer your remarks," said Tussi. "This board approved the construction of Phase Two in December, two years ago. My client was seeking Department of Environmental Protection approval and that was received. We then went to the Planning Board and the plan was changed in terms of parking and a reduction in the number of units. This board heard those changes and denied the plan. I'm not asking for approval of the special exception today, but to give the applicant a chance to provide information to counter the abutters' concerns, as we have done with the Planning Board. The board can then make its decision."

"This is the second time I've heard an appeal," said Rachel. "The first time, it was lopsided in the applicant's favor. There was not as much organized information available as there was the last time around. I approved it back then, but I had major concerns. The applicant originally asked for approval of everything, but the board just approved one phase. I don't think it's fair to go back and do this all over again.

"The abutters were here for many hours, listening to the applicant who had a lot of people here in suits who knew their stuff, as well as the people who live in CHS's apartments who love the place where they live. They all talked about it. I think the applicant got a fair hearing. I would not vote to reconsider because I feel that the board really heard all of it last time. It was not an easy decision for me, and I was aggressive with my concerns. This is a huge development, and for the applicant to say they have been blindsided by organized opposition who are concerned with the scope of such a project is foolish.

A developer coming forward with something the size of this project has to be prepared for opposition."

"I think *we have* been prepared," said Kurt Tussi. "The one thing that wasn't agreed upon was the trip counts.

"Mr. Tussi stated the changes made to their plans were per the order of the Planning Board," said Michael. "They weren't voluntary changes made by the developer."

"Some of the changes were the applicant's changes and some were in response to abutter's concerns," said Tussi.

"My main concerns were the traffic, the length of the one road cul-de-sac requiring a waiver, and the lack of a second access road to the property," said Jane Emery. I think these can be solved by a traffic study. Another concern is when the board approved this two years ago, there was only one abutter here who was somewhat interested in what was happening. One of my statements at that meeting was that I would not approve all the phases because I was interested and concerned about the impact that phase would have on the abutters. At the last meeting on this project, this public hearing room was full. That's very telling. There was great concern amongst the abutters about property value and high density. I think the developer has had an opportunity over the last year to think about what is happening to the neighborhood and to consider if this is what the neighborhood wants to happen. I'm tired of some of the rhetoric, and I don't want to hear any more arguments. This board sat here at the last hearing for over three hours listening to the banter back and forth. I think we've heard enough until more studies are done."

"We only have four voting members tonight but that number qualifies as a quorum. Under those conditions we need at least two board members to vote in favor to rehear it," said Bolduc.

"The applicant is asking the board to revisit this," said Michael. "The board's findings contained the reasons why the board said no. If the developer has new evidence that refutes it, can't they just reapply?"

"No, not for the same thing," replied Chairperson Bolduc. "There would have to be substantive changes. According to the Land Use Ordinance Code, the board can't hear the same application within a year."

Turning to face the Code Enforcement Officer, the chairperson asked, "Mr. Treble, when is the board's next scheduled meeting?"

"In another three weeks from tonight, in the beginning of April."

"Thank you, Mr. Treble." He looked at his fellow board members. "So, if we vote to reconsider the previous decision, the hearing will be scheduled at our next available date in April."

"Does everyone feel as though it's fair to put the abutters through this again?" asked Rachel. "Is it fair to have all these people put aside another night, plus all the organizing they have done? Is it fair to ask them to do that?"

"I don't think it's a matter of what's fair to anyone," Chairperson Bolduc replied. "The issue is whether or not there's something that was not presented before that may have changed the vote. I don't care who it puts out: the little guy, the big guy. I'm more concerned with fairness. I personally don't really want to hear this again. I would rather have the applicant appeal the board's decision and have the Maine superior court figure it out. But we have an obligation to see this through, and we will do that."

"Fair or not fair," Eleanor interjected, "this is a process that exists. Sometimes you may not like the process, but the board has to follow it. If anyone thinks it's unfair, there are political resources through the Town Council to have the ordinance changed. I don't think 'fair' is a correct assessment of the process, because the applicant has every right to do this."

"Yes, it's a State law," said Bolduc.

"I'm just asking you to consider the time that people put into it," said Rachel. "Now they have to make the same arguments all over again."

"At this point," said Bolduc, "I'd like a show of hands as to whether or not this application is to be reconsidered. How many are in favor of a reconsideration for approval of this project?"

With a show of hands, Chairperson Bolduc and Michael Grady showed support for the reconsideration, and Rachel Greene and Jane Emery opposed it. Eleanor Adley attempted to vote showing her support, but as she raised her hand,

Chairperson Bolduc reminded her she couldn't vote either way.

"From the show of hands," said Bolduc, "I see there are at least two Board members who are in favor of a reconsideration for this application. Therefore, since it was a draw and not a negative vote, this board will hold another hearing. This will essentially be going back to the beginning for both the applicants and the abutters."

Allen Treble quickly stood, interjecting, "Nothing else can be submitted in writing from the applicant because tomorrow is fourteen workdays days prior to that meeting, so it will have to be oral testimony. Written material from an applicant has to be provided prior to a fourteen-day period in accordance with the Land Use Code Ordinance. Abutters, however, can submit material up to five days prior to the next hearing."

"Will the abutters get a copy of what the applicant has submitted to this Board so they can respond?" asked Rachel.

Allen responded. "It's public information, so anyone can come to the Town Hall and look at it."

"I would ask that the board focus on Phase Two for this discussion," said Eleanor. "Maps were presented at the last hearing for the entire phased project."

"The board can't set the rules for the hearing, as it will be a new hearing," said Bolduc.

"My understanding for scheduling this hearing once again is so it can be heard within forty-five days," said Nancy Stacy. "Can that timeline be extended if the applicant agrees? My concern is that Mrs. Emery previously indicated concerns about traffic, and I know that's a major issue with the abutters. I also know the abutters have done their own traffic study. Mr. Tussi has advised me there is a traffic engineer performing another study now. I think the additional traffic study would be helpful and would like to be able to submit the information once it is available."

"I don't think State law allows the board to go outside the forty-five days," said Bolduc.

"That time period will have to do then, as long as the information can be presented by the applicant or their representative through oral testimony," said Stacy.

"Yes, that's acceptable," Chairperson Bolduc said.

And with that curt answer, the public hearing was adjourned.

Nelson looked up at the wall clock and realized it had been another long evening. He donned his winter coat and before he could start toward the exit, a reporter from the Laslo Journal blocked his path, he presumed in order to get his response to the results of the hearing.

"Mr. Quip. What do you think about the reconsideration by the ZBA for this project? It looks like the developer is getting a second chance for their appeal to the Zoning Board."

"You could call it a retrial at this point," Nelson responded. "I've heard some of the CHS residents are saying I'm opposed to them as neighbors. That's not the issue; I'm not objecting to them. Elderly housing run by a charity would be an asset to the community. But it seems to me it's about money being generated by a high cluster density housing project rather than by an elderly housing unit. CHS is listed as a non-profit company that is developing real estate. Because of their status they don't have to pay state, federal, and in some states, local property taxes."

The reporter scribbled on the notepad in her hand while Nelson was talking, then asked, "How non-profit is CHS?"

"Well, a neighbor of mine asked the director of CHS for a copy of their tax-exempt 501(c)3 organization's Form 990 tax return, exercising her rights under the Federal Tax Code. She got a letter back from their attorney stating that as an abutter she wasn't entitled to request tax information from them. She didn't know it at the time, but such information is public knowledge. I believe question 83a of the Federal Tax Form 990 asks whether or not the organization complies with public inspection requirements for returns and exemption requirements. They answered Yes on their tax return last year. If they answer Yes this year, then they would be filing a false tax return because she was denied access to review the tax forms."

"Why should a tax-exempt organization be required to show its finances?"

"Because they could possibly get a free ride if such information wasn't available for scrutiny. Taxpayers and the residents of this town actually subsidize such companies. Last year, CHS paid just over two-thousand dollars in service fees in lieu of property taxes. They called it a service fee contribution. Based on their real estate asset worth of five plus million, they should have paid over a hundred-thousand dollars to the town. That would add up to about a million dollars over the last ten years in which they haven't been paying property taxes."

"Does CHS deserve its tax-free status?"

"If they provided a charitable service to the community, such as special services for sick or elderly disabled citizens that would otherwise be paid for by the taxpayer, then yes. But none of the residents have seen any evidence of that. They merely provide a nice place to live—at least that's what I've heard. And they charge rents at market rates just like any other landlord. The town's tax assessor is currently reviewing their tax-exempt status."

As Nelson completed his last few words, he saw Kurt Tussi talking with Attorney Stacy. The reporter noticed them as well. She quickly thanked Nelson for his comments and rushed over to talk with them before they left.

Nelson zipped up his coat, and as he turned to leave the conference room, he overheard a portion of Kurt's conversation with the reporter. "The last ZBA meeting was the worst public hearing in my life. Mr. Dumas and I just weren't prepared for a voluminous package of objections filed by the abutters just five days before the hearing. We also didn't expect the meeting room would be packed with residents who object to the plans."

I wonder what they really thought we'd do? Nelson asked himself as he exited the town hall.

It was late the following evening when Nelson e-mailed Maxwell a new chapter of his book based upon the results of the ZBA public hearing. It was difficult to believe there would be another.

ii.

The remainder of March passed quickly, and the ZBA hearing began in April as scheduled—a retrial, so to speak. The public hearing hall was full. Nelson squirmed in his chair, unsettled about the next round of discussions. "Oh, by the way," he said, as he turned in his chair to face Joe Vaschon. "I found out why Chairperson Bolduc recused himself from voting on this special exception during the first ZBA hearing."

"I had almost forgotten about that. It was so long ago. Why?"

"Because he apparently had done some legal work in the past for Caring Home Services. He actually did the right thing by recusing himself—conflict of interest."

"At least he's an upstanding guy for doing that," replied Joe. "I just don't understand why he keeps voting in their favor. And I don't see Eleanor Adley here tonight, just a scrawny little guy with thick coke bottle eyeglasses who is in her seat."

"Her tenure on the board was up and she decided not to return," Sarah responded. "I understand she was replaced by that man. His name is Thomas Hatfield. It's on his nameplate. He was temporarily appointed by the Town Council until the next elections, per the article I read in the paper.

"I wonder if he will be able to vote tonight since he is new," Joe questioned.

"Since this is a new hearing, Mrs. Adley could have voted if she were still here. But since she isn't, Mr. Hatfield will be voting."

Nelson's thoughts of Eleanor Adley's runaway wig from the last ZBA hearing were interrupted by Chairperson Bolduc opening the hearing and reading the application.

"This public hearing is a reconsideration of Caring Home Services, Incorporated, requesting a special exception to the terms of Title 10, Section 14.060, Subsection E.1 and E.2 of the Land Use and Development Code Zoning Ordinance to expand the existing Phase One into Phase Two, to include forty-two units in four buildings—one multi-complex building consisting of twenty-six units, two six-plex buildings consisting of twelve units, and one four-plex building consisting of four units, accessed off Route 2, Map 2, Lot 35, Laslo, zoned urban residential."

When he stopped speaking, Attorney Dumas stood to address the board members.

"Everyone is quite familiar with the details of this project by now, and hopefully our team can provide specific information to enable you to take a second look at the application for a special exception. All I am asking is for the board to listen carefully to the evidence and to keep an open mind on this situation, then come to the best possible decision based on that information and not on feelings. The applicant will make a thorough presentation starting with Phil Dwyer, the agent for the Caring Home Services project, who will talk about the development in general and the specific need for it in Laslo. After Mr. Dwyer speaks, David Hemp, a professional real estate appraiser, will talk about the need for affordable housing in the Laslo area. Then Kurt Tussi of Tussi Engineering and Architecture will go through the approval criteria and show that each one can be met. Mr. Peter Townsend, a traffic engineer, will also talk about the project."

The attorney continued. "There are two issues I would like to address first. I would like the issue of the tax-exempt status of the project to be off the table. I know that was the consensus at a prior hearing, but it still keeps coming up in submitted material. I would also like the board to consider the issue which I raised in the submittal, of rebuttal papers presented to the board at the last hearing—that this review should be limited to the changes that were brought about from feedback from the DEP and the Planning Board.

"I want to remind you that this project was approved by this board earlier. Since then, some minor tweaks have occurred and, hopefully, those will be the scope of the board's review tonight. The applicant has come too far and has worked in good faith with the town, and hopes the board and the audience will work in good faith with the applicant. The organization behind Caring Home Services intends to treat the abutters as good neighbors. That being said, if there are steps that can be taken to receive approval, the applicant would like to hear about them. At this point, Mr. Dwyer will now address the board."

Phil Dwyer stood and with his rasping, high-pitched voice began to speak. "As you all know, I am the director of CHS. I'd like to address some points about the need for this type of facility, especially Phase Two—one that definitely serves the local area and the local people.

"The median age of people being served by CHS is eighty: frail elderly people who need affordable housing. Our apartments are for the greatest number of people with the greatest need. This facility has been completely full for over ten years, and there is a waiting list, which indicates the need for housing like this. This is not a subsidized unit, and there are other high end expensive condos like Coastal Estates and New Dawn Towers that are good for people who can afford them. But the majority of elderly people can't. Half the residents are directly from Laslo or have come here because of someone else who lives here, like their adult children. Many of the residents have been here most of their lives, or retired to a warm spot and later wanted to come back.

"Some of the residents are very frail and close to needing assisted living. CHS provides supportive services and a supported lifestyle so they can remain in their apartment, with some level of independence. If you look at what CHS is charging for rent compared to what the market rate would be for these units, it is twenty-four percent below the market rate on the North Campus and twelve percent below on the South Campus. Over time, that gap will grow, and these apartments will be even more affordable. Mr. David Hemp has more information regarding the advantages to these rental costs, so I'll return to my seat and let him speak to you."

"Thank you, Mr. Dwyer. And thank you board members for giving me an opportunity to speak on behalf of Caring Home Services. I'm a professional real estate appraiser and former planner. I've undertaken a survey for CHS in order to see how their rents compare to that of other apartment developments in this metro statistical area. I have put together a grid based on information obtained from HUD which has about thirty check points that can be used when comparing CHS with other apartment developments, and can be adjusted for elements that they both have or don't have.

"I have reviewed those comparisons for the one bedroom and two bedroom apartments on the North and South Campus relative to five other apartment complexes in the area. The result is that after all of the adjustments, a one bedroom apartment comparable to a North campus apartment is $925 per month and the CHS apartment rent for a one bedroom apartment is $703. A similar rent for a two bedroom apartment is $1100 per month versus a CHS apartment for $831. That means the difference for a one bedroom is $222 a month and the two bedroom is $269 a month. The difference between the market rents and the CHS apartments on the South Campus is not as significant because those units are newer.

"The divergent conditions will grow as the years pass because CHS has no need for a profit. This project is an investment for future affordable housing. The need for affordable housing becomes obvious when you examine the options available. When you realize the cost of rents being charged and the current market rates, Caring Home Services is affordable housing."

Phil Dwyer returned to his feet. "There was a survey done in February to determine the income level of the elderly residents, and it was found that sixty percent fall below the low-income guidelines set by the Maine State Housing Authority. In addition, twenty-six percent were below the median income, which means that eighty-six percent of the residents are needy and fall into the category of very low income people." He looked at the other man waiting to speak to the board to make sure he was ready. With a slight nod, Dwyer returned his attention to the board members. "I'll turn this over to Mr. Tussi now."

"I'll bet their residents really like being called 'needy'," Sarah whispered to Nelson while making the quotation marks with her fingers.

"Thank you, Mr. Dwyer," replied Kurt. "I realize there's a lot of information out there, and the board is looking for answers, so I appreciate the chance to respond. I'll try to run through the information quickly and answer any questions.

"It's important for the members involved to understand exactly what is being voted upon. The board previously approved a plan for Phase Two with forty-four units in five buildings. The plan in front of the board tonight shows Phase Two consisting of forty-two units in four buildings. This board also approved parking for Phase One and the North Campus that was perpendicular to the buildings. The Planning Board felt this type of parking could result in an unsafe condition by causing the residents to have to back out into the street so it was all changed from perpendicular to either parallel parking or to a larger parking lot. A note was added to the Phase Two construction plan for reconstructing these spaces.

"Yet another change to the last plan was that the units would be redesigned to provide greater setbacks from the buildings to the abutters. Most of the abutters were concerned about the structures being so close. The distance was increased to one hundred and forty feet where only fifteen feet was required, as a show of good faith. Those are the changes since the board's December approval, two years ago, and those are the changes that I'm asking the board to review tonight."

Pointing to a large copy of the site plan that had been set on a stand in front of the board members, Rachel Greene asked, "Mr. Tussi, would you address this new additional area on the plan?"

"It's an off-street parking area. The total number of parking spaces the Planning Board had previously approved was sixty spaces. We are now asking for seventy-four spaces for Phase Two."

"Thank you."

Kurt continued. "I've been asked by this board to provide information in response to some of the abutters' concerns, as provided by Mr. Quip since he's apparently coordinated and summarized most of the concerns. The first is the adverse effect on the scenic or natural beauty of the area and aesthetics and wildlife.

"Some of the abutters raised concern that Inland Fish and Wildlife didn't do a site visit, and that's correct. On each project we do there is a site location permit process with the Department of Environmental Protection, the DEP. It requires me to request information from Inland Fish and Wildlife, Maine Natural Areas program and Maine Historic Preservation Commission. The Inland Fish and Wildlife and the Maine Natural Areas program found the project would not increase the adverse effect on the environment. The Inland Fish and Wildlife also didn't have any information on rare species on this parcel, although there is wildlife on it.

"If this project is allowed to go forward, the wildlife will simply move to another portion of the project. When a project is developed, it does displace wildlife, but there are not rare, threatened, or endangered species on this parcel. The Maine Natural Areas program found there were no endangered species on the project as far as the survey provided for this county area was concerned. Also, the Maine Historic Preservation Commission requires documentation of all structures over fifty years old for their evaluation. This is done using photographs of the structures on adjacent parcels that are fifty years or older. After several requests for information, the Commission concluded the project would not have an adverse effect on historical properties.

"Another concern of the abutters is the high-density cluster housing development. Under the ordinance, if the board grants a special exception, this development can support eight units per acre of net developable area. I've determined that the net developable area is about 28.7 acres. That acreage includes deductions for the road right-of-way and fifty percent deduction of hydric soils. If the board approves Phase Two, there would therefore be 2.36 units per acre.

"An additional concern raised is on the number of trips per day. I'll leave that up to Pete Townsend, our traffic engineer, to answer in depth later. I will give a brief overview now. When I first contacted Mr. Townsend about a traffic survey, it had nothing to do with two means of access. At that time, Mr. Townsend determined the number of trips per day based upon the 6th and 7th edition of the ITE standards at 2.15 trips per day. Laslo's Head of Public Works, Mr. Norman Blake, wrote a letter saying he agreed with Mr. Townsend's number and asked that the traffic from a nearby office complex using the same access road into the Phase One property be considered. The Planning Board didn't find that a second means of access was required, even when adding the office complex that shares the same access road because their parking lot is very close to Route 2.

"As Attorney Dumas stated earlier, if the board requires an emergency access and doesn't kill the project for the developer, one could be constructed with a gate at the end of Baker Street. We've mentioned that before. There was a concern with this because of a narrow entrance and other road issues. Improvements for future phases, such as a center turning lane, an acceleration/deceleration lane, and a signalized intersection could alleviate that concern.

"The abutters have pointed out that these buildings are being constructed on fifteen feet of fill, which is working against the land. That isn't entirely accurate. The larger multiplex building consisting of twenty-six units in Phase Two is fifteen feet higher than its finished elevation, that part is true. But there's a finished basement, so there will be only three to four feet of fill, not fifteen. As we've discussed with the Planning Board, most of these buildings have basements with foundation footings.

"I've read the latest information submitted by the abutters. A lot of what I haven't touched on has to do with traffic, which Mr. Townsend will address. There is a comment in there by Mr. Quip about the trips per day and the category used. Mr. Quip states that the storm water management plan for the development is based on it being a retirement community, but the category on the traffic plan is congregate elderly housing. He said on the permit it uses the words retirement community for people over the age of fifty-five. In three other categories and in the title it's called a congregate care elderly housing project, which is what this is.

I believe we can address Mr. Quip's concerns by addressing the fact that this project meets the sixteen criteria under Section 14.21.050 of the Land Use Ordinance Code. I can go through the criteria that this board has issues with if the board would like or I can just answer questions."

"Why don't you continue to go through your presentation and the board will ask questions when the time comes."

"Thank you, Mr. Chairperson," replied Kurt. "We'll continue then with Mr. Peter Townsend, who will discuss the traffic study he performed."

Pete rose upon Kurt's introduction and slowly walked over to the podium facing the board members.

"I did the original traffic study for the developer, which was for all the phases. To clarify, a traffic engineer usually looks at peak hour traffic. The average daily traffic doesn't enter into the analysis. Somewhere along the line in these discussions, the question came up as to what is daily traffic. My initial reaction was who cares? But it's in the Town's Land Use Code that daily traffic has an impact, so I calculated that from the trip generation manual put out by the Information Technology Equipment Safety Standard, or ITE as we call it. This manual takes all the studies submitted by engineers and categorizes it into types of land use and provides definitions for each. It is for sale for traffic engineers to use.

"When this discussion started two years ago, I was looking at the 6th edition of the manual; there were categories of elderly housing detached, elderly housing attached, and congregate care facilities. It was decided to use the elderly housing detached category. Elderly detached housing would be a separate cottage unit, and it was thought the duplexes had similar characteristics. I do peak traffic counts from 7:00 a.m. to 9:00 a.m. and from 4:00 p.m. to 6:00 p.m. There was data available for peak hour information, but at that time there was nothing available on daily traffic. To fill in for the lack of information, daily traffic can be estimated by taking the peak hour estimate and determining what percentage on an average day that peak hour represents. Based on the numbers I obtained after completing my peak traffic analysis, I selected the highest percentage of daily trips during the peak hours which would give the highest daily traffic and made an estimate on that.

"After the abutter letters were submitted to the board, Mr. Tussi came back with more questions. We looked at the standards again and discovered the number system was changed and additional categories were added. I looked at all this and went back to Mr. Tussi and asked him for a description of what was happening here. It was decided that the multiplex building containing twenty-six apartments was congregate care and the other units are attached and detached senior housing resulting with an overall average trip count rate of 1.93. Phase Three will kick that rate up to over two hundred trips. That addresses where these numbers came from."

"At this point," said Kurt, returning to the podium after Pete left, "I'd like to address a few of the sixteen criteria that I believe the board had issues with at the last meeting, starting with the Second Criteria.

"The Second Criteria is in regard to the conservation of property values and the encouragement of the most appropriate uses of land. After the construction of Phase One, the Planning Board asked the developer to look at this as a cluster housing development. That was done for Phase Two. There's a note on the plan showing that after Phase Two, the total open space remaining after construction, which is the amount of land undisturbed, is ninety-two percent. The setbacks for the Phase Three buildings were increased, if and when the project gets there, to offer additional conservation and buffer area to the abutters. At the request of the Conservation Commission, the wetland on the south parcel was put into a conservation easement.

"The Third Criteria is in regard to the effect that the location of the proposed use might have upon the congestion or undue increase of vehicular traffic congestion on public streets or highways. Mr. Townsend has explained that for this type of development, the traffic counts are relatively low.

"The Ninth Criteria is in regard to the inaccessibility of the property or structures for the convenient entry and operation of fire and other emergency apparatus. This project has been reviewed by both the Fire and Police Chiefs. Neither one felt at this time that a second means of access is needed for Phase Two, nor did either one have any issues with this expansion. If the board feels this is something it wants to require, I don't have a concern with that. The developer would be glad to build a road to the Fire Chief's specifications.

"The Tenth Criteria is in regard to whether the use, or the structures to be used, will cause an overcrowding of land or undue concentration of population. Phase Two is just slightly over the density allowed for a straight subdivision. In one of the CHS units, there are probably less people living in it than you would see in a single-family dwelling. There are usually one to two residents per apartment.

"The Fifteenth Criteria, which is the last factor the board had an issue with, is in regard to whether the proposed use anticipates and eliminates potential nuisances created by its location. I have some background information on this for the North Campus and for Phase One of the South Campus. To my knowledge, it doesn't create a nuisance. The buildings are heavily buffered by trees, and I don't think the residents living there create a nuisance by requiring the police to break up wild parties."

Kurt's last remark about wild parties brought chuckles from a few of the CHS residents, a somewhat welcome relief to everyone, as evidenced by the look on their faces. It was then that Chairperson Bolduc called a five-minute recess, providing an opportunity for people to stretch their legs and talk amongst themselves about the oral presentations.

iii.

Nelson and the others were back in their seats when

Chairperson Bolduc called the meeting to order after five minutes.

"I want to remind everyone present the board isn't here to decide if elderly housing is good or bad for the Town of Laslo. The board isn't here to decide if this facility should be tax exempt or not. That has nothing to do with this appeal. The board's criteria is for a special exception for the number of units allowed to be built. I am asking that speakers keep their comments as much as possible to the Criteria Factors contained in the ordinance for a special exception. If people have comments that are consistent with what someone else has said, please say that, along with your name and address. That will save time. We'll now open the meeting to comments for, against, or about this proposed project."

"The board will first hear from the Conservation Commission because their representative isn't feeling well tonight. Mrs. Landers, would you begin on behalf of the Laslo Conservation Commission?"

"Thank you, Mr. Chairperson. The Commission appreciates Mr. Tussi's willingness to have the least amount of impact on the wetlands. However, the applicant has not provided any details to the Conservation Commission on the amount of disturbance to the wetlands by the proposed roadways, making it difficult to determine the actual amount of impact. We need some clarification from the applicant." She sat down, showing she was finished with her comment.

"Thank you, Mrs. Landers. Is there anyone else interested in speaking about the application?"

Nelson recognized the first person responding to Chairperson Bolduc's request. She lived in the Phase One development and had previously spoken to the Planning Board in favor of the plan.

"I'm Marsha Moran. I live in the apartments owned by CHS, and I would like to reiterate what Mr. Dwyer has said about this type of housing being needed. I hope the board approves it." She sat down as quickly as she stood.

Ned Garth was the next person to be recognized.

"There are many residents here tonight who live in the apartments owned by Caring Home Services. I was born in Laslo eighty-seven years ago, was educated here, and raised my family here. I've been a resident of CHS for four years. I searched for several months to find a place that was peaceful and quiet at a moderate price. There was nothing available in Laslo, or in any of the nearby towns except for these apartments. These apartments are owned by a non-profit church organization, and these additional units will have an immense impact on the town. This facility is well managed locally by the director of development, and I'm sure they will do all they can to cooperate with the Zoning Board."

Another person from the same row of seats stood and addressed the board members.

"I'm Jeffrey Arnold and I live in the Phase One apartments. This is affordable housing. I don't know if the current board members were sitting on the board when the original proposal was done, but the board has allowed this type of housing in town. I would like them to keep it going. This is a great place, and it's needed. I think the board needs to listen to what I'm saying even though Mr. Quip and the others will have reasons for not listening to us."

Nelson looked at the group of people where Jeffrey Arnold was sitting. Turning to Sarah, he whispered, "They've brought a whole bunch of people to speak up for them this time, but there's not a lot of substance in their addressing the real issues at hand."

Randy Myers, a resident of the South Campus stood in support of the development. "I've been to places where people rent apartments in like circumstances, but I've never lived in a rented complex where the residents are anywhere near as happy as they are on the South Campus. You can't knock happiness."

"I'm Meghan Moore and live in Phase One of the South Campus. I heard a remark that I'd like to address." She kept her eyes forward, never glancing around the room. "I've never been called a nuisance before, but that happened when CHS was called one. The board probably thinks we're nuisances because we are associated with Caring Home Services, who keeps coming back, but they have to to make everyone understand the need for such housing. It would be great if this could be resolved and they could construct their development."

"Yeah, I'll bet it would," whispered Mary Vaschon to Joe.

"The other thing I've heard from the opposition is that

they wouldn't be caught dead living in this development," said Meghan.

"Wow. They've got to be making this stuff up," whispered Nikki Williams, who was sitting next to Will Penton. "I've never heard anyone say that." Nelson could hear her comment even though he sat two rows down from her. "It's like having a political party saying someone's gonna throw grandma off a cliff. It's amazing how some people will believe this kind of bullshit."

Meghan continued. "The CHS apartment complex is not a cemetery but a place where the residents are alive and well. I love being with my friends, and I want to see more people live there."

Several other people from the same group stood and reiterated similar responses until there was a pause from the audience, at which point Chairperson Bolduc asked, "Is there anyone else who would like to speak in behalf of the proposed development, perhaps with more information relative to the pending issues?" There were no further responses. "Now, are there any members of the public who would like to speak in opposition to this proposed expansion?"

Bolduc looked directly at Nelson as he finished asking the question, anticipating he would be the first to speak.

iv.

Nelson was prepared to argue his case and as he stood and walked over to the podium. Bolduc remarked, "Yes Mr. Quip, go right ahead."

"Mr. Chairperson, it's hard to know where to start with all the misguided information that's been presented relevant to this proposed development. On behalf of many of the residents and taxpayers of Laslo, including, I might add, the elderly living in their own homes, I am requesting the board to deny this application.

"I realize my objection is no surprise to this board. This project doesn't fit into the urban residential zone and is in violation of the zoning ordinances, and those ordinances applied by the Planning Board, as previously discussed. I personally have taken some abuse in the ongoing discourse regarding this development as someone who dislikes the elderly, which is not true. I've continued to pursue stopping this expansion because it's the right thing to do. We need to look out for the residents of this town, and that includes the elderly as well as the taxpayers.

"I don't see how the continued expansion of Phase Two or any further phased expansions is good for this town. There will be increased costs in terms of services for fire, police, sewer, water, pumping stations, and to facility expansions due to increased demand loads. Our own Comprehensive Plan currently indicates that our town is over forty-three percent more than what is needed for elderly housing. There already has been a precedent set in our state, stipulating that a town's Comprehensive Plan, as required by the state of Maine, prevails over zoning laws. Since our town already has exceeded what is required, the expansion of additional elderly housing shouldn't be allowed. There's also a provision in the Comprehensive Plan stating that cluster type of housing developments should be allowed at a density up to four units per net residential acre, not eight units, which is what the developer is asking for with a special exception. There's even a section in the Land Use Ordinance that states that a development should conform to the Comprehensive Plan.

"There are already several other elderly housing projects available in the area and more being developed in nearby towns. There's nothing special about this project. Even the independent Peer Review performed earlier stated the proposed development doesn't take advantage of the existing topographical features and noted that there would be an extensive amount of fill used to accommodate the proposed development. According to the applicant's site plans, it's a mess of buildings that myself, as an engineer, would be ashamed to propose. This is actually a high rent housing development.

"I've reviewed the ITE standards, and this development simply doesn't qualify as a congregate elderly care facility. It doesn't even meet Title 36 of the Maine Revised Statutes Annotated for property tax exemption. The advertising brochures and literature promoting the apartments for CHS refer to their campuses as a retirement community, as did the DEP. The independent Peer Review referred to it as an elderly housing complex. Even Mr. Tussi called the facility an elderly housing project. The traffic engineer, Mr. Townsend, however, referred to it as a congregate care facility, and in the past, it's been referred to as elderly housing detached. It appears as though the designations keep changing in order to fit a particular trip count so a second access road isn't required. Back last August, Chairperson Tunney of the Planning Board said Phase Two required a second access road. But I guess that was before the ITE numbers and definitions kept changing.

"By definition, this development isn't a congregate care facility. According to the ITE Standards, a congregate care facility is defined as having dining, housekeeping, and transportation among other amenities, which this facility does not have. The combined number of units for Phase One at twenty-six units, along with the proposed Phase Two at forty-two units results in a total of sixty-eight units. Using the congregate care ITE standard of 2.02 results in one hundred and thirty-seven trips. Using the previous elderly housing-attached ITE standard of 3.48 for the North Campus results in two hundred and thirty-seven trips, which, of course, means a second access road is required for the South Campus, according to our Land Use Ordinance Code. Using that designation with an ITE standard of 2.02 versus the 3.48 originally used for Phase One, simply gets the count down so a second access isn't required—an interesting ploy on the developer's part.

"The trip counts have changed at least three times now, and all notations to traffic counts were removed from the original plan, which brings up other issues. The CHS representative, Mr. Tussi, makes light of a very informational and non-professional traffic study count that the residents did when he noted that more consideration should be given to the professionals. We were actually surprised at the volume of traffic on Route 2, which serves as the only entrance into Phase One of their South Campus. That count was an actual count based on a direct observation by the residents, not something taken from a book. Phase One, itself, barely meets the necessary traffic counts. A 5.86 traffic count from the ITE standard as a retirement community would actually be a more appropriate number to use. It's also interesting to note the traffic assessment report written by Mr. Townsend states that the South Campus will be accessed via Route 2 and Baker Street. Previously, Chairperson Bolduc said the use of Baker Street wasn't allowed—an issue constantly ignored by the applicant."

Nelson paused, looked at his notes, and continued.

"There are seventy-four abutters representing almost the entire population encompassing this development who have signed a petition submitted to this board, asking you to deny this application. The abutters believe there is a problem with this high-density housing development and its impact on property values, traffic, and safety. I've found no additional evidence that would make the board's decision to deny this any different than your previous decision. There have been a lot of changes to Phase Two since it was originally proposed two years ago. Those changes include the number of buildings, the number used to define trip counts, parking and access areas, and even the total acreage used to determine the density calculations. Twelve acres from the separately deeded North Campus were added to Phase Two of the South Campus, changing the ground rules by adding additional land to the original plans, ensuring a maximum building density.

"You've heard from the applicant that site surveys were done in several areas, but we haven't seen any evidence of that. I've written to the State of Maine Inland Fish and Wildlife Bureau requesting confirmation of any site surveys performed. I received copies of the letters sent to the applicant and included copies in the evidence package I previously submitted to this board. Sentences in those letters from the State Bureau were omitted, changing the actual context. I believe Kevin Sparks will have a comment about that. I just want to add that with development projects, an applicant always has the upper hand in that they can review the packets of information presented to the Planning and Zoning Boards and reply to them at the hearings. They can then introduce new issues that the residents don't have time to research prior to a hearing. Also, after the public hearings are closed, there can be times when the applicant can be asked questions by board members during their deliberations. If they provide answers that simply aren't true, the public doesn't have the opportunity to respond. So those board members may never know the real truth, only what they are told by the developer."

"Sounds like the rest of the country, doesn't it?" Nikki

whispered to Will.

Nelson heard her comment, causing him to pause and think about how her words paralleled those of Maxwell's previous correspondence before continuing.

"This expansion proposal doesn't meet those Criticality Factors discussed earlier, which includes Sections 14.21.050.B1, B2, B3, B9, B10, B15, and B16 of the Land Use Ordinance. This board has already agreed it doesn't. This type of high density clustered housing development simply doesn't belong in the urban residential zone. I hope this board looks closely at the evidence packet I've submitted and denies the request for a special exception for this development."

Nelson was relieved to complete his oration and returned to his seat, noting there appeared to be several people anxious to address the board members. He looked at Nikki and smiled, thinking briefly about her whispered comment as Will Penton stood to speak.

"We appear to be here tonight because Caring Home Services was unprepared at their last try at this. The request by the Conservation Commission for more information regarding the amount of disturbance to the wetlands hasn't been fully satisfied. I also question the policy of taking some land from the previously approved North Campus development and using the additional unused acreage to calculate the density for the South Campus. You can't take away land from something that has been already approved; that would make the previously approved development less in compliance."

Kevin Sparks stood abruptly, surprising Will. "I have a couple of points I wish to address." He turned toward Will and added, "I apologize to Mr. Penton for my interruption, but I just can't sit here any longer with something I need to say that's been festing under my craw."

"No problem," replied Will. "I know what that feels like. Go right ahead." He extended his arm and indicated for Kevin to continue.

"Thanks, Will," said Kevin. He turned back to the board members. "I question the evidence in a letter from the Department of Inland Fish and Wildlife because I've seen salamanders and turtles that are the type of species protected by state law. I called the State House and asked how their information was derived. That office corroborated my doubt. They used old satellite photos and no on-site surveillance in order to determine the possibility of wildlife on the site. The board should take consideration that no survey was performed.

"Mr. Tussi mentioned that no botanical features were documented, but failed to mention the next sentence in the state's letter stated there was a lack of data, which indicated a minimal effort was used to confirm the absence to rare botanical features. The letter also stated there should be an on-site review done by the Department of Conservation. That information was omitted from Mr. Tussi's discussion with this board. I'm not trying to place blame on misleading statements. I'm just trying to keep the conversation honest, something I wish more people would do. That additional declaration from the state should never have been omitted from this board. I just think this development proposal is too large and shouldn't be expanded any further."

"I also have something I want to add to this discussion," said Mary Vaschon. "I want to mention that there are discrepancies with the elevations on the plan. Mr. Tussi has stated that the larger multiplex building in Phase Two would have only three to four feet of fill, yet the independent Peer Review noted that the same multiplex building would be constructed on eight to fifteen feet of fill. That's quite a discrepancy. And the area where the developer is talking about filling only fifteen feet is actually a thirty-foot gully. I have photos of this area, and I'd like to provide them to the board, showing these deeply recessed ravines."

"Chairperson Bolduc, is the board going to accept the photos presented by Mrs. Vaschon?" asked Dumas.

"Yes."

There was a brief pause after Bolduc's one word response, then John Silverman stood to speak.

"I own property that abuts this development. I think the first phase of this project has been an asset to the community and hasn't created any known problems. I've even helped some of the people move into the Phase One apartments. I read through the letter from Attorney Dumas to the ZBA, which of course is a public record that I obtained from the Code enforcement officer, Mr. Treble, and it appears to get nasty at the end. Mr. Dumas mentions what the board did went against its decision two years ago. I've personally not talked to the board members outside the Council Chamber other than to say hello, but I think the Zoning and Planning Boards deserve a lot of credit. They've had a lot of things dumped in their laps.

"Many of the board members are ordinary citizens who don't know all the rules and regulations. It's up to the engineering companies and the applicants to give the board members all the information they need so they can make a fair and honest decision, so the applicant doesn't have to keep coming back. As it stands now, the board members can say that when they made their decision two years ago, they didn't have all the information necessary for the good of the town. The board should now review the information more fully and make a decision based on that. I think it's important that the board does this, as there are a lot of questions that haven't been answered.

"The recent submission letter from Tussi Engineering and Architecture disputes everything we've said. I'm not against Caring Home Services or the elderly. Their appraiser, Mr. Hemp, stated that the apartment rentals for CHS were twenty-four percent below market rental prices. I did a simple check comparing apartment and house rentals advertised in our local newspaper for costs associated with available rents in this area. I found the average price of rentals to be at least fifteen percent lower than the cost of rentals available from CHS. In other words, they are a high cost rental apartment complex, and people would save more money if they rented elsewhere," Silverman added.

"Mr. Tussi's submission letter states there are no adverse effects on the forested environment, and he provided quotes from several State of Maine Department letters to back this information. He said the agencies reviewed the areas and determined there would be no adverse effect on historical properties and no identified wildlife habitat on this site. I believe evidence *has been* presented to show how poorly that study was done, and that the ZBA only has the information the developer wants it to have. I've seen wild turkeys, fox, raccoons, possums, and deer in that area. Mr. Tussi says the studies show the animals aren't living out there, so he must have yelled at all of them to go somewhere else beforehand."

There was an outburst of chuckles from the public. John Silverman sat down and looked around the room, smiling at the results of his last statement.

After Silverman sat down, Marie Paterson stood and added, "CHS is presenting this expansion project as elderly housing when in actuality it's a high density clustered apartment development. According to their plans, there are twenty buildings and over one hundred apartments proposed in Phases Two through Seven. Normally, high-density cluster housing allows four units per acre, but elderly housing, as an exception, can allow eight units per acre. If it's considered as elderly housing, the number of units can be doubled for profitability even though the applicant considers themselves as a non-profit organization. As Mr. Quip already noted, the town's Comprehensive Plan states that an urban residential cluster development with open space can be allowed a density of four units per acre, not eight. Mr. Tussi responded by saying ninety-two percent of the parcel is open space after the completion of Phase Two. What Mr. Tussi doesn't say is the open space that is put aside as conservation land will be developed in the future. *This* is not an elderly care facility but an apartment complex for people older than fifty-five. It should not be given consideration for a special exemption."

Returning to her seat, Marie nodded to Nikki, as if giving her an affirmation to continue.

Nikki quickly walked to the podium, notes in hand. "I've been involved with this debate for a while now, and I've listened to what is happening between the two public hearing boards and the citizens. I've noticed that some people have shifted the focus from the violation of zoning and land use codes to an attitude of what is being done to elderly people. This is not a discrimination issue. Everyone matters in this discussion. These people, tonight, opposed to this project, don't have a problem with Phase One as it stands now. They believe it's a nice piece of property that has been taken care of, even though CHS should be paying property taxes. The North Campus is pleasing to the eye and the residents seem happy, but there's not the conglomeration of buildings and pavement that the developers want to make the South Campus into.

"Phase One of the South Campus is acceptable as it is already built. To raze and level the remaining land and clear out the trees and then replace them with enormous building complexes is unacceptable. There's been stories made up about how some residents want to kick the elderly people out of town, and that's just mean and malicious hearsay. I personally resent being thought of in that manner. They're currently in a retirement community where they appear to know many of their fellow residents personally. They should be concerned, however, that their community remains small and doesn't become just a matter of numbers lost in a large corporation, trying to muscle its way through small town ordinances.

"If this expansion is allowed to continue into Phase Two, despite repeated protests by abutters and residents of our town, another access road suitable for regular and emergency vehicle traffic is required. Even now there is speculation on whether the current road into just Phase One of their South Campus is sufficient for the traffic flow into and out of that complex. The plans for Phase Two also call for a dead end road, not a cul-de-sac. Trying to maneuver an emergency vehicle in order to exit the complex could be difficult at best, especially during the winter months. Earlier in this hearing, Mr. Tussi brought up the fact that Fire Chief Gerard had no problems with this expansion. That's not entirely true. I have a copy of a letter written from the Fire Chief to our town planner, Mr. Hatch, stating he had a concern as to the size of the development in relation to hydrant water availability. You have a copy of that letter in your information packages submitted by Mr. Quip. I'm referring to that letter just in case you haven't had a chance to read over the information he submitted. Fire Chief Gerard stated that the development is rapidly depleting the current water main capabilities. I don't know about you, but that statement says to me that he did have some concerns.

"As I mentioned in February, I talked with Mr. Albert Diamond from Coastal Realty about the effect of this development upon the value of abutters' properties. He's been a real estate broker for over twenty years and a copy of his letter is in your information packets. I read you his letter during that hearing. But I wanted to remind you what it indicated. He stated in his opinion, property which abuts wooded open space is more valuable than the same property abutting multi-unit housing. He said that's the reason for zoning. It maintains the character and subsequently preserves the value of like property. He also noted that there is more activity in retirement type of complexes, like those of CHS, with residents and visitors always coming and going, and that would certainly be a negative factor that any buyer would likely consider due to increased traffic flow.

"I attended the last ZBA hearing and was very disappointed that CHS was granted a reconsideration to rebuke the evidence presented by a group of us concerned residents. I have seen the response that the applicant is calling new evidence, but I don't believe it's any different than what you've heard before. It's really disheartening when all the information we have supplied is manipulated by the applicant to fit whatever scenario is deemed applicable. This project keeps bouncing from one board to another for continuous appeals because of nonconformance to ordinance codes. It seems to me that when all the evidence is reviewed and the hearings aren't just one-sided in favor of the applicant, the board should see the lack of merits for a project of this scope for our town.

"The group of residents opposing this Phase Two project is not trying to make this into a controversy about banning our elderly population. Some people might want to spin the facts in order to make others believe that. That type of manipulation happens all the time, especially if you watch the news regarding national issues. These arguments are about a corporation trying to manipulate and grievously disregard our town's Zoning and Land Use Ordinances, in order to build a development that's not needed and is too big for this area. It's like many national policies I've listened to lately, where executive orders are rampant and no one is paying attention to what the people want. I trust the members of this board have read all the information we have submitted so you have sufficient and true facts in order to maintain your original decision for denial."

Her closing words were succinct. "Thanks for listening." With notes in hand, she returned to her seat.

Tugging at his sleeve, Sarah whispered, "That was quite a speech Nikki gave."

"She did a bit of research and preparation for that," Nelson said. "She's normally more rowdy than what we just witnessed. She always surprises me 'cause I just never know what she's going to say next."

The room was quiet. There were no further comments in opposition.

V.

Chairperson Bolduc appeared to reflect on the statements made by Nikki. Then he broke the silence.

"The board members may either say they haven't heard anything to change their mind tonight regarding their previous decision, or if they have questions, they can ask those now."

Attorney Dumas briskly stood and asked, "If Caring Home Services didn't need the high cluster density, which I believe this is, and just wanted to do four units per acre in this zone, would it even come before this board?"

"It would have to go before the Planning Board for a cluster development," Chairperson Bolduc replied. "The special exception is just for the elderly housing aspect of it."

"The reason for the elderly housing is to go from four units per acre to eight, doubling the number of units per acre," said Rachel. "Mr. Hatch, could the applicant still develop the CHS complex at four units per acre?"

"Yes, with Planning Board approval."

"But it still might need a special exception from this board," suggested Rachel. "There are other things that could arise with respect to zoning concerns with the density issue being the basic issue. It's fabulous to hear people say how much they love their apartments. That matters a lot to me. I feel the facility should be able to expand, but not at eight units per acre in this zone, where the surrounding neighbors have stated with fact and emotion that this is not the kind of development that fits in with their neighborhood. There are sixteen criteria to look at, and there are a few of those Criteria Factors that I feel the proposed expansion doesn't meet. I'm not opposed to expansion, but I think that Caring Home Services should fall under the same guidelines as anyone else at four units per acre, not eight."

"The Town Planner, Todd Hatch, has previously stated this application is before this board, no matter what, as elderly housing," said Dumas.

"If the use is for elderly housing, a special exception is needed," said Bolduc. "If the applicant goes for regular housing, not fifty-five, or older, or elderly, the most units per acre allowed is four. That's Mrs. Greene's point."

"Look," said Rachel, "I'm not suggesting to the people here that it shouldn't be elderly housing. I'm just saying that CHS could still continue to remain as it is by not having such a high density. It isn't the elderly housing aspect that I'm against but the density of the development."

"If this is not over the density for a clustered subdivision but a developer wants to provide housing for people over fifty-five years of age, is a special exception needed?" Kurt asked.

"Yes," replied the Town Planner, "because a clustered subdivision and elderly housing aren't the same."

"What I understand Mr. Todd is saying," Kurt reiterated, "is that whether or not it's one unit, or four units, or eight units per acre, it still has to go before the Zoning Board of Appeals."

"That may be the case," said Rachel, "but it wouldn't be as big an issue to most of the abutters and probably not to most of the board members because the issue is the density and scale of the project. There's no way around that issue. I appreciate the fact that CHS fulfills a certain niche in the market. If I go down that road, considering eight units per acre when the zone only allows four, I would want to see subsidized housing and workforce housing. I've been involved in issues around town about there not being enough low-income housing. There are some not for profit organizations that can speak to the need for elderly housing, especially subsidized housing. Why didn't Mr. Hemp talk about something like that? Mr. Hemp is a paid consultant. The discussion would have carried more weight to have a third party come in and say we really need this, instead of someone who is paid to say *this* is needed."

David Hemp stood to defend himself against Rachel's comment. "I've been involved with the workforce housing task force for many years, so I'm not just speaking as a paid consultant but as a person who has been a planner in this area and who knows about the critical need for housing. My study was based on what the rental costs are in various developments around here, with a conclusion that this is affordable housing. I just did a study of rents and the market rates using HUD guidelines, so it was objective."

Jane Emery looked directly at Phil Dwyer and asked, "What services are provided by Caring Home Services?"

Phil quickly stood to respond and justify his position. "There are all types of social programs, such as art classes, and blood pressure clinics, and foot clinics where people can come in and talk about health issues. There are a lot of amenities other than just an apartment. They include an exercise room, billiard room, library and computer facilities, a garden plot, a monthly newsletter, choirs, funeral seminars, and several different church groups that come in."

"Are there dining facilities for the residents?" Jane asked.

"There is no dining hall, but residents who want to, can make arrangements with the Laslo Community Hospital."

"So the answer to my question is no. Then are housekeeping services offered to the residents?"

"Well, no, although there is housekeeping for the common areas."

"Again, your answer is no to my question. Let me ask you another question. Is transportation offered so the residents can get to doctors and dentists?"

"No, not directly, but there is public transportation that comes and picks up the residents."

Jane appeared to be perturbed with the answers from Dwyer. With a noticeable scowl, she responded, "Then your development doesn't qualify under the ITE standards as a Congregate Care facility."

She turned her gaze toward Kurt Tussi. "Mr. Tussi, according to the ITE Standards a Congregate Care facility is defined as providing social activities, security, meals, housekeeping services, and transportation. It's pretty obvious CHS doesn't provide any of those things. Look, it's getting late, and here's where I'm at with this thus far.

"I'm concerned with Criticality Factor Three, which states consideration must be given as to the effect the location of the proposed use may have upon the congestion or undue increase of vehicular traffic congestion on public streets or highways. Things have changed since the original approval of Phase One, two years ago. One critical item is the trips per day and the need for a second access road. The CHS proposed development is *not* a congregate care facility because it doesn't have dining, housekeeping and transportation among other amenities, so it doesn't meet the 2.02 trips per day as a Congregate Care facility. It appears this facility would fall under the 3.48 trips per day of elderly housing attached, which is what Phase One used as its original guideline. That would put the added facility of Phase Two over the two hundred trips per day that is required by the ordinance, which means you need to have a second access road. There is no second access on the plan and that affects my decision greatly.

"The next thing I'm concerned about, among other things, is Criteria Factor Two, regarding the conservation of property values. There was an article in the local newspaper earlier this month entitled 'Selectmen Remove Homeowner's Problem'. The article was about an issue that happened in our neighboring town, Kimball Crossing. I'm not saying the incident is the exact same thing as what we've been discussing here, but it makes me nervous about property values. It was about a couple who asked their town to drain a pond that formed on their property after an abutter built a house next door seven years prior. During the construction, the abutter brought in massive amounts of fill, elevating that property by twelve feet. As a result, rainwater drained into their yard creating a pond above their septic tank. We just don't know what will happen with all the fill that is being brought in for this project. My concerns therefore are in regard to property value and the fact that there is no secondary access road."

Jane looked over at the other board members, indicating she was finished. Michael Grady picked up where she left off.

"I'd like to congratulate Mr. Tussi and his team, as well as the abutters, for presenting very detailed and complete cases," said Grady. "I voted to deny approval in February because there were too many things left unanswered. In March, I did vote to have a new hearing. People may agree or not agree with how I vote, but I believe I have all the information I need now. My comment will be brief. I agree a hundred percent with the reasons presented by Mrs. Greene, that this is not a good fit because of the density. I love that this is elderly housing, but, in my opinion it doesn't fit the area. If this was less dense overall, I wouldn't have that much of a problem with it. There will be too many units and too many people on that wooded site, and I'm only talking about Phase Two. That's the only issue I have, but I feel it's a big one." He looked at the other board members, indicating he was done.

"I haven't changed my mind from the last time I voted," said Bolduc. "I don't believe it's significantly different than what I voted for two years ago. My concern is with Mrs. Greene's and Mr. Grady's comment regarding the density. The decision to allow eight units per acre for elderly housing was made by the Planning Board. I don't think we have the authority to question that or change it. I can only look at the situation and see if it is proper for this development. This area is already fairly dense, but I don't think the density issue is a legal reason to deny this. I was on this board when the request to use Baker Street wasn't allowed because there were too many questions regarding safety. I would still say no to the use of Baker Street, but I'm not convinced that this phase of the project has any safety or other concerns."

"I understand your position, Mr. Bolduc, but I disagree with you," Rachel said. "You can't overlook the density issue when being asked to consider a special exception for elderly housing. Part of that comes with the knowledge that the units per acre are going from four to eight. Because of that, the project has to be up to the Land Use Code standards. We also shouldn't overlook the requirements set forth in the town's Comprehensive Plan that apparently takes legal precedence over the Land Use Code. I think an argument can be made that looking at the density is part of the decision-making process. There are a number of conditions that come along with the granting of that use, and we have to consider them."

"I have a point of order here," said Dumas. "Does the applicant have an opportunity to amend the plan and add a second entrance or juggle the density and come back at a later date so they don't have to go back to square one? I'll have to talk to the people in authority to see if they agree with doing that, but rather than blow off all the work that's been done, to continue this, like the Planning Board does, the applicant could come back with a modification."

<u>*vi.*</u>

Peter Bolduc rubbed the palms of both hands down over his eyes as if to clear his vision in order to start anew, then responded to the attorney's comment.

"The applicant can always come back with a new plan, something that's different than what has been presented today. The board can't tell the applicant how to go about it, but the applicant can take the board's comments and change the plan accordingly."

"I'm open for compromise," interjected Rachel.

"Is Eleanor Adley still on the board?" asked Attorney Dumas.

"No. Her term expired and she didn't reapply," said Bolduc.

"Did any board members have any outside contact on this project?" asked Attorney Dumas. "Or any communication with a third party? I would like this board polled to find out if anyone has discussed this application outside this hearing. The applicant is entitled to know that."

"I'll ask each board member to indicate if they have had any discussion with other people regarding this application," replied Bolduc, looking somewhat irritated at the request.

"I've not had any," said Thomas Hatfield.

"I've discussed it," said Jane Emery.

"No," said Michael Grady.

"Absolutely, I've had discussions about every case I look at," said Rachel. "Otherwise, I wouldn't have taken this job. To me, it would be a matter of negligence if matters weren't discussed."

"I have as well," said Bolduc.

"I'd like to learn a little more about those discussions," said Dumas.

"Have any of the board members had discussions with the applicant or opposing abutters?" asked Bolduc.

"My discussions have been with general members of the public," said Emery.

"That's the same for me," said Rachel. "My discussions were not with the abutters or the applicant. I do my research and talk to people on the Planning Board and to my husband. If people approach me on the street and give me their two cents, I tell people I can't discuss the issues. People can tell me their feelings, but I can't tell them mine. I absolutely do my research. I read the entire packets of information provided by both parties prior to voting upon something. Otherwise, I shouldn't be voting at all. I also look at the property, and talk to the Conservation Commission. That's part of this job."

"My talk was with Mr. Tussi after the last meeting," said Bolduc. "I believe we talked about the substance of the meeting, but that was it."

"Where is it written that we can't, to the best of our ability, look into this, other than talking to those involved?" asked Rachel Greene.

"The board sits in the capacity of a judge," said Attorney Dumas. "A superior court or district court judge doesn't get information out of the courtroom."

"I agree, that's the law, but this isn't a court room. It's a town board meeting," said Bolduc.

"That isn't possible for these hearings," said Rachel. "We live in a small community and people want to talk."

"It isn't so much about talking but about making decisions prior to the meeting or using information that isn't presented at the meeting and making a decision based on that," said Bolduc.

"In my case, I've not been contacted by anyone on either side," said Jane Emery. "People I've talked to have had nothing to do with the applicant or the abutters. The board is presented with material up to fourteen days prior to the meeting by the applicant and up to five days prior from the abutters. It's only appropriate that the board look at both sides of the issue. I was especially interested in the traffic issue. After the last meeting, it was made clear I was going to have to follow up on that because it was a safety concern for me. I've spent a lot of time on this issue, even reading newspaper articles about property values. I'm a homeowner, and I've had to deal with situations regarding landfill in my family. That's worrisome for me because it was stated at the last meeting that all the new buildings would be on landfill. Over the last month, I've thought about where I stood in regard to the Land Use Code. There hasn't been anything nefarious about my discussions. Taking the applicant's word for everything is not what the board does. The board takes what the applicant has submitted and what the abutters have submitted and tries to come to some conclusion."

There was a pause among the board members as Mrs. Emery finished her commentary. It was then that Michael Grady spoke up.

"Apparently, our discussions are concluded. I move that the application for reconsideration of Caring Homes Services, requesting a special exception to the terms of Title 10, Section 14.060, Subsections E.1 and E.2 of the Land Use and Development Code Zoning Ordinance be put to a vote."

Thomas Hatfield seconded the motion and Chairperson Bolduc then asked, "With a show of hands, how many are in favor of the motion to accept the reconsideration of this special exception for zoning?"

Only Chairperson Bolduc raised his hand. The room grew quiet with surprise and apparent relief on Nelson's part, and that of the abutters as evidenced by the look on their faces.

"How many are opposed to this motion?"

Rachel Greene, Jane Emery, Michael Grady, and Thomas Hatfield all raised their hands.

Chairperson Bolduc looked first at Phil Dwyer, then Kurt Tussi, and finally at Attorney Dumas, then matter-of-factly responded, "The board has denied the reconsideration to approve a special exception to zoning on the same grounds as given in the Findings of Fact and Conclusion at the original denial in February. You will receive written notice confirming the board's decision within one week. The applicant or any interested party withstanding may appeal the decision of this board within fifteen days in Superior Court. This public hearing is adjourned."

"It's finally over," uttered Nelson to Sarah as he stood, stretched, and donned his coat.

"Hopefully," replied Sarah with a look of concern.

"What do you mean? Why the non-jubilant frown?"

"Well, I looked at the agenda for the Planning Board and Zoning Board hearings and CHS is currently scheduled for a Planning Board hearing in early May."

"Maybe they were just projecting a positive outcome from tonight's hearing. I would assume they'll just cancel that hearing."

Will Penton overheard Sarah and Nelson's conversation as he approached. He said, "I overheard Attorney Dumas talking with Kurt Tussi just now, after the board's denial of the special exception. Their attorney said they're going to continue their discussions with the Planning Board."

"Why and how come?" Nelson asked, slightly perplexed with the news. "They've been denied the special exception twice now. What good does it do for them to proceed?"

"Good question. I don't know," replied Will. "One of us will have to talk with the town planner and see if we can find out what's going on."

Nelson shook his head in disbelief as he left the town hall. Upon his arrival at home, a short e-mail message from Maxwell was waiting to be read.

To: NelsonQuip – April 18
From: Mdraper
Subject: Zoning Board Hearing—Chapter Reviews

Nelson,
I received several of the chapters from your manuscript this week involving the discussions between the two public hearing boards. Please keep me updated on what happened in tonight's public hearing. I think people will find all the rhetoric somewhat unusual and hard to believe—stuff that can really happen to any one of us.

There are some other issues you also might consider adding to your story about foretold events. When Alex visited me during his March semester break, he told me he was thinking about entering the Boston marathon. That's when I told him I was concerned about disturbing news traffic I read regarding terrorist groups overseas. We had a radio broadcast from our satellite, Turing-B, about an attack that occurred in Boston. There was no date referenced; only a few words about an explosion. But I was never able to confirm if such an incident had ever occurred. Unfortunately, as you know, just last week, a tragic bombing did take place. With such acts of terrorism, I'm concerned about future forecasts. In this same month, it's been reported that Iran has begun operations at two uranium mines and a uranium ore-processing plant, furthering its capacity to produce nuclear material—again, my concern about nuclear proliferation and our future.

Dora has also noted that a new terrorist organization called ISIS (Islamic State in Iraq and greater Syria) has formed, splintering off from the al-Qaeda jihadist movement. I just hope this country is taking a concerned look at that organization and what's really going on in the middle-east. This is not the time to make light of terrorist organizations.

Keep me posted on your public hearings. Doesn't sound like you came to a final resolution at your last meeting. Hopefully things went better tonight. I've made a few comments on your recent chapters, and I'll get them to you shortly. Still real busy at the lab.

My best
–Max

Chapter Fifteen

Recapitulation

i.

It was the seventh day of May on a late Tuesday afternoon, almost two weeks after the Zoning Board hearing, when Nikki Williams walked into Todd Hatch's office at the Town Hall.

"If you have a few minutes, I've got a few questions I'd like to ask," she said.

Todd, who'd been the town planner for ten years, looked up from his cluttered desk, recognized her from previous discussions, and politely responded. "Sure, ask away. I'll *try* to answer your questions."

"Caring Home Services was scheduled for a Planning Board hearing this month even though the ZBA had disapproved their request for a special exception. I checked the posted schedule yesterday and found out they cancelled their public hearing. Are they finally going to stop trying to get approval for their Phase Two expansion because of disapproval by the Zoning Board?"

"I think they may have been unprepared to completely answer the questions still pertaining to traffic counts and a second access road."

"Is it correct that they can't go back to the ZBA with the same plans because they have been denied their special exception twice now?"

At that question, Todd cleared his voice, stroked his short, gray beard, and with a slight gruffness in his voice responded.

"The ZBA has to make the determination of whether or not a plan is repetitive. If so, they reserve the right not to hear it again. If the plan is deemed different, then they could rehear the proposal, or in that case, hear it for the first time."

Not particularly liking the response and determined to get a more definitive reply, Nikki continued her questioning.

"If Caring Home Services changed their elderly housing plans from eight units per acre to four units per acre, do they have to appear before the ZBA again, or just the Planning Board?"

"That would probably create some questions from the Planning Board as to why they are changing plans. Any approvals granted by the Planning Board would remain conditional on the ZBA."

"If they revise their plans from elderly housing to an over fifty-five age cluster type of housing development, do they lose their elderly housing status?"

"Most likely."

"If they revise their plans to cluster housing, is it in the town ordinances that they must designate fifty percent of the land, not including wetlands, for conservation land that is not developable?"

Todd was starting to show his impatience at what he must have thought would be only a few questions. With an outward sigh, he replied, "Yes. They must designate a portion of the land for conservation.

"Let me ask you another question," Nikki said. "Is Caring Home Services required by our town codes to state what they are calling themselves? Or are they able to keep switching around until they find something that fits their solution? For instance, are they a retirement community, an elderly housing complex, or cluster housing?"

"It basically comes down to what I have to say about it as the town planner. If they continue to switch around, as you put it, and let's say the permit is denied, then it would go back before the ZBA, and the board might have some legitimacy issues with the project."

At that point, Nikki decided to switch topics and asked, "If CHS changes from elderly housing to let's say a retirement community of over fifty-five years of age, or even apartments, or residential housing, the trips per day count would definitely increase requiring a second access road to the property. Is that correct?"

"Yes. A road of some fashion would be required."

Noting that Todd was getting slightly perturbed at her

continued questioning, Nikki asked one last question.

"At the last ZBA meeting, it was noted that cluster housing specified a density of four units per acre. I know Caring Home Services wishes to build as many apartments as they can in order to get eight units per acre. But I thought that *cluster housing* was actually three units per acre per the Land Use Code, not four units per acre. Which is correct?"

"The correct density for cluster housing is three units per acre, not four."

"Thanks for your time and for answering my questions, Todd." she said, and left his office.

She imagined Todd would be happy to see her leave.

ii.

The late afternoon air was warm for mid-June, and Joe Vaschon was clearly agitated by the probability that there could be more public hearings. Joe's wife, Mary, Nikki Williams, Will Penton, Emmy Anderson, Kevin Sparks, Nelson, and Sarah sat around the picnic table in Marie Paterson's backyard to regroup and discuss their collective information subsequent to April's ZBA hearing.

Joe was the first to speak.

"Mr. Tussi and his client have been awfully quiet lately. I was hoping we were done with all these public hearings. Is that why we're all here this afternoon—to discuss the continued efforts of Mr. Tussi in getting their project approved by the town?"

"Yes," blurted Emmy. "Two days ago, I found out what CHS has been up to. Katrina Scott from the Laslo Journal was doing a follow up story about the CHS project. I've known her for several years. She called and told me that Kurt Tussi is redrawing the site plans. That's why we haven't heard from anyone since the ZBA public hearing in April. He's removed sixty apartments from Phases Five, Six, and Seven, which is probably equivalent to two wings of the massive one hundred and eighteen unit apartment complex that was originally shown on the plans for those phases."

"You mean they're redrawing the plans and they're changing three proposed phases so it looks like one smaller complex?" asked Nikki. "My God! Aren't we supposed to only be talking about Phase Two for approval? I swear that Kurt Tussi's asshole must be larger than his mouth, 'cuz he keeps talkin' out of it!"

Emmy chuckled at Nikki's remark, and continued her report to the group. "Katrina said she was informed that they are going to use Baker Street as their second access and emergency road. So they plan to be back before the Planning Board by August to get all these plans approved. I've already called the people who live on Baker Street and requested that each of them write a letter to the Planning Board members, stating they didn't want Baker Street used as an access road. I told them to make five copies and get them to the town hall by the end of July, at the latest. I think most of them will do that."

"How do they keep getting away with using Baker Street as a means of access?" Will asked. "They keep getting told they can't use it. Yet, they continue to put it in their plans, and the boards continue to let them do it even after they've told them they can't. How does that even happen?"

"I certainly can't figure that out either," replied Nelson. "It's exasperating. It's like big brother is ignoring the little guy. If I were chairperson on either of those boards, I'd tell them to flat out remove the idea of using Baker Street in any capacity."

"I guess at this point," replied Will, "it's urgent we get a letter out to our town tax assessor asking about the evaluation of CHS's property taxes. I know the Planning Board doesn't want to address the issue, but it does have some bearing on the welfare of the town. Besides, it's been quite a while since this issue was brought up and nothing yet has been determined."

"How utterly depressing. So, because they are changing the plans, there will be another public hearing." Emmy commented. "Since I seem to have such a great rapport with our town tax assessor, now that I've told him how to do his job, I'll write the letter to Mr. Duncan reminding him about CHS's exemption from property taxes. I don't think he'll forget my previous conversation with him."

"I'll put together a 'bullet' type list in a letter regarding violations to the town ordinances so the Planning Board has something to think about," Nelson replied. "Anything else?"

"Yeah," said Nikki. "I talked with Todd Hatch in his office last month, after the last ZBA meeting, and I wanted to fill everyone in on what he said. I wrote it all down so I wouldn't miss anything and made copies for everyone to read."

"I was just at the town hall this morning and spoke to Todd Hatch," said Kevin. "I didn't know you had also talked with him. He wasn't in a very cooperative mood. I think he's getting tired of talking to us. He told me there's no additional information regarding *any* changes to Phase Two. I'll pick up a copy of the latest blueprints when they're revised so we can review them prior to the next Planning Board meeting, whenever that is."

"Thanks, Kevin, that'll be a big help," said Nelson.

"I was also talking with our Code Enforcement Officer," Kevin continued, "and he said that Joan Landers of the Conservation Commission has already sent three letters to CHS regarding wetlands issues with their current plans. Evidently, at some point, CHS still wants to build a bridge connecting their North and South Campuses over the extensive wetland area that divides the two properties. That's why they never removed the annotation about a bridge from their plans as they were asked to do."

Nelson gestured his disapproval by slightly shaking his head from side to side, and loudly mumbled, "This thing never seems to end does it?"

iii.

David Jakes, the town manager of Laslo, knocked on the open door to Todd's small, cluttered office and entered. "I just read a copy of an e-mail that Mr. Quip sent you. Did you answer him yet?"

"Have a seat, Dave. No, I haven't answered him yet. You know how it is. Preparing for the Planning Board meetings is always hectic for my office. Mr. Quip believes the Planning Board might be in violation of the Land Use and Development Code Zoning Ordinance, pertaining to the order of review. I'll have to remind him that the ordinance states that where action of the ZBA is required, such action is *encouraged* prior to a Planning Board review or request. The word 'encouraged' is operative. Besides, the Planning Board has not yet approved any portion of the Phase Two development currently before them. So there is no order of review relevance."

Dave leaned back is his chair as he faced Todd. "I would surmise the Planning Board would rather have an applicant's approval in hand from the ZBA prior to undertaking their review."

"That would be ideal, but it's not required," he agreed. "Nor is it uncommon for any given applicant to be working their way through the review process on a parallel course."

"So you're telling me we're talking about more than a Phase Two development. They anticipate succeeding and moving ahead with other phases no matter what."

"Look, when the Planning Board approves an application, their approval is based on condition that all the other necessary permits and approvals are complete. That includes local, state, and federal levels. The members of the Planning Board are well aware that Caring Home Services has been twice denied their Special Exception from the ZBA for a portion of their proposed project."

"Doesn't that waste the Planning Board's time? If the ZBA denied the Special Exception the company needs in order to make it economically feasible, why continue and delay other groups from getting approval for their projects?"

"As I understand it, the Planning Board feels the application before them should not be confused or combined with the Special Exception that's sought. Their review is totally independent of the ZBA, whether or not it makes sense to stop the process until it's resolved, one way or another."

"Todd, Mr. Quip cited another section of the Code about the timing of repetitive applications that perhaps disqualifies CHS from submitting another special request to the ZBA."

"It's entirely up to the Zoning Board to determine whether or not a subsequent application is a repetitive petition for the project. The ZBA has to agree that the project is significantly different from a previous presentation, or from other circumstances as stated within that particular section of the ordinance in order to be considered. As I understand it, neither board can or will deny acceptance of an application for review."

"It seems to me there should be some sort of caveat in the ordinance to stop a parallel process from occurring if one board has denied part of the requirements for a development. They should fix whatever has to be resolved then continue on their parallel course. What about the property tax issue questioned by Mr. Quip?"

"Well, regarding the property tax issue, it's my understanding that the town attorney and the tax assessor are in receipt of a report from CHS in regard to their eligibility for tax-exempt status. Mr. Simon has informed me they are evaluating that report and hope to make a determination in the near future. I'll send an e-mail to Mr. Quip regarding the current status."

"Okay. Thanks, Todd."

iv.

Nikki knocked on Todd Hatch's door and entered his office. Four weeks had passed since she had attended a meeting with her neighbors, and it had been over two months since her last visit with Todd. Nikki noticed the papers scattered throughout his office hadn't changed position much. Unfolded layers of blueprints on both his desk and a nearby table made his office look even more disorderly.

"Have you got a few minutes for me?" Nikki asked. She stood at the front of his desk, looking down at him. "It looks like you're really busy, but I wanted to make sure you were aware of several issues prior to the Planning Board hearing I understand is being held sometime in August. I've been involved with the CHS proposed expansion for a period of time now."

"Yes, you have."

"I've been to most, if not all, of the board meetings, both Planning Board and ZBA. If you are feeling a little angst about seeing me again, I feel your pain."

Todd sighed. He stroked his short beard with one hand as he often did, and mumbled softly more to himself than to her, "Yep, so can I."

Nikki smiled at his low toned remark and the earnest way it showed how he felt. She paced from one edge of his desk to the other while she carefully thought about how she wanted to phrase her next remarks.

"You understand that Caring Home Services was denied

their Special Exception to continue with the construction of Phase Two, not once, but twice now, don't you? The plans they presented hadn't changed enough to warrant any further discussion. They simply hadn't changed anything to fix what the ZBA had told them was problematic. They seemed to have simply ignored the board. Probably because they thought they would only have to address the Planning Board and circumvent everything else."

"That's speculation on your part," said Todd.

"Yeah—well, I've recently seen the new plans the developer is submitting for the August Planning Board hearing. I assume you've reviewed them as well?" She glanced over at the layers of blueprints on a nearby table.

"They're on the table over there. And, yes, I've reviewed them."

"It's been said that this is a phased project. However, we should only be discussing Phase Two. When I look at the latest plans, the only changes I can see to Phase Two are the addition of Baker Street as a second access road and the elimination of two parking spaces. So why are these plans going before the Planning Board again without addressing any of the ZBA's concerns?"

She continued talking without allowing Todd a chance to respond.

"Since both boards have repeatedly denied CHS the use of Baker Street as a secondary access road, why is it back in the plans? I realize with the trip counts being what they are, this project requires a secondary access road, something the developer never wanted to admit to while they were discussing the bogus trip count numbers they kept presenting for Phase Two. How many more times is Baker Street to be denied before being removed from the plans? It appears to me if CHS keeps arguing for the same plans until they wear down the board members, they will obtain approval they are looking for. It seems to be a great tactic that works for them."

Todd sat listening to Nikki, not contributing to the one-sided conversation; she continued.

"I'm really concerned that although this South Campus development project was originally approved as a phased project, CHS will start grouping all the phases and future expansions together into one development. The developer should not be allowed to combine them if that's what they have up their sleeve. The overall density numbers have been reduced, but in actuality they have only removed two wings from one massive building, which was to be the last apartment complex constructed if the last phase of the project was approved. I personally think that CHS will be trying to gain approval wholly, rather than by individual phases." She leaned forward and met Todd's eyes, "You must know something about what they are planning. What's the story?"

"I really can't tell you what those private conversations were about," Todd responded.

"You can't or won't?"

"Both."

"From what I can see," Nikki replied, attempting to pry what information she could from the reluctant town planner, "according to their new set of plans, this project has been reduced from seven phases to four phases now. It's great they've reduced the number of phases, but unfortunately the size of the development hasn't changed much. They're trying to convince the boards we need more elderly housing, even though the town's comprehensive growth plan says we already have forty-three percent more elderly housing than what the town needs. According to the minutes of the ZBA meeting held in April, Mr. Dwyer told the board the median age of their residents is eighty years old and that they are getting frail. Mrs. Emery of the ZBA then asked him about what they offered for services for these people. They discussed the definition of congregate care and concluded that CHS simply doesn't offer services indicative of a congregate care facility.

"So you have residents whose median age is eighty, getting frailer, and soon won't be able to live by themselves. Instead of offering those residents a place to live where they can receive assistance, they want to build additional rental apartments where only self-sufficient people can live. In my world, a charitable and benevolent organization would help them and not kick them out when they can no longer live on their own. It makes you wonder what their actual purpose really is."

"Why are you telling me all this? I thought you had some issues you wanted to discuss with me. Shouldn't you be addressing your concerns with the Planning Board?"

"I don't want to monopolize your time. I just wanted you to think about these things before Kurt Tussi and his client's arsenal of attorneys filled your plate. Don't forget, there are a lot of discrepancies with this project that are still questionable, including wetland delineation, wildlife ignorance, and taxes. I just want you and the town to consider all the information before taking the word of one architectural firm and their client trying to push through a huge project."

"Put this all in writing and submit it to the board for their review."

"I already have. Several other abutters have also submitted packages that discuss each Land Use and Development Code that doesn't appear to be met in their continued attempt to get approval for Phase Two. I just don't understand why the board is reviewing a set of plans that have no changes to Phase Two."

"I'm not sure what they propose to submit, only that they have some changes that they're working on," Todd curtly replied. "It's up to the board to decide what changes can be submitted."

"Mr. Duncan has also been given a comprehensive package by Mr. Quip, regarding property tax exemptions," Nikki said. "The state laws are very specific. If a company is not incorporated within the state, they are not eligible. Since, for some unknown reason, no assessment reviews have been done for the last ten years or so, it would be interesting to know whether or not back taxes can be applied."

Todd stroked his short beard once again. He appeared disgruntled and somewhat impatient by the continued diatribe.

"All I can tell you is Mr. Duncan and our town attorney are working on that particular issue now; they anticipate completing their study later this fall. At that time the determination will be made public and you'll be welcome to get a copy of it."

Nikki realized Todd had shut down their conversation with his statement and didn't want anything more to do with her quest for information. She quietly left his office after an abrupt good-bye.

After Nikki left, she paused just outside and listened. She heard Todd's chair creak when he sat back, pictured him stroking his beard, then heard the phone lift from its cradle. She left before hearing who he was calling because a door down the hall opened and she didn't want to get caught eavesdropping.

V.

It was the latter part of August when the Planning Board reconvened. The board members hadn't changed nor had the plentiful supply of hard metal chairs, accommodating the increased number of interested residents of Laslo. Nelson looked about the room and noted the key opposing players were all there—Kurt Tussi, Phil Dwyer, John Townsend, and Attorney Dumas.

Chairperson Tunney introduced the project once again in order to formally address the hearing. This time, however, Nelson noted the project was introduced as a Phase Two, Major/Cluster Subdivision for Elderly Housing, a somewhat different introduction from previous meetings.

"I'd like to bring the board members up to date on the modifications we've made to our site plans," said Kurt with his revised proposal. "I will also have Mr. Townsend discuss his study of traffic counts. Afterward, I'd like the board to discuss these changes and respectfully consider approving these plans since I believe they now meet the town's requirements. The biggest modification is the reduction of sixty units over the entire plan. Before us, proposed in total, are now four phases versus seven. We reduced the larger multiplex building proposed as Phases Five, Six, and Seven by sixty units. We also reduced parking. Other than the reduction of a few parking spaces, Phase Two remains the same for your consideration and approval. Your town planner, Mr. Hatch, and I have discussed this and decided to leave Phase Two essentially the same. There is one modification to that, however. On our plan, although I don't believe we need it, we've included an emergency gated access to Baker Street. The Public Works director, Mr. Norman Blake, and the Fire Chief, Mr. Gerard, support this inclusion. The emergency gated access would also provide a secondary way to Baker Street."

Nelson could overhear an exasperated Nikki Williams whispering to Will Penton. "How can they just keep ignoring the fact that they're not supposed to be using Baker Street as an access or anything else for that matter? This is like having big brother doing whatever they want and to hell with everyone else. Gee, where have I seen that lately? Not within our own government—nah. It's like a virus. It just keeps growing. And duh, sure, why wouldn't a Fire Chief want an emergency access? It would sound pretty stupid if he didn't want one, wouldn't it? These people are just unbelievable!"

The volume of Kurt's voice increased with deliberate conviction. "In the past, there have been a number of comments from the abutters. I believe we have provided adequate responses to their statements.

"The first concern involves the amount of fill needed. The main floor for one of the buildings in the plan is fifteen feet higher than ground level, but there is a finished basement, so there is only three feet of fill. Another concern is about the vernal pools. The abutters say there are three vernal pools. They now say there *could* be three. Big difference between are and could be. The point here is not to debate each of their concerns. There is some truth based on fact and some concern based on emotion.

"I would like to move forward with the new information and will be glad to answer any questions the board may have at this time. If there are no questions, our traffic engineer, Mr. Townsend, will make his presentation. Traffic has been a big element of this subdivision, and Mr. Townsend is more than qualified to answer those questions. The Ordinance is not based on someone going out and counting traffic. They are supposed to calculate it with the ITE manual, which he has done."

"A little condescending to all of us who did our own traffic count, wouldn't you say?" mumbled Nikki to Will.

"Go ahead, proceed with your discussion, Mr. Townsend," said Chairperson Tunney, looking a little annoyed at the background noise from the public.

"Traffic generation from this project will be minimal. When I initially prepared this information, I focused on peak hour traffic, and said everything that is not a duplex will be considered a senior adult attached development. I now consider the duplexes to be senior adult detached. Based on my previous experience, I'm looking at this facility as congregate care with some independent living and communal activities. Based on our traffic count, Phase One and Phase Two would be less than two hundred trips daily."

"Mr. Townsend," interjected the chairperson, "the board members will probably have some questions regarding your trip count. I suggest we go to this right now for discussion."

"Thank you, Mr. Tunney," said Elaine Graft. "I do have a question. With a number less than two hundred trips per day, the applicant is apparently using the figures for congregate care facility for the bulk of the units. If the applicant used the number for senior attached, that number is well over two hundred trips per day. Mr. Townsend, how many dwelling units will there be in the South Campus when Phase Two is completed?"

"There will be sixty-eight units. We figure forty-two of those units are elderly housing attached and twenty-six of those units are congregate care. The figure for elderly housing attached is 3.4 trips per day. The figure for congregate care is 2.02 trips per day per the ITE Standards."

"I think congregate care facilities typically offer dining," said Elaine.

"Not always."

"That's how the ITE Standards define it," she replied. "That issue was discussed at the ZBA hearing in April. I read the minutes of that meeting. You should know that was addressed since you were involved in the discussion. If you're talking about congregate care, you're talking about a facility where people don't need to leave, where they have services provided for them, like what was discussed at the April hearing. That certainly doesn't describe this applicant's development."

"I'd like to explain," he replied.

"I bet he would," Nikki mumbled to herself.

"Cooking facilities are provided in the apartments," continued Townsend, "so residents can prepare their own meals. Congregate care facilities are typically populated by those who don't have automobiles but they could have meal services delivered to them. They can also have meal services linked with care, which will be available in later phases, where the person could eventually go to a nursing home. But even if the figure for elderly housing attached was used entirely, instead of congregate care, requiring two access points, the applicant has that."

"How in the hell did they just get a second access point?" Nikki asked as she turned to Will and poked him in the arm.

"The issue in traffic is not daily traffic," added Townsend. "It would be like telling Mr. Tussi to design drainage based on the yearly amount. You do it based on peak flow."

Drew Laden had a concerned look on his face as he spoke up for the first time in the hearing. "I'm having trouble understanding why we're going through this argument. If we look at the definitions at face value, there's a difference between the ITE Standard for a congregate care facility and a senior housing detached unit. I think Mr. Townsend is pushing the definition as far as he can in one direction, seemingly trying to get away from the total of two hundred trips per day, and now he says that the discussion is moot because the applicant is providing the second access anyway. If the applicant is doing that anyway, then why are we debating the nuances of these definitions?"

"I agree with Mr. Laden," said Brett. "I think discussing the trip counts is a moot point. Just go with the higher number of trips. And the fact is that they have provided a secondary access, unless we don't think that's enough."

"The issue *is* the access and that hasn't been discussed with us before this," said Tunney. "Certainly, we have some members of the public who oppose the use of a gated access."

"If they didn't have a second access, I'd feel more strongly about a resolution to this issue," said Brett Manley. "I really think the actual trip count number that should be used is somewhere in the middle."

"I agree this is an argument that we don't need to have," said Tunney.

"I sure think it's an argument that's necessary," mumbled Nikki, "'cause I still don't understand how they now have a secondary access point."

Don Morgan said, "I have two conclusions from this discussion. One is that a second entrance is needed, and the second is that the numbers are higher than those that Mr. Townsend gave us."

"We're not at a level of this project where there's a problem requiring a secondary access," said Brett.

"We seem to be depending on which ITE standard is being used," replied Don.

"I don't have a problem with accepting the presentation regarding the trip count issue," said Tunney. "Some of the board members may disagree, and I respect their opinion. But we don't need to worry about the trip counts at this point. It's somewhere in the range, perhaps at the higher end of the range. What about the use of Baker Street? What exists there now at the end of Baker Street and what changes would occur?"

"Norman Blake, the town's Public Works Director, wanted a turnaround placed at the end of Baker Street that extends onto the old wood's road on the applicant's property, where they would have a gate," said Kurt Tussi. "The wood's road would join the Baker Street pavement."

"Would Baker Street be extended?" asked Tunney.

"No," replied Kurt, "just an area for turnaround when they plow Baker Street in the winter."

"This is a bit different than what you show on your new site plans," said Tunney.

"That's because the site plans were created before we reached a compromise with the town planner."

"Have any parking or number of apartments been reduced in Phase Two?"

"There's been no decrease in the number of units," replied Kurt, "but the number of parking spaces have been reduced by four spots."

"Has there been any shift in the placement of buildings or pavement?"

"No," replied Kurt.

"There may be a few aspects of this discussion that members of the public will want to comment on," said Tunney. "Are there any other comments from board members before those discussions?"

"There's a wetland crossing near the turnaround being proposed at the gated entrance onto Baker Street," said Drew.

"The turnaround is on high ground," said Tussi.

"How much of that old wood's road would have to be upgraded for Phase Two?"

"It's difficult to say. We'd construct a new gravel road,"

said Tussi.

"Will you be putting a gravel road where you're thinking about putting a permanent road?" asked Don.

"Yes."

"I'd like to ask for public comments on the new aspects of the plan," said Tunney. "There's been extensive public comment as to the plan already presented, and I'd like to hear only comments about the new aspects of the plan. With respect to anything that has been addressed before, I'd ask that the public keep their comments very brief."

vi.

"I'll keep my comments brief," said Kevin Sparks. He stood and pushed the thick black frame of his glasses back from the edge of his nose. "For the record, I never said there are vernal pools on the property. I've always stated that there are potential vernal pools. What I'd like to know is what effect the changes at the end of Baker Street will have on future phases, as well as water runoffs to the wetlands. That's all I have for now." He looked in Nelson's direction. "I believe Mr. Quip has something he wanted to say."

With the odd introduction from Kevin, Nelson stood to address the board members.

"I'll keep my comments brief, as well. The ZBA denied the special exception for this development at two independent hearings. There are also at least a half a dozen zoning criteria not met under the town's Land Use and Development Codes. From what I've heard tonight, there are basically no changes to Phase Two. During a previous meeting with this Planning Board, I was told that the use of Baker Street wasn't to be addressed and access was not to be allowed. This development has now been proposed to become four large, toxic pills rather than seven little ones. None of the issues with the Criteria Factors have been corrected. I trust the board members have read the information letter I submitted. I won't get into the congregate care matter. However, I find it interesting that brochure information from Caring Home Services refers to themselves as a retirement community. The town's Comprehensive Plan suggests four buildings per acre for such a facility. In short, it's time to discontinue deliberations on plans that have not been corrected."

"Thank you for your written submission, Mr. Quip," said Tunney.

"Just for the record, I wasn't given a copy of Mr. Quip's letter," said Kurt Tussi.

"Mr. Hatch, do we have an extra copy for Mr. Tussi?" asked Tunney.

"It went out in the packet for the others," replied Todd. "But my secretary didn't put it in with the abutters' letters for Mr. Tussi."

"I have an extra copy." Kevin Sparks maneuvered his large frame around the chairs and handed Kurt a copy.

"If CHS owns a piece of property that borders the end of Baker Street, what's to prevent them from opening a gate to access that property any time they want?" asked Millie Hodgdon. "And how will they be taxed?"

"The tax situation will be worked out with the Town Manager," said Tunney. "As far as a gate and its use, if it's an emergency gate, a lock box will be available for firemen to use only, with a break away fence that you have to drive through. It would say it was restricted on both the plans and the gate, and that is sufficient assurance that it won't be used otherwise."

Persistent with her questioning, Millie continued. "Why did you wait this long before mentioning that?"

"I can't answer that."

Millie sat down, appearing to Nelson to be somewhat distraught with the evasive answer to her question.

Someone else was waving their hand, trying to get recognized so they could speak before the board members.

The chairperson motioned for the person to speak.

"My name is John Silverman. I spoke against this project during what you might consider to be the April retrial of the ZBA. My property abuts this development. I don't envy this board's responsibilities. I know there's a lot to consider. But as Mr. Quip noted, the ZBA did deny this project a Special Exception, and that denial encompasses the same criteria which applies to these site plans tonight. The applicant has presented a mishmash of information which changes like the weather. I think the trip count changes depending on what will appease whichever board the applicant is before. Caring

Home Services had Baker Street in the original plans, and it has been denied several times by the ZBA. Now the applicant is digging up the same grave. I don't understand how this board can keep agreeing to listen to that argument. This board has a list of discrepancies in front of it. I don't know if the separate boards intermingle their facts, but ZBA had a package of information that the Planning Board should have read instead of skim coating the issues. If the members of this board haven't read all of the information, then any decisions made are bogus.

"The ZBA found that what they voted on recently wasn't what they voted on originally several years ago, and they changed their minds for additional approvals. This board should ensure it's being presented with a full factual package before it approves or disapproves this project. As far as the wetlands are concerned, I don't believe the DEP has looked into it to question the amount of wetlands and vernal pools. I've lived in this area for many years; it looks wet to me. I think it should be reevaluated."

"The Planning Board and ZBA would probably agree that the present way of doing business is not satisfactory, with the bouncing back and forth between two boards at the same time," said Tunney. "We're not all in the same room at the same time and not getting the same packets of information. The Town Council should be looking to change the procedures. I would propose that Special Exceptions would go to the Planning Board as well as site reviews, and not to the ZBA."

"That would sure make things a lot easier for the Planning Board to approve, wouldn't it?" Nelson queried Sarah. "It would be just like having executive orders signed with no one managing the store, so to speak—perhaps somewhat of a dictatorship."

"In terms of what the ZBA did or did not do, and understanding the basis for their decision," the chairperson continued, "we don't second guess their process and procedure. It is not our role to do so. The town ordinance currently requires two bodies of review. It does not clearly indicate on the order in which the review is performed. We feel in this instance the ZBA approval will remain a condition. If the condition never gets resolved, this phase won't get built."

Anxious to make a public statement, Nikki Williams stood

to address the board members. "I have a question in regard to Mr. Townsend's presentation. He said he deals with peak hours and not trip counts. There's been a lot of waffling back and forth on the numbers being used. I'd like him to re-explain his traffic numbers."

With a heavy sigh, the chairperson asked, "Would you care to explain your numbers again, Mr. Townsend?"

"Sure. The peak hours for the development will not occur during normal peak hours of the adjacent roadway, which is Route 2. Everyone in the development is probably out after 9 a.m. and back before 3 p.m. Since their peak hour traffic is different, they probably have little impact on the peak hours that occur on the adjacent major roadway. I've done no studies in terms of counts. I've only used the ITE Standard's manual to see how much traffic would be generated in the morning and in the afternoon."

"I'd like to clarify that Mr. Townsend was following the ordinance," said Tunney after Nikki sat down, "which requires the use of a standard's manual, in this case the ITE standard. That standard can be referred to for the information relating to traffic counts for peak hours."

"Mr. Townsend came up with a low enough number that he didn't need to discuss two entrances in his original study", said Drew Laden. He said that he considers the twenty-six unit multiplex building as a congregate care facility."

"If they don't drive cars, why do they need all the parking spaces?" stated Don Morgan.

Noticing no answers to Don's question, Sarah re-introduced what she and many others had previously asked without getting a satisfactory response.

"In previous ZBA hearings, the chairperson said that Baker Street wasn't to be used as access to the develop-ment. Why is that access still being addressed?"

"Was that in regard to a secondary access or emergency access?" asked Brett Manley.

"I have the minutes of that hearing with me," Sarah re-plied as she read through sections she had highlighted. "They discussed the use of Baker Street as a secondary emergency access. At that time, the chairperson of the ZBA, Mr. Bolduc, stated that Baker Street was not to be used for access to the property even before they saw the plans. Either type of access means you are still trying to use Baker Street."

"There are two issues here," said Tunney. "Does the traffic require a secondary access or does it only require an emergency access? What I understood the engineer to say is the amount of traffic generated by this does not meet any threshold of concern or anything in our ordinance that would require something of the developer. What we did need was a secondary emergency access." Glancing around the room, he added, "I see three other hands up. After addressing those questions we'll proceed with the board's discussion. Mr. Sparks, go ahead once again."

"I don't understand why you don't count in all the traffic for all phases now? In the last phases of the proposed development, their new site plans show there are little foot-bridges running from one area to another, which brings us back to discussing wetland issues. Mr. Tussi may be an expert, but things do change, especially since Phase One was completed. What's to keep them from pushing through all of the phases without addressing the traffic issue? They have already."

Emmy Anderson was one of the three who had her hand raised to speak. Chairperson Tunney quickly recognized her, eluding Kevin's question.

"I also was at one of the former meetings with the Zoning Board. Mr. Tussi stated that he did a wetland study on this property ten years ago. I'd like to see it done by an independent company and flagged. I think there could be a conflict of interest here. The Land Use Code says to do a study within two years of building."

"That study was done before the first phase was built," replied Kurt.

"My point," said Emmy.

Chairperson Tunney didn't respond to Emmy's statement. Instead, he recognized Joan Landers of the Laslo Conservation Commission.

"Mrs. Landers, you had your hand up to be recognized. Did you have a comment from the Conservation Commission?"

"Has the board received our letter?"

"I think it's in our information packet."

"I e-mailed it to you."

"Oh, we didn't print it. We'll need a copy to go into the record."

"I read the e-mailed letter from them," Brett interjected. "They remain concerned about many of the issues they've raised previously, and stated they haven't been properly addressed by the developer. Should Phase Two be approved, they want the wetland crossing removed from the site plan. They're concerned it will cause future confusion and may show tacit approval of the crossing if it remains on the plan. They stated they've repeatedly asked that reference to the crossing be removed."

"I'd be happy to accommodate the request from Mrs. Landers and the Conservation Commission," said Kurt.

"Why didn't you do that when you were asked to before, you asshole," Nikki mumbled, just loud enough for the two rows in front of her to hear. She had a habit of doing that.

Kurt continued. "The reason we made revisions to the plan is in response to the second meeting with the ZBA. After the second meeting, we had discussions with Mr. Dwyer who thought the March meeting went much better than the one in February. The ZBA said it was too dense and needed a secondary access. When Phase Two was originally proposed almost three years ago, the ZBA chairperson told me he would consider a secondary access off Baker Street."

"That never happened during the public hearing," Sarah whispered to Nelson.

"The guy's lying through his teeth," Nelson said, "unless there was some back door deal going on."

"Let's proceed with the board's deliberation," continued Chairperson Tunney. "I'm not sure where to begin."

Nelson saw Emmy look across the room to where Kevin was seated. She caught his glance and both shrugged their shoulders in obvious wonderment on why their questions hadn't been answered.

"I'd like to start with a discussion about this project as a cluster residential development and about the written statements we have, which I don't have in front of me at the moment," said Brett Manley.

"Is the reduction in the number of apartments done in order to get out of the cluster development requirements?" asked Chairperson Tunney.

"For clustered residential buildings, the applicant can't exceed three units per acre," said Elaine Graft.

"If you approve Phase Two, then you are at only 2.36 units per acre," said Tussi.

"Then how would you come up with the project as clustered housing for future expansion?" asked Brett. "Some of the things that you would have preserved in the beginning are not preservable anymore. Down the road, are you saying the future expansion will come under cluster elderly housing?"

"It would come under elderly housing," said Kurt.

"We also need to look at the preservation of natural features," said Brett. "When you come back to add more Phases, the natural features in Phases One and Two disappear."

"We're preserving ledges and wetlands," said Kurt.

"That's because they're not blowing them up or filling them in entirely," mumbled Nikki.

"I'm concerned about going from a non-cluster development to a cluster development, depending on the time of an expansion. I think we need to make that decision now as to whether or not cluster housing is allowed," said Brett. "I thought the applicant was coming before us today with verbiage on how they would do cluster housing for the whole thing, and that they would set a section of property aside so in the future we would see a second cluster. If we don't call it cluster today, we can't do it in the future."

"The cluster development issue has come up a couple of times periodically," said Tunney. "I'm still not sure the applicant has agreed on how it is categorized. What does the board want to do about this cluster issue?"

"It's a cluster all right," mumbled Nikki, visibly fidgeting in her chair.

"If they want to take the entire South Campus for density purposes, then the cluster rules should apply," said Don Morgan. "They should declare now whether or not they are going to use up their reserve of land area for this development."

"When we apply the open space allowances proposed against the numbers in our ordinance, how do they add up?" asked Tunney.

"Looking at the site plan, it does appear they have made a number of changes to accommodate the cluster issue," said Elaine. "They may not be exactly what we're looking for, but they have made a lot of changes and preserved some areas."

"The buffer areas are restricted and recorded," said Kurt. "We have not put the wetlands into a conservation ease-ment, but we'd be willing to do that. The existing wood paths are shown on the plan, the ledge outcrops will be preserved, and basically all the wooded areas will be preserved. We have no problem putting those in easements. I think we are complying with the cluster requirement. If the total develop-ment meets the ordinance, then each construction phase meets the ordinance."

"If they keep building the entire development, there won't be any woods left out there," Sarah whispered to Nel-son. "It'll look like the borough of Queens."

Nelson nodded his head in agreement.

"We keep dancing around the issues," said Drew Laden. "One of the things we have to do in approving a plan like this is to conclude whether it meets the Land Use Code ordinance, the Comprehensive Plan, and any other plan that applies."

"Look, it's already 11 p.m.," said Chairperson Tunney. "Should we continue or set up another hearing time to finish deliberation on these?"

"We still have to discuss the addition of Baker Street as an access," Elaine exclaimed.

"We still need to discuss the wetland crossing," added Don.

"And we need to memorialize where we are in delibera-tions before we stop," remarked Brett. "Can we put a memo together with help from Mr. Hatch addressing the board's deliberations?"

"Yes. I think we should do that," replied Chairperson Tunney. "It's getting really late, and this session concludes our hearing for tonight. Mr. Hatch, when can we continue these deliberations?"

"We can't meet again until at least the first week of No-vember. We have a very full schedule."

"That would be fine with us," replied Kurt. "With the win-ter months approaching, we can't really start on anything until next spring."

"Thank you, gentlemen," said Tunney. "This board will meet once again to discuss this development during the first week of November, to be scheduled by Mr. Hatch."

Chapter Sixteen

Conversations

i.

It was early October when Nelson decided it would be informative and productive to discuss the public hearings and property tax exemption issues with Dave Jakes, the town manager, Todd Hatch, the town planner, and Simon Duncan, the town tax assessor. The notion raised about the Planning Board handling Special Exceptions instead of the Zoning Board of Appeals was bothersome. He thought it would be a good idea to involve Nikki Williams, Emmy Anderson, and Kevin Sparks in the conversations so he'd have a little back-up support.

"Thanks for taking the time to meet with us this afternoon, Mr. Jakes," Nelson said after he and the others walked into the town manager's office. The town manager was alone in his office. "During the last Planning Board hearing, Mr. Tunney recommended that the town's Land Use Code be changed so that the Planning Board handles Special Exceptions instead of the Zoning Board of Appeals. He said it would make it less confusing for an applicant going before two different boards at the same time. I just wanted to say that I think that is a really *bad* idea. I don't believe it's smart to have one branch of government making a decision that affects so many people. A smarter approach would be to require that an applicant receive approval from the ZBA for a Special Exception and not allow both boards to continue their review simultaneously. If the time limit is exceeded whereas the Planning Board hasn't approved a project and changes were subsequently made to a development requiring ZBA review again, then the Planning Board deliberations should be suspended until the ZBA approves the application with those additional changes. That would be a more logical approach."

"You have an interesting point, Mr. Quip. We should go over to Todd's office to discuss this further," replied Dave.

The walk to the town planner's office was brief. It was located at the end of a narrow corridor, around the corner from the town manager's office. With a brief knock, Dave entered the small room first, followed by Nelson and his support group.

Todd looked up from behind a stack of blueprints. The state of disorder was nothing new according to Nikki's description from previous visits.

"Mr. Quip and party have a few things they want to discuss," said Dave, at which point Nelson politely reiterated his concern over the simultaneous approval process by both the Planning and Zoning Boards.

Todd grimaced. Nelson assumed it was because of the group's continued persistence.

"Mr. Quip, the Land Use Code addresses the continuation of a review for an application, and it doesn't imply any cumulative time limit. That section of the Land Use Code allows for the continuation of reviews with the concurrence of both the applicant and the board. So the applicant and each town board can continue what they are doing."

"I just think that's kind of crazy," replied Nelson.

"As I mentioned to Mr. Jakes, the chairperson of the Planning Board also suggested that *they* should handle Special Exceptions instead of the Zoning Board. It appears the Planning Board is already inundated with plans," Nelson said as he glanced at the stack in front of Todd. "I don't believe that board should take on more work by adding the review of Special Exceptions. There are still an awful lot of issues with the proposed development by CHS. The discussion regarding Phase Two has been going on now for at least three years. And the plans keep getting band-aided by the Planning Board. It's also quite noticeable that the ordinances always appear to be compromised by allowing waivers as well as allowing direct violations to the Land Use Code. The ordinances are written for a reason; not to go around them by exceptions. This local board is operating just like the federal government at times—doing whatever they want to do—whether it's the IRS, the EPA, or even the White House."

Before Todd could answer, Emmy Anderson turned to

face the town manager. "While we're here, Mr. Jakes, I wanted to talk with you about the property tax exemption investigation. I e-mailed our town tax assessor, but he's never gotten back to me, which is unacceptable."

"That's a complicated on-going investigation, and any future correspondence should be directed to me as the tax collector, not our tax assessor," said Dave.

"Then I guess I'm finally talking to the right person, now aren't I," Emmy quipped. "I'm anxious to hear if the town actually got an updated Form 1023 from Caring Home Services. You know, that's the form that spells out what a company states they are going to do in order to receive a non-profit status. Anyway, on their current form, CHS stated they would provide short-termed skilled care and the residents would have the use of an on-site nursing home. Mr. Duncan provided me a copy of the original form filed over fifteen years ago. It doesn't corroborate their current statement on the care provided. They don't provide any type of care at all. Therefore, their form is not relevant to their situation today."

"I'm actually the one who asked for that form," Kevin interjected. "When I first asked Mr. Duncan for it, he said it wasn't available and he didn't have a copy. He then asked me to put the request in writing, which I did. I also requested via e-mail that he put together a statement for my records indicating that he didn't have the form available. Right after I sent that request, he somehow came up with a copy. I gave it to Emmy once I received it."

Emmy kept her eyes locked on Dave. "After Kevin gave me that copy from Mr. Duncan, I discovered it was missing pages ten through twenty-two, as well as several attachments pertinent to the form." Still facing him, she asked, "Can you furnish those missing pages to us?" Crossing her arms in front of her, she continued. "I don't understand how you can be basing a property tax decision on an incomplete, fifteen year-old document. Why haven't you requested a more recent and up-to-date copy of their form 1023 from the IRS? To make a true assessment, a current document is pertinent. If they're a legitimate 501(c)3 company, they should have no problem furnishing it. Caring Home Services made over $820,000 last year in rental income according to last year's IRS annual 990 tax form. That form is available to the public because they file as a non-profit organization. They take their so called non-profit income, purchase more abutting land, expand their development, and don't add to the property tax rolls of the town."

Not giving Dave a chance to answer, Nikki joined the conversation. She spoke directly to Todd. "We really need to have CHS decide on what type of facility they really are. I personally think they're a clustered housing retirement institution. They also need to designate what land they are giving to conservation. And it sure seemed like their traffic consultant manipulated the traffic counts and associated terminology to fit their needs. Seems to me it's all smoke and mirrors."

"That's not a very nice thing to say," Todd quickly responded.

"Like I said, it sure seems that way," replied Nikki. "There's a section in the Land Use Code stating that any development expected to generate an average daily traffic of two hundred-one or more trips per day shall have at least two street connections with existing public streets. This is the more restrictive part of the town code that takes precedence. A gated access for emergency use doesn't resolve any traffic considerations. It's not a true second access. You might want to bring that point up with the Planning Board. This is a major issue that CHS is trying to skirt around, and they've been pretty proficient in doing that. Why are ordinances simply ignored? The Zoning Board of Appeals has already refused their Special Exception for elderly housing. So what gives?"

"Look, you'll all have to discuss this at the next public hearing."

Nelson turned to face the town manager. "Mr. Jakes, before we leave, I'm giving you a tax package that I've compiled; you can provide a copy to our tax assessor and the town's attorney. This is a sixty-seven page packet of information regarding the property tax exemption issue. If you compare CHS's Form 1023 against their annual tax Form 990, you'll find some of the information is not entirely accurate. I thought it best to bring several items to your attention as well as Mr. Duncan's. Public hearing boards in our town continue to believe everything they're told by CHS without doing any further research on the issues at hand. At least it appears that way, especially when documents are missing information and the context of information provided appears to get somewhat twisted."

Dave looked at the papers handed to him, then at Nelson. "Okay. Let's talk about this with Mr. Duncan." Dave nodded toward the town planner then turned to leave the room. "Thank you for your time, Todd. We'll get out of your way so you can work and head over to Simon's office, where Mr. Quip and Ms. Anderson can discuss property tax exemption issues."

ii.

Simon Duncan looked up over his half-reading glasses as Emmy Anderson was the first to enter his office, followed closely by Nelson and the rest of the group. David Jakes quickly spoke before Emmy could say a word; he knew that Simon hadn't appreciated Emmy's previous disquisition concerning the responsibilities of his job.

"Simon, Ms. Anderson and Mr. Quip and party would like to talk about the property tax exemption issue regarding Caring Home Services."

"Sure, I have a few minutes." Leaning back in his chair and not looking at Emmy, he asked, "What did you want to talk about, Mr. Quip? You do realize I'm already looking into that matter?"

"I believe it's important to note that although CHS currently has a 501(c)(3) status for exemption of income taxes, it doesn't mean they're automatically exempt from property taxes. I'm a tax accountant, and I've reviewed CHS's current Form 990 versus their Form 1023 originally filed with the IRS over fifteen years ago. It appears they do not meet the qualifications for income tax exemption under 501(c)(3) regulations, let alone qualify for a property tax exemption. But that is a matter for the Internal Revenue Service, and not our town. What is of concern for this town, however, is that the decision for property tax exemption is being based upon information that was filed fifteen years ago and not on more current information. Form 1023 only has to be filed once in order to obtain 501(c)(3) status for income tax exemption unless the purpose and actual function of the organization changes, which in this case it has. Since conditions under the original Form 1023 don't apply to CHS's current business practices, only the annual Form 990 should be used."

"I can assure you, Mr. Quip, the town is not basing its decision on old information. We've been reviewing documentation provided by their attorney in response to specific questions we asked."

"I'm aware of that. Since the information is available to the public, Emmy was able to get a copy of their responses. Part Three of CHS's Form 990 indicates the organization's primary exempt purpose is continuing care for the elderly and Part Seven of that form requests an explanation of how the derived income contributes to the organization's exempt purposes. CHS states on their form that their organization is structured to provide elderly individuals an affordable housing alternative within a suitable environment. The distinction between these two sections is such that CHS does not appear to provide any charitable or benevolent services to their tenants."

"I suggest we go over some of the answers provided by their attorney to the questions asked from my office."

"Sounds like a good idea to me," Emmy said. She abruptly sat down then raised her eyebrows as Simon's furrowed. "Go ahead, Mr. Duncan, let's talk about their answers to you."

He took a gulp of his coffee then set the cup down on the desk.

"Okay, I asked them to detail all qualifications and requirements necessary to become a tenant, including any age requirements and any financial minimum or maximum income or minimum or maximum assets requirements in order to qualify for residence, as well as any benevolent services they provide. Their attorney stated that applicants must be fifty-five years or older and be capable of maintaining independent living. He said they cater to seniors of modest means, and they will offer up to twenty households some rental assistance. He also stated that they provide exercise rooms, a library, desktop computers access, and common areas as included services."

Emmy was quick to respond to Simon. "They've never subsidized their tenants, at least not at this point. That's a fact. If people can't pay their rent, they have to move out. Even if they did help subsidize a few people, it would only help to lower the rent they charge to that which is comparable in the area. Their answer to you also substantiates the fact that no health care services are available or provided."

"The part about not providing health care services is in direct conflict with their Form 1023, which was filed over fifteen years ago and has never been amended," Nelson quickly added. "They don't provide dining, transportation, or housekeeping services."

Emmy's eyebrows raised once again upon hearing Nelson's remark. "As I recall, during the ZBA hearing last March, Mr. Dwyer of CHS was asked by board member Jane Emery what services are provided by CHS to those who live there. Mr. Dwyer said there are all types of social programs, such as art classes, and blood pressure clinics and foot clinics where people can come in and talk about health issues. He said there were a lot of amenities other than just an apartment, including an exercise room, billiard room, library, computer facilities, and a garden plot. Benefits such as exercise rooms and common areas are nothing out of the ordinary. Other rentals in the area provide amenities like pool facilities, laundry facilities, and exercise rooms, but don't consider themselves as providing benevolent services. Those amenities are all part of included rent. Then she asked if there were dining facilities for the residents. Mr. Dwyer said there was *no* dining hall. He said residents could make arrangements with our local hospital for meal services. She then asked if housekeeping services are offered to the residents. He said there weren't. She asked if transportation was offered to get to doctors and dentists. Mr. Dwyer said *no*, not directly, but there was public transportation that comes and picks up residents. At that point Ms. Emery concluded that by the definition of congregate care, Caring Home Services was not a congregate care facility."

"What are you both trying to imply?" asked Simon.

"We're trying to *emphasize*," countered Nelson, "the fact that CHS provides no services for elder care. What they claim as services are not unique from other amenities by other rentals in this area. Other elderly housing projects have similar amenities, yet those facilities pay property taxes to the towns in which they're located. Whatever happened to the assisted care that's referenced in their Form 1023?"

Emmy pressed on. "I noticed in your list of questions that

you asked for reasons why CHS believed they were considered to be a charitable and benevolent organization under Maine law Title 36, Section 652."

"Yes," said Simon, "and as you know from the information I gave you, they said that the Maine statute stated benevolent and charitable institutions include, but are not limited to, nonprofit nursing homes, nonprofit boarding homes, and licensed boarding care facilities. They stated that the word non-profit meant a facility exempt from taxation under IRS Section 501(c)(3). They said that although affordable senior housing is not specifically itemized in Section 652, that section expressly states that the list of institutions is not exhaustive. They said they conduct their operation for a purely benevolent and charitable purpose. By providing affordable housing costs for the area's senior population, they implied that served a tremendous benefit to the community."

"What a bunch of hogwash," Nikki suddenly interjected. Nelson knew she had been quiet for too long and couldn't hold back her thoughts any longer. Both he and Emmy quickly glared at her, hoping Simon wouldn't become too upset and ask them all to leave his office. But Simon surprised everyone by not immediately responding to her outburst.

Nelson took advantage of the moment.

"Simply stated, Mr. Duncan, the town of Laslo is not relieved of any burden by virtue of activities conducted or services rendered by CHS. In contradiction, there are increased costs to our town in terms of services for fire, police, sewer, water services, pumping stations, and increased costs to facility expansions due to increased demand load, as well as imposing higher taxes to other residents in order to compensate for what CHS should be paying. CHS has only been paying two percent of their revenue in lieu of property taxes. They are not paying two percent to the town because they are benevolent, but because it is a state of Maine law. They are not doing us any favors from the kindness of their hearts. Title 36 MRSA Section 652 allows the town to levy a service charge of two percent of their revenues. Therefore, by the town allowing this tax exemption all these years, CHS has had a pretty sweet deal."

Nelson paused to let his words sink in before he continued.

"They've been paying just over six-thousand dollars to

the town for their entire South Campus in lieu of property taxes based upon several million dollars in real estate value. I would imagine that exemption has saved them well over a hundred-thousand dollars a year. All the forms mentioned by CHS may have originally been established with a charitable purpose in mind, but they've never operated in that capacity. They have never established any of the criteria mentioned in Schedule F of Form 1023. In my opinion they actually should owe back property taxes to the town of Laslo. But we're here simply to ask that you consider all this information and assess CHS for future property taxes. There should be no exemption allowed. Caring Home Services is perhaps the most lucrative landlord in Laslo because of the things they've been allowed to do."

Dave leaned forward and placed his elbows on the desk. Steepling his fingers, he looked first at Simon and then back at Nelson.

"Mr. Quip, the decision on the tax exemption will be made by the town assessment team and while your information might be useful, the town is doing its own review for the property tax determination. Your materials are not considered town documents for retention purposes as there was no hearing or request for public information on the issue. We will have our town determination on the tax question in the very near term. But thanks again for your efforts."

Heat rose to Nelson's face at the blatant dismissal. He inhaled deeply and exhaled slowly to calm himself before speaking.

"Mr. Jakes, my intent was only to provide additional information regarding CHS so you could make an informed decision. The questions recently raised should have been asked years ago by the town tax assessor. I'm familiar with many of the tax rules and regulations. From the little information available at the town hall, I was worried that the current depth of review might be insufficient. I'm concerned that a blind eye to limited information could be detrimental in forming a valid conclusion. I have always found it wise to take all information into account whether or not solicited before making decisions. You never know when there is an item that was never considered before, that just might lead to a wiser decision. I'm just trying to help. This decision affects all the taxpayers of Laslo."

"I certainly appreciate the work you've done, and it will be reviewed by staff and others. Your interest and assistance are always welcomed. However, the final decision will be made by our tax assessor with assistance by our legal counsel."

That was a very politically polite way of dismissing us, Nelson thought, as he turned to leave, thanking the two men for their time. His first words to Sarah when he arrived home late that afternoon were—"I've got to tell Max about our conversations this afternoon."

೮ ೮

It was early in the evening when Maxwell saw Nelson's incoming e-mail and several hours later when he replied.

E-mail: Oct 7 – 21:23
To: NelsonQuip
From: Mdraper
Subject: Public Hearing Minutes & Discussions

Hi, Nelson,
Got your e-mail regarding the discussions you had with the town manager, planner, and tax assessor, and thanks for sending me a copy of the minutes from the last public hearings. It amazes me how your opposition can spin versions of their project and twist words so the board members believe them. Just like our federal laws, ordinances are written for a reason; not to go around by exception—very disconcerting. Good luck with your November hearing before the Planning Board—again.
One note of continuing concern. I've noticed a lot of government e-mails and reports about many negotiations on a structured approach to resolving the IAEA's concerns about the possible military dimensions of Iran's nuclear program. Our new Secretary of State is having meetings with Iran, China, France, Germany, Russia, and the U.K. I worry about what we're willing to give up—probably everything, with nothing in return except for kicking the proverbial can down the road, as the saying goes. Kind of reminds me about our former Secretary of State who presided over dropping the

idea of a missile defense system in Eastern Europe in ex-change for nothing. We keep following the same scenarios.

By the way, why don't you come up for a visit? I'm only a few hours away. We can review your manuscript together and discuss the parallels of small town government and large national government as well as the concepts I've been at-tempting to correlate and understand about time dilation, gravity effects, and the relevance to our satellites.

I've been thinking a lot about the past lately, about my wife (her short life), about Alex, about our college days and all the difficult courses we managed to get through together, even about our Area 52 construction—very therapeutic for both Alex and myself at the time. I also think about the fu-ture and the problems we all face, about the contorted events distorted by time and still yet to happen, and perhaps a perception of what I could do to better understand the real-ity of it all. So here I am, getting a little sentimental about everything. Even though we don't see each other very often, I guess I just want you to know how much I value our friendship.

–Max

It had been a long day for Maxwell. Exhausting philo-sophically and technically. He had a few innovative ideas about time dilation and a possible link to the lab's particle accelerator, weighing the options of experimentation. When he checked his e-mail before retiring early for the night, he found an unexpected reply; short and quick—one line—and smiled.

E-mail: Oct 7 – 21:29
To: Mdraper
From: NelsonQuip
Subject: Zoning Board Hearing This Time—Reply

Max,
"I'll be there tomorrow—late morning."
–Nelson

Chapter Seventeen

Pale Blue Dot

i.

It was late morning when Nelson arrived at Maxwell's home. It had been almost ten years since his last visit. Sunshine gleamed from the metal arches of Area 52 and a single green steel door at the front of the building faced Nelson as he reached the end of a long driveway. Everything appeared the same, with one exception—a large parabolic dish mounted on a single pedestal was positioned next to the side of the structure. Area 52 had no windows and only a single outside camera, alerting any occupants inside of arriving company. Nelson smiled and stepped from his car into the crisp October air, looking forward to his visit.

The green steel door opened and Maxwell stepped outside. "Great to see you again," Nelson said, followed by a quick handshake and a brief hug.

"You too. It's been a long time. Come on in. We have a bit to discuss regarding your manuscript. I also called the lab earlier and arranged a quick tour of our research center for later this afternoon. You probably have to get back home later today, but I thought you'd find the facility of interest. Neither of my assistants will be there this afternoon. It's Saturday, and we all need a little time off at some point." He grinned back at Nelson then continued toward the building. "So it's just you and me this afternoon. I was hoping Alex could be here, but he's finishing up some research material for his thesis."

Nelson hadn't been in the building since he had helped with its original construction, and memories of days working closely together engulfed his thoughts. The tiled hallway, sheetrock, mudding, paint, Ethernet cabling, electrical, wall to wall benches, and the fleeting days of focused, yet enjoyable labor—it all came back.

Although Nelson perceived the main computer room to be a conglomeration of servers, monitors, oscilloscopes, scanners, and a few pieces of unidentifiable equipment, his first remark was in regard to the outside of the building.

"I noticed you installed a large parabolic dish to create your own rendition of a radio telescope. You said you were going to do something like that after we completed this structure. It really makes this building look like it came out of some sci-fi movie. Have you been listening for ET?"

"Yeah, in a way." Maxwell smirked. "That's what some of this equipment is for. Alex and I put the parabolic antenna together and then designed a receiver with the help from several universities. Of course, it's only a very small unit and not as sensitive as any large array, but it gives us the opportunity to study the radio frequency portion of the electromagnetic spectrum from astronomical objects. It took us a couple of years to make it functional, but most importantly, it brought us together more." Then as an afterthought, he added, "We do get some interesting radio signal images at times, though."

Nelson smiled at Max's comment, thinking of the difficulty in raising a child alone. When he looked about the room, a large framed image of 'the pale blue dot' caught his attention.

"I see you still have that image of earth from Voyager I."

"That was the last image it sent," said Maxwell. "The satellite was about six billion kilometers away when it took that image on Valentine's Day in 1990. Then the cameras were turned off to save power and memory for the instruments. Doesn't seem possible that Voyager I was launched back in September of 1977. Now it's over twenty billion kilometers from earth and it's still sending scientific information about its surroundings, taking over seventeen hours to reach the Deep Space Network."

"But weren't your two satellites, Sagittarius-A and Turing-B sent before that?"

"Yes, by almost twenty years. They were private, experimental launches about six years apart. Back then, they were named Sagittarius-A-21132 and Sagittarius-B-21133. A few years ago we changed the name of Sagittarius-B to Turing-B. I'll elaborate on the reason for the name change during our tour of the particle accelerator, where you'll find the explanation more interesting. Right now, we should take the time to review a few portions of your manuscript. Then we'll go to the lab. It's only about a thirty-minute drive from here."

ii.

As Maxwell stood at the entrance to the fourth level of the research complex, his conversation with Nelson was interrupted by the southern accent of a tall, thin security guard.

"Afternoon, Dr. Draper, unusual to see you here on a Saturday afternoon. Usually, I see you either late at night or early mornings."

"Hi, George," Maxwell said. "Good to see you, too. This is my friend Nelson Quip. What are you doing on an afternoon shift?"

"On weekends, sometimes my shift gets rotated, particularly if they have a shortage of security personnel. This time it was my turn. I've got the identity badge for your friend, Mr. Quip, so he can tour the entire four and five levels with you."

"Thanks, George."

Max led him through each level, ending at level four which housed the main computer servers and Max's work station.

"This hadron collider is impressive," Nelson exclaimed.

"We're quite proud of what we've managed to accomplish so far," said Max. "This particle accelerator is a larger version of the one located with French European Council for Nuclear Research, or CERN for short. They operate the particle physics laboratory known to most scientists."

Even after all these years, Nelson still saw awe on his friends face when he spoke about his work.

"Many people don't realize that CERN is also the birthplace of the World Wide Web because of the need to make data analysis available to researchers everywhere. At some point, we'll offer our data processing facilities as well," Max continued. "Our hadron collider is similar to CERN, where the term hadron is defined as any elementary particle that is subject to strong interactions. We also hope to uncover new particles through strong interactions, anticipating those properties will give us new insights into physics. We just don't know what those new particles will be as we keep trying to find matter's underlying elements and their interactions."

"From what you've shown me this afternoon, I understand that's one portion of your studies. But what's the status of your time dilation experiment?" asked Nelson; they sat across from each other at Maxwell's desk. "You certainly have had some interesting radio transmissions and predictions that have come to fruition."

"Do you remember some of our late-night discussions at college about the fact that time is not regarded as a completely separate concept?" asked Max. "That time is actually combined with space in a four-dimensional aspect called space-time. Space-time contains the laws that govern electric and magnetic fields as well as the laws that govern the motion of bodies. Einstein called space-time theory the new theory of relativity. Time doesn't just flow on forever. Space and time can be warped, you might say, distorted by matter and energy in the universe so that the nature of time is shaped by it.

"I believe time starts as a singularity where a gravitational field is infinitely strong. It means that time would either begin in the past as an expansion of the universe or in the future as a gravitational collapse of stars. Which leads one to the question: does time have a beginning and an end? Mathematically, you could continue time past a singularity, but its concept related to consciousness would come to an end. I guess you could call it imaginary time—a concept derived from Einstein's special relativity and quantum mechanics, mathematically convenient in connecting quantum mechanics to statistical mechanics. It's a difficult concept to visualize. If you imagine regular time as a horizontal line that runs between the past in one direction and the future in another, then imaginary time would run perpendicular to that line. It's not really imaginary in the sense it's made up, but simply runs in a direction different from the time we normally experience. The concept allows you to look at time as if it were a dimension of space. You can move forward and backward along imaginary time just like you can move right and left in space."

Maxwell paused in his disquisition, just long enough for

Nelson to interrupt his thoughts.

"You said there was a reason for the name change to your second satellite: Sagittarius-B to Turing-B. Why the change?" asked Nelson.

"I'll show you." He entered his security password into his workstation and accessed a specific file. The large LED monitor instantly came to life with a detailed constellation map. As Maxwell pointed to the image, he explained, "This is why I thought it would be more interesting to discuss the reason for the name change here at the lab. This map shows the programmed and projected courses of those two satellites and where we believe they are now."

Nelson eyed the coordinate positions on the progressive grid circles. Frowning, he fixed a quizzical look on Max. "At one point it appears that each satellite suddenly moved billions of kilometers from one another in totally different regions of space."

"Yes, both did. We don't know why or how. Our satellites are further from us than they should be. Like I mentioned once before—it's almost like they decided to take a faster vehicle in order to make such a long trip. I believe, however, that they encountered a black hole where the gravity is so strong even light can't escape, but with a pull that may have altered the position and speed of the satellites. Somehow Sagittarius-A managed to return on its preprogrammed course. Sagittarius-B, however, appears to have been caught in a traversable wormhole, one that can be crossed in both directions, which is only possible if exotic matter with negative energy density could be used to stabilize it.

"If negative matter does physically exist, it could bend and shape space-time, allowing faster than light travel. Tachyons were at one time considered by physicists to have faster than light speed properties. Many don't believe in them now; but it's been proposed that when tachyons lose energy, they gain speed, and when they gain energy, they slow down. If they existed, they would have imaginary masses, meaning their mass is only meaningful at speeds greater than light, and move backward in time, which would affect the time of travel. But we're getting into a philosophical discussion and getting away from my explanation of why we changed the name of our second satellite."

Maxwell paused to reflect upon his next choice of words.

"About seven years ago, we found that as Sagittarius-B approached the intense gravity of the black hole's event horizon; the original radio broadcasts sent from earth were returned altered. We started to receive broadcasts about events that had not yet occurred. At first the time differences between when an event was reported and when it actually occurred were short—sometimes days, sometimes weeks. However, as the satellite encountered stronger gravitational conditions, the effects of time dilation became more pronounced. The time between an event forecasted and when it actually occurred were further apart—weeks to months, months to many months, and then even to years. Trying to understand the effect of the apparent time dilation and the enigma of those prophesied broadcasts brought about the name change from Sagittarius-B to Turing-B. We named it after Alan Turing, the person who decrypted Germany's enigma machine coding. Since we're trying to unravel our own mystery of gravitational time dilation and what the messages mean, it just seemed an appropriate name change.

"We are witness to an enigma that we haven't been able to explain. In time, perhaps only another year, we'll eventually lose Turing-B to the black hole's event horizon and its singularity. Sagittarius-A continues on its course, even though it hasn't transmitted a radio broadcast back to us in several years. We don't know why. At some point, we'll lose any ability to contact it, as well. It will probably be decades before we fully understand the elements behind the protracted events foretold, long after we lose access to these satellites that may tell us of our future."

Chapter Eighteen

Disappointment

L

Nelson looked around the room as he sat down, still chilled from the early November air. He noticed Nikki Williams was perched directly behind him. She caught his glance and responded with her grinning smile and matching attitude of frizzy hair. He couldn't help but smile about how she approached things. He just never knew what she was going to say or do next. She'd probably purposely sat behind him just so she could mumble her disagreements in his ear during the Planning Board members' discussions. Nelson's thoughts about Nikki's seating location were interrupted by Chairperson Tunney's voice as he introduced Kurt Tussi and offered him time to speak before the board.

"I've purchased a few new easels for tonight's discussion," Kurt said. He carefully eyed the face of each board member and attempted to establish a personal connection. "I've brought Phil Dwyer, the Director of Caring Home Services, Mr. Stanley Dumas, their attorney, and Connie Parker, a landscape architect from Parker Associates. Miss Parker has worked with us on several developments, similar to this one in other towns. I'd like Miss Parker to talk about her landscaping suggestions.

"We went to her and asked for a critique, especially about possible trails on this property and how the site works with the natural features and topography. In this set of plans is a revised site and grading plan for Phase Two. I've got drawings of these plans on the new easels for our discussion. One is Miss Parker's rendering and the other is my CAD rendering of the site for Phase Two. We've moved the multiplex building an additional twenty-five feet back from the wetland. This plan, including the rendering, is what we're asking you to approve tonight. Your town planner, Mr. Hatch, also asked me to review the cluster subdivision ordinance with the board."

He pointed in the direction of the new plans then continued.

"We've reduced the number of units and parking spaces. Originally, we had proposed two hundred and thirty-five additional units with three hundred and fifty-eight parking spaces. Those numbers have been reduced to two hundred and eight new units with two hundred and seventy parking spaces."

Tussi returned his attention to the board members.

"I appreciate all the time the board members have spent on this proposal. What I'm hoping to do tonight is to bring this to a vote. During every meeting, I feel as though we almost get there. I therefore respectfully ask the board to consider moving this project along its way this evening. I'd now like to bring Miss Parker up to discuss her rendering for landscaping."

Nelson had never heard of Parker Associates or Connie Parker for that matter. Her most noticeable feature was the tight wrap of hair wound around the back of her head into a bun that had highlighted strands of light-blue hair exiting at various angles. One pronounced blue strand exited about three inches straight out the back. Nelson wondered what sort of fashion statement was intended and what would happen if someone pulled on that strand. Would the bun unravel or would some rodent exit the nest? He knew he was being cynical about her appearance just because she was there to support CHS. His mistrust toward her presence heightened as she began her presentation.

"Good evening. I'm Connie Parker. I'm licensed in the State of Maine as a landscape architect and I've been practicing for over twenty years. I do quite a bit of design work for Tussi Engineering and Architecture. Most of it is residential in nature. They asked me to walk the site and comment on the appropriateness of the development, and to look at potential walking trails.

It's a lovely site: gently rolling hills, woodlands for the most part, a benign site suitable for many types of development. When I looked at the master plan, I was pleased to see that the majority of the development is centered with surrounding buffers. The buildings are similar in scale to a residential development—not big, and with the exception of one, a good scale for buildings on the site. I think the treatment of landscaping is very appropriate for what it is."

"Yeah, I just bet she does, depending on how much she got paid," mumbled Nikki, somewhat distracting Nelson from his focus on the presentation.

"On the whole, it's a good plan. It does draw itself away from the abutters. When Mr. Tussi told me it was zoned for residential, I thought this plan was highly superior. As far as the trail system goes, there are existing paths that come from offsite and go across the existing site. They are bucolic and it is wonderful to walk through that woodland."

"While it still exists," countered Nikki, not entirely under her breath.

"Caring Home Services wants to allow the neighboring abutters and those people who live in the development the ability to access that property, and to be able to walk through it as they do now, but on newly manicured pathways. You can see two or three major access points, one of which is down by an old cemetery that abuts the northern part of the complex, and the other which is by an office complex that shares the same road into the current Phase One portion from Route 2. These paths will come across the wetland areas with little bridges that will be constructed for use.

"In Phase Two, Mr. Tussi is suggesting to retain the trails that are already there and link them into a new trail system. Additionally, CHS is proposing a second pathway that comes around the back-side of the site, through the wetland, along to the other side of the wetland. I envision the paths as blaze paths, not graded, but tagged so people can find their way through."

Again, Nikki was quick to respond to the comment, and whispered, "I wonder how many folks they're going to lose in the forest?"

Nelson smiled, envisioning people stumbling through the trees in the dark, then once again focused his attention on the discussion.

"I looked at the master plan to consider what else could be done. On the existing site plan, you can see that a few trails exist. There's even a trail through the wetland, which is not on the plan, but which I walked. That trail has little bridges."

"I wonder where she found little bridges," whispered Sarah to Nelson.

"I've walked throughout all those pathways over several years," said Nelson. "There aren't any little bridges—anywhere. I wonder what she was smok'n during her walk, or if she was even on the correct piece of property."

Nikki overheard their conversation. She tapped Nelson on the shoulder, and said, "I'm surprised she didn't find any small trolls under those bridges."

Miss Parker hesitated, slightly distracted by the whispers in the audience, then continued.

"There is a potential to connect the trails around the proposed Phase Two to the wetlands surrounding the area. I hope that works for everyone." She returned to her seat and Kurt stood once again.

"Thank you, Miss Parker," Kurt said. "I think it's important to note that this development can be accessed not only to the residents, but also to the abutters and citizens of Laslo. With Miss Parker's guidance, that trail system will be an asset. That's all I have to comment upon at this point. I've tried to answer all the board members' concerns. Again, I appreciate the board's time and effort that's been spent on this proposal."

"Kurt Tussi is one smooth talker," Nelson whispered to Sarah. "I'll give him that."

There was a slight pause before Chairperson Tunney spoke.

"To the extent of the new information that has been provided tonight, I'll allow a short public comment period. At the last meeting, we had some comments on the Baker Street issue. The paths are also a change, and there is the reduction in the number of units as well. If there is public comment that is germane to those changes, the public is welcome to speak on any of them."

Nelson stood and asked for recognition to address the board.

"I've provided a very detailed package to this board about this project, and I hope each member has had a chance to read it before this hearing. In these hearings, we seem to discuss issues and never come to a conclusion on any of them. One of the things addressed at the last Planning Board meeting was the density issue. I did some calculations and showed that the density for Phase Two alone is over ten apartments per acre. Those calculations were done using a planimeter to determine actual area per their site plan, and I did so just to ensure the board was aware of the density in just that phase alone."

"What's the page number for that information?" asked Chairperson Tunney.

Disheartened at the thought that no one read the packet, Nelson sighed before he replied.

"It's in enclosure one, the last page. There's a paragraph in there that talks about it. I was really hoping everyone had a chance to read it over before this hearing. Page three, the second paragraph on that page, talks about the individual phases as well as the entire development. Ten units per acre for that particular area of land is greater than what the ordinance allows. The ordinance also states that wetlands should be considered a severe constraint on development. Baker Street is another issue. Last February, the Chairperson of the ZBA said that Baker Street couldn't be used. Such a statement means that Baker Street shouldn't be used as either a road or as an emergency access.

"I'm not going to go over everything that I've provided in the packet of information to this board. The information was provided so it could be read prior to this hearing. There's still a problem with having only one access and egress to Phase Two without the use of Baker Street."

"That access," replied Chairperson Tunney, "is for locked, gated use, and for emergency use only."

"I understand that, but you keep forgetting that Chairperson Bolduc said it was not to be used as an access. Whether or not it's for emergency should be irrelevant. You should also recognize the fact that there are wetlands on both sides of the proposed emergency access onto Baker Street. There are so many questions about the extent of the wetlands that I think they should be re-surveyed. That determination affects net developable area. I also think that a survey should be done by a third party; not the firm that has a vested interest in the development. I trust this board will take the time to deliberate those issues that haven't been resolved to date."

"Does anyone else wish to say something?" Chairperson Tunney asked.

Mary Vaschon stood just as Nelson sat down. Her face was flush and her voice was noticeably angry.

"I find the addition of pathways across the back of our property lines and almost in our backyards utterly reprehensible. You should look at this from our perspective. How would you like more than two hundred people from nearby apartments walking along the backside of your property? I can't believe the totally, unmitigated gall of these people. I certainly hope you won't allow them to do that!"

Will Penton, who sat next to Mary, stood and spoke.

"I have a couple of other concerns, as well," he said. "The Baker Street issue should be a moot point by this time. It was denied and denied and denied, but it still appears and appears and appears in the plans. And you keep talking about allowing that road as an access. I don't get it! You should also look at whether there is sufficient water for the project. That was also discussed once before, and I'd like to hear the board's opinion on that. Now there are walking paths with bridges proposed throughout the wetlands with openness to their residents.

"I've read the packet Mr. Quip has provided. The lack of surveys performed by various departments of the state is addressed on page six of the information Mr. Quip has given you. Satellite photos and hearsay don't cut it. I think someone from the state should come down and look at the area. I think you'd find they would agree that there are more than just people on those pathways. There are a lot of animals that live out there. I think the animal population should be taken into consideration.

"There's a lot of valid points that have still not been answered. I think that Mr. Tussi, the director of the CHS, and their attorneys have been here representing this project simply because there are so many problems with it."

"Anyone else have something to say?" asked Chairperson Tunney, as Will returned to his seat.

"Yes, *I do*. My name is Kevin Sparks. I've addressed this

board on several occasions. I want to say that I agree with all these objections to this project, and the fact that I believe a lot of misinformation has been provided to both Zoning and Planning Boards by this developer. I would like to reiterate what's been said about the use of Baker Street. If the use as an emergency access is approved, even after the ZBA announced it couldn't be used, we'll all find that eventually, after Phase Two is built, Baker Street will turn into a fully accessible connection. I believe this because of the way they push and push and push the rules to the limits.

"The applicant also has an unfair advantage over the people who rent around the area. The real estate person that talked about rental prices at the last hearing went way off the deep end and distorted the facts. I think this board should just put the whole proposal to a rest and say enough is enough."

"Thank you for your comment, Mr. Sparks," said Chairperson Tunney. "I'd like to address information contained in a letter from the Conservation Commission now. The Commission is requesting that conservation easements be implemented on the wetlands, with language prohibiting buildings and structures, soil disturbance, and plant disturbance. This request will go into the record. I also want to thank the applicant for removing a couple of the invasive species and showing concern that the storm water treatment facilities are inadequate."

"Did he just blow off Sparks' statement?" asked Nikki, as she nudged Nelson from behind. Nelson, not saying anything, simply threw up his hands just enough to indicate agreement with her remark and his frustration that he couldn't do anything about it.

Kurt stood to address the board members again. "First of all, it's kind of entering the realm of hearsay regarding the ZBA, where everyone is quoting Chairperson Bolduc about something he might have said."

"I didn't ask folks to stop talking about that, but I am asking that your response be brief, Mr. Tussi," said Chairperson Tunney.

"I've already spoken to Chairperson Bolduc about re-filing once again for ZBA approval."

"Oh, not again," moaned Nikki, loud enough so that the

two rows of people in front of her could hear, which was nothing out of the ordinary for her.

"I was told by Chairperson Bolduc that as far as he knew, the ZBA approved Baker Street as an emergency access and didn't see it as a problem. My client plans on filing for that approval from the ZBA as soon as this site plan is approved by this board. I've also contacted the Director of Public Works, Mr. Blake, and he thought it was acceptable to use Baker Street for an emergency access, as well—for occasional use. We're only proposing use for an emergency. I also don't know how Mr. Quip did his density calculations. If he used the phase lines drawn on the site plan, they are incorrect. The phase lines show which buildings will be constructed on a particular portion of the land. The phase lines do not show the perimeters of the entire parcel. That doesn't mean that the remainder of the lot just goes away. As for the Conservation Committee's request, I have no issue in putting the open spaces into conservation easements. I will send the proposed easements to the Laslo Conservation Committee for review prior to recording them."

"And what do you have with respect to density calculations, Mr. Tussi?" asked Chairperson Tunney. "What are *your* calculations based upon for Phase Two?"

"My calculations would be based on Phases One and Two."

"Is that a cumulative density calculation?"

"Yes. The cumulative density of all units is 5.9 units per acre if all future expansion is done. For Phases One and Two, it would be 2.5 units per acre of net developable area."

"Mr. Quip, what are you using to get your figures?"

"Mr. Chairperson, you need to understand that Mr. Tussi is using the entire acreage in order to get his numbers for just Phases One and Two. That remaining open space will disappear as they construct additional buildings for additional Phases."

"Mr. Quip, I want to know what *you* are using to get your figures."

"When the density issue was discussed at the last hearing, I thought it would be useful to calculate the density for each individual phase. I therefore calculated it based upon how the Phase lines were drawn for the area. If you calculate the density for the areas designated as Phase One and Two, it would be a little more than six units per acre. That number exceeds what the ZBA recommended of four units per acre, without the current eight units per acre requested as a special exception. Just look at the site plan. It's very dense in that one area of land where they're putting all those buildings."

"Mr. Tussi, do you have a reply for Mr. Quip's comment?"

"I just want it to be clear that those phase lines shown on the plan are just drawn around a particular phase of the property. They are not necessarily representing a specific portion of the land to be used. It's just a designation of a phase to be built."

"Thank you, Mr. Tussi. Are there any more public comments on the new aspects to this project?" The room was still.

Nelson sat bewildered by the fact that his arguments had been evasively and tactfully ignored.

"Since there are no show of hands, the public comment portion is now closed. The board members will now deliberate."

ii.

Brett Manley was the first board member to speak.

"I think the fact that CHS has increased the setbacks of the buildings from the wetland areas, shown on this site plan, is a step in the right direction, protecting those buffers. We are looking at Phase Two here and assuming that they will want to go further. I want to make sure that we don't lose something right off the bat that we'll want to maintain. I believe the Laslo Conservation Commission is requesting that we have some sort of language on the site plans regarding conservation easements."

"The plans are currently marked," replied Drew Laden.

"I think what we're talking about here is not an easement, but a covenant not to build or disturb the wetland buffers with a note on the plan," said Tunney. "Let's move on to the issue of Baker Street. Is there an existing wood's road that connects the northern part of their South Campus to Baker Street? What improvements are needed in order to connect the property to Baker Street for use as an emergency access for Phase Two? Do we need a sixteen or eighteen foot wide gravel road?"

Kurt was quick with a reply, anxious to take advantage of a continued discussion.

"Mr. Tunney, Fire Chief Gerard would like a sixteen foot wide gravel road that is maintained year round. That request may require replacement of the current culvert that runs under the old wood's road. It's an old culvert that allows water from the wetland on one side to pass to the wetland on the opposite side. The fire Chief doesn't think the old culvert would support the town's fire trucks in its current condition."

"I noticed that Mr. Quip has included a few photographs of that area in his packet to us," said Chairperson Tunney. "Have you seen his pictures?"

"Yes," replied Kurt.

"Mr. Tussi, are you creating any side slopes on either side of the road?" asked Drew. "Since there are wetlands on both sides of this old wood's road, are you creating a wetlands issue?"

"We'd want to replace the old culvert and do that during a time of year when there was no water in the culvert. We would put a silt fence down on both sides of the road, and the actual crossing would be wider than the current woods road. It would be an extension to Baker Street."

"Does this have any impact on the wetland?" asked Brett.

"The old wood's road crosses the wetland now, doesn't it, Mr. Tussi?" asked Tunney.

"Yes. There should be a foot of gravel cover over the culvert, and there isn't now, so that would change."

"Wouldn't adding a foot of gravel create a bit of a side slope?"

"It would steepen up the side slopes."

"If you increase the width of that wood's road, won't you need a wetland crossing permit?"

"The only disturbance would be the replacement of the old culvert, and that would be considered a maintenance issue," noted Brett.

"The Land Use Ordinance Code explicitly states that if there is repair or maintenance to an existing structure, you don't need a wetlands permit as long as you don't remove more than ten cubic yards of gravel and the existing wetland hydrology is maintained," said Laden. "We can consider this as a repair and maintenance of existing drainage facilities."

"I agree with, Mr. Laden," said Brett. "I don't think a permit is needed in this case. The existing culvert doesn't work at this point. I think the proposed plan works as long as the applicant is not going into the wetland with the side slopes of gravel."

"I'm satisfied with that conclusion," said Drew.

Nikki leaned over whispering to Sarah. "So they're going to get around the issue of a wetlands permit by calling the replacement of a culvert a repair? The only reason the current culvert needs repair is because they want to create a road for the development. Wow!"

"That's exactly what they're doing," said Sarah. "I think we're being railroaded again."

"Let's move on then," said Chairperson Tunney. "What are your thoughts, Mr. Manley, regarding the cluster issue?"

"Well, the applicant has agreed to put areas of Phase Two into conservation easements, or whatever you want to call them. That would include the wetland buffer, and part of that area would be designated as no cut."

"Mr. Manley, are we going back to what we were discussing about recordable covenants?" asked Elaine. "I'm just trying to understand where we are."

"So am I," muttered Nikki.

Nelson smirked, thinking the same thing and wondering how they could still continue going from one topic to another without resolving any one issue.

"I think Mr. Manley is alluding to the remaining land not built upon in Phase Two," said Tunney. "I'm not suggesting a covenant, but rather a note on the plan that says there is no removal of vegetation except for the creation of paths or to remove hazards until further review, or something like that. I would just like some assurance that the applicant could not clear-cut this area under our ordinance without permission from the town."

"I think they'd need to get a permit," said Elaine Graft.

"I don't think it's the applicant's intent to clear cut more area," said Tunney.

"It didn't really cross my mind," replied Kurt.

"Yeah, I bet it didn't," mumbled Sarah.

"If Mr. Tussi is coming back before the Planning Board for

developing more buildings and wants the additions to be seen as a cluster development, he needs to preserve enough land for use," said Tunney. "The driver behind this discussion is to follow the ordinance code in order to build a cluster development downstream. We also need a note on the plan that the access to Baker Street will be used for emergencies only, will have a locked gate, and that the road will be maintained throughout the year."

"For emergency fire access, you should also include a statement regarding the maintenance of the gate as well," said Elaine.

"It's a given that the road and gate are to be maintained," said Chairperson Tunney.

"I think a note stating that fact needs to be added to the plan for the future," said Elaine.

"You may have a point. If we don't do that we'll be back to arguing about trip counts. I also want to mention that one abutter has also raised concern over the location of the proposed walking paths adjacent to or running by a property line or home. I'd like the applicant to allow that abutter to have some input. There may be a way to move the path or allow vegetation to mitigate a loss of privacy. I'd like the applicant to mark a proposed path and then walk it with the individual before it is finalized."

"Could the applicant have the path follow the roadway and then go to one of the other parking lots?" asked Brett.

"That wouldn't be very natural," interjected Ms. Parker.

"Sure it would," countered Brett. "It would be a straight shot from the back of one parking lot to another."

"The path is on the plan because their residents want to walk through the forest area," said Drew. "If they don't want the paths, then remove them."

"Did you hear any of their residents saying they wanted to walk through the forest?" Nelson asked Sarah. "Are they even interested in doing that?"

"Nope, none of them ever mentioned walking in the forest, and if some of them were interested, they could get lost."

"There's really no difference from what there is right now," Kurt said to Drew.

"On our last site walk," Drew said, "when we got lost, we walked on one of those old pathways."

Nelson smiled at Drew's comment, thinking about Sarah's reply to his question.

"One of our jobs on this board is to buffer the residents who have concerns," said Elaine. "If that works for you, then it's a real easy solution. Just find another way to keep the pathway."

"There are several ways we can do this," said Connie Parker.

Mary Vaschon, visibly upset, stood and with deliberate conviction addressed the board members. "You should just get these new pathways out of our backyards."

"There are people walking around down there all the time right now," said Ms. Parker.

"You don't know that," Mary continued. "You don't even know where we live. You don't see what we see."

Marie Paterson abruptly chimed into the conversation. "Some of the paths you are proposing are at the bottom of some steep ravines. The ground is soft and soaking wet at the bottom of those ravines. You can't walk down there. It's always wet."

"I don't want us to get too far off track with this discussion," said Tunney.

"There's no pathway at the bottom of the ravine Ms. Paterson is talking about," said Drew. "It's a natural place where if you follow the natural path, you'll either get your feet wet or climb a steep hill to the top."

"If there had been a path on the other side, then we might not have ended up in someone's back yard," said Brett Manley.

"It's actually quite simple," said Tunney. "The applicant needs to pull away from the abutters and make sure their privacy concerns are addressed. Look, I have a couple of general things that I want to address, such as the water sufficiency issue. Let's move on to that topic. Is there sufficient water for this Phase Two project, Mr. Hatch? You're the town planner."

"Yes. I believe there's a letter from the Water and Sewer Department saying that there is sufficient capacity."

"I'm asking that question because I believe Mr. Quip has cited a letter from the Fire Department stating something different to that effect. Are you aware that Fire Chief Gerard has stated there is insufficient water?"

"No."

"Okay then," said Tunney. "Does the board want to address anything to do with the issue on density calculations or is the board satisfied with what has been presented in that regard?"

"So I guess the chairperson totally disregards what I told him?" Nelson asked Sarah, incredulous to the short reply and abrupt end to any further discussion regarding any water issue.

"Why can't they stick to one topic at a time?" whispered Nikki, obviously exasperated with the chairperson's question. "They're not aware of a problem with water so they just ignore any information and continue?"

"I don't think they're capable of resolving one issue at a time," replied Nelson as he turned toward Nikki, shaking his head from side to side negatively.

"I've struggled with the density issue," said Elaine. "Looking at the evidence before us, I'm asking whether we can rely on what has been presented by the applicant. Is that more reliable than the other evidence that has been presented?"

"I don't see that there's any conflict," said Drew. "The main question is what does the code intend? If you go to the definitions section of the Land Use Code, I think you can answer that question."

"Look," said Elaine, "when the peer review was done, they also quoted directly from the ordinance on this. You look at the gross area minus the area required for streets or access minus areas of site suitable for development with respect to the whole site. You have to do a net residential acreage calculation."

"The question is," said Tunney, "does the acreage requirements meet the ordinance today?"

"Are you using the whole parcel or are you limited by the outline on the site plan of Phase Two," asked Elaine. "You don't want everything crammed down into one corner unless you're going to have a recreation area for the rest of the acreage. The applicant has to decide what they want the development to look like. They've made some big adjustments during this whole process. They have open space requirements and other things they have worked through. The other argument concerns the net residential density. They've had discussions with the ZBA and have to decide where they will proceed from here."

"I don't want to be too narrow-minded about this," said Chairperson Tunney. "If we feel reasonably assured that the cluster requirements could be met in the future, we should ask for a note to be added to the plans regarding the preservation of the natural features of the land."

"I know that there are a lot of the members of the public who have reviewed this," Elaine interrupted. "Throughout this process, the applicant has to keep in harmony with the features of the land, the water, and the development. As they encroach closer to each single family residence, they have a responsibility to create a buffer or neutral area as best they can, and the board and the town must help them with this."

"The density discussion will take them into a cluster type of development the next time," said Drew.

"I want the board to take note of Mr. Quip's hard work and the information he has provided in his memorandums and letters to us," said Tunney. "He's raised a lot of issues over a long period of time and has been very thorough. I'm very impressed with his work."

"I think he's trying to placate you," whispered Sarah as the chairperson continued.

Nelson winced at her comment.

"Some of the issues Mr. Quip has raised have caused the applicant to make substantial changes in their proposal, or at least the application has moved in a way that addresses those points. I've looked at the files, however, and did not see a water issue. Also, I've looked at the traffic issue, and in my opinion the numbers do not trigger the need for a traffic study. The other issue is conformity with local ordinances and plans. Those are the types of issues that this board has to address.

'   "After hearing all this for many meetings, considering it, looking at the Comprehensive Plan, and deliberating, our judgment will be reflected in how we vote. In terms of the mapping of small wetlands, vernal pools, and a more extensive inventory of wildlife, I would say that there is no indication that the original information is wrong. I think there may be some areas that aren't designated, but I don't believe they are large wetlands. And I think there is quite a bit of area that is not being built on and that issue may be back before us. At that point we may need to remedy the usable land inventory.

"Does the board have any other issues?" Chairperson Tunney asked, raising his eyebrows as he spoke. He glanced to his left and right at the board members.

"Are there any outstanding waivers?" asked Drew.

"I believe there was a waiver for the length of the road into Phase Two and something about the material being used for sidewalks."

"I believe the board members were favorable to those waivers," said Kurt.

"Does the board want to discuss the street length waiver?" asked Tunney.

"I don't see a problem with it," replied Brett. "I assume all these waivers are doable."

"Well then," said the chairperson, "there may be more to discuss, but I would like to entertain a motion to approve the waivers."

Brett Manley took the opportunity to make the motion requested and Drew Laden seconded it.

"Are there any other discussions from this board?" asked Chairperson Tunney. Hearing nothing from the members, the chairperson continued. "Then I ask for all those in favor of accepting the waivers, please raise your hands."

Nelson sat there, knowing what the outcome of the vote would be. There were none opposed.

"Are there any other issues with the plans beyond the waivers?" asked the chairperson.

"What do you mean by that," asked Drew.

"I mean, is there anything else?"

"What do we have for conditions of this development right now?" asked Don Morgan.

"Mr. Laden has been writing them down," said Tunney.

"There's ZBA approval needed, designated wetland areas, new walking paths to be designed in consultation with adjacent abutters in order to address privacy concerns, a note to be added on the plans that Baker Street access is allowed for emergency access only, with a locked gate, and a note to the effect that the gate and roadway are to be maintained year-round, also..."

"You should also include," interrupted Brett, "putting a note on the plan that the sixteen foot gravel emergency access and gate will be maintained year round for emergency access, and the upgrade of the road will not encroach any further upon the wetland. There should also be a note stating there will be no removal of vegetation without Planning Board review except for the maintenance of the road, trails, and removal of hazards."

"Are we going to be approving all of the plans?" asked Drew.

"Just Phase Two," Brett said.

"I guess that means it's all a done deal no matter what we do," Nelson whispered to Sarah.

"This is like the President doing whatever he wants to do—the hell with Congress or anyone else for that matter," Sarah replied. "The people of this board have spoken—so who cares about everyone else! I'm sick of being ignored."

"Several sheets of the site plans have future expansions shown, but we are approving only Phase Two of this subdivision," said Tunney.

"Having reviewed the proposed development plans," said Brett, "I move that we find it in substantial compliance with the town's Comprehensive Plan, the Laslo Land Use and Development Code in general, and the Conservation of Wetlands Zoning. I move that we approve the site subdivision plan for Caring Home Services."

"Keep in mind that we've been taking a lot of notes," said Tunney, "and we should take a look at the complete set of plans and their applicable revisions and make sure they're complete. Otherwise this motion might have to be amended at our next meeting."

"How about adding the findings of fact from the approval of the board members?" asked Brett.

"That's done after we approve the plans."

"Then I second Mr. Manley's motion to accept the plans," said Drew.

"All in favor then?" Chairperson Tunney asked. He watched for hands as all members voted their approval. Fixing his gaze on the members of the public, he announced, "Any aggrieved party can appeal this decision to the Superior Court within forty-five days. I do request that the applicant accept the minutes of this meeting when the approved findings of facts are included."

"Are there any findings of facts?" asked Attorney Dumas.

"That's not been our practice in the past. But we're trying to clean up the minutes of the meeting and use those. At this point, the applicant will have to refer to the ruling of the Zoning Board of Appeals. This meeting is now adjourned."

iii.

It was only 9 a.m. on the following morning when Nelson heard chainsaws searing their way through trees that abutted the back of his property.

"I like taking a few Fridays off now and then, when I get a chance," exclaimed Nelson to Sarah, "but now I get to hear chainsaws in the forest first thing in the morning. What are they doing over there anyway?" he asked. "It sounds like they're starting to clear cut a path for CHS's new roadway for Phase Two. Just because the Planning Board foolishly approved their plan to screw up the forest doesn't mean the project is approved for development—at least not yet, anyway."

iv.

The menacing sound of chainsaws cut through the morning's silence. "What now?" I muttered out loud, expressing my frustrations and concerns to the surrounding trees and hurried along the familiar trail on the top of the ridge that overlooked the expanding development. *Can't even take a quiet morning stroll any more*, I thought to myself.

From earlier discussions of my neighbors in their backyard get-togethers, I had thought the project was on hold for the time being, waiting for ZBA approval. I wondered if Nelson had heard the all too familiar whine of the saws and what he might be thinking about this new situation.

I approached the two-man crew and watched as tree after tree fell to the ground from the sharp teeth of unrelenting steel. I watched in dismay and amazement how quickly a wide path was being cleared in so little time, considering the sad reality that it took several decades for those trees to grow.

Then, to my surprise, the harsh rasping sounds suddenly ceased as someone yelled for the two men to stop cutting. They shut off their saws, turned around, and walked back several hundred yards to their truck. They talked among themselves, and then drove out of the woods.

v.

Sarah was just as upset as Nelson at the sound of chain-saws in the early morning, particularly because they were emanating from what seemed to be their own backyard. "They still don't have the Zoning Board of Appeals approval," she exclaimed to Nelson as he looked out toward the forest, shaking his head in disbelief. "I'll call the Code Enforcement Officer and ask him what's going on. I think CHS has to have approval before they can just start to clear-cut a roadway. And they certainly don't have full approval yet."

It was Sarah's phone call to the town and the discussion with Allen Treble that brought about the quick discontinuance of the trees being clear cut that morning.

"We should have a meeting with our neighbors before our next encounter with the Zoning Board," said Nelson, after Sarah had called the town and the sound of chainsaws stopped. "At some point, CHS has to go back before the Zoning Board for an appeal. I just don't know when that will happen. I guess we all better discuss where we stand while everything is still fresh in our minds. I'll call everyone and tell them about the presumptuous tree cutting and ask them if we can all get together for tomorrow afternoon. Saturday would probably be the best time to get most everybody in one place."

vi.

It was mid-afternoon the next day when Nelson managed to get eight of his neighbors to meet at his backyard patio. Emmy Anderson, Kevin Sparks, Marie Paterson, Joe and

Mary Vaschon, Nikki Williams, Will Penton, and Donny sat around the flames of the fire pit, providing warmth to a chilly November afternoon. I was there as well.

Emmy Anderson was the first to start the conversation.

"Before we start talking about another ZBA hearing, I just want everyone to know that I got an e-mail from our town tax assessor, with an attached copy of a letter that had been sent to CHS. Simon told me he would keep me informed, and he did."

"Oh, this should be interesting," said Joe.

"Well, for once, it's good news. The town has denied the tax exemption status for Caring Home Services."

"Wow, I'm really surprised," said Joe, his face expressing complete surprise to the news. He turned quickly and faced Nelson. "Have you heard anything from the IRS about their non-profit status?"

"No," Nelson replied. "Actually, that's between the IRS and them. I really doubt if anything will ever be done, even if they're not compliant with the tax laws. At this point in time, the IRS appears to be more involved with targeting tea party and conservative organizations."

"It seems like there's never anything done unless there is enough pressure from the public," said Emmy. "Believe it or not, the letter from Simon Duncan was well written. I still can't believe that CHS said they were being benevolent by paying a two percent service fee to the town when it's actually a State Law. They had no choice but to pay that fee. Our town is actually the benevolent party because Simon's letter stated they aren't going to request back taxes from the rental properties, even though they should have been paying the town for all those years and didn't. The taxpayers of Laslo should be happy about this outcome, though. I understand a new property tax assessment will be conducted prior to the next tax bills being issued. If it weren't for us, CHS would never have paid any property taxes."

"I guess payback can be a bitch sometimes," said Nikki in her normally unabashed tone.

"Just so everyone knows," Nelson added, "when Sarah called the Code Enforcement Officer about CHS's non-permitted tree cutting, she asked if there was going to be another ZBA hearing."

"Mr. Treble was very nice," Sarah said. "He told me that he expected CHS to apply for another hearing, but he had no idea as to when that might occur. He said that he understood they were amending their plans once again. If it's a new appeal, he thought it would be a while before we'd hear anything."

"With that news," said Nelson, "I thought it would be best if I put together another evidence packet for the ZBA Board members, just to ensure the facts we have at this point are complete and up to date. I've already written a letter to the people who live on Baker Street defining problems with the ordinance on wetland setbacks and their issues. I've asked them to write a joint letter to the ZBA as an opposing group. I'm not sure if they'll let us speak during the hearing. It may not be up for public discussion at that point. Since the Planning Board has already approved the CHS plans, regardless of what we've had to say, we should have an organized front in case we get an opportunity to speak."

"Kevin and I," said Joe, "are annotating a map of the so-called South Campus in order to provide as much detail as possible for wetland delineation. We'll compile that information and add it to your packages, Nelson. Kevin and an old friend of his who is an environmental engineer and has a Professional Engineering license in another state have also written a letter to the ZBA for us, stating that their rendition of the wetland delineations has been misconstrued."

"That's a nice way of putting it," said Nelson.

"What are you going to say to the ZBA if they even give you a chance to speak?" asked Will.

"Well, the packet of information I'll put together will be quite large, so I'll have to quickly summarize some of that information for the public to hear. I'll break up the packet into discussions regarding misleading information, density issues, secondary access road requirements, wetland issues, and the Planning Board's decision to violate the town's own Comprehensive Plan, in that the town has already exceeded the number of elderly units mandated. And I'll remind them that the Comprehensive Plan is supposed to take legal precedence over the Land Use Code.

"Next, I'll remind them that the ZBA denied a special exception for zoning for Phase Two back in February of this year, and then again in March for the same reasons. Specifically, they failed to meet seven of the town's Land Use Ordinance Criteria Factors. Then I'm going to identify the fact that since those public hearings, there have been no significant changes to Phase Two of their project. There were a few items changed during the last two Planning Board meetings, which included reducing the number of phases by two so there is no longer a Phase Six and Seven. But that change doesn't affect Phase Two. An emergency gate and occasional use access from Baker Street was also added, when on countless occasions before, Mr. Tussi was told they could not do so by the ZBA.

"I'll point out to them that by adding an emergency access, a currently functioning culvert that allows the flow of water from one wetland area to another will have to be replaced with a new culvert that will withstand the weight of a fire truck. That action alone violates the ordinances regarding the disturbance of wetlands. You don't repair something when it doesn't need to be fixed. I'll mention that walking paths have now been added, causing more concern for people's privacy as well as further property de-valuation.

"The reasons for the ZBA denial for a Special Exception to Zoning for Phase Two has simply not changed. The high-density cluster housing number of units has remained the same. The safety, nuisances, and traffic concerns have also not been alleviated, and it appears that these conditions have actually worsened.

"Then I'll talk about the inconsistencies and discussions taken out of context by the developer and the misinformation provided to both boards during this process."

Nelson looked at the others sitting around the fire, paused to let his words sink in, then continued.

"As an example, the trip counts have been modified and reverse engineered on at least four occasions. In fact, the original number of 3.48 trips per day was removed from the original plans, and then verbally changed many times after that. In addition, the definition of congregate care was misconstrued to both boards when in fact the terms elderly housing or retirement community are more appropriate to determine trips per day counts. Of course, lowering the trips counts per day was done on purpose. We all know that it removes the necessity of a second access road.

"Another example of twisted truths started several years ago in a letter from the Assistant Ecologist from the State of Maine Department of Conservation. The letter to the developer stated there were no rare or botanical features documented specifically within the project area. That statement is what the developer used in order to confirm the state didn't see any problems. They conveniently left out the next sentence which stated the lack of data might indicate minimal survey efforts rather than confirm the absence of rare botanical features. The state's letter actually suggested that the site should be inventoried by a qualified field biologist to ensure no undocumented rare features were inadvertently harmed. It continued to state that in the absence of a specific field investigation, the Maine Natural Areas Program could not provide a definitive statement on the presence or absence of unusual natural features at the site. No site surveys were ever subsequently requested by Mr. Tussi's company."

"Are you going to say anything about the density calculations?" asked Joe.

"Yes, I'm including the details of the density calculations I researched. If allowed to speak, I'll tell the board that my review resulted in a density of ten units per acre for Phase Two alone, not eight as proposed by the applicant, and certainly not four as recommended by the ZBA Board. I'll also mention that there's almost two acres of buildings and paved impervious surfaces covering about forty-two percent of the area in Phase Two. Planning Board members seem to ignore the fact that Mr. Tussi keeps trying to add the already developed land in their North Campus to the land in the South Campus in order to calculate the net developable area. Those are two distinct pieces of property with separate deeds."

"Didn't Kurt Tussi give you a hard time about the numbers you used to calculate density at the last Planning Board hearing?"

"Yeah, Tussi said that since the Phase lines sketched on the site plans were only used to define the area for Phase Two, my calculations weren't valid. I used the actual area on the plans that was allocated to that portion of the development. My determination actually gave Tussi additional land area, including setback areas from wetlands. Using the actual acreage and Land Use Code requirements of four units per acre, there should only be an estimated sixteen units built versus the proposed forty-two. But that wouldn't be very profitable for them, would it?"

Will Penton spoke up. "Members of the ZBA Board need to remember that they previously ruled the proposed Phase Two would cause overcrowding and that a more appropriate use would be to build four units versus eight units per acre."

"Let's hope they remember what they said last time," said Sarah. "And the Planning Board now wants to let them add walking paths along the borders and adjacent to abutter's properties, violating people's privacy as well as further de-valuing their homes."

"That addition was a real kick in the ass," said Nikki. "Nothing like adding insult to injury."

"I can see why you want to get this packet of information put together now," said Joe. "We'll never remember all these details if we don't write them down."

Donny sat quietly, looking out over the forest, deep in thought. Then turned his attention back to his neighbors and in a low tone of voice said, "You've done all you can to stop the destruction of this forest. You've all fought this battle for well over five years now. We've all been involved with opposing the development in some capacity. At least we haven't just been sitting around letting things happen. At least we've paid attention to what's been happening in this town—even better than most people who haven't paid much attention to what's been happening in our own country."

I looked at Donny, thought about the acquiescence of his statement, and then carefully observed my neighbors' facial expressions. All eight neighbors seemed lost in their own silence; each wore a reflection of concern of what the future might bring: both short and long term.

Year Six

"Beware lest you lose the substance by
Grasping at the shadow"

– Aesop

Chapter Nineteen

Irrelevance

i.

Over the next nine months, everyone became preoccupied with their individual lives, each reluctant to think about ever wanting to attend another public hearing, but fearing the developer was apparently gathering a strategy in order to obtain approval for their project from the ZBA. Nelson was busy with tax clients, outside landscaping, and spending time with his family; including occasional visits with his sons to Treasure Rock. The forest remained intact. Maxwell was constantly working at his research facility with Dora, Harold, and their team, hardly noticing the passing of time, except, of course, for the continued satellite reports and changing news content.

The past winter's short days of little light, constant cold, and high snowdrifts interrupted my travels along the wooded pathways, often making it difficult to walk. Winter cold, spring wetness, and summer heat were the typical seasons of change as they traded places with one another and the year slid quickly into the start of another fall.

Nelson and Maxwell were completely attuned to one another through their writing. They grew to know each other more than they ever had before, and they worried about those things that could come true. Maxwell continued to monitor obscure and bizarre radio signals and tried to interpret their meaning. Both men worried that the story they wrote might be more than entirely fictional.

Nelson's attention was no longer focused on local public hearings but rather diverted by Maxwell to concentrate on the steady increase in continued negotiations with Iran about their nuclear program, almost on a monthly basis. Steps to waive specific economic sanctions and release a schedule of payments for Iran to receive oil money withheld by other countries were part of the agreement framework being discussed by policy makers. In August, Iran missed deadlines to complete actions on areas of concern to the IAEA, and by September failed to provide them with information about past activities with possible military dimensions. Nevertheless, negotiations continued.

Nelson's reprieve from never ending public hearings, however, ended unexpectedly in mid-September when he received a letter from the town of an impending Zoning Board of Appeals hearing.

ii.

"Where's Chairperson Bolduc?" Nelson asked as he sat down next to Sarah. "Looks like the newest member of the board, Thomas Hatfield, has replaced him as chairperson of the ZBA."

"And there's a new member in Hatfield's old seat," said Nikki Williams as she sat down in her favorite spot, directly behind him. "Her name is Becky Bertrim," she said. "I went to grade school with her. See her slightly hooked nose? We used to call her Becky Bird Beak because of that nose. I saw her name on the list of changes for the ZBA on the town's website just before I came tonight. Evidently, Mr. Bolduc's tenure was up and he decided not to participate any longer as a member of the board."

"I wonder where that leaves us now?" asked Sarah.

As the new chairperson peered over the metal frame of his thick coke bottle round lenses, he called the meeting to order.

"Tonight, we have Caring Home Services requesting a special exception to the terms of Title 10, Section 14.060 of the Land Use and Development Code Zoning Ordinance. They wish to construct Phase Two of their proposed development, which includes forty-two units in four buildings accessed off Route 2, Map 2, Lot 35, in our town of Laslo, zoned as urban residence. This is a new appeal, but it's bringing up the same type of appeal that this board has already heard twice before. This appeal falls under a special category, so I'll remind everyone how the board's procedure works."

Hatfield eyed the public over his glasses, but his eyes lingered especially on Nelson.

"The Land Use Code states that if the ZBA denies an appeal or request, a second appeal or request of a similar nature shall not be brought before the ZBA unless the appellant submits new evidence and the ZBA, by formal action, decides the evidence is significant and warrants a new hearing, or unless the ZBA finds in its sole and exclusive judgment that an error or mistake of law or misunderstanding of facts has been made.

"It's important to note that I haven't opened up the public part of this meeting yet. All those members of the board who were here when the board heard this appeal the last time need to decide if enough has changed in this application to warrant the board to hear it again. Those board members would be Ms. Greene, Mr. Grady, Ms. Emery, and myself. It will not include Ms. Bertrim, because she was not a board member at the last hearing and therefore did not vote during the last appeal.

"There will be no presentation from Caring Home Services, the applicant, at this time. Members of the board can ask questions of anyone regarding this application. When there are no further questions, one of the four members who participated in voting last time will have to make a motion to hear the appeal. If and when a motion has been made, then a majority of the four members will have to vote 'yes'. If that happens, then a regular appeal will be heard. If that doesn't happen, then the appeal won't happen. Do the board members have any questions?"

Rachel Greene was the first to speak. "I've read over the information packet received from the applicant and I see that some changes have been made, but it's my understanding that there haven't been any changes to the two most important aspects of the plan. Phase Two still has forty-two units."

Attorney Dumas stood quickly to respond to her remark. "I'd like the opportunity for my client to make a brief presentation about the changes. The applicant has worked hard to be here tonight, has gone to many, many Planning Board meetings and has held at least three site walks, and has listened to what this board has said. The applicant is prepared to address the comments that have been made. I think it would be more helpful to all concerned if the board would allow the applicant a brief amount of time to be heard."

"I understand your comment," said Chairperson Hatfield, "but in the issue of fairness, I don't think the abutters would consider it fair to only listen to the applicant. This is not in deference to the abutters, but the board will go by the law."

"In deference to my client, this is a new application for a special exception and not an appeal. I think the applicant should be under the old rules of procedure and should be allowed to make a presentation. I don't believe the applicant should be confined to the written material which has been presented to the board members."

"Mr. Dumas, this request is of a similar nature to ones we've had before. If the applicant doesn't like the board's decision, they can appeal whatever decision is made within forty-five days. With the controversy surrounding this project, the board will go completely by the book and not err on anyone's side or vary either way."

Board member Michael Grady addressed the chairperson's remarks. "This hearing is not to be a lobbying session for attorneys, and we certainly don't want to turn it into a debate forum. I don't think it would be detrimental to anyone if the applicant explains what the differences are in the plan."

"I have the minutes from last February's public hearing as well as the re-considerations from March and April," said Chairperson Hatfield, "which were the last times this application was heard by this board. The Findings of Facts and Conclusions in the letter sent to the applicant states why their request for a special exception was disallowed. The board concluded that this project did not meet several of the Land Use Code Criteria Factors. Perhaps we should review those findings."

"Then let's go through them, one at a time."

"Okay, Mr. Grady. I don't have a problem with that. The finding for Criteria Factor One stated that the character of this elderly housing development was too dense for this property. Not meeting that criteria could also affect property values in the area, which is in reference to Criteria Factor Two. Therefore, the First and Second Criteria could not be met. So we need to ask the question of whether or not the density of what is now proposed is less than it was before."

"I don't think the applicant should be able to deliver an entire presentation," said Rachel Greene, "but if it's done that way, it would be more than fair to them."

"If that's what the board members want to do, then we can do it that way," said the chairperson. "Mr. Dumas, would you care to address the density issue?"

"I believe Mr. Tussi, the project engineer, can address that issue for you," said the attorney.

Kurt Tussi stood and walked over to the podium.

"Before you speak, Mr. Tussi, remember this is not a hearing," said the chairperson. "Allowing your comment is purely to answer the board's questions. I will stop your discourse if you start to vary from the topic. The question at hand is about the density. There were forty-two units before; what is it now and how has it changed?"

"Mr. Chairperson, there were forty-two units proposed in Phase Two and there are still forty-two units proposed. There has been a reduction of fifty-two units in the proposed assisted living building in one of the later phases, as well as other reductions, for a net reduction of sixty units. The parking has also been drastically reduced and there is more green area."

"Mr. Tussi, are any of these changes associated with Phase Two?"

"No. There are forty-two units proposed for Phase Two and there still are forty-two units proposed. The Planning Board felt any changes in Phase Two would be looked at unfavorably by that board because they were already eleven months into that part of the process.

Rachel Greene addressed the board members. "Eight units per acre is what is allowed for elderly housing as a special exception. The developer has reduced that number down to six units per acre for the entire development, and only three units per acre are allowed *without* a special exception. The town planner, Mr. Hatch, has told Mr. Tussi, however, that the Land Use Ordinance requires a special exception because the development meets the definition requirements as elderly housing. Mr. Tussi, what will the numbers of units be per acre when Phase Two is completely developed?"

"If the board approves Phase Two and the forty-two units are built, plus the twenty-six units already completed in Phase One, it's 2.36 apartments per acre. Out of the 32.7 acre parcel for the South Campus, after taking out fifty-percent for hydric soils and road area, the net density is 26.7 acres. At the end of *all* building phases, the build-out would be at six units per acre."

"I understand how frustrating this is for the developer," said Rachel.

"That's an understatement for the rest of us," mumbled Nelson to Sarah.

"This board must look at only Phase Two, because that's what we're approving," continued Rachel. "The Planning Board and this town also want to look at the entire project. Mr. Tussi said the Planning Board decided that even though they are looking at approving Phase Two, they want to see the whole plan in order to know what the future holds. Even though the entire plan was shown to the Planning Board in that light, Mr. Tussi has said it was fair that the Zoning Board should also see it in the same light. If you look at only Phase Two, this is it, as it is shown on this plan. Mr. Tussi has pointed out the wetlands, undisturbed buffer areas, and the development areas of Phase One and Phase Two. Mr. Tussi has said the project currently exceeds the open space requirement for Phase Two and also when it's totally built out, it's as a clustered subdivision. Mr. Tussi said he wrestled with the density issue and that sixty units have been taken out of the total because he believes this board is looking at Phase Two and the master plan, even though the board isn't approving anything but Phase Two."

"What has been discussed so far covers Criteria One and Two of the Land Use Code," said Chairperson Hatfield. "Criteria Factor Three concerns the question of traffic. I realize there's been a lot of discussion on the number of trips per day, and that the number seems to have been changed to fit the moment. Mr. Tussi, has anything changed in regard to the actual number of trips per day?"

"At the last Planning Board meeting, our traffic engineer, Mr. John Townsend, told the board members that the trips per day would be in the range of 2.02. The Planning Board members believed that figure was too low. Most of the board

members agreed the actual number was somewhere between the 2.02 and the 3.48 figure per the proper ITE standard. A lot of material has been introduced about using the
3.48 trips per day figure. To resolve a secondary road access
issue, the Planning Board approved our plan with a sixteen-
foot wide emergency access road to Baker Street. We have
letters from both Fire Chief Gerard and the Director of Public
Works, Mr. Blake, in support of the emergency access. I've
talked to the former chairperson of this board, Mr. Peter
Bolduc, with the understanding that an emergency access
would be agreeable, but not as a regular access."

"Typical bureaucratic bullshit," whispered Nikki, "behind
closed door discussions without public input, if what he's saying is true at all."

"Not unlike a lot of other issues," replied Nelson. His
thoughts and concerns momentarily drifted to recent conversations with Maxwell.

"Who said that the Baker Street access has been agreed
upon?" asked the chairperson.

"The Planning Board agreed upon it," replied Kurt. "The
site and subdivision plans show a sixteen-foot wide access.
There's a note on the plan stating there will be an emergency
break-away gate which would be maintained year-round. A
turnaround would also be constructed by the developer so
that the town snow plows can turn around at the end of
Baker Street."

"Would that emergency access gate be built during construction of Phase Two, Mr. Tussi?"

"Yes."

"Looking through my notes," remarked the chairperson,
"I noticed there were three or four decisions on the number
of trips. Without the emergency access to Baker Street, there
are just too many trips for access to this development. The
change for Criteria Factor Three is that Baker Street access
wasn't on the previous plan."

"That's true, Mr. Chairperson. That's one of the changes.
For Phase Two, the total number of trips would be two hundred and thirty-one, which is over the two hundred trip limit
per the Land Use Ordinance."

"What about the different numbers used to calculate the
number of trips, Mr. Tussi?" asked Rachel.

"The number of 3.48 is the maximum that could be used, which amounts to two hundred and thirty-one trips per day. As you know, the ordinance requires a secondary means of access at two hundred trips per day."

"Will the emergency access be maintained by the town?" asked Jane Emery.

"No, by the developer. The developer will have to take this property and construct a turnaround so the plow can turn and back around."

"This board has pretty much talked about all the reasons why this project was denied the last time," said Chairperson Hatfield. "I'd like some comments from the board members."

Jane Emery was the first to speak.

"Last time this board's concerns had to do with the density, the property values, safety, and a second access. I want everyone here to know that I've agonized over this now for the third time. I've read everything the applicant and abutters have provided to this board. I have reviewed the maps here and the changes that have been proposed. This project has now gone from seven phases to four and has been in the works for years. I keep asking myself, however, why has this process been so difficult? If it's a good project, it shouldn't be this hard.

"I reviewed the Town's Land Use and Development Code and there are conditions that the board must use as a basis for a decision. One of the conditions stands out among all the others. That's condition Criteria Factor Four, which states that the use will be in harmony with and promote the general purposes and intent of Title 10 of the Land Use Code. This board has to think about whether this project is in harmony with Title 10.

"It states, and I quote: '*This title is designed for all the purposes of zoning embraced in Maine Revised Statutes, and has been created as an integral part of a comprehensive planning process for the town to promote the health, safety, and general welfare of its residents. Among other things, it is designed to encourage the most appropriate use of land and water throughout the town, to promote traffic safety, to provide safety from fire and other elements, to provide adequate light and air, to prevent overcrowding of real property, to prevent housing development in unsuitable areas, to pro-*

vide an adequate street system, to control and manage the coordinated development of unbuilt areas, to encourage the formation of community units, to provide an allotment of land area in new developments sufficient for all the requirements of community life, to conserve energy and natural resources and protect the environment, to preserve land values, and, to provide for adequate public services.'

"I've looked at the plan, and I've visited the site. It's filled with vegetation and trees and wetland, and as I look at this proposal, I see parking lots, apartments, more apartments, and roads, roads, roads. It's simply not in harmony with the land, and that's the crux of everything. If this project was in harmony with the land, I don't believe we would have been sitting here for over three years discussing this. It would have gone through the public hearings and everyone would have been happy with it: both the abutters and the developer. I don't feel there have been enough changes to warrant the board taking another look at it again in this hearing.

"I feel that elderly housing is extremely important in Laslo, but I don't think this is the piece of land for it, unless it's redesigned to be in harmony with the land itself. I know my comments make some people here tonight unhappy and some happy, but that's how I feel about this. I have seen other projects in nearby towns that have turned out to be inharmonious, and it makes you want to cry after seeing the land before and after development. I don't believe this project is harmonious with the land."

Chairperson Hatfield said, "In reviewing the six criteria where the earlier board didn't feel the project fit, it breaks into two issues: three of the Criteria Factors were about density and a "big city feel" and the other three had to do with trips per day and emergency access. In my opinion, if the developer had changed enough of Phase Two, we could rehear this project. But in reality, the reason the board turned down Phase Two was the density, and that hasn't changed. I feel the project is still very dense and is a very unfitting, inharmonious application for the area. In my opinion, it doesn't fit in well. I'm glad the numbers of phases have been reduced, but Phase Two is too dense."

"I'd like to make a point about this procedure," said Attorney Dumas, his face flushed. "There's a real question on the comments made about relying on the general purpose section of the ordinance. There are several cases in Maine that say those standards are too broad to be applied. Before the board votes this down, I would respectfully request a postponement until the Town Attorney can give an opinion. I would rather take a pass on a vote than have a negative decision."

"Mr. Dumas," Hatfield calmly replied, "if no one makes a motion, or if a motion is made and the board decides not to hear it, a vote simply doesn't happen. As I stated previously, this board is deciding on whether or not to hear the appeal."

"If the board's vote is based on the general purpose standards," said Dumas, "there are several cases which state that that's not sufficient basis on which to make a decision. In that case, I would ask for a postponement."

Mr. Hatfield's comment is one board member's feeling on the project," said Rachel Greene. "It's not how I'm basing my opinion. Chairperson Hatfield has given his reason why he won't rehear it. I thought that Jane Emery also made some valid points, but the reason for her decision would fall into more with what Chairperson Hatfield has said. The board has very strict guidelines about whether or not we hear a case. Mr. Tussi has tried to respond to the board's concerns and the abutters' concerns, and I respect that."

"I don't," whispered Nikki to Nelson in a low voice. "A lot of those responses were half-truths."

"Mr. Tussi is in a tough place," Rachel continued. "An applicant can't just keep coming back, and this applicant has been back many times. In my opinion, the last time the applicant was here there were no changes, but the board heard it again. Other people in this town, who get turned down, have to wait a year before they can continue to have something reheard each time. The number of units is the same. The applicant has addressed some of the traffic and safety issues but not the density issue, which is the main issue for me. It just hasn't changed. I believe the applicant has already received special treatment by being heard at least twice for the same proposal. I don't believe the plan has sufficiently been changed enough in order to be heard again. I'm not hanging my hat on the definition of the purpose of Title 10 that Jane talked about, but rather on the fact that an applicant has to have substantial changes in order to be heard again."

"At this time," asked Chairperson Hatfield, "would anyone like to make a motion to hear this appeal?"

Nelson cringed at Hatfield's question and quickly scanned the board members for telltale facial expressions. There were none. The room was quiet, yet the stillness was deafening. No motion came forth.

The chairperson looked at each member for some sign or comment. There were none. After a long unbearable pause, he finally interrupted the silence and addressed the public.

"With no motion being made, the ZBA will not hear this appeal. I believe the result of this hearing still falls under the applicant having forty-five days to appeal this non-decision.

"The board will issue a Findings of Fact letter regarding the results of this appeal, which will address the following: One—the applicant is asking for an appeal of a similar nature to one that was previously denied by the board regarding their Phase Two expansion. Two—testimony was given by the applicant's representative that considerable changes have been made to the emergency access, the amount of trips per day, and traffic control. Three—testimony was given by the applicant's representative that the number of units in Phase Two has not changed since the last hearing, in that there are still forty-two units proposed. Four—in accordance with the Land Use Code, you need to make significant changes to the plan in order for the ZBA to hear an appeal. As there weren't enough substantial changes to prompt the board to hear the appeal again, no motion has been made to hear it. These findings will be sent to the applicant. That concludes our hearing tonight and we are adjourned."

"Is that it?" asked Sarah. "Are we done? Are they done?"

"I simply don't know at this point," said Nelson, shaking his head from side to side in a questioning manner. "Knowing CHS, I wonder what's next, if anything?"

Year Seven

**"We and the trees and the way
Back from the fields of play
Lasted as long as we could
No more walks in the wood."**

– John Hollander

Chapter Twenty

Allegory

i.

The sun was setting when I saw Nelson and Sarah standing at their back yard patio, looking out over the forest. He glanced away from the sunset and at Sarah as she smiled and announced, "We got an e-mail from Maxwell. He's stopping by tomorrow afternoon to attend our yearly fall neighbor get together. He wants to meet our neighbors and talk about what we managed to accomplish at all the public hearings we've attended. He said he also had a package of reports he thought you should read and consider including in your final manuscript. He mentioned that he wants to discuss more of the idiosyncrasies from some radio transmissions, as well."

It was early afternoon the following day when Nelson, Sarah, Nikki Williams, Emmy Anderson, Marie Paterson, Will and Barbara Penton, Joe and Mary Vaschon, Josh Gosling, and Donny sat in a circle around the small fire pit on Nelson's small backyard patio, just as they had done many times already. The warmth of the flames and smell of apple wood from old branches of pruned fruit trees brought everyone closer together to ward off the slight chill of the September afternoon.

It had been just over one year since the ZBA had last decided not to rehear the developer, and it was with heightened trepidation that Nikki Williams had decided to ask the town planner for an updated status. The conversation started with Nikki Williams' report to the group about her meeting. Everyone was interested to hear what she had learned.

I listened to their conversations with great interest. There were a lot of things that I hadn't been privy to.

"What did you find out from Todd Hatch?" Nelson asked.

"We've heard nothing from anyone about another Planning Board or ZBA hearing. I just keep waiting for the other pro- verbial shoe to drop. Things have been too quiet. There's been no word from the Planning Board since last November when they approved Phase Two and nothing from the ZBA since they voted not to hear another appeal."

"Well," she started, "Mr. Hatch told me that after a lot of discussion, the Planning Board decided not to sign the site plans for approving the development. They figured that since the ZBA didn't hear an appeal again, they couldn't give final approval of the plans. One of the conditions was to get ratifi- cation from the ZBA. Since CHS had to wait for a year and make substantial changes to get another hearing from the ZBA, the approval process from both boards would have to start all over again. There has been no application for any additional hearings submitted to Mr. Hatch. Evidently, there are no substantial changes that can be made to Phase Two to make it economical for development."

"The Zoning Board is the one board we've been able to count on," Joe said. "During this whole process, the Planning Board couldn't seem to focus on any one topic at a time. They seemed to address a variety of topics, hardly ever com- ing to a conclusion about anything. That caused the entire board to lose sight of the problematic issues that many of us talked about. It seems like it was done on purpose, to keep us unfocused and confused, like the past seven years of po- litical bullshit we've had to live with—one scandal and one bad decision after another—until you forget about the previ- ous one. That's my perception, anyway.

"There were several instances when it was obvious to me that the board members never even read the material we provided, not unlike Congress voting on a Bill before reading it. Why would you even vote on something if you never read the information on the issue at hand? Time after time they also accepted waivers to the town ordinances in order to pro- ceed with the applicant's plans, simply ignoring why the or- dinances were written that way in the first place."

"The problem I had with that board," said Marie, "was that the public didn't always get a chance to speak out about falsely made statements by the developer. That board is supposed to represent both the applicant as well as the residents. And it sure didn't seem that way. I even overheard one board member tell another that they thought the Land Use Code should be changed so that a developer wouldn't have to go through the ZBA to get a special exception for zoning. It appeared that they wanted to make decisions by themselves and eliminate any form of checks and balances."

"Gee, that sounds familiar, doesn't it," said Joe.

"Did you notice that CHS has been advertising their apartments for rent?" asked Emmy. "I wonder what happened to that long list of applicants waiting to move into their facility. Since they now have to pay property taxes and they can't just establish high density housing, I doubt if it's economical for them to continue any expansion at all."

"Ironically, in the long run, we may have saved them financially from themselves," said Sarah.

It was at that moment when Maxwell Draper walked around the side of the house toward the group. Everyone looked up, surprised by the interruption.

ii.

"How are you doing, Maxwell?" Nelson stood to greet his old friend and introduced him to his neighbors. "It's been almost two years since I visited you. I guess our continued correspondence has made that time interval seemingly less."

"I'm doing okay," Max replied. "I've been immersed with my research at the lab."

"And how's Alex? I was hoping to see him during my brief visit the last time I was there, but I know he was inundated at the time with graduate course work."

"I'm very proud of Alex. He's just completed his doctorate in Applied Physics, and he's thinking about taking a position at the same research center where I'm working, with a different group."

"Have a seat," said Nelson. He pulled an extra lawn chair into the circle and both he and Maxwell sat down.

"We almost feel like we've met you before," Joe cheerfully said. "Nelson has mentioned your name several times and has even shared with us some of what both of you have been writing." His expression changed to one of concern. "Your forecasts of events and insight to actual occurrences have given us a lot to think about." Joe turned to smile at Nelson and added, "We're looking forward to reading the final manuscript."

"Well, you've all been paying attention to what's been happening around you on the local level. I commend you all on your perseverance, and I congratulate you all on the well-deserved success in your fight. For the last six years, you all have been involved with opposing something that you determined was harmful to your town, its residents, and the wildlife. During that same period of time, I've observed just the opposite on a countrywide basis, where it seems that very few people have paid any attention at all to harmful policies, resulting with a nation that appears to be in a state of deterioration."

Donny gave Nelson a knowing glance and spoke up, breaking the group's momentary silence.

"The continual deliberations we've had over the last several years have been very frustrating for all of us. The same issues were repeatedly discussed with no immediate resolution. And all the developer has had to say was that our concerns were ones of emotion. But our concerns were more than that. We've had real concerns about wildlife, wetlands, property values, high-density cluster housing, the impact to safety and traffic, and also the cost of services to our town. If this project had somehow been approved, there would have been several violations to the town's Land Use Codes and waivers to previously established ordinances. Those kinds of circumstances make you want to ask yourself, why have any rules at all?

"Our concerns and questions throughout all the hearings have been countered by distorted responses and misleading answers. Truths have been fabricated and facts have been taken out of context from sources. What has been most frustrating is the erroneous and exaggerated information supplied to both boards in order to achieve approval."

"I'm simply amazed the ZBA members stuck to their guns," Nelson said, "and followed the town's ordinances and rejected appeals. And since the Planning Board didn't sign the final site plans, the developer would have to come back to the ZBA, substantially modify the plans, and start all over again with the Planning Board."

"I don't think that's going to happen," Maxwell said in a somewhat subdued tone. "As Emmy already mentioned, it would not be cost effective for them to add more apartments. And from what Nelson told me earlier, they are continually advertising apartments for rent. If they can't increase the number of units for rent, can't conceivably install two access roads per an ordinance, and now finally have to start paying property taxes to the town for their millions of dollars worth of real estate, they will not find it economical to continue a fight. I believe it's all about the money for them, although they'll never admit to it. You've won your fight. You've managed to stop something bad from happening."

Joe exhaled a brief sigh: a sign of pent up frustration and recurring desperation.

"Maxwell, have you observed the same kind of problems while analyzing news broadcasts?" he asked. "I'm talking about distorted responses, misleading answers, or fabricated facts in order to achieve a particular *national* agenda."

"Unfortunately, yes. One thing you have to consider is the fact that it takes a lot more people to pay attention to national issues than it does for a single local issue in order to make any difference. You were able to draw attention to your dissention. It's more difficult on a national level if people are dispassionate."

"I understand the President now wants authority to reorganize the government at his discretion," Joe said.

Nelson, understanding the intent of Joe's remark, quickly added, "Well, I believe his actual quote was: '*The government we have is not the government that we need.*' And he went on to say, '*Our economy has fundamentally changed— as has the world—but our government, our agencies, have not.*'"

Nelson glanced at Maxwell before continuing.

"From what Maxwell has told me, it appears the country will not be the same if we continue with current policies, or lack thereof. We saw what happened in our particular situation; our fight was on a much smaller scale than what is actually happening in the country as a whole. If people don't wake up soon, they're going to find themselves living in a country foreign to them, just like the animals in this forest behind us, and it's not for the better. If the country continues on the same path we're on, I'm not sure where we'll end up."

Nelson shrugged his shoulders, exhibiting a thoughtful expression, knowing that the abutters and friends he had come to acquire during their personal siege had survived overwhelming odds in the fight against a corporation, its attorneys, and its hired experts, not unlike dealing with a government bureaucracy. Joe's remark about the reorganization of government had prompted Nelson's ongoing dialog.

"Just a few years ago a gallon of gas was $1.79. The price went up to around $4.00, and with mid-east issues the price has fluctuated significantly. Then, even though everyone was against fracking, the slang term for hydraulic fracturing, otherwise known as a drilling process used for extracting oil, natural gas, geothermal energy, or water from deep underground, we developed more of our own resources, helping to bring the price down to about two bucks or so. The establishment was against fracking, and they still are, but they certainly seem to have taken credit for the country's reducing its oil prices. In only a few years, food stamp recipients are at a thirty-five percent increase to at least forty-seven million people, and our unemployment has soared from about 2.6 million people to 6.4 million. Those are pretty staggering numbers for a 'hope and change' agenda, don't you think?"

Without hesitation Nelson went on.

"Did you know that the number of U.S. citizens living in poverty has risen another four million people in the last few years? And to make matters worse, our national debt is escalating towards twenty trillion dollars and continues to climb—that debt consists of about fourteen trillion in public debt and another five trillion in debt the government owes to itself. The total will have doubled in only about eight years. At one point, Standard and Poors even cut the U.S. long-term credit rating from triple A to a double A-plus as a result from concerns about the nation's budget deficits and climbing debt burden. Most people seem to ignore that, or have forgotten about it.

The support for our capitalistic system has waned where many millennials, *but not all*, either support socialism or don't understand it at this point in time. We've had a health care bill called the Affordable Health Care Reform Act that appears to violate our own constitution with a lot of back door deals.

"In the past few years, we've had an administration that has obstructed oil drilling in the Gulf of Mexico as well as the east coast and established abusive moratoriums, spent over a trillion dollars on so-called shovel ready jobs that were admittingly not shovel ready, tried to enforce a major manufacturing company from being able to choose in which state they were allowed to locate a factory, federally filed lawsuits against several of our states who are simply trying to enforce federal law and stop illegal immigrants from crossing our borders, encouraged racial discrimination and intimidation at polling places, attempted to pass a cap and trade bill that would have economically crippled America more than it already is, withheld progress on the construction of a pipeline from our friendly neighbor, Canada, that would be in our national interest, and withdrew coal permits that had previously been properly issued."

Nelson drew a quick breath and continued before any comments could be said.

"Another pet peeve of mine is that we have curtailed our NASA space program, inhibiting our ability to put an astronaut into space. Our government cancelled the Constellation rocket-capsule program, and, because of that insane decision, the control of manned space flight has been graciously ceded to Russia and China. We have to rely on hitching a ride on one of the Russian Soyuz tubs. What a sad day *that* is!"

"It actually gets a little worse," said Maxwell. "It's my understanding that several years ago the President gave the administrator of NASA a prime directive that would focus primarily on making Muslims feel good about themselves."

"What the hell does that mean?" asked Nikki.

"Well, I guess it means that if the Iranians launch a rocket piloted by a Muslim suicide bomber service, then NASA would have the distinct job of having a technical specialist along, guiding them during the Allah Akbar portion of the reentry phase."

"Ouch!" replied Joe, as he winced from Maxwell's intended connotation.

"I'm not sure if it's true or not," said Nelson, "but all in all, we have a weakened comprehensive NASA strategy."

"Apparently so," replied Max. "We'll have wasted much of our previous investment with the loss of many years that will be required to recreate the equivalent of what we have discarded. The lack of rocket development and spacecraft will assure that our ability to go beyond earth orbit destines our nation to become one of second or even third-rate stature, and also will assure that the ability to do so will not be available for several years. We even have to purchase rocket engines from Russia in order to get our payloads into space. Hopefully, more private firms will step up to continue research." Maxwell lowered his head slightly at his last statement and in a noticeably low tone added, "I'm afraid we're on a downward slide to mediocrity."

"And to make matters worse," Emmy said, "imagine receiving a Nobel Peace Prize for making multiple global apology tours! Most recipients have actually had to work many years to achieve such an honor. And what about our former Secretary of State saying she was broke upon leaving the white house, or that she was once under sniper fire, or she was allowed to use personal e-mails for work—a serial liar with no constraints and no accountability. And people keep making excuses for the lies, not questioning any sort of competency."

Nelson was astutely aware of the intended consequences of government growth.

"We're even trying to screw up our education system with federal common core standards," he said. "Some people like it, some don't. But I honestly believe there's nothing like taking simple math and making it complicated—unbelievable! Don't people understand any of these things? And don't get me started about making a mockery of our constitution, about exceeding laws by executive orders. It's been done before but not at these levels. We also don't seem to get real news anymore. We seem to get a lot more liberal propaganda than we used to. I'd just like to get news that is factual—not political, and I don't need celebrities telling me how I should vote. We've been lied to about being deficit neutral, lied to about keeping your doctor, lied to about lower health insurance premiums, and lied to about real unemployment rates with numbers that simply aren't true. The actual participation in finding jobs is the lowest it's been in years. In other words, many people have given up looking for jobs. The unemployment number is really higher than what's being re-ported—more propaganda. What are we becoming? Looks like your predictions were right," Nelson added, turning to-ward Maxwell.

"Which ones?"

"Well to start, it wasn't that long ago when you said the Internal Revenue Service would be caught targeting con-servative groups and delaying their applications for non-profit status. That event actually occurred, and they have publicly acknowledged that practice. It looks like the very agency charged with enforcing the new Health Care law was systematically targeting those groups, and they were doing it for two years before the new law came into existence. The IRS's role implementing a highly partisan law rammed through Congress has fundamentally transformed the tax agency."

"That must have just been a coincidence," said Joe, belching a noticeable laugh.

"The Ways and Means and Government Oversight Com-mittees have had a lot of hearings about the targeting is-sues," said Maxwell. "It's all politics in this case. In short, like I told you once before, nothing will ever come of it. It will be forgotten. It's analogous to the public hearings you've at-tended. There will be a deliberate effort to maximize and ob-fuscate facts rather than admit any misconduct."

Nelson replied sarcastically, "I can't believe there would be a smidgen of corruption in the IRS targeting."

"What you may not have heard," Max said, "is that the Treasury Inspector General was supposedly investigating pos-sible criminal activity at the IRS. Investigators uncovered over thirty-thousand e-mails relating to the targeting scandal. In the future, I'm sure you'll hear about hard drive failures and missing files. We've also got to start paying attention about cyber attacks from countries like Russia, Iran, and China. Our electrical grid could be affected at some point. And another thing—getting back to scandals and e-mails—the former Sec-retary of State had highly classified e-mails that were hidden from the public on private home servers that were supposed to be government controlled for national security reasons. Even with the understanding of gross negligence, there will be no responsibility accounting for what was done."

"That sounds like an awful politically partisan statement to make," said Nikki. "I happen to like the former Secretary of State."

"There's nothing partisan about it," said Max. "I'm actually an independent voter and what I have said are simply the facts. The real issue here is one of total incompetence. It makes no difference what party you're affiliated with, at least it shouldn't. And I'm not sure if we're any better off with the current Secretary of State trying to negotiate a nuclear deal with Iran."

"How do you know all this?" asked Nelson.

"I listen—a lot—to many sources."

Maxwell paused, looking to Nelson as if he was considering the fact that he had been allowed access to several sources unavailable to everyone else, particularly news broadcast from Turing-B that hadn't yet occurred.

"There are a bunch of things we all need to worry about, including many national issues evaluated by the Supreme Court. I worry about many of the decisions that have been made," he added finally.

"What do you mean?" Nelson questioned.

"Well, the courts have embraced their duty to ratify and even facilitate lawless discretion exercised by administrative agencies. The judiciary has written rules that stack the deck to favor government overreach in cases of statutory construction. The courts appear to be obligated to do whatever is required to make a law efficient, regardless of how the law is written. The Supreme Court seems to be legislating, not judging, enlarging executive discretion. It seems as though there is a judicial function to construe laws in ways that make them perform better. That deference becomes judicial dereliction with anti-constitutional consequences. I believe this is progressivism's central objective, the overthrow of the Constitution's architecture.

"What really worries me is the fact that so few people are aware of it. The last several years have certainly changed the direction of our country. When did we start glorifying a criminal over their victims? Why do we continue to divide ourselves versus unite ourselves? Why doesn't our Congress read a Bill before voting on it? And why does the Supreme Court now have the courage to explain that although the intent of a law is good, it is significantly flawed and requires re-writing? Much of the press has been in a coma for several years now, yet their power to influence families has become stronger. The family's power to influence the media has in turn become weaker. Children are learning an alternate set of values that pits them against their parents and their own common sense."

"Speaking of common sense," said Nelson, "there are some people who are often wrong but never doubt them-selves because they're overcome by their own sense of self-worth. Confident ignorance is a dangerous quality of anyone in a leadership position. And a leader's greatest accomplish-ment shouldn't be getting their golf handicap down to the teens."

"It sounds like you and Maxwell are condemning the cur-rent administration," protested Marie.

"It may seem that way," said Max, "because everything that has happened to you locally has occurred during the same period of time when your issues indirectly relate to mine. The point is such events in our government could hap-pen under any administration, if gone unchecked. Nelson and I have written a story to remind people of events that have already occurred as well as warn people of events that could still occur."

"What do you mean by our local issues relating indirectly to yours?" asked Marie, clearly upset her political philoso-phies were being threatened.

"There are similarities," Maxwell answered. "Let me give you just a few examples. First, your opposition deliberately stated they contributed a charitable service fee, never telling you that it was actually required by law. How many times have you been misled and found that information had been deliberately falsified during national public hearings? Second, how many times has the law of the land been circumvented by exception? Laws are written for a reason, just like town ordinances; and still they're bypassed. Third, many members of both boards apparently didn't read the material your group provided before they voted, not understanding all the infor-mation required to make a proper decision. Neither does Congress at times. Fourth, you have witnessed distorted re-sponses, misleading answers, and fabricated facts to achieve a particular agenda—in your case the destruction of a forest and development of land. In my case, one of partisan politics, anything said to meet an agenda. Fifth, there's the obfuscation of information, locally or nationally, whether from omitted information from the Maine Department of Fisheries and Wildlife, the Maine Department of Conservation, or the lies about Benghazi or classified e-mails. Sixth, you've had one board that's shifted from one topic to another, never resolving anything. That's similar to the many scandals we've witnessed on a national level; so many that people simply forget that they've ever occurred. Seventh, you've had a situation where one regulation board wants to take over one of the duties of the other—more power to dictate.

"There are just so many incongruities; whether it's the IRS 501(c)(3) versus 501(c)(4) comparisons or even a redistribution of wealth where the local taxpayers will have to bear the burden and pick up the tab for an organization that should be paying its own property taxes.

"If you look at all the arguments you've been through during the public hearings, you'll actually find more examples, but I believe I've made my point. If people don't speak out, harmful events can happen—excessive regulations, loss of your second amendment rights, restrictions on our production of energy. The list goes on.

"If you hadn't paid attention to the Special Exception requested by a developer, you would have lost a forest and its wildlife. If we don't pay attention as a country, we'll lose a lot more than that," Max stressed. "There will always be changes depending upon the leadership we have or lack thereof in this country and others. I just want to emphasize the fact that people need to pay attention in order to make the changes necessary and avoid more scandals, failures, unintended consequences, negligence, and radical ideals. We appear to have become complacent. As a result, we're sleepwalking through history."

iii.

It was late in the afternoon when Nelson's neighbors left for their respective homes. I stayed and listened to Nelson and Maxwell's continued conversation for several hours. Even though the drive from Maxwell's home to Nelson's was only two hours, and although invited to stay over for the night, Maxwell insisted on returning home. Before he left, however, he handed Nelson a package.

"Look over what I've written. It's for your novel. Include whatever you wish. There are some things that I need to better understand about the particle accelerator we've built, the trials we've been running with proton collisions, and the possibility of creating the effect of a black hole. I also need to review some of the modified as well as new radio transmissions I've received and when they were actually transmitted. I'll send you the audio files later. I may be a little preoccupied so you may not hear from me for a while."

After Maxwell left, Nelson remained outside with me and opened the large package. It contained several marked-up chapters of Nelson's manuscript, a letter from Maxwell, and numerous reports accumulated by Dora. Dates, times, events—all were organized in sequential order of initial transmission and actual occurrence. He read through the contents of the box and the letter out loud, allowing me to hear the context:

Nelson, I apologize for my obstreperous personality at times. But we've known each other for a long time now, so perhaps it's allowed. I guess my variation in tone comes across in the letters and e-mails I've written you. If we continue to be unaware of what is happening around us, our situations will undoubtedly worsen. We simply need to be aware that we are unaware. Is that so difficult to understand?

With that thought in mind, I would think we are done with these letters of political misgivings. Your battle has ended. You've won—at least for now. The problems you've encountered with your hometown development issue are what you might consider to be an allegory to the national issues we are facing. In both situations misinformation is presented, which amounts to actual lies told to people and the resulting consternation from such actions. People's indifference is apparent, and I worry about consequences to their inattention. It seems that if people don't want to hear about an issue they disagree with, they become monosyllabic and glance around for the exits.

Our country is becoming an ideological wasteland. We are likely to give weapons and equipment to radical governments believing they will become our friends. We continue dialogs beyond their effective results. And the time wasted with such continued irresponsible actions will ultimately have a negative effect on the country. Nuclear proliferation will be dramatic. We continue to treat terrorism within a legal system that protects the perpetrators as if they were a victim of circumstance. We're becoming a hysterical nation willing to bend.

Furthermore, violence may take an organized movement toward a dangerous form of identity politics. There will be no reasoning arguments, only a perversion and alteration to our basic institutions. Using violence instead of articulate political discourse will thus cause a lessening of ethics, society, and past values. Sinister claims from unproven anonymous sources will also occur in attempts to block, interfere, and undermine any improvements for the welfare of the country. Political tactics will stoop to new lows in order to perpetrate an agenda and subvert the very fabric of government.

I fear that perpetual disorder could become a prescription to destroy a nation from within. There is a real danger that abusive power will be put ahead of principle and ambition put ahead of conviction, establishing a two tier type of justice system within the government. Journalism will have its own agenda using uncorroborated news and scandals, and social media will be used for further disruption.

Over the past few years, Dora has managed to be quite proficient at scrutinizing everything from conflicts to scandals. We appear to have lost control over our economy, our borders, health care, immigration, the Department of Justice, the State Department, the Internal Revenue Service, medical treatment for our Veterans, terrorism, foreign policy (in that we don't seem to have much of any real policy), welfare expenditures, the national debt, unemployment, our military capabilities, and so much more—mostly all in a matter of only a few short years.

So long as people don't follow the factual portions of national news and understand the events of each day, whether good or bad, then they will be unaware of those events that will dramatically affect or alter their lives. Their health insurance, taxes, gun laws, immigration, energy costs, environmental regulations, even the terms we use to define things like terrorism by calling it 'workplace violence', are subject to the erosion of a strong society.

In order to contain harmful events, people need to be aware of them. Is it just a case of pure laziness, simply a matter of not caring, or are people becoming troglodytes? The latter two scenarios are more worrisome. Is everyone simply distracted from life or simply, don't they care?

If you pay close attention, you will notice that bureaucratic 'mishaps' and controversial issues are diverted and downplayed in order to distract the individual from perceiving cause and effect. People simply need to pay attention. They will care once they learn they've lost control over their lives. But will it be too late to correct that which has been corrupted? That's when people will simply ask, 'What happened?' Sooner or later as government becomes larger, it will become out of control. Without true leadership qualities, subordinates in the numerous departments of bureaucracy will run amuck with abuse of power, along with an increase in their arrogance and stupidity. It shouldn't be about politics, but rather about survival.

You must keep in mind that in the future there will be groups formed to oppose our ways of governing, our laws, and a process that has been in place for decades; a total disrespect of an established government. Such organizations will create movements to organize communities for progressive change; an overreach by shadow organizations aimed at resisting and tearing down our Constitutional Republic.

Just as a Roman legion once crossed the Rubicon River in 49 BC, the country has been progressing toward an irrevocable course from where there is no point of return. Once crossed, 'Ãlea Iacta Est', —'the die has been cast'. There is a natural order to the world, and we are on the cusp of its beginning or possibly its end.

We will continue to try and make agreements with apocalyptic countries wanting to annihilate other countries, including us. Our continued actions of placation will guarantee that such countries will be nuclear states, willing to destroy anyone else's way of life. We will unfreeze assets and loosen *sanctions in order to convince them to delete their programs to enrich uranium.*

In doing so, we will provide them with the ultimate opportunity of time and the economic means to change their part of the world forever and eventually ours. Our actions will weaken and empower radical changes in the earth's future. Such countries will deceive the world based upon their religious philosophies and will complete their nuclear development plans.

Don't ever underestimate the difference one person can make. You've experienced that yourself. Tell that in your story. People need to pay attention to those things happening around them. I can't emphasize that enough. They need to be aware of issues in order to make a difference. Each person may only play a minor role, but each minor role is a contribution that encompasses and becomes essential for major change.

You and your neighbors have managed to succeed in making your voices heard. As a small group, you have achieved what the people in our entire country need to understand and achieve, as well. Perhaps your story will warn people about the greater issues across the country that could occur. I certainly hope so. Perhaps in my journey to understand the science behind all of what is predicted, I'll manage to find those elusive tachyons.

Regards,
Maxwell

Chapter Twenty-One

The Woods

i.

The cool morning air felt refreshing. It stimulated the mind and provided the opportunity to let the worries about the future fade into the background. Yet Nelson still thought about the previous afternoon's discussions with Maxwell.

He took his first few steps toward the woods and saw morning doves at the back of the house, eating sunflower seeds that had spilled onto the ground below the hanging bird feeders. The doves—fairly docile birds—were rather unique because he knew they kept the same partners throughout life.

Watching them brought a smile to his face at the remembrance of researching the kinds of food they ate. That was the day when he had looked for the answer in an old ornithology book from his office library. Before coming to the word Dove, he had noticed there was a species called Dither birds; a strange name for a bird with very little information about them.

Curiosity ensued, and he had expanded his search to the internet in order to locate additional material. There were no photographs, and once again very little information. It appeared there were just a few of them remaining, and the majority of those lived in isolated pockets in Central and South America.

What intrigued him was the fact these birds were noted to be lackadaisical in nature, always vacillating from any decision.

"A fitting name for many people," Nelson mumbled out loud, his breathe floating cloudlike in the crisp air. "An affliction *many* people have nowadays."

He stepped onto the well-worn forest pathway for a brief

walk to start his day and did what Donny often did: he talked to the forest as though it was a person. The forest never objected to whatever he had to say. It usually helped to clear his mind. Today, his thoughts were on his writing and the politics and concerns that Maxwell had discussed. It weighed heavily on him. He spoke quietly to no one.

"It must be more than shear demographics," he lamented. "I just don't understand why so many people are fixated about getting free stuff all the time. Are people that shallow—or worse yet, gullible? Don't people understand we can't continue on a downward economic path? We're acquiring more debt every day. We keep spending and creating bureaucratic, non-manufacturing jobs, and we keep supporting countries that brutalize their own people. There will come a time when the borrowing will have to stop. And then the free stuff will disappear. It doesn't go on forever; it can't. And when people don't get any more free stuff because there simply isn't any left, then what? I just don't get it. Sooner or later, someone has to pay for it. Increasing the spending on new social programs will marginalize the country. The idea that weaker is less provocative is a fallacy that we will come to regret."

Completely wrapped up in his thoughts, Nelson paid little attention to his progress along the path until he found himself in front of the old maple tree that sheltered the names Donny had scrawled into its bark so many years ago. He smiled as he slowly viewed the names, distorted by withered bark, and whispered each one to a listening forest. At the same time, animals voiced their own distinct cries in the early morning, not unlike the many cries within our own society.

The animals of the forest, however, had no voice against those intervening with their lives. They couldn't argue their case in front of Planning Boards or Zoning Boards or people who would disrupt their way of living. They could only accept what was dealt them, not having the ability to do anything about it.

Nelson realized there were some things a person might not be able to fix, but also understood that people could try. As long as they tried, there was hope.

ii.

It was late afternoon when I saw Donny entering the forest. I was on a ridge slightly above and opposite the old trail he always traveled. As usual, he didn't see me. He seemed to be in a hurry, and I couldn't catch up to him, nor could he hear my call. At the edge of his property line, he stepped off the trail to face a large oak tree and hauled himself up onto an adjacent old stump. I waited and watched with great interest as he reached up and inserted metal clips into the bark. Once done, Donny turned slowly around, and scanned the forest to see if anyone was watching. He didn't see me. On all his excursions throughout those years I lived near him, he never noticed our parallel paths. I always managed to stay well hidden from sight because I simply didn't like to intrude upon his quiet time.

The contrasting fall colors made his blue eyes twinkle brighter than usual, and his normally slight smile was more exuberant. He turned back and quickly hung fixtures onto the clips he had attached to the great old oak. Once completed, he stepped down off the stump and retraced his steps to the old trail. He stopped and looked back once more at the oak tree. He smiled that mischievous smile of his and slowly walked away, continuing along the well-traveled path.

I was curious about his actions and decided to take a closer look at what his task had been. That mischievous looking smile was just too much to simply ignore. The oak tree now had a face on it, consisting of two large eyes with noticeable eyebrows, a large nose, and a mouth with a distinct tongue hanging out, accompanied by two hands pulling back a pair of lips, showing disdain to those who saw it. I guess it was Donny's way of saying his neighbors had been successful in stopping the additional phases and the destruction of a forest, its inhabitants, its pristine wetlands, and a way of life we both loved.

The oak tree and its newly attached image directly faced the existing Phase One of the southern portion of the apartment complex. No one could remove the image. It would remain for many years; the tree was on his property.

I followed him once again until he came to the large maple tree that sheltered the many names he had inscribed onto its weathered skin. I decided not to interfere.

He guided his hand lightly over the rough bark, as if reaching out to a dear friend, then leaned slightly against the tree. At that moment, Donny looked old and fragile. He paused, his head bowed, then turned to walk away. He disappeared from sight just as I noticed he had left his walking staff leaning against the aged tree. But I didn't say anything. The whisper of leaves from a passing breeze interrupted the silence of the approaching dusk, only to be muffled once again by the sound of branches swaying overhead. The day was at an end.

iii.

Three weeks later, Nelson received another letter from Maxwell accompanied by a transcript and a flash drive. The letter read as if it was first intended as an e-mail.

To: NelsonQuip – October 19
From: Mdraper
Subject: Audio File and Concerns

Nelson,

For the last several years we have been witness to an obfuscation of information pertinent to events in our country. I remember when it was said we couldn't keep troops in Iraq—there could be no agreement. Apparently, that was false. It was our own decision not to support those people. Our own former Secretary of State actually allowed that to happen.

Remember when I e-mailed you that we had received a transmission from Turing-B, the satellite approaching the wormhole, about an embassy in Libya being attacked? Well, we all now know that incident actually happened. And before it happened, Dora identified multiple requests for added security from the embassy in Libya. Nothing was ever done by the State Department to support those requests.

I know that there will be investigations as to the cause of lives lost and that lies throughout those investigations will be substantiated. But very few people will understand or care. No matter how many hearings are held, nothing will happen. People responsible will never admit to any wrong-doing. Di-

rect lies as to the cause of such an attack, for the most part, will simply be ignored. At best, we are but a bystander in collusion. Everything is now upside down. Where do the lies stop? What about the victim's families?

And if you believe the number of victims ends there, you're wrong. We have made a historic mistake in signing a nuclear agreement with Iran. Such an agreement does nothing about Iranian behavior and leaves an infrastructure intact. Unless nullified, such an agreement will eventually cause nuclear proliferation of other countries. Our ban on arms sales will be lifted as part of the agreement as well as economic sanctions. That country will even be able to purchase ballistic missiles, as well. They've already started testing some. And they're still shouting 'death to America'.

I don't understand the lackadaisical idea of creating any type of agreement with that country. An embargo should never have agreed to be lifted. I wouldn't be surprised if the Iranian regime is allowed to gather their own samples when it comes time for nuclear inspections! There probably have been covert deals done as well by the United Nations IAEA.

What's sad is the fact that the congressional review period of the Iran agreement ended without passage of a resolution of approval or a resolution of disapproval. Did you know that Iran tested a medium-range ballistic missile just a week ago, capable of carrying a 1650 pound payload just over 1000 miles? That's a violation of a UN Security Council Resolution 1929 agreed to in 2010, which prohibits Iran from testing nuclear-capable ballistic missiles.

Yet, just yesterday we formally adopted the Joint Comprehensive Plan of Action (JCPOA); a one-sided transaction that is supposed to delay IRANS's nuclear program, which is a better deal for IRAN than us. The deal didn't even include prohibiting the testing of nuclear capable missiles. Everything was given to them up front; even cash!

Don't forget about North Korea, either. You haven't seen the end of their nuclear-capable status or ballistic missile testing, or the fact that they'll have satellites with trajectories that locate them daily over this country. They could be capable of performing an electromagnetic pulse attack that would affect our national electrical grid. And when they address their next congress, they'll praise themselves for accomplish-

ing their first hydrogen bomb test. We have done little to prepare for such issues.

There's also ISIS, which will cause refugees to seek new homes. And among them will be terrorists disguised, finding a stealthful way into this country, who will sooner or later perform immeasurable damage. It's alarming to know that our government doesn't even know where those people are, who have violated their VISAs. Our vetting system has not kept up with technology, and there are violent criminals who should be deported and have not been.

There will be countries like Russia ready to fill the vacuum left by us and a takeover of the middle-east. Misguided policies—that's what we've had over the last several years. During one of our discussions, I mentioned I didn't understand why the term ISIL was used more often by some government officials than the term ISIS. I finally understand why the term ISIL was used.

Our leaders tend to refer to the mid-east terrorists as ISIL versus ISIS because an administration would rather eliminate the connection between the chaos in Iraq with inaction in Syria. The term Levant associated with the term ISIL describes a territory much greater than simply Iraq and Syria. It consists of parts of other countries including Lebanon, Palestine, southern Turkey, and others. An army of more territorial magnitude takes the focus off the two countries that many believe define our continued failure in the middle-east, which are Iraq and Syria. Because our administration has dithered, we've lost the opportunity to engage with those who oppose the leader of Syria. And if the ISIS organization is eventually overcome, the ideology will still continue under other names.

We continue to deceive ourselves. I'm worried those deceptions will catch up to us, particularly with Iran.

If over 70% of the people are dissatisfied with the way the country is going, then why in the world do the people keep voting the way they do? I'll tell you why. They're simply not paying attention to what is happening around them. Perhaps they simply believe in all the rhetoric they listen to and don't care to understand the specifics.

I find our situation, and the fact that I can't seem to do much about it, very frustrating. We appear to lead from be-

hind, creating instability in the world. We've created a vacuum by removing troops in questionable regions, indicating our military is weak. Our allies don't trust us—can you blame them? Our enemies don't fear us; apparently there is nothing to fear from us. I worry that we have created a short pathway for an irrational country to gain nuclear weapons. Why would you befriend an enemy that will always be your enemy?

I'm spouting off about these latest concerns because of a curious radio transmission we just received from the first of our two satellites: Sagittarius-A. Remember, that's the one that continues toward the black hole in the center of our Milky Way galaxy. That satellite never encountered anything like the wormhole which the second satellite, Turing-B, appears to have. (We discussed that during your last visit.) Therefore the effect of any gravity anomalies is insignificant in comparison.

The wormhole that satellite Turing-B traveled into still remains open, and its transmissions have resulted in many more perplexing renditions from the original versions of radio signals transmitted from earth; almost like we've received radio transmissions from a vanished civilization.

I wanted to send you the enclosed audio file received from Sagittarius-A. Sagittarius-A hasn't transmitted a radio news broadcast back to us for several years now, until recently. It was strange to receive a radio signal that we originally broadcasted in 1996. It's as if it has been waiting—silent—for the right moment in time. This recent transmission seems to convey a unique summary of my concerns.

The message was from a radio broadcast by Paul Harvey, a well-known news commentator from the past. The content, a prophetic essay, sheds an eerie reflection on the conversations we've been having. It seems to address my earlier concerns as well as those I've touched upon in this letter. Unfortunately, it appears we have now lost all communications with it.

The essay makes one ponder about the issues you and I have discussed over the last few years. Enclosed is the audio file on a flash drive as well as a transcription. It's almost like we sent ourselves a warning from years ago. Even with the scratchy background sounds, the audio is fairly clear. I'll put this letter and the audio file in our outgoing mail slot tonight.

I know it sounds like an antiquated method to converse versus an e-mail, but sometimes our server halts e-mails containing certain wording—for security reasons. The message itself—well, you'll have to arrive at your own conclusion.
    Regards,
    Max

Year Eight

October 19 - Afternoon

"It's no use in an ending to proclaim from the start
That the moral of the story is to begin—"

—Gilbert O'Sullivan

Chapter Twenty-Two

Sunrise

i.

Large windows identical to ones Nelson observed in the outer office extend along the entire wall behind Paul Whitman's desk, providing a breathtaking view of the city. The gray clouds in the fall sky shield the early setting of the sun, and shadows sneak from ledge to window, changing the perspective and character of each building from one moment to another.

Discussions about the storyline and the philosophical and political ramifications from Maxwell Draper's communications have continued throughout a working lunch, and the conversation continues into the late October afternoon.

There's another storm coming, Nelson thinks to himself. He turns his gaze away from the darkening clouds and faces Paul.

"Perhaps I *should* include Max's letter, the one you mentioned earlier this morning, the last one he mailed exactly one year ago from today, which I left out of the original manuscript."

"Nelson, you've actually delivered *your* message as well as Maxwell's in your story. I believe that was his intention all along."

"I agree with you. My story provides a conduit for his message to everyone without his direct involvement. His message is a lament for the decadence of the country and a changing society. He doesn't want to be available, doesn't want to have to explain his thoughts or how he happens to know about certain events. It's not that he's shy. In most aspects, he's just a very private individual. He has simply used *me* to express his concerns."

"Perhaps Maxwell was unsure about a possible security

breach in his own research. More probable is what you stated: the fact that he wanted you to explain his concerns without having to explain it himself." Paul's voice adjusts to a
low, more serious tone. "So how was *he* able to make the
predictions he did, regarding national issues?"

"I asked Maxwell the same question," replies Nelson.
"Maxwell told me he fed data into their lab's computer system from hundreds of media outlets as well as government
sites, and he referred to an assistant by the name of Dora,
who assimilated all that information. At first, I assumed she
was a colleague who analyzed trend information using a
newly developed software application that functions as a so-
phisticated algorithm. I didn't have the actual facts until only
a few days ago. It was Max's computer technician, Harold
Lang, who put a wrinkle in my understanding of who Dora
really was. I'll explain everything about who she was in a few
minutes.

"Maxwell had told me that Harold had his own fantasy
about their associate—even had a picture of her on his desk.
The results of all the intelligence she gathered from so many
diversified and somewhat classified sources allowed predictions based upon particular scenarios. Max's team had a substantial amount of information for analysis, and Harold
worked closely with Dora. Apparently, their lab's computer
system is one of the largest data crunching facilities in the
world, at least that's what I discerned from several of Max's
e-mails.

"What's strange is the fact that I haven't been able to get
in touch with Maxwell for several weeks now. The research
facility he works for can't *even* locate him. It seems he just
stopped going to work, like he fell off the planet. Their security system doesn't indicate he ever logged out of the main
lab complex. According to their log entries, he went into the
lab and never came out. But I also understand it isn't the
first time the lab's security system failed to log a person out.
All they would tell me is Dora told the lab's administration
board that Maxwell had gone.

"I wanted to discuss the letter he sent me last year,
along with the original radio transmission from 1996 received
from the Sagittarius-A satellite. It was a warning to America
from the well-known radio broadcaster, Paul Harvey. As I

was completing the final draft of the manuscript, I needed to ask Maxwell's opinion on how it would be best related to this story. I sent you a copy of the transcript from the radio transmission."

"Yes, I have it," says Paul as he removes the letter from a thick folder on his desk and reads it aloud, as if refreshing his memory of its contents. He reads the accompanying transcript and peers over the top of his glasses without raising his head. "Nelson, I haven't heard the actual audio file Maxwell sent you, which was transmitted so many years after it had been originally broadcast. Did you bring a copy of it so you can play it for me?"

"I did," Nelson replies. "I thought you might want to hear the actual sound bite." He hands the flash drive to Paul and the audio hisses to life as he inserts it to the USB port on his laptop.

The words are scratchy but distinct and clear. A solitary voice deafens the silence of the room.

"If I were the prince of darkness, I would want to engulf the whole world in darkness.

I'd have a third of its real estate and four-fifths of its population, but I would not be happy until I had seized the ripest apple on the tree—thee.

So, I would set about however necessary to take over the United States.

I'd subvert the churches first, and I would begin with a campaign of whispers.

With the wisdom of a serpent, I would whisper to you as I whispered to Eve, "Do as you please."

To the young, I would whisper that the Bible is a myth. I would convince the children that man created God instead of the other way around. I'd confide that what's bad is good and what's good is square.

And the old, I would teach to pray after me, "Our Father, which are in Washington ..."

Then, I'd get organized, I'd educate authors in how to make lurid literature exciting so that anything else would appear dull and uninteresting.

I'd peddle narcotics to whom I could. I'd sell alcohol to ladies and gentlemen of distinction. I'd tranquilize the rest with pills.

If I were the devil, I'd soon have families at war with themselves, churches at war with themselves, and nations at war with themselves until each, in its turn, was consumed.

And with promises of higher ratings, I'd have mesmerizing media fanning the flames.

If I were the devil, I would encourage schools to refine young intellect but neglect to discipline emotions. I'd tell teachers to let those students run wild. And before you knew it, you'd have drug-sniffing dogs and metal detectors at every schoolhouse door.

With a decade, I'd have prisons overflowing and judges promoting pornography. Soon, I would evict God from the courthouse and the schoolhouse and then from the houses of Congress.

In his own churches, I would substitute psychology for religion and deify science. I'd lure priests and pastors into misusing boys and girls and church money.

If I were the devil, I'd take from those who have and give to those who wanted until I had killed the incentive of the ambitious.

What'll you bet I couldn't get whole states to promote gambling as the way to get rich?

I'd convince the young that marriage is old-fashioned, that swinging is more fun, and that what you see on television is the way to be.

And thus, I could undress you in public and lure you into bed with diseases for which there are no cures.

In other words, if I were the devil, I'd just keep right on doing what he's doing."

This is Paul Harvey—and now you know—the rest of the story—Good Day"

The hissing noise blends into a background of silence as the audio fades. Both men pause to think about what they've just heard.

"So who's the devil in this reference? What's the inference?" Paul asks. "Is it about one person, someone like Robert Mugabe, the President of Zimbabwe, who some say stifled democracy and subjected his people to hyperinflation? It has been said that his disgraceful record was proof alone that one man could ruin a country."

"Anyone can interpret the transmission to be attributed to one person," replies Nelson. "But I personally don't believe it is. I think that commentary from our past is one of foreboding. It refers to what is happening in this country and where our government policies are taking us, and to those politicians who apparently don't understand the actual issues but are more concerned about partisan politics and quite simply, just looking out for themselves and their own jobs.

"The inference involves more than the actions of just one person. *People* have *allowed* our decadence to happen. I think the message *is* coincidental for this time period, but nevertheless ominous. That's why Maxwell wanted me to hear it. People need to pay attention to world affairs and to the results from an overabundance of government rules and regulations. That's what Maxwell was trying to say. Hell, some people don't even know who George Washington was or the year this country gained its independence, or even from whom. They don't even understand what socialism really is. We're causing our own problems. Many people just don't see that. Perhaps they're too busy texting, tweeting, or doing whatever on social media. If we don't change the path we're on, new versions to the same old problems will still be waiting at the end.

"There is no collective outrage. Our downward trend will be progressive if people don't start paying attention and begin to understand what they are doing to themselves and others. Our withdrawal from any strategy of foreign policy will show itself over time. We are becoming a different country, and not in a positive way. It will take time for people to understand that. Hopefully it won't be too late."

"Don't you think you should include the words of this transmission in your story and include Maxwell's concerns expressed in his letter to you? Do you think adding this message received from the past might make people take notice?"

"Perhaps—yes. Paul, you mentioned you thought Max had purposely wanted me to tell my story so his would be indirectly conveyed to the reader. He was somewhat subtle about it, but I understand what he was trying to do. I just wasn't sure if I should include that communication—perhaps too symbolic as a prediction."

"How would you explain the accuracy of Max's so-called predictions?"

"As I mentioned previously, his assistant, Dora, had the computer processing capabilities necessary to simulate outcomes predicated from a series of interrelated events. Max had told me that sequential data was fed into their system from an abundance of media outlets and from a continuous progression of periodic news events. Dora aptly assimilated and interpreted those sources, analyzed the sequential algorithms, and arrived at a possible conjecture of possibilities."

"Who *was* this assistant Dora? You said you found out who she really was."

"Yes. Sorry I didn't explain who she was to you sooner. I finally understood who she was when Maxwell's son, Alex, called to tell me he had a letter for me that Maxwell had started writing but hadn't finished. He had intended to send it before he simply disappeared. Alex has been trying to locate Maxwell and remembered his father kept a daily journal at their computer complex, which is a separate outbuilding at their home, the complex they called Area 52. When Alex went to look for the journal, he found the letter with another flash drive in a large manila envelope addressed to me, not yet sealed. It seems as though Maxwell was going to add more information to the letter once he returned from performing some sort of test at his research lab. Apparently, he never returned. Alex thought I should read it and mailed it only a few days ago."

Nelson looks out the window, lost in thought for a moment before returning his attention to the discussion at hand.

"When Alex called me, I asked about Dora. He told me that DORA isn't a person. He said the name is an abbreviation for the Defense Of the Realm Act. It was a legislative act passed by the British parliament four days after the country entered World War I back in 1914. It gave the British government wide-ranging powers to requisition buildings or land needed for the war effort or make regulations creating criminal offenses. It ushered in a variety of social control mechanisms like censorship. The law was designed to help secure people's safety and prevent communications from being harmful and prevent invasion. But looking at everything, it was a bit extreme in its application. DORA is the nickname

Max used for his computer system at work because it reviewed everything and was always there to help them figure things out."

"So what did Maxwell have to say in his unfinished letter to you?"

"Here, take a look," Nelson hands the letter to Paul. "I thought you should read it. That's why I brought it with me, as well as the audio output from the transmission they received. Now that we've discussed including the last letter he actually mailed, perhaps we should include this letter, as well.

To Nelson - Oct 5, 2016

Nelson, this letter is my own perspective of realities that I have observed. If you believe any of my comments are worth sharing, then by all means include them in your final manuscript. I realize it's pretty much ready for the publisher.

As we all know, the Mayan apocalypse didn't occur on the 21st of December 2012 as predicted. That's a fact. We're still here. The end-date of a 5,125 year cycle in the Mayan Long Count calendar simply stopped. Perhaps the individual working on the calendar died or perhaps lost his or her job due to a poor economy and was never replaced by anyone else. I guess we'll never know. (I just know how you will appreciate my attempt at humor.)

What was most disturbing about such an ominous event, however, was the lack of concern people had and the fact that many thought it was a joke. Whether or not it was something to worry about, at least there were many people aware of the potential event. Yes, many people talked about it. Not many were really concerned, but people were at least aware.

The scientists' conclusion is that the end of the Mayan calendar did not imply the end of the world, only the end of the Mayan long-count period that is part of the Mayan calendar shaped like a wheel. When you reach the end of the wheel, it will turn to the beginning again.

That premise reinforces the idea to analyze events for trends in order to predict potential outcomes from actions or non-actions. There exist news media data sets that can be observed as a multivariate time series, such as diagnostic data, video, and audio recordings—radio signals we transmit around the earth at or near the speed of light. Our search capability software responds to queries for potentially complex behaviors and analyzes time shifts between variables and returns a possible match for possible outcomes.

The last news event that Dora collected from such media, in order to deduce a consequential outcome, was the political lessening of sanctions and removal of economic pressures and the unfreezing of assets from a country—Iran—that wants to enrich uranium, creating an apocalyptic country bent upon the annihilation of other countries. Dora predicts that radical terrorism will escalate in the future. We will pay a price for not taking adequate actions. By removing more sanctions in order to receive a pause in uranium enrichment, the software algorithms indicate that we give away the ultimate opportunity of time. This will, in turn, weaken and empower radical changes to the earth's stability of power and increase deception based upon religious philosophy.

These actions basically appear to guarantee that a mideastern country will become a nuclear state. Our creditability as a country has been lost over only a few short years. Commitment has become only a word, with no real meaning. Attention will continue to be diverted from one scandal to another in order to avoid focus on any one particular issue, and that diversion is a deliberate obfuscation of the facts, analogous to what you witnessed during public hearings. If we are to believe in the lies that surround us, then we will become a part of those lies and in turn we will fail. Those lies can start at the lowest level. You've witnessed that yourself at your town meetings, and I've witnessed that at higher governmental levels. Nevertheless, they're all still lies.

In my studies of time causal relationships, I have learned not to focus on just those relationships between events but rather on the pattern of events as a whole. Time dilation, however, seems to have interceded with my observations, providing outcomes I didn't expect nor completely understand. I found that as Turing-B got closer to what I believe is the event horizon of a wormhole, the greater the time disparity and distortion of the re-transmitted media.

I'm enclosing a radio transmission that I've downloaded

onto a flash drive from a very garbled and partial broadcast we received from Turing-B, which I believe is caught in an event horizon. This second satellite was in an area with a much greater gravitational pull than the first, and therefore encountered an apparently more aggressive space-time continuum where time is somewhat folded in on itself.

It's unsettling to note that we're losing the transmission capability of that satellite, probably due to its approach toward what appears to be an open wormhole. Ultimately that satellite will simply disappear into the event horizon forever. But as it has continued on its journey, its re-transmissions from our own earth originated radio signals have become bizarre—altered. The last transmission we received from that satellite is one that we apparently have not yet sent. The message seems to be a harbinger of things to come. I can't explain it.

I've also been trying to understand why some of those same radio transmissions networked into my Area 52 systems from the lab are also linked to sporadic radio signals received by my five-meter radio telescope. I've received 'multiple' unidentified coded signals from the radio telescope.

It makes me wonder what would happen if the main lab's particle accelerator could create 'multiple' simultaneous particle collisions. Could we actually create a quantum black hole using our collider and produce particles in the collisions of pairs of protons? And what would happen if we could create more than one singular event; simultaneous events so to speak? Can a wormhole artificially be created? We discussed the idea of negative mass. Such a possibility also makes me wonder if you could create a tiny wormhole and then inflate it to a macroscopic size by negative mass.

I still have another test I need to perform tonight on the accelerator before I complete this letter. It may explain a few things I had never before considered doing. I'll try to resolve some of the questions I have and derive a plausible explanation. I'll finish this letter and mail it to you in the morning; just writing this now so I don't omit anything or forget what I wanted to convey while I have these thoughts.

Pay attention to this audio portion of the transmission file I'm sending you. I haven't played it back to anyone yet. Again, I can't explain its content since I believe it has never *been sent. There's no referral from any source. Perhaps we should pay attention to the past in order to ensure we have a future. Perhaps it's not the indifference we have, but rather the resolve to do something about it. We can't go back and change the past, but we can change the future. We never seem to learn anything from history, which is why we're always doomed to repeating it.*

I worry there will come a point in time when people eradicate writings and symbols from our past, no matter whether good or bad. Then we will never remind ourselves of our mistakes so we can improve. Enough of my ranting though.

To date, this is the last broadcast received from Turing-B. The words are very garbled and some are difficult to understand. I worry about what this transmission means...

"So Maxwell had another audio file for you?"

"He did. The one Alex sent to me. The message and prediction it conveys are more disturbing than any of the others."

"What do you mean by that?" Paul asks. "Some of Maxwell's so-called predictions have already been strange enough. He warns us about dilemmas we have created for ourselves over the last seven years; situations that escalate toward harmful consequences. Is this prediction stranger than the others because Maxwell believes it hasn't been sent yet? Is the information from the transmission that much more significant?"

Nelson frowns as he looks down at the flash drive in his hand, and responds, "This audio file... It's even more perplexing and relevant to my story. After our discussion today, I think it should be included. It's what Maxwell would call a riddle wrapped in a conundrum—a catastrophic event that should have never happened. Want to hear it?"

"By all means." Nelson hands him the flash drive to install.

The sharp sibilant sounds and the deafening volumes of static dampened by time and distance creates a foreboding effect as the words parse from one incomplete sentence to another, with random and somewhat incoherent words. The commentator's voice is faint, and solemn, and Paul listens intently to the crackling transmission.

The distant words begin:

"...a tragedy...proportions...incomprehensa...nuclear explo-sions... occurr...d...bo...coasts...major cities...mid-east...with...n minutes of...millions...   This...moment...history...someone should have seen coming...because...national policies. No one anticipa...te...d...the...other...wise, the mid-east... It's im-portant...understand...circum...stances...avoided..."

The voice fades and only static is left from the cacophony of space.

Paul Whitman stares at Nelson, his face showing he real-izes full well what the audio file means. He pauses purposely to avoid an impromptu remark, and carefully contemplates the choice of his next words.

In a low solemn voice, he asks, "Do you think the inclu-sion of these radio transmission transcriptions will make a difference to the reader?"

"I don't know. I just don't know. I think Max was hoping that it might. That last transmission is the one event that has never happened, at least not yet. If it had, we wouldn't be meeting here today. Think about the catastrophic implica-tions."

"I'd rather not," Paul replies, then adds, "I'm hoping those words are the result of some future audio trailer from your book after it's published, and not an actual incident. Af-ter listening to that sound clip and reviewing all of Max's ear-lier predictions, I believe he knew about events because of his experimentation and investigations with particle accelera-tors, black holes, and gravity anomalies. Or should his pre-dictions be considered to be based upon science fiction, fan-tasy, or some best guessed accounts from a deranged genius?"

"Paul, you know as well as I do that there is a key differ-ence between science fiction and fantasy. Science fiction is science that's possible; things that could happen, given our understanding of reality. Fantasy, on the other hand, in-volves events that are impossible according to that same un-derstanding of reality.

"I don't believe there's any science fiction type of situa-tion here that you would relate to fantasy. I'm just not sure how to explain that time can be compressed in on itself due to infinite gravitational forces, so that a radio transmission is received from a future time before it's actually sent from the present time. We don't even know if wormholes are real. But they *are* a part of science that *could* be real.

"I know that Max was experimenting with causal time relationships by analyzing transmissions sent to satellites near forces of enormous gravity deflections. We've already established that fact. However, that's all I know. Obviously, he was trying to understand time dilation effects as well as validate the existence of tachyons, you know, particles traveling faster than the speed of light. I think what you're witnessing here is something entirely different—an assimilation of data trends defining an event."

"I'm not so sure," replies Paul. "We agree that your book will be published, and after today's discussion, we even have an idea as to a scheduled date of publication. But an audio portion of your book or some radio or news report from the media about some catastrophe could have been transmitted at any time after that. We don't really know the date of the original broadcast, if there *was* one, or even if an undated event actually happens based upon a signal received from some so-called space-time gravity hypothesis. Maxwell may have been simply extracting logical extensions of the technology he was seeking to understand in order to provide a warning to avoid a bleak future. We don't know if Maxwell's warning is real."

"That's true," replies Nelson. "That's the rub. We just don't know."

"Look, we'll include everything as we edit the manuscript. Your story gives us all a lot to think about. I guess that's all we can do for now."

As both men stand to conclude their discussion, Paul warmly shakes Nelson's hand and says, "I look forward to working with you on this project. Let me know if you hear from Maxwell. Together, we'll ensure people get the message. I just hope they understand it. The story will serve as a reminder to never put ourselves in a position like this again."

"I hope so. I really hope so." Nelson walks toward the wide double doors of Paul's office, looks back, and renders a slight smile.

"I wonder if we can avoid what appears to be an existential eventuality?"

Paul pauses, giving reflection to Nelson's question. He returns a thoughtful, yet solemn nod, and replies, "Only time will tell. I guess we both understand the future's comprised of events that only the present can influence."

ii.

Maxwell Draper steps into multiple beams of the collider, witnesses the convergence to a single point, and looks up into the heavens. The black sky is unencumbered, an instance that exists now and forever, a night that falls into stillness. Blackness and suns from distant galaxies glitter, surround him, and tell their stories of creation as well as of their inevitable endings. Memories of past dreams are but one brief instant and bring him an understanding smile of finality about the last radio transmission he had received, the last one he had saved for Nelson, a last message he will not be able to finish.

There is a natural order to the world, and Maxwell knows he is on the cusp of a new beginning—his entire life now at a singular point. Time exists in all directions where history and moments occur simultaneously. Seconds to minutes, hours to days, days to years, time into time. Like a dream where all the details get fainter the harder you try to grasp them. He is in a place where time slows, folds in upon itself, and the future becomes the past.

Maxwell turns and looks back to where he had once been and beholds multiple sunrises on a fragile, majestic blue sphere. He now understands the reality of the last transmission received, that faint and parsed broadcast—a warning of destruction beyond comprehension.

As the earth fades into a singular pale blue dot, Maxwell realizes at this moment, he is witness to the concept of observing dilated time; an event that has yet to occur; a philosophical conundrum. Perhaps an event that can be prevented, if only people would pay attention. He knows now that his journey is just beginning, one in which nothing really ends but only begins once again. An awareness that nothing is lost forever.

iii.

The sun is slowly dissolving into the early evening while Nelson returns from his walk in the forest along one of the few remaining paths that approach his home. The sopping footpath from the previous night's rain is deep with leaves. The cool air is a reminder of fall once again, giving time for repose. His previous day's discussion with Paul Whitman was exhilarating, exhausting, troublesome, and had left him much to reflect upon.

A slight breeze tickles the tops of the trees and progressively waifs from one tree to the next, not unlike the steady and continuous swells of a recalcitrant ocean. The thinner birches sway ever so gently, as if caressed by a gentle hand. The forest whispers its message; the air is transformed into sounds funneled by the leaves. And unknowing eyes watch as he walks along the old woodland trail.

Nelson has been this way before, but those visits have recently been too infrequent. This is not his daily routine. This is his quiet time to clear his head and unwind.

The time for arguments with people about a development is over, at least for now. The individual battles had been frustratingly and painfully long. There were too many moments when he had thought that all arguments would be lost. But the more overwhelmed by opposition and half-truths, the more he had held onto his own personal ethics—the conviction to always try and do the right thing.

He had struggled to write about the local issues that affected the people in his small community, about the national issues that affected the country, and about the possible consequences of inaction to either. He can only hope that people will listen to the message that dwells within the pages of his book.

Dusk descends as Nelson travels upon the same worn path Donny often tread upon. Only the whisper of leaves from a passing breeze interrupts the silence. He passes by the old bench where Donny often stops to rest and finds last winter's battering snowstorms and neglect have taken their toll—it is a place no longer able to support a weary traveler. *There is no respite to time,* he thinks and continues along the pathway until stopping in front of a large maple tree that is separate from all the others. Facing its wide trunk, he notices the many names etched into the weathered bark. Drawn simply by their existence, he quietly and methodically whispers the names inscribed.

It's getting late, yet he takes on one more task before he leaves the forest. He opens a small pocketknife, kneels down beside the tree, and etches one last name into the aging bark—Donny. He finishes the last letter and an old wooden staff from the side of the tree slides to the ground next to him—as if handed to him by its former owner.

The ending sunshine of the day exposes the real beauty of the wood, defining its fine grains, smooth to the touch. He picks it up and a warmth fills the palm of his hand. Nelson instinctively knows the owner has left it on purpose—for him, perhaps to carry on the hope that time offers. With staff in hand, he continues on the same path, knowing he won't see Donny again. He had died earlier that winter, his journey at an end.

Nelson approaches the edge of the forest near his home when the rush of wings startles him. A bird, unique and distinctive in appearance, much larger than the black crows or red tailed hawks abundant in the forest, takes rapid flight. Fading sunlight glistens upon the contrasting bright reds, light blues, and blacks of strong, great wings—a spectacular statement at day's end.

The Dither bird climbs high above the impending dusk covering and protecting the forest, then ever so slowly disappears from sight as the evening sky touches the horizon.

He stands motionless with a steadfast gaze, unable to divert his attention from the spectacle. His eyes follow the steady, swift ascent of the bird until it disappears above the trees and blends into the ubiquitous, diminishing rays of the sun. The minutes of flight seem like hours have passed, only to encompass that singular rapid occurrence—an instant in one's life that is always remembered.

Nelson feels a sense of silence—waiting—in awe of what he's seen. Worrisome thoughts, apprehension tied to Maxwell's warning, separating past events from those hidden in the future. All temporarily forgotten by an uplifting moment that somehow concludes with the preservation of a forest before it has been changed forever.

People had become aware before it was too late to correct the unrepairable.

iv.

I have observed Nelson and Donny for several years now and have listened to their conversations about their attempts to save this forest; even their discussions about their national worries.

On occasion, I take my walks in the woods with both men and am thoughtful to never interrupt their conversations. I'd like to think of myself as a good neighbor to have around. I'm quiet, not demanding, and mostly stay away from discussions, especially those of political discord. I listen a lot but very seldom contribute to the conversations around me; it just isn't my nature.

I have listened to Nelson and his neighbors' discussions about their limited tolerance to a crippled political environment. Those conversations have given me the opportunity to understand their concern that people tend to look at things with a predetermined point of view at times, developing opinions based upon incomplete or biased information and on nothing but sheer rhetoric.

I've enjoyed my days in the forest, traveling along the old trail that runs along the top of the ravine. I've traveled it for several years, during many seasons, watching Donny and listening to him talk to the forest. I think about late afternoons when Nelson sat in back of Donny's house, reading his manuscript to him, asking for opinions and reactions to his words. Donny seems to enjoy those sessions with Nelson. I eavesdrop once in a while and listen with interest to Nelson's story, and I understand that we all have a connection to the concerns he writes about.

Looking up at the face that Donny placed on the old oak tree brings a smile to my face, knowing that in some small way, a large overbearing corporation failed in its efforts to change the forest. And then there is the sad realization that similar events on a much grander and more complex scale are occurring within the country. My own thoughts become entangled with the extremes that our own society has placed upon us.

Things are not as simple as they were in previous years when I was much younger. At least, it seems that way. Perhaps I am starting to pay attention to what is occurring around me as I get older, more than I ever did before.

The possibility of people not being able to stop the abuse of local regulations and the increase of global socialization troubles *even* me. For on a grander scale, I know that actions to poorly thought out changes and the lack of understanding actual facts could eventually lead to a collapse of any nation—destruction from within. These are the thoughts that invade the peace that dusk brings to the end of my day.

It is the individual person who must become aware. It is the collection of those individuals who can bring about corrective change and the return to ethical and moral values. One must realize that their own demise can occur if they don't pay attention to their surroundings.

Perhaps Dither birds are more prevalent in this part of the world than one might think. Perhaps they are not few or endangered after all. But if they're not paying attention to their current conditions and surroundings, how long can even *they* continue to exist?

I realize that many people are like Dither birds in so many ways when they simply choose to ignore what is occurring around them, and as a result *they* are the *ones* who may become the endangered species, not the Dither bird.

Perhaps I've stayed here for too many seasons already and have weathered more cold winters than I should have. I've watched and learned that some people do care about their surroundings and the things that affect their lives. Once they become aware, they can make a difference, but only then.

Maybe it's time for me to move a little further south, at least for this winter. The winters chill me more than they did before. This forest will be here in the spring, thanks to people like Nelson and his neighbors, and then I can return to its peaceful beauty. I guess I'm one of the few that prefers this part of the world, but now it is time that I connect with others like me.

I should tell those at home that they need to pay attention to what is occurring around them. They might not be able to make changes, but maybe some can make a difference by simply living in places that draw attention. Perhaps the rare occurrence of being seen will incite someone to take action. If the course of things doesn't change in these divisive times, the memory of this place may be the only thing left.

I notice a myriad of acorns from nearby majestic oaks in the clearing of a premature road. New growth emerges from those acorns, but it will be many years before the new trees can establish themselves and correct the damage already done. A slight warm breeze searches for me and hugs me as if to say we'll somehow get back to where we once were.

The loneliness of dusk is upon me, waiting for a new day to start. In retrospect, we all look at things we should have done, or perhaps should have done differently.

And perhaps too often, we wish we had paid more attention.

It's time to go. I can feel autumn sinking into a winter still to come.

I look down at the forest below as the air currents lift me higher, a resolute force beneath my wings. The cardinal-red hue from a sinking sun illuminates the tops of trees as I travel toward my own event horizon.

I look back over the forest I dearly love, leaving behind the lives of those people who have become aware of their surroundings, aware of those things they cherish, and aware of their individuality.

Perhaps everything will be all right after all. The forest is still here, at least for now. But we all need to understand and be aware of what's in the forest. Maxwell's predictions can occur. Perhaps they will. Hopefully they won't. People had better start to look around and become aware of events as they happen in our world. And try not to become biased either, although that can be difficult at times.

People need to understand that circumstance and truth can be easily misconstrued and manipulated by others. They need to understand the facts, whether they like them or not. They should not ignore the harmful circumstances that surround us on a daily basis. It's up to them to save the forest, not me.

If people don't pay attention and believe only in the rhetoric that keeps us from understanding real meaning, then perhaps we all might witness more than one sunrise on a single day—on this singular pale blue dot, in this space where we exist.

Our story begins in a forest where there are many paths from which to choose...

About the Author

Russell H. Plante is an Engineering Physicist with a diverse engineering and academic background in Engineering Physics, Electrical Engineering, and Business Administration. A skilled technical writer, he is a previously published author of non-fiction with John Wiley & Sons, Inc. and Academic Press (Elsevier).

His first novel, *Journey Home – A Cat's Tale* was published by Whimsical Publications. *Beware the Dither Bird* is his second novel, and he continues to write in both non-fiction and fiction genres.

He resides with his wife Kathy and their now more than three cats (another interesting story) in Kittery, Maine where there's always a chance of a blizzard during the cold winter months and time to contemplate and create meaningful stories.